By now, with this the seventh volume of Isaac Asimov's remarkable retrospective series of the great science fiction of past years, it has become obvious that this encyclopedic series is invaluable to everyone who reads and likes SF. Each year of the Golden Age produced the classic marvels that are the foundation stones of the widespread world of science fiction today.

In this volume from the year in which atomic energy was first liberated—a truly pivotal moment in human history—appear unforgettable tales by *Fredric Brown, Fritz Leiber, Murray Leinster, Bertram Chandler, Henry Kuttner, and Isaac Asimov* himself among others. . . .

ISAAC ASIMOV

Presents

THE GREAT SCIENCE FICTION STORIES

Volume 7, 1945

Edited by
Isaac Asimov and
Martin H. Greenberg

DAW Books, Inc.
Donald A. Wollheim, Publisher

1633 Broadway, New York, N.Y. 10019

Cover design by One Plus One Studios.
Cover art by Bernal.

Complete list of copyright acknowledgments for the contents will be found on the following page.

FIRST PRINTING, JULY 1982

1 2 3 4 5 6 7 8 9

DAW TRADEMARK REGISTERED
U.S. PAT. OFF. MARCA
REGISTRADA. HECHO EN U.S.A.

PRINTED IN U.S.A.

ACKNOWLEDGMENTS

Brown (THE WAVERIES)—Copyright © 1945 by Street and Smith Publications, Inc. Copyright renewed. Reprinted by permission of the agents for the author's estate, the Scott Meredith Literary Agency, Inc., 845 Third Ave., New York, NY 10022.

Padgett (THE PIPER'S SON)—Copyright © 1945. Reprinted by permission of the Harold Matson Company.

Leiber—Copyright © 1945 by Street and Smith Publications, Inc. Copyright renewed. Reprinted by permission of the author and his agent, Robert P. Mills, Ltd.

Asimov—Copyright © 1945 by Street and Smith Publications, Inc. Copyright renewed. Reprinted by permission of the author.

Brackett—Copyright © 1944 by Love Romances Publishing Co.; © 1972 by Leigh Brackett; reprinted by permission of Blassingame, McCauley & Wood.

Jones—Copyright © 1945 by Street & Smith Publications, Inc. Copyright renewed. Reprinted by permission of the author and his agents, the Scott Meredith Literary Agency, Inc., 845 Third Ave., New York, NY 10022.

Leinster—Copyright © 1945 by Street & Smith Publications, Inc. Copyright renewed. Reprinted by permission of the agents for the author's estate, the Scott Meredith Literary Agency, Inc., 845 Third Ave., New York, NY 10022.

del Rey—Copyright © 1945 by Street & Smith Literary Agency, Inc. Copyright renewed. Reprinted by permission of the author and the author's agents, the Scott Meredith Literary Agency, Inc., 845 Third Ave., New York, NY 10022.

Kuttner—Copyright © 1945. Reprinted by permission of the Harold Matson Company.

Leinster—Copyright © 1945 by Street & Smith Publications, Inc. Copyright renewed. Reprinted by permission of the agents for the author's estate, the Scott Meredith Literary Agency, Inc., 845 Third Ave., New York, NY 10022.

Kuttner (WHAT YOU NEED)—Copyright © 1945. Reprinted by permission of the Harold Matson Company.

Chandler—Copyright © 1945 by Street & Smith Publications, Inc. Copyright renewed. Reprinted by permission of the author and his agents, the Scott Meredith Literary Agency, Inc., 845 Third Ave., New York, NY 10022.

Leinster—Copyright © 1945 by Standard Magazines, Inc. Copyright renewed. Reprinted by permission of the agents for the author's estate, the Scott Meredith Literary Agency, Inc., 845 Third Ave., New York, NY 10022.

Brown (PI IN THE SKY)—Copyright © 1945 by Standard Magazines, Inc. Copyright renewed. Reprinted by permission of the agents for the author's estate, the Scott Meredith Literary Agency, Inc., 845 Third Ave., New York, NY 10022.

299-AL

TABLE OF CONTENTS

1945 Introduction

In the world outside reality, it was a momentous year. U.S. forces invaded the Philippines on January 9, while on January 31 Private Eddie Slovik became the first American soldier to be executed for desertion since the time of the Civil War. Dresden was firebombed in an attack on February 13 that killed an estimated 135,000 people; Kurt Vonnegut, Jr., then a prisoner of war, helped to fight the fires. U.S. forces crossed the Rhine on the last remaining bridge at Remagen on the same day. Iwo Jima fell to American forces on March 16.

President Franklin D. Roosevelt died on April 12, and Harry Truman took office the next day. In Europe, Soviet troops reached the outskirts of Berlin by April 21, while Benito Mussolini and his mistress were executed on April 28. Two days later Adolph Hitler committed suicide inside his bunker in Berlin—his "1,000 Year Reich" in shambles. Germany surrendered on May 7, although May 8 was declared V-E Day.

The Philippines were cleared of Japanese troops by July 5 and massive bombing raids began on the Japanese home islands on July 10. On July 18 the world changed when the first atomic "device" was successfully tested at Alamogordo, New Mexico. A few weeks later, on August 6, the *Enola Gay* dropped an atomic bomb on Hiroshima, killing 100,000 instantly, with tens of thousands dying later. On August 9

Nagasaki felt atomic power as a second bomb killed almost as many people. Japan asked for peace on August 10, and V-J Day was declared on the 14th. The formal Japanese surrender took place on the U. S. battleship *Missouri* in Tokyo Bay on September 2.

The Nazis had killed an estimated 14,000,000 human beings; total dead from all causes in World War II was estimated at more than 54,000,000.

During 1945 Conrad Hilton opened a hotel of the same name in Chicago. The Detroit Tigers took the World Series from the Chicago Cubs four games to three. Frozen food became widely available in American supermarkets while the Coca-Cola company registered "Coke" as a trademark. Menachem Begin directed his IZL in attacks against British troops occupying Palestine. Penicillin and streptomycin became commercially available. Diego Rivera painted *The Market in Tiangucio* and "Meet the Press" debuted on radio. *Black Boy* by Richard Wright was published. Army was the national college football champion but golf's Masters Tournament was again called off because of the war. "Till the End of Time," "Laura" and "I'm Beginning to See the Light" were popular song hits. Jean-Paul Sartre published *The Age of Reason.*

Joe Louis was still the heavyweight boxing champion of the world, but the record for the mile run was now the 4:01:4 recorded by Gunder Haegg of Sweden. Ballpoint pens went on the market. Symphony Number 5 in B Flat Major by Serge Prokofiev and Symphony Number 9 by Dmitri Shostakovich were performed for the first time. Kathleen Winsor's *Forever Amber* was published. An army air force bomber crashed into the Empire State Building in New York City, killing 13 people. There were 5,000 television sets in the United States. Phil Cavarretta (how quickly we forget) led the majors with a .355 average. *The Glass Menagerie* by Tennessee Williams opened on Broadway, while Toronto won the Stanley Cup. Alexander Calder constructed his "Red Pyramid." Hoop, Jr., with Eddie Arcaro up, won the Kentucky Derby, and the Washington Redskins won the National Football League Championship. George Orwell published *The Animal Farm.* Top films of the year included *The Story of G.I. Joe, The Lost Weekend*, Alfred Hitchcock's *Spellbound, State Fair*, and *A Walk in the Sun.* Richard Rodgers and Oscar Hammerstein's *Carousel* opened on Broadway, while *The*

Madwoman of Chaillot by Jean Giraudoux was performed for the first time. Grand Rapids, Michigan became the first American community to have its water fluoridated.

Mel Brooks was still Melvin Kaminsky.

In the real world it was a good year. Donald Wollheim edited the *Portable Novels of Science,* and *The World of Ā* by A. E. van Vogt was serialized in *Astounding. That Hideous Strength* by C. S. Lewis was published.

On the other hand, "I Remember Lemuria" by Richard S. Shaver appeared in *Amazing,* beginning a series of stories that helped sales but damaged science fiction.

More wonderful people made their maiden flights into reality: in the summer, Jack Vance with "The World Thinker"; in December, Rog Phillips (Roger Phillips Graham) with "Let Freedom Ring"; and in the winter, Bryce Waltorn with "The Ultimate World."

Death took Malcolm Jameson, Franz Werfel and Charles Williams, but distant wings were beating as Michael Bishop, Dean R. Koontz, George Zebrowski, M. John Harrison, Robert Chilson, Karl Edward Wagner, Jack Dann, Hank Stine, Edward Bryant, Charles Platt, Gordon Eklund, Robert E. Toomey, and Vincent DiFate were born.

Let us travel back to that honored year of 1945 and enjoy the best stories that the real world bequeathed to us.

THE WAVERIES

by Fredric Brown (1906-1972)

ASTOUNDING SCIENCE FICTION,
January

Fredric Brown produced a number of excellent science fiction stories in the 1940s, including this gem on the effects of technology-reversal on an already sophisticated society. Astounding's *editor, John W. Campbell, Jr., wanted his writers to focus on the consequences of applied science, and in "The Waveries" Brown gave one of his characteristic twists to this commandment, with results that may surprise you. An outstanding mystery and suspense writer, Brown was a reporter for the* Milwaukee Journal *before making the decision to become a fulltime writer in 1947. Although primarily and rightfully known in sf for his short stories, he also wrote several excellent sf novels, including* What Mad Universe *(1949),* The Lights in the Sky Are Stars *(1953), and* Martians go Home. *(1955).*

(Well, now, I think I'll have to put in a bit of dissent on this story. No, no, I don't contend that it doesn't belong here at all. I mean I want to dissent on the thesis because I'm a technophile [that is, I love advancing technology] and don't think that walking backward is the route to a Golden Age.

I just want to refer to one small passage in the story where Pete Mulvaney says that the air in New York City is "better than Atlantic City, without gasoline fumes" because the automobiles are gone. The next question from George Bailey is, "Enough horses to go around yet?" and the answer is "Almost."

Well, I've passed the horses at Central Park that pull the buggies, two or three of them, and I have to hold my breath every time. They stink *of sweat and manure. That's two or three. Fill the city enough to take care of even the "last million people" the story speaks of and everyone will long for gas fumes again. Particularly in the summer when there will be no air-conditioning [something Fred, writing in 1945, says nothing about].*

Enjoy the story, but keep your perspective, that's all. I.A.)

Definitions from the school-abridged Webster-Hamlin Dictionary, 1998 edition:

wavery (WA-vĕr-i) n. a vader—*slang*
vader (VA-dĕr) n. inorgan of the class Radio
inorgan (in-ÔR-găn) n. noncorporeal ens, a vader
radio (RA-di-ō) n. 1. class of inorgans 2. etheric frequency between light and electricity 3. (obsolete) method of communication used up to 1957

The opening guns of invasion were not at all loud, although they were heard by millions of people. George Bailey was one of the millions. I choose George Bailey because he was the only one who came within a googol of light-years of guessing what they were.

George Bailey was drunk and under the circumstances one can't blame him for being so. He was listening to radio advertisements of the most nauseous kind. Not because he wanted to listen to them, I hardly need say, but because he'd been told to listen to them by his boss, J. R. McGee of the MID network.

George Bailey wrote advertising for the radio. The only thing he hated worse than advertising was radio. And here on his own time he was listening to fulsome and disgusting commercials on a rival network.

"Bailey," J. R. McGee had said, "you should be more familiar with what others are doing. Particularly, you should be informed about those of our own accounts who use several networks. I strongly suggest . . ."

One doesn't quarrel with an employer's strong suggestions and keep a two hundred dollar a week job.

But one can drink whisky sours while listening. George Bailey did.

Also, between commercials, he was playing gin rummy with Maisie Hetterman, a cute little redheaded typist from the studio. It was Maisie's apartment and Maisie's radio (George himself, on principle, owned neither a radio nor a TV set) but George had brought the liquor.

"—only the very finest tobaccos," said the radio, "go *dit-dit-dit* nation's favorite cigarette—"

George glanced at the radio. "Marconi," he said.

He meant Morse, naturally, but the whisky sours had muddled him a bit so his first guess was more nearly right than anyone else's. It *was* Marconi, in a way. In a very peculiar way.

"Marconi?" asked Maisie.

George, who hated to talk against a radio, leaned over and switched it off.

"I meant Morse," he said. "Morse, as in Boy Scouts or the Signal Corps. I used to be a Boy Scout once."

"You've sure changed," Maisie said.

George sighed. "Somebody's going to catch hell, broadcasting code on that wave length."

"What did it mean?"

"Mean? Oh, you mean what did it mean. Uh—S, the letter S. *Dit-dit-dit* is S. SOS is *dit-dit-dit dah-dah-dah dit-dit-dit.*"

"O is *dah-dah-dah*?"

George grinned. "Say that again, Maisie. I like it. And I think you are *dah-dah-dah* too."

"George, maybe it's really an SOS message. Turn it back on."

George turned it back on. The tobacco ad was still going. "—gentlemen of the most *dit-dit-dit* -ing taste prefer the finer taste of *dit-dit-dit* -arettes. In the new package that keeps them *dit-dit-dit* and ultra fresh—"

"It's not SOS. It's just S's."

"Like a teakettle or—say, George, maybe it's just some advertising gag."

George shook his head. "Not when it can blank out the name of the product. Just a minute till I—"

He reached over and turned the dial of the radio a bit to the right and then a bit to the left, and an incredulous look came into his face. He turned the dial to the extreme left, as far as it would go. There wasn't any station there, not even the hum of a carrier wave. But:

"*Dit-dit-dit*," said the radio, "*dit-dit-dit*."

He turned the dial to the extreme right. "*Dit-dit-dit*."

George switched it off and stared at Maisie without seeing her, which was hard to do.

"Something wrong, George?"

"I hope so," said George Bailey. "I certainly hope so."

He started to reach for another drink and changed his mind. He had a sudden hunch that something big was happening and he wanted to sober up to appreciate it.

He didn't have the faintest idea *how* big it was.

"George, what do you mean?"

"I don't know what I mean. But Maisie, let's take a run down to the studio, huh? There ought to be some excitement."

April 5, 1957; that was the night the waveries came.

It had started like an ordinary evening. It wasn't one, now.

George and Maisie waited for a cab but none came so they took the subway instead. Oh yes, the subways were still running in those days. It took them within a block of the MID Network Building.

The building was a madhouse. George, grinning, strolled through the lobby with Maisie on his arm, took the elevator to the fifth floor and for no reason at all gave the elevator boy a dollar. He'd never before in his life tipped an elevator operator.

The boy thanked him. "Better stay away from the big shots, Mr. Bailey," he said. "They're ready to chew the ears off anybody who even looks at 'em."

"Wonderful," said George.

From the elevator he headed straight for the office of J. R. McGee himself.

There were strident voices behind the glass door. George reached for the knob and Maisie tried to stop him. "But George," she whispered, "you'll be fired!"

"There comes a time," said George. "Stand back away from the door, honey."

Gently but firmly he moved her to a safe position.

"But George, what are you—?"

"Watch," he said.

The frantic voices stopped as he opened the door a foot. All eyes turned toward him as he stuck his head around the corner of the doorway into the room.

"*Dit-dit-dit*," he said. "*Dit-dit-dit*."

He ducked back and to the side just in time to escape the flying glass as a paperweight and an inkwell came through the pane of the door.

He grabbed Maisie and ran for the stairs.

"Now we get a drink," he told her.

The bar across the street from the network building was crowded but it was a strangely silent crowd. In deference to the fact that most of its customers were radio people it didn't have a TV set but there was a big cabinet radio and most of the people were bunched around it.

"*Dit*," said the radio. "*Dit-dah-d'dah-dit-dahditdah dit—*"

"Isn't it beautiful?" George whispered to Maisie.

Somebody fiddled with the dial. Somebody asked, "What band is that?" and somebody said, "Police." Somebody said, "Try the foreign band," and somebody did. "This ought to be Buenos Aires," somebody said. "*Dit-d'dah-dit—*" said the radio.

Somebody ran fingers through his hair and said, "Shut that damn thing off." Somebody else turned it back on.

George grinned and led the way to a back booth where he'd spotted Pete Mulvaney sitting alone with a bottle in front of him. He and Maisie sat across from Pete.

"Hello," he said gravely.

"Hell," said Pete, who was head of the technical research staff of MID.

"A beautiful night, Mulvaney," George said. "Did you see the moon riding the fleecy clouds like a golden galleon tossed upon silver-crested whitecaps in a stormy—"

"Shut up," said Pete. "I'm thinking."

"Whisky sours," George told the waiter. He turned back to the man across the table. "Think out loud, so we can hear. But first, how did you escape the booby hatch across the street?"

"I'm bounced, fired, discharged."

"Shake hands. And then explain. Did you say *dit-dit-dit* to them?"

Pete looked at him with sudden admiration. "Did you?"

"I've a witness. What *did* you do?"

"Told 'em what I thought it was and they think I'm crazy."

"Are you?"

"Yes."

"Good," said George. "Then we want to hear—" He snapped his fingers. "What about TV?"

"Same thing. Same sound on audio and the pictures flicker and dim with every dot or dash. Just a blur by now."

"Wonderful. And now tell me what's wrong. I don't care what it is, as long as it's nothing trivial, but I want to know."

"I think it's space. Space is warped."

"Good old space," George Bailey said.

"George," said Maisie, "please shut up. I want to hear this."

"Space," said Pete, "is also finite." He poured himself another drink. You go far enough in any direction and get back where you started. Like an ant crawling around an apple."

"Make it an orange," George said.

"All right, an orange. Now suppose the first radio waves ever sent out have just made the round trip. In fifty-six years."

"Fifty-six years? But I thought radio waves traveled at the same speed as light. If that's right, then in fifty-six years they could go only fifty-six light-years, and *that* can't be around the universe because there are galaxies known to be millions or maybe billions of light-years away. I don't remember the figures, Pete, but our own galaxy alone is a hell of a lot bigger than fifty-six light-years."

Pete Mulvaney sighed. "That's why I say space must be warped. There's a short cut somewhere."

"*That* short a short cut? Couldn't be."

"But George, listen to that stuff that's coming in. Can you read code?"

"Not any more. Not that fast, anyway."

"Well, I can," Pete said. "That's early American ham. Lingo and all. That's the kind of stuff the air was full of before regular broadcasting. It's the lingo, the abbreviations, the barnyard to attic chitchat of amateurs with keys, with Marconi coherers or Fessenden barreters—and you can listen for a violin solo pretty soon now. I'll tell you what it'll be."

"What?"

"Handel's *Largo*. The first phonograph record ever broadcast. Sent out by Fessenden from Brant Rock in 1906. You'll hear his CQ-CQ any minute now. Bet you a drink."

"Okay, but what was the *dit-dit-dit* that started this?"

Mulvaney grinned. "Marconi, George. What was the most powerful signal ever broadcast and by whom and when?"

"Marconi? *Dit-dit-dit*? Fifty-six years ago?"

"Head of the class. The first transatlantic signal on December 12, 1901. For three hours Marconi's big station at Poldhu, with two-hundred-foot masts, sent out an intermittent S, *dit-dit-dit*, while Marconi and two assistants at St. Johns in Newfoundland got a kite-borne aerial four hundred feet in the air and finally got the signal. Across the Atlantic, George, with sparks jumping from the big Leyden jars at Poldhu and 20,000-volt juice jumping off the tremendous aerials—"

"Wait a minute, Pete, you're off the beam. If that was in 1901 and the first broadcast was about 1906 it'll be five years before the Fessenden stuff gets here on the same route. Even if there's a fifty-six light-year short cut across space and even if those signals didn't get so weak en route that we couldn't hear them—it's crazy."

"I told you it was," Pete said gloomily. "Why, those signals after traveling that far would be so infinitesimal that for practical purposes they wouldn't exist. Furthermore they're all over the band on everything from microwave on up and equally strong on each. And, as you point out, we've already come almost five years in two hours, which isn't possible. I told you it was crazy."

"But—"

"Ssshh. Listen," said Pete.

A blurred, but unmistakably human voice was coming from the radio, mingling with the cracklings of code. And then music, faint and scratchy, but unmistakably a violin. Playing Handel's *Largo*.

Only suddenly it climbed in pitch as though modulating from key to key until it became so horribly shrill that it hurt the ear. And kept on going past the high limit of audibility until they could hear it no more.

Somebody said, "Shut that God damn thing off." Somebody did, and this time nobody turned it back on.

Pete said, "I didn't really believe it myself. And there's another thing against it, George. Those signals affect TV too, and radio waves are the wrong length to do that."

He shook his head slowly. "There must be some other explanation, George. The more I think about it now the more I think I'm wrong."

He was right: he was wrong.

"Preposterous," said Mr. Ogilvie. He took off his glasses, frowned fiercely, and put them back on again. He looked through them at the several sheets of copy paper in his hand and tossed them contemptuously to the top of his desk. They slid to rest against the triangular name plate that read:

B. R. OGILVIE
Editor-in-Chief

"Preposterous," he said again.

Casey Blair, his best reporter, blew a smoke ring and poked his index finger through it. "Why?" he asked.

"Because—why, it's *utterly* preposterous."

Casey Blair said, "It is now three o'clock in the morning. The interference has gone on for five hours and not a single program is getting through on either TV or radio. Every major broadcasting and telecasting station in the world has gone off the air.

"For two reasons. One, they were just wasting current. Two, the communications bureaus of their respective governments requested them to get off to aid their campaigns with the direction finders. For five hours now, since the start of the interference, they've been working with everything they've got. And what have they found out?"

"It's preposterous!" said the editor.

"Perfectly, but it's true. Greenwich at 11 P.M. New York time; I'm translating all these times into New York time—got a bearing in about the direction of Miami. It shifted northward until at two o'clock the direction was approximately that of Richmond, Virginia. San Francisco at eleven got a bearing in about the direction of Denver; three hours later it shifted southward toward Tucson. Southern hemisphere: bearings from Capetown, South Africa, shifted from direction of Buenos Aires to that of Montevideo, a thousand miles north.

"New York at eleven had weak indications toward Madrid; but by two o'clock they could get no bearings at all." He blew another smoke ring. "Maybe because the loop antennae they use turn only on a horizontal plane?"

"Absurd."

Casey said, "I like 'preposterous' better, Mr. Ogilvie. Preposterous it is, but it's not absurd. I'm scared stiff. Those lines—and all other bearings I've heard about—run in the *same direction* if you take them as straight lines running as tangents off the Earth instead of curving them around the surface. I did it with a little globe and a star map. They converge on the constellation Leo."

He leaned forward and tapped a forefinger on the top page of the story he'd just turned in. "Stations that are directly under Leo in the sky get no bearings at all. Stations on what would be the perimeter of Earth relative to that point get the strongest bearings. Listen, have an astronomer check those figures if you want before you run the story, but get it done damn quick—unless you want to read about it in the other newspapers first."

"But the heaviside layer, Casey—isn't that supposed to stop all radio waves and bounce them back?"

"Sure, it does. But maybe it leaks. Or maybe signals can get through it from the outside even though they can't get out from the inside. It isn't a solid wall."

"But—"

"I know, it's preposterous. But there it is. And there's only an hour before press time. You'd better send this story through fast and have it being set up while you're having somebody check my facts and directions. Besides, there's something else you'll want to check."

"What?"

"I didn't have the data for checking the positions of the planets. Leo's on the ecliptic; a planet could be in line between here and there. Mars, maybe."

Mr. Ogilvie's eyes brightened, then clouded again. He said, "We'll be the laughingstock of the world, Blair, if you're wrong."

"And if I'm right?"

The editor picked up the phone and snapped an order.

April 6th headline of the New York *Morning Messenger*, final (6 A.M.) edition:

RADIO INTERFERENCE
COMES FROM SPACE,
ORIGINATES IN LEO

May be Attempt at Communication by Beings Outside Solar System

All television and radio broadcasting was suspended.

Radio and television stocks opened several points off the previous day and then dropped sharply until noon when a moderate buying rally brought them a few points back.

Public reaction was mixed; people who had no radios rushed out to buy them and there was a boom, especially in portable and table-top receivers. On the other hand, no TV sets were sold at all. With telecasting suspended there were no pictures on their screens, even blurred ones. Their audio circuits, when turned on, brought in the same jumble as radio receivers. Which, as Pete Mulvaney had pointed out to George Bailey, was impossible; radio waves cannot activate the audio circuits of TV sets. But these did, if they *were* radio waves.

In radio sets they seemed to be radio waves, but horribly hashed. No one could listen to them very long. Oh, there were flashes—times when, for several consecutive seconds, one could recognize the voice of Will Rogers or Geraldine Farrar or catch flashes of the Dempsey-Carpentier fight or the Pearl Harbor excitement. (Remember Pearl Harbor?) But things even remotely worth hearing were rare. Mostly it was a meaningless mixture of soap opera, advertising and off-key snatches of what had once been music. It was utterly indiscriminate, and utterly unbearable for any length of time.

But curiosity is a powerful motive. There *was* a brief boom in radio sets for a few days.

There were other booms, less explicable, less capable of analysis. Reminiscent of the Wells-Welles Martian scare of 1938 was a sudden upswing in the sale of shotguns and sidearms. Bibles sold as fast as books on astronomy—and books on astronomy sold like hotcakes. One section of the country showed a sudden interest in lightning rods; builders were flooded with orders for immediate installation.

For some reason which has never been clearly ascertained there was a run of fishhooks in Mobile, Alabama; every hardware and sporting goods store sold out of them within hours.

The public libraries and bookstores had a run on books on astrology and books on Mars. Yes, on Mars—despite the fact that Mars was at that moment on the other side of the sun and that every newspaper article on the subject stressed the fact that *no* planet was between Earth and the constellation Leo.

Something strange was happening—and no news of developments available except through the newspapers. People waited in mobs outside newspaper buildings for each new edition to appear. Circulation managers went quietly mad.

People also gathered in curious little knots around the silent broadcasting studios and stations, talking in hushed voices as though at a wake. MID network doors were locked, although there was a doorman on duty to admit technicians who were trying to find an answer to the problem. Some of the technicians who had been on duty the previous day had now spent over twenty-four hours without sleep.

George Bailey woke at noon, with only a slight headache. He shaved and showered, went out and drank a light breakfast and was himself again. He bought early editions of the afternoon papers, read them, grinned. His hunch had been right; whatever was wrong, it was nothing trivial.

But *what* was wrong?

The later editions of the afternoon papers had it.

EARTH INVADED, SAYS SCIENTIST

Thirty-six line type was the biggest they had; they used it. Not a home-edition copy of a newspaper was delivered that evening. Newsboys starting on their routes were practically mobbed. They sold papers instead of delivering them; the smart ones got a dollar apiece for them. The foolish and honest ones who didn't want to sell because they thought the papers should go to the regular customers on their routes lost them anyway. People grabbed them.

The final editions changed the heading only slightly—only slightly, that is, from a typographical viewpoint. Nevertheless, it was a tremendous change in meaning. It read:

EARTH INVADED, SAY SCIENTISTS

Funny what moving an S from the ending of a verb to the ending of a noun can do.

Carnegie Hall shattered precedent that evening with a lecture given at midnight. An unscheduled and unadvertised lecture. Professor Helmetz had stepped off the train at eleven-thirty and a mob of reporters had been waiting for him. Helmetz, of Harvard, had been the scientist, singular, who had made that first headline.

Harvey Ambers, director of the board of Carnegie Hall, had pushed his way through the mob. He arrived minus glasses, hat and breath, but got hold of Helmetz's arm and hung on until he could talk again. "We want you to talk at Carnegie, Professor," he shouted into Helmetz's ear. "Five thousand dollars for a lecture on the 'vaders.' "

"Certainly. Tomorrow afternoon?"

"Now! I've a cab waiting. Come on."

"But—"

"We'll get you an audience. Hurry!" He turned to the mob. "Let us through. All of you can't hear the professor here. Come to Carnegie Hall and he'll talk to you. And spread the word on your way there."

The word spread so well that Carnegie Hall was jammed by the time the professor began to speak. Shortly after, they'd rigged a loud-speaker system so the people outside could hear. By one o'clock in the morning the streets were jammed for blocks around.

There wasn't a sponsor on Earth with a million dollars to his name who wouldn't have given a million dollars gladly for the privilege of sponsoring that lecture on TV or radio, but it was not telecast or broadcast. Both lines were busy.

"Questions?" asked Professor Helmetz.

A reporter in the front row made it first. "Professor," he asked, "have all direction finding stations on Earth confirmed what you told us about the change this afternoon?"

"Yes, absolutely. At about noon all directional indications began to grow weaker. At 2:45 o'clock, Eastern Standard Time, they ceased completely. Until then the radio waves emanated from the sky, constantly changing direction with reference to the Earth's surface, but *constant* with reference to a point in the constellation Leo."

"What star in Leo?"

"No star visible on our charts. Either they came from a point in space or from a star too faint for our telescopes.

"But at 2:45 P.M. today—yesterday rather, since it is now past midnight—all direction finders went dead. But the signals persisted, now coming from all sides equally. The invaders had all arrived.

"There is no other conclusion to be drawn. Earth is now surrounded, completely blanketed, by radio-type waves which have *no point of origin*, which travel ceaselessly around the Earth in all directions, changing shape at their will—which currently is still in imitation of the Earth-origin radio signals which attracted their attention and brought them here."

"Do you think it was from a star we can't see, or could it have really been just a point in space?"

"Probably from a point in space. And why not? They are not creatures of matter. If they came here from a star, it must be a very dark star for it to be invisible to us, since it would be relatively near to us—only twenty-eight light-years away, which is quite close as stellar distances go."

"How can you know the distance?"

"By assuming—and it is a quite reasonable assumption—that they started our way when they first discovered our radio signals—Marconi's S-S-S code broadcast of fifty-six years ago. Since that was the form taken by the first arrivals, we assume they started toward us when they encountered those signals. Marconi's signals, traveling at the speed of light, would have reached a point twenty-eight light-years away twenty-eight years ago; the invaders, also traveling at light-speed would require an equal of time to reach us.

"As might be expected only the first arrivals took Morse code form. Later arrivals were in the form of other waves that they met and passed on—or perhaps absorbed—on their way to Earth. There are now wandering around the Earth, as it were, fragments of programs broadcast as recently as a few days ago. Undoubtedly there are fragments of the very last programs to be broadcast, but they have not yet been identified."

"Professor, can you *describe* one of these invaders?"

"As well as and no better than I can describe a radio wave. In effect, they *are* radio waves, although they emanate from no broadcasting station. They are a form of life dependent on wave motion, as our form of life is dependent on the vibration of matter."

"They are different sizes?"

"Yes, in two senses of the word size. Radio waves are measured from crest to crest, which measurement is known as the wave length. Since the invaders cover the entire dials of our radio sets and television sets it is obvious that either one of two things is true: Either they come in all crest-to-crest sizes or each one can change his crest-to-crest measurement to adapt himself to the tuning of any receiver.

"But that is only the crest-to-crest length. In a sense it may be said that a radio wave has an over-all length determined by its duration. If a broadcasting station sends out a program that has a second's duration, a wave carrying that program is one light-second long, roughly 187,000 miles. A continuous half-hour program is, as it were, on a continuous wave one-half light-hour long, and so on.

"Taking that form of length, the individual invaders vary in length from a few thousand miles—a duration of only a small fraction of a second—to well over half a million miles long—a duration of several seconds. The longest continuous excerpt from any one program that has been observed has been about seven seconds."

"But, Professor Helmetz, why do you assume that these waves are *living* things, a life form. Why not just waves?"

"Because 'just waves' as you call them would follow certain laws, just as inanimate *matter* follows certain laws. An animal can climb uphill, for instance; a stone cannot unless impelled by some outside force. These invaders are life-forms because they show volition; because they can change their direction of travel, and most especially because they retain their identity; two signals never conflict on the same radio receiver. They follow one another but do not come simultaneously. They do not mix as signals on the same wave length would ordinarily do. They are not 'just waves.' "

"Would you say they are intelligent?"

Professor Helmetz took off his glasses and polished them thoughtfully. He said, "I doubt if we shall ever know. The intelligence of such beings, if any, would be on such a completely different plane from ours that there would be no common point from which we could start intercourse. We are material; they are immaterial. There is no common ground between us."

"But if they are intelligent at all—"

"Ants are intelligent, after a fashion. Call it instinct if you will, but instinct is a form of intelligence; at least it enables them to accomplish some of the same things intelligence would enable them to accomplish. Yet we cannot establish communication with ants and it is far less likely that we shall be able to establish communication with these invaders. The difference in type between anti-intelligence and our own would be nothing to the difference in type between the intelligence, if any, of the invaders and our own. No, I doubt if we shall ever communicate."

The professor had something there. Communication with the vaders—a clipped form, of course, of *invaders*—was never established.

Radio stocks stabilized on the exchange the next day. But the day following that someone asked Dr. Helmetz a sixty-four dollar question and the newspapers published his answer:

"Resume broadcasting? I don't know if we ever shall. Certainly we cannot until the invaders go away, and why should they? Unless radio communication is perfected on some other planet far away and they're attracted there.

"But at least some of them would be right back the moment we started to broadcast again."

Radio and TV stocks dropped to practically zero in an hour. There weren't, however, any frenzied scenes on the stock exchanges; there was no frenzied selling because there was no buying, frenzied or otherwise. No radio stocks changed hands.

Radio and television employes and entertainers began to look for other jobs. The entertainers had no trouble finding them. Every other form of entertainment suddenly boomed like mad.

"Two down," said George Bailey. The bartender asked what he meant.

"I dunno, Hank. It's just a hunch I've got."

"What kind of hunch?"

"I don't even know that. Shake me up one more of those and then I'll go home."

The electric shaker wouldn't work and Hank had to shake the drink by hand.

"Good exercise; that's just what you need," George said. "It'll take some of that fat off you."

Hank grunted, and the ice tinkled merrily as he tilted the shaker to pour out the drink.

George Bailey took his time drinking it and then strolled out into an April thundershower. He stood under the awning and watched for a taxi. An old man was standing there too.

"Some weather," George said.

The old man grinned at him. "You noticed it, eh?"

"Huh? Noticed what?"

"Just watch a while, mister. Just watch a while."

The old man moved on. No empty cab came by and George stood there quite a while before he got it. His jaw dropped a little and then he closed his mouth and went back into the tavern. He went into a phone booth and called Pete Mulvaney.

He got three wrong numbers before he got Pete. Pete's voice said, "Yeah?"

"George Bailey, Pete. Listen, have you noticed the weather?"

"Damn right. *No lightning*, and there should be with a thunderstorm like this."

"What's it mean, Pete? The vaders?"

"Sure. And that's just going to be the start if—" A crackling sound on the wire blurred his voice out.

"Hey, Pete, you still there?"

The sound of a violin. Pete Mulvaney didn't play violin.

"Hey, Pete, what the hell—?"

Pete's voice again. "Come on over, George. Phone won't last long. Bring—" There was a buzzing noise and then a voice said, "—come to Carnegie Hall. The best tunes of all come—"

George slammed down the receiver.

He walked through the rain to Pete's place. On the way he bought a bottle of Scotch. Pete had started to tell him to bring something and maybe that's what he'd started to say.

It was.

They made a drink apiece and lifted them. The lights flickered briefly, went out, and then came on again but dimly.

"No lightning," said George. "No lightning and pretty soon

no lighting. They're taking over the telephone. What do they do with the lightning?"

"Eat it, I guess. They must eat electricity."

"No lightning," said George. "Damn. I can get by without a telephone, and candles and oil lamps aren't bad for lights—but I'm going to miss lightning. I *like* lightning. Damn."

The lights went out completely.

Pete Mulvaney sipped his drink in the dark. He said, "Electric lights, refrigerators, electric toasters, vacuum cleaners—"

"Juke boxes," George said. "Think of it, no more God damn juke boxes. No public address systems, no—hey, how about movies?"

"No movies, not even silent ones. You can't work a projector with an oil lamp. But listen, George, no automobiles—no gasoline engine can work without electricity."

"Why not, if you crank it by hand instead of using a starter?"

"The spark, George. What do you think makes the spark."

"Right. No airplanes either, then. Or how about jet planes?"

"Well—I guess some types of jets could be rigged not to need electricity, but you couldn't do much with them. Jet planes got more instruments than motor, and all those instruments are electrical. And you can't fly or land a jet by the seat of your pants."

"No radar. But what would we need it for? There won't be any more wars, not for a long time."

"A damned long time."

George sat up straight suddenly. "Hey, Pete, what about atomic fission? Atomic energy? Will it still work?"

"I doubt it. Subatomic phenomena are basically electrical. Bet you a dime they eat loose neutrons too." (He'd have won his bet; the government had not announced that an A-bomb tested that day in Nevada had fizzled like a wet firecracker and that atomic piles were ceasing to function.)

George shook his head slowly, in wonder. He said, "Streetcars and buses, ocean liners—Pete, this means we're going back to the original source of horsepower. Horses. If you want to invest, buy horses. Particularly mares. A brood mare is going to be worth a thousand times her weight in platinum."

"Right. But don't forget steam. We'll still have steam engines, stationary and locomotive."

"Sure, that's right. The iron horse again, for the long hauls. But Dobbin for the short ones. Can you ride, Pete?"

"Used to, but I think I'm getting too old. I'll settle for a bicycle. Say, better buy a bike first thing tomorrow before the run on them starts. I know *I'm* going to."

"Good tip. And I used to be a good bike rider. It'll be swell with no autos around to louse you up. And say—"

"What?"

"I'm going to get a cornet too. Used to play one when I was a kid and I can pick it up again. And then maybe I'll hole in somewhere and write that nov— Say, what about printing?"

"They printed books long before electricity, George. It'll take a while to readjust the printing industry, but there'll be books all right. Thank God for that."

George Bailey grinned and got up. He walked over to the window and looked out into the night. The rain had stopped and the sky was clear.

A streetcar was stalled, without lights, in the middle of the block outside. An automobile stopped, then started more slowly, stopped again; its headlights were dimming rapidly.

George looked up at the sky and took a sip of his drink.

"No lightning," he said sadly. "I'm going to *miss* the lightning."

The changeover went more smoothly than anyone would have thought possible.

The government, in emergency session, made the wise decision of creating one board with absolutely unlimited authority and under it only three subsidiary boards. The main board, called the Economic Readjustment Bureau, had only seven members and its job was to co-ordinate the efforts of the three subsidiary boards and to decide, quickly and without appeal, any jurisdictional disputes among them.

First of the three subsidiary boards was the Transportation Bureau. It immediately took over, temporarily, the railroads. It ordered Diesel engines run on sidings and left there, organized use of the steam locomotives, and solved the problems of railroading sans telegraphy and electric signals. It dictated, then, what should be transported; food coming first, coal and fuel oil second, and essential manufactured articles in the order of their relative importance. Carload after carload of new radios, electric stoves, refrigerators and such useless articles were dumped unceremoniously alongside the tracks, to be salvaged for scrap metal later.

All horses were declared wards of the government, graded according to capabilities, and put to work or to stud. Draft horses were used for only the most essential kinds of hauling. The breeding program was given the fullest possible emphasis; the bureau estimated that the equine population would double in two years, quadruple in three, and that within six or seven years there would be a horse in every garage in the country.

Farmers, deprived temporarily of their horses, and with their tractors rusting in the fields, were instructed how to use cattle for plowing and other work about the farm, including light hauling.

The second board, the Manpower Relocation Bureau, functioned just as one would deduce from its title. It handled unemployment benefits for the millions thrown temporarily out of work and helped relocate them—not too difficult a task considering the tremendously increased demand for hand labor in many fields.

In May of 1957 thirty-five million employables were out of work; in October, fifteen million; by May of 1958, five million. By 1959 the situation was completely in hand and competitive demand was already beginning to raise wages.

The third board had the most difficult job of the three. It was called the Factory Readjustment Bureau. It coped with the stupendous task of converting factories filled with electrically operated machinery and, for the most part, tooled for the production of other electrically operated machinery, over for the production, without electricity, of essential nonelectrical articles.

The few available stationary steam engines worked twenty-four hour shifts in those early days, and the first thing they were given to do was the running of lathes and stampers and planers and millers working on turning out more stationary steam engines, of all sizes. These, in turn, were first put to work making still more steam engines. The number of steam engines grew by squares and cubes, as did the number of horses put to stud. The principle was the same. One might, and many did, refer to those early steam engines as stud horses. At any rate, there was no lack of metal for them. The factories were filled with nonconvertible machinery waiting to be melted down.

Only when steam engines—the basis of the new factory economy—were in full production, were they assigned to running machinery for the manufacture of other articles. Oil lamps, clothing, coal stoves, oil stoves, bathtubs and bedsteads.

Not quite all of the big factories were converted. For while the conversion period went on, individual handicrafts sprang up in thousands of places. Little one- and two-man shops making and repairing furniture, shoes, candles, all sorts of things that *could* be made without complex machinery. At first these small shops made small fortunes because they had no competition from heavy industry. Later, they bought small steam engines to run small machines and held their own, growing with the boom that came with a return to normal employment and buying power, increasing gradually in size until many of them rivaled the bigger factories in output and beat them in quality.

There *was* suffering, during the period of economic readjustment, but less than there had been during the great depression of the early thirties. And the recovery was quicker.

The reason was obvious: In combating the depression, the legislators were working in the dark. They didn't know its cause—rather, they knew a thousand conflicting theories of its cause—and they didn't know the cure. They were hampered by the idea that the thing was temporary and would cure itself if left alone. Briefly and frankly, they didn't know what it was all about and while they experimented, it snowballed.

But the situation that faced the country—and all other countries—in 1957 was clear-cut and obvious. No more electricity. Readjust for steam and horsepower.

As simple and clear as that, and no ifs or ands or buts. And the whole people—except for the usual scattering of cranks—back of them.

By 1961—

It was a rainy day in April and George Bailey was waiting under the sheltering roof of the little railroad station at Blakestown, Connecticut, to see who might come in on the 3:14.

It chugged in at 3:25 and came to a panting stop, three coaches and a baggage car. The baggage car door opened and a sack of mail was handed out and the door closed again. No luggage, so probably no passengers would—

Then at the sight of a tall dark man swinging down from the platform of the rear coach, George Bailey let out a yip of delight. "Pete! Pete Mulvaney! What the devil—"

"Bailey, by all that's holy! What are you doing here?"

George wrung Pete's hand. "Me? I live here. Two years now. I bought the *Blakestown Weekly* in '59, for a song, and I run it—editor, reporter, and janitor. Got one printer to help me out with that end, and Maisie does the social items. She's—"

"Maisie? Maisie Hetterman?"

"Maisie Bailey now. We got married same time I bought the paper and moved here. What are you doing here, Pete?"

"Business. Just here overnight. See a man named Wilcox."

"Oh, Wilcox. Our local screwball—but don't get me wrong; he's a smart guy all right. Well, you can see him tomorrow. You're coming home with me now, for dinner and to stay overnight. Maisie'll be glad to see you. Come on, my buggy's over here."

"Sure. Finished whatever you were here for?"

"Yep, just to pick up the news on who came in on the train. And *you* came in, so here we go."

They got in the buggy, and George picked up the reins and said, "Giddup, Bessie," to the mare. Then, "What are you doing now, Pete?"

"Research. For a gas-supply company. Been working on a more efficient mantle, one that'll give more light and be less destructible. This fellow Wilcox wrote us he had something along that line; the company sent me up to look it over. If it's what he claims, I'll take him back to New York with me, and let the company lawyers dicker with him."

"How's business, otherwise?"

"Great, George. *Gas*; that's the coming thing. Every *new* home's being piped for it, and plenty of the old ones. How about you?"

"We got it. Luckily we had one of the old Linotypes that ran the metal pot off a gas burner, so it was already piped in. And our home is right over the office and print shop, so all we had to do was pipe it up a flight. Great stuff, gas. How's New York?"

"Fine, George. Down to its last million people, and stabilizing there. No crowding and plenty of room for everybody.

That *air*—why, it's better than Atlantic City, without gasoline fumes."

"Enough horses to go around yet?"

"Almost. But bicycling's the craze; the factories can't turn out enough to meet the demand. There's a cycling club in almost every block and all the able-bodied cycle to and from work. Doing 'em good, too; a few more years and the doctors will go on short rations."

"You got a bike?"

"Sure, a pre-vader one. Average five miles a day on it, and I eat like a horse."

George Bailey chuckled. "I'll have Maisie include some hay in the dinner. Well, here we are. Whoa, Bessie."

An upstairs window went up, and Maisie looked out and down. She called out, "Hi, Pete!"

"Extra plate, Maisie," George called. "We'll be up soon as I put the horse away and show Pete around downstairs."

He led Pete from the barn into the back door of the newspaper shop. "Our Linotype!" he announced proudly, pointing.

"How's it work? Where's your steam engine?"

George grinned. "Doesn't work yet; we still hand set the type. I could get only one steamer and had to use that on the press. But I've got one on order for the Lino, and coming up in a month or so. When we get it, Pop Jenkins, my printer, is going to put himself out of a job teaching me to run it. With the Linotype going, I can handle the whole thing myself."

"Kind of rough on Pop?"

George shook his head. "Pop eagerly awaits the day. He's sixty-nine and wants to retire. He's just staying on until I can do without him. Here's the press—a honey of a little Miehle; we do some job work on it, too. And this is the office, in front. Messy, but efficient."

Mulvaney looked around him and grinned. "George, I believe you've found your niche. You were cut out for a small-town editor."

"Cut out for it? I'm crazy about it. I have more fun than everybody. Believe it or not, I work like a dog, and like it. Come on upstairs."

On the stairs, Pete asked, "And the novel you were going to write?"

"Half done, and it isn't bad. But it isn't the novel I was going to write; I was a cynic then. Now—"

"George, I think the waveries were your best friends."

"Waveries?"

"Lord, how long does it take slang to get from New York out to the sticks? The vaders, of course. Some professor who specializes in studying them described one as a wavery place in the ether, and 'wavery' stuck—Hello there, Maisie, my girl. You look like a million."

They ate leisurely. Almost apologetically, George brought out beer, in cold bottles. "Sorry, Pete, haven't anything stronger to offer you. But I haven't been drinking lately. Guess—"

"*You* on the wagon, George?"

"Not on the wagon, exactly. Didn't swear off or anything, but haven't had a drink of strong liquor in almost a year. I don't know why, but—"

"I do," said Pete Mulvaney. "I know exactly why you don't—because I don't drink much either, for the same reason. We don't drink because we don't *have* to—say, isn't that a *radio* over there?"

George chuckled. "A souvenir. Wouldn't sell if for a fortune. Once in a while I like to look at it and think of the awful guff I used to sweat out for it. And then I go over and click the switch and nothing happens. Just silence. Silence is the most wonderful thing in the world, sometimes, Pete. Of course I couldn't do that if there was any juice, because I'd get vaders then. I suppose they're still doing business at the same old stand?"

"Yep, the Research Bureau checks daily. Try to get up current with a little generator run by a steam turbine. But no dice; the vaders suck it up as fast as it's generated."

"Suppose they'll ever go away?"

Mulvaney shrugged. "Helmetz thinks not. He thinks they propagate in proportion to the available electricity. Even if the development of radio broadcasting somewhere else in the Universe would attract them there, some would stay here—and multiply like flies the minute we tried to use electricity again. And meanwhile, they'll live on the static electricty in the air. What do you do evenings up here?"

"Do? Read, write, visit with one another, go to the amateur groups—Maise's chairman of the Blakestown Players, and I play bit parts in it. With the movies out everybody goes in for theatricals and we've found some real talent. And there's the chess-and-checker club, and cycle trips and picnics—there isn't time enough. Not to mention music. Everybody plays an instrument, or is trying to."

"You?"

"Sure, cornet. First cornet in the Silver Concert Band, with solo parts. And—Good Heavens! Tonight's rehearsal, and we're giving a concert Sunday afternoon. I hate to desert you, but—"

"Can't I come around and sit in? I've got my flute in the brief case here, and—"

"*Flute?* We're short on flutes. Bring that around and Si Perkins, our director, will practically shanghai you into staying over for the concert Sunday—and it's only three days, so why not? And get it out now; we'll play a few old timers to warm up. Hey, Maisie, skip those dishes and come on in to the piano!"

While Pete Mulvaney went to the guest room to get his flute from the brief case, George Bailey picked up his cornet from the top of the piano and blew a soft, plaintive little minor run on it. Clear as a bell; his lip was in good shape tonight.

And with the shining silver thing in his hand he wandered over to the window and stood looking out into the night. It was dusk out and the rain had stopped.

A high-stepping horse *clop-clopped* by and the bell of a bicycle jangled. Somebody across the street was strumming a guitar and singing. He took a deep breath and let it out slowly.

The scent of spring was soft and sweet in the moist air.

Peace and dusk.

Distant rolling thunder.

God damn it, he thought, *if only there was a bit of lightning.*

He missed the lightning.

THE PIPER'S SON

by "Lewis Padgett" (Henry Kuttner [1914-1958] and C. L. Moore [1911-])

ASTOUNDING SCIENCE FICTION,
February

Henry Kuttner and his wife, Catherine L. Moore, were arguably the dominant writers in sf in the mid to late 1940s, writing many stories under their own names and others as "Lewis Padgett" and "Lawrence O'Donnell," and this selection is the first of three in this book. All stories under all of their names should be approached with caution—it is likely that both had something to do with every one of them (after 1940), even those signed by Kuttner or Moore alone.

"The Piper's Son" was the first of their "Baldy" series of stories (published as Mutant *in 1953) about humans mutated and endowed with special powers as a result of an atomic war. All are powerful treatments of the situation of the outsider in society, split among themselves over the uses to which their unique talents should be put.*

(The year 1945 was the Year of the Bomb and mutant stories went into high gear. We knew that radiation could damage the body's genetic mechanisms, but we intended to imagine dramatic mutations that, from the standpoint of sober science, were utterly unlikely, while ignoring the obvious result—radiation sickness and death.

Then, too, looking back on the stories of a generation ago, it is remarkable how many stories bear the clear mark of John Campbell's notions. I wonder if he published any stories at all that he didn't put his mark on, usually by indoctrinating his writers beforehand. I know he labored for hours indoctrinating me but I was never really aware at the time that other writers were subjected to the same process.

Campbell had the distinct impression that mutants with superhuman characteristics would be cut down and destroyed by ordinary human beings. We had it in A. E. van Vogt's "Slan" most notably and in Robert Heinlein's "Methuselah's Children." Campbell may have thought this because I suspect he felt he had been scapegoated in youth for the crime of being mentally superior and many science fiction writers went along with him because they perhaps had also experienced an uncomfortable childhood for the same reason.

Come to think of it, I was occasionally scapegoated when I was young, but not for being superior—just for being a pain in the neck, which I was, till I learned better. I.A.)

The Green Man was climbing the glass mountains, and hairy, gnomish faces peered at him from crevices. This was only another step in the Green Man's endless, exciting odyssey. He'd had a great many adventures already—in the Flame Country, among the Dimension Changers, with the City Apes who sneered endlessly while their blunt, clumsy fingers fumbled at deathrays. The trolls, however, were masters of magic, and were trying to stop the Green Man with spells. Little whirlwinds of force spun underfoot, trying to trip the Green Man, a figure of marvelous muscular development, handsome as a god, and hairless from head to foot, glistening pale green. The whirlwinds formed a fascinating pattern. If you could thread a precarious path among them—avoiding the pale yellow ones especially—you could get through.

And the hairy gnomes watched malignantly, jealously, from their crannies in the glass crags.

Al Burkhalter, having recently achieved the mature status of eight full years, lounged under a tree and masticated a grass blade. He was so immersed in his daydreams that his father had to nudge his side gently to bring comprehension into the half-closed eyes. It was a good day for dreaming, anyway—a hot sun and a cool wind blowing down from the white Sierra peaks to the east. Timothy grass sent its faintly musty fragrance along the channels of air, and Ed Burkhalter was glad that his son was second-generation since the Blowup. He himself had been born ten years after the last bomb had been dropped, but second-hand memories can be pretty bad too.

"Hello, Al," he said, and the youth vouchsafed a half-lidded glance of tolerant acceptance.

"Hi, Dad."

"Want to come downtown with me?"

"Nope," Al said, relaxing instantly into his stupor.

Burkhalter raised a figurative eyebrow and half turned. On an impulse, then, he did something he rarely did without the tacit permission of the other party; he used his telepathic power to reach into Al's mind. There was, he admitted to himself, a certain hesitancy, a subconscious unwillingness on his part, to do this, even though Al had pretty well outgrown the nasty, inhuman formlessness of mental babyhood. There had been a time when Al's mind had been quite shocking in its alienage. Burkhalter remembered a few abortive experiments he had made before Al's birth; few fathers-to-be could resist the temptation to experiment with embryonic brains, and that had brought back nightmares Burkhalter had not had since his youth. There had been enormous rolling masses, and an appalling vastness, and other things. Prenatal memories were ticklish, and should be left to qualified mnemonic psychologists.

But now Al was maturing, and daydreaming, as usual, in bright colors. Burkhalter, reassured, felt that he had fulfilled his duty as a monitor and left his son still eating grass and ruminating.

Just the same, there was a sudden softness inside of him, and the aching, futile pity he was apt to feel for helpless things that were as yet unqualified for conflict with that extraordinarily complicated business of living. Conflict, competition, had not died out when war abolished itself; the business of adjustment even to one's surroundings was a conflict, and conversation a duel. With Al, too, there was a double problem. Yes, language was in effect a tariff wall, and a Baldy could appreciate that thoroughly, since the wall didn't exist between Baldies.

Walking down the rubbery walk that led to town center, Burkhalter grinned wryly and ran lean fingers through his well-kept wig. Strangers were very often surprised to know that he was a Baldy, a telepath. They looked at him with wondering eyes, too courteous to ask how it felt to be a freak, but obviously avid. Burkhalter, who knew diplomacy, would be quite willing to lead the conversation.

"My folks lived near Chicago after the Blowup. That was why."

"Oh." Stare. "I'd heard that was why so many—" Startled pause.

"Freaks or mutations. There were both. I still don't know which class I belong to," he'd add disarmingly.

"You're no freak!" They didn't protest too much.

"Well, some mighty queer specimens came out of the radioactive-affected areas around the bomb targets. Funny things happened to the germ plasm. Most of 'em died out; they couldn't reproduce; but you'll still find a few creatures in sanitariums—two heads, you know. And so on."

Nevertheless they were always ill-at-ease. "You mean you can read my mind—now?"

"I could, but I'm not. It's hard work, except with another telepath. And we Baldies—well, we don't, that's all." A man with abnormal muscle development wouldn't go around knocking people down. Not unless he wanted to be mobbed. Baldies were always sneakingly conscious of a hidden peril: lynch law. And wise Baldies didn't even imply that they had an . . . extra sense. They just said they were different, and let it go at that.

But one question was always implied, though not always mentioned. "If I were a telepath, I'd . . . how much do you make a year?"

They were surprised at the answer. A mindreader certainly could make a fortune, if he wanted. So why did Ed Burkhalter stay a semantics expert in Modoc Publishing Town, when a trip to one of the science towns would enable him to get hold of secrets that would get him a fortune?

There was a good reason. Self-preservation was a part of

it. For which reason Burkhalter, and many like him, wore toupees. Though there were many Baldies who did not.

Modoc was a twin town with Pueblo, across the mountain barrier south of the waste that had been Denver. Pueblo held the presses, photolinotypes, and the machines that turned scripts into books, after Modoc had dealt with them. There was a helicopter distribution fleet at Pueblo, and for the last week Oldfield, the manager, had been demanding the manuscript of "Psychohistory," turned out by a New Yale man who had got tremendously involved in past emotional problems, to the detriment of literary clarity. The truth was that he distrusted Burkhalter. And Burkhalter, neither a priest nor a psychologist, had to become both without admitting it to the confused author of "Psychohistory."

The sprawling buildings of the publishing house lay ahead and below, more like a resort than anything more utilitarian. That had been necessary. Authors were peculiar people, and often it was necessary to induce them to take hydrotherapic treatments before they were in shape to work out their books with the semantic experts. Nobody was going to bite them, but they didn't realize that, and either cowered in corners, terrified, or else blustered their way around, using language few could understand. Jem Quayle, author of "Psychohistory," fitted into neither group; he was simply baffled by the intensity of his own research. His personal history had qualified him too well for emotional involvements with the past—and that was a serious matter when a thesis of this particular type was in progress.

Dr. Moon, who was on the Board, sat near the south entrance, eating an apple which he peeled carefully with his silver-hilted dagger. Moon was fat, short, and shapeless; he didn't have much hair, but he wasn't a telepath; Baldies were entirely hairless. He gulped and waved at Burkhalter.

"Ed . . . *urp* . . . want to talk to you."

"Sure," Burkhalter said, agreeably coming to a standstill and rocking on his heels. Ingrained habit made him sit down beside the Boardman; Baldies, for obvious reasons, never stood up when nontelepaths were sitting. Their eyes met now on the same level. Burkhalter said, "What's up?"

"The store got some Shasta apples flown in yesterday. Better tell Ethel to get some before they're sold out. Here." Moon watched his companion eat a chunk, and nod.

"Good. I'll have her get some. The 'copter's laid up for today, though; Ethel pulled the wrong gadget."

"Foolproof," Moon said bitterly. "Huron's turning out some sweet models these days; I'm getting my new one from Michigan. Listen, Pueblo called me this morning on Quayle's book."

"Oldfield?"

"Our boy," Moon nodded. "He says can't you send over even a few chapters."

Burkhalter shook his head. "I don't think so. There are some abstracts right in the beginning that just have to be clarified, and Quayle is—" He hesitated.

"What?"

Burkhalter thought about the Oedipus complex he'd uncovered in Quayle's mind, but that was sancrosanct, even though it kept Quayle from interpreting Darius with cold logic. "He's got muddy thinking in there. I can't pass it; I tried it on three readers yesterday, and got different reactions from all of them. So far 'Psychohistory' is all things to all men. The critics would lambaste us if we released the book as is. Can't you string Oldfield along for a while longer?"

"Maybe," Moon said doubtfully. "I've got a subjective novella I could rush over. It's light vicarious eroticism, and that's harmless; besides, it's semantically O.K.'d. We've been holding it up for an artist, but I can put Duman on it. I'll do that, yeah. I'll shoot the script over to Pueblo and he can make the plates later. A merry life we lead, Ed."

"A little too merry sometimes," Burkhalter said. He got up, nodded, and went in search of Quayle, who was relaxing on one of the sun decks.

Quayle was a thin, tall man with a worried face and the abstract air of an unshelled tortoise. He lay on his flexiglass couch, direct sunlight toasting him from above, while the reflected rays sneaked up on him from below, through the transparent crystal. Burkhalter pulled off his shirt and dropped on a sunner beside Quayle. The author glanced at Burkhalter's hairless chest and half-formed revulsion rose in him: *A Baldy . . . no privacy . . . none of his business . . . fake eyebrows and lashes; he's still a—*

Something ugly, at that point.

Diplomatically Burkhalter touched a button, and on a screen overhead a page of "Psychohistory" appeared, enlarged and easily readable. Quayle scanned the sheet. It had code notations on it, made by the readers, recognized by Burkhalter as varied reactions to what should have been straight-line explanations. If three readers had got three different meanings out of that paragraph—well, what *did* Quayle mean? He reached delicately into the mind, conscious of useless guards erected against intrusion, mud barricades over which his mental eye stole like a searching, quiet wind. No ordinary man could guard his mind against a Baldy. But Baldies could guard their privacy against intrusion by other telepaths—adults, that is. There was a psychic selector band, a—

Here it came. But muddled a bit. *Darius*: that wasn't simply a word; it wasn't a picture, either; it was really a second *life*. But scattered, fragmentary. Scraps of scent and sound, and memories, and emotional reactions. Admiration and hatred. A burning impotence. A black tornado, smelling of pine, roaring across a map of Europe and Asia. Pine scent stronger now, and horrible humiliation, and remembered pain . . . eyes . . . *Get Out!*

Burkhalter put down the dictograph mouthpiece and lay looking up through the darkened eye-shells he had donned. "I got out as soon as you wanted me to," he said. "I'm still out."

Quayle lay there, breathing hard. "Thanks," he said. "Apologies. Why you don't ask a duello—"

"I don't want to duel with you," Burkhalter said. "I've never put blood on my dagger in my life. Besides, I can see your side of it. Remember, this is my job, Mr. Quayle, and I've learned a lot of things—that I've forgotten again."

"It's intrusion, I suppose. I tell myself that it doesn't matter, but my privacy—is important."

Burkhalter said patiently, "We can keep trying it from different angles until we find one that isn't too private. Suppose, for example, I asked you if you admired Darius."

Admiration . . . and pine scent . . . and Burkhalter said quickly, "I'm out. O.K.?"

"Thanks," Quayle muttered. He turned on his side, away from the other man. After a moment he said, "That's silly—turning over, I mean. You don't have to see my face to know what I'm thinking."

"You have to put out the welcome mat before I walk in," Burkhalter told him.

"I guess I believe that. I've met some Baldies, though, that were . . . that I didn't like."

"There's a lot on that order, sure. I know the type. The ones who don't wear wigs."

Quayle said, "They'll read your mind and embarrass you just for the fun of it. They ought to be—taught better."

Burkhalter blinked in the sunlight. "Well, Mr. Quayle, it's this way. A Baldy's got his problems, too. He's got to orient himself to a world that isn't telepathic; and I suppose a lot of Baldies rather feel that they're letting their specialization go to waste. There *are* jobs a man like me is suited for—"

"*Man!*" He caught the scrap of thought from Quayle. He ignored it, his face was always a mobile mask, and went on.

"Semantics have always been a problem, even in countries speaking only one tongue. A qualified Baldy is a swell interpreter. And, though there aren't any Baldies on the detective forces, they often work with the police. It's rather like being a machine that can do only a few things."

"A few things more than humans can," Quayle said.

Sure, Burkhalter thought, if we could compete on equal footing with nontelepathic humanity. But would blind men trust one who could see? Would they play poker with him? A sudden, deep bitterness put an unpleasant taste in Burkhalter's mouth. What was the answer? Reservations for Baldies? Isolation? And would a nation of blind men trust those with vision enough for that? Or would they be dusted off—the sure cure, the check-and-balance system that made war an impossibility?

He remembered when Red Bank had been dusted off, and maybe that had been justified. The town was getting too big for its boots, and personal dignity was a vital factor; you weren't willing to lose face as long as a dagger swung at your belt. Similarly, the thousands upon thousands of little towns that covered America, each with its perculiar specialy—helicopter manufacture for Huron and Michigan, vegetable farming for Conoy and Diego, textiles and education and art and machines—each little town had a wary eye on all the others. The science and research centers were a little larger; nobody objected to that, for technicians never made war except under pressure; but few of the towns held more than a few hundred families. It was check-and-balance in most efficient degree; whenever a town showed signs of wanting to become a city—thence, a capital, thence, an imperialistic empire—it was dusted off. Though that had not happened for a long while. And Red Bank might have been a mistake.

Geopolitically it was a fine setup; sociologically it was acceptable, but brought necessary changes. There was subconsicous swashbuckling. The rights of the individual had become more highly regarded as decentralization took place. And men learned.

They learned a monetary system based primarily upon barter. They learned to fly; nobody drove surface cars. They learned new things, but they did not forget the Blowup, and in secret places near every town were hidden the bombs that could utterly and fantastically exterminate a town, as such bombs had exterminated the cities during the Blowup.

And everybody knew how to make those bombs. They were beautifully, terribly simple. You could find the ingredients anywhere and prepare them easily. Then you could take your helicopter over a town, drop an egg overside—and perform an erasure.

Outside of the wilderness malcontents, the maladjusted people found in every race, nobody kicked. And the roaming tribes never raided and never banded together in large groups—for fear of an erasure.

The artisans were maladjusted too, to some degree, but they weren't antisocial, so they lived where they wanted and painted, wrote, composed, and retreated into their own private worlds. The scientists, equally maladjusted in other lines, retreated to their slightly larger towns, banding together in small universes, and turned out remarkable technical achievements.

And the Baldies—found jobs where they could.

No nontelepath would have viewed the world environment quite as Burkhalter did. He was abnormally conscious of the human element, attaching a deeper, more profound significance to those human values, undoubtedly because he saw men in more than the ordinary dimensions. And also, in a way—and inevitably—he looked at humanity from outside.

Yet he was human. The barrier that telepathy had raised made men suspicious of him, more so than if he had had two heads—then they could have pitied. As it was—

As it was, he adjusted the scanner until new pages of the typescript came flickering into view above. "Say when," he told Quayle.

Quayle brushed back his gray hair. "I feel sensitive all over," he objected. "After all, I've been under a considerable strain correlating my material."

"Well, we can always postpone publication." Burkhalter threw out the suggestion casually, and was pleased when Quayle didn't nibble. He didn't like to fail, either.

"No. No, I want to get the thing done now."

"Mental catharsis—"

"Well, by a psychologist, perhaps. But not by—"

"—a Baldy. You know that a lot of psychologists have Baldy helpers. They get good results, too."

Quayle turned on the tobacco smoke, inhaling slowly. "I suppose . . . I've not had much contact with Baldies. Or too much—without selectivity. I saw some in an asylum once. I'm not being offensive, am I?"

"No," Burkhalter said. "Every mutation can run too close to the line. There were lots of failures. The hard radiations brought about one true mutation: hairless telepaths, but they didn't all hew true to the line. The mind's a queer gadget—you know that. It's a colloid balancing, figuratively, on the point of a pin. If there's any flaw, telepathy's apt to bring it out. So you'll find that the Blowup caused a hell of a lot of insanity. Not only among the Baldies, but among the other mutations that developed then. Except that the Baldies are almost always paranoidal."

"And dementia praecox," Quayle said, finding relief from his own embarrassment in turning the spotlight on Burkhalter.

"And d. p. Yeah. When a confused mind acquires the telepathic instinct—a hereditary bollixed mind—it can't handle it all. There's disorientation. The paranoia group retreat into their own private worlds, and the d. p.'s simply don't realize that *this* world exists. There are distinctions, but I think that's a valid basis."

"In a way," Quayle said, "it's frightening. I can't think of any historical parallel."

"No."

"What do you think the end of it will be?"

"I don't know," Burkhalter said thoughtfully. "I think we'll be assimilated. There hasn't been enough time yet. We're specialized in a certain way, and we're useful in certain jobs."

"If you're satisfied to stay there. The Baldies who won't wear wigs—"

"They're so bad-tempered I expect they'll all be killed off in duels eventually." Burkhalter smiled. "No great loss. The rest of us, we're getting what we want—acceptance. We don't have horns or halos."

Quayle shook his head. "I'm glad, I think, that I'm not a telepath. The mind's mysterious enough anyway, without new doors opening. Thanks for letting me talk. I think I've got part of it talked out, anyway. Shall we try the script again?"

"Sure," Burkhalter said, and again the procession of pages flickered on the screen above them. Quayle did seem less guarded; his thoughts were more lucid, and Burkhalter was able to get at the true meanings of many of the hitherto muddy statements. They worked easily, the telepath dictating rephrasings into his dictogarph, and only twice did they have to hurdle emotional tangles. At noon they knocked off, and Burkhalter, with a friendly nod, took the dropper to his office, where he found some calls listed on the visor. He ran off repeats, and a worried look crept into his blue eyes.

He talked with Dr. Moon in a booth at luncheon. The conversation lasted so long that only the induction cups kept the coffee hot, but Burkhalter had more than one problem to discuss. And he'd known Moon for a long time. The fat man was one of few who were not, he thought, subconsciously repelled by the fact that Burkhalter was a Baldy.

"I've never fought a duel in my life, Doc. I can't afford to."

"You can't afford not to. You can't turn down the challenge, Ed. It isn't done."

"But this fellow Reilly—I don't even know him."

"I know of him," Moon said. "He's got a bad temper. Dueled a lot."

Burkhalter slammed his hand down on the table. "It's ridiculous. I won't do it!"

"Well," Moon said practically, "your wife can't fight him. And if Ethel's been reading Mrs. Reilly's mind and gossiping, Reilly's got a case."

"Don't you think we know the dangers of that?" Burkhalter asked in a low voice. "Ethel doesn't go around reading minds any more than I do. It'd be fatal—for us. And for any other Baldy."

"Not the hairless ones. The ones who won't wear wigs. They—"

"They're fools. And they're giving all the Baldies a bad name. Point one, Ethel doesn't read minds; she didn't read Mrs. Reilly's. Point two, she doesn't gossip."

"La Reilly is obviously an hysterical type," Moon said. "Word got around about this scandal, whatever it was, and Mrs. Reilly remembered she'd seen Ethel lately. She's the type who needs a scapegoat anyway. I rather imagine she let word drop herself, and had to cover up so her husband wouldn't blame her."

"I'm not going to accept Reilly's challenge," Burkhalter said doggedly.

"You'll have to."

"Listen, Doc, maybe—"

"What?"

"Nothing. An idea. It might work. Forget about that; I think I've got the right answer. It's the only one, anyway. I can't afford a duel and that's flat."

"You're not a coward."

"There's one thing Baldies are afraid of," Burkhalter said, "and that's public opinion. I happen to know I'd kill Reilly. That's the reason why I've never dueled in my life."

Moon drank coffee. "Hm-m-m. I think—"

"Don't. There was something else. I'm wondering if I ought to send Al off to a special school."

"What's wrong with the kid?"

"He's turning out to be a beautiful delinquent. His teacher called me this morning. The playback was something to hear. He's talking funny and acting funny. Playing nasty little tricks on his friends—if he has any left by now."

"All kids are cruel."

"Kids don't know what cruelty means. That's why they're cruel; they lack empathy. But Al's getting—" Burkhalter gestured helplessly. "He's turning into a young tyrant. He doesn't seem to give a care about anything, according to his teacher."

"That's not too abnormal, so far."

"That's not the worst. He's become very egotistical. Too much so. I don't want him to turn into one of the wigless Baldies you were mentioning." Burkhalter didn't mention the other possibility: paranoia, insanity.

"He must pick things up somewhere. At home? Scarcely, Ed. Where else does he go?"

"The usual places. He's got a normal environment."

"I should think," Moon said, "that a Baldy would have unusual opportunities in training a youngster. The mental rapport—eh?"

"Yeah. But—I don't know. The trouble is," Burkhalter said almost inaudibly, "I wish to God I wasn't different. We didn't ask to be telepaths. Maybe it's all very wonderful in the long run, but I'm one person, and I've got my own microcosm. People who deal in long term sociology are apt to forget that. They can figure out the answers, but it's every individual man—or Baldy—who's got to fight his own personal battle while he's alive. And it isn't as clear-cut as a battle. It's worse; it's the necessity of watching yourself every second, of fitting yourself into a world that doesn't want you."

Moon looked uncomfortable. "Are you being a little sorry for yourself, Ed?"

Burkhalter shook himself. "I am, Doc. But I'll work it out."

"We both will," Moon said, but Burkhalter didn't really expect much help from him. Moon would be willing, but it was horribly different for an ordinary man to conceive that a Baldy was—the same. It was the difference that men looked for, and found.

Anyway, he'd have to settle matters before he saw Ethel again. He could easily conceal the knowledge, but she would recognize a mental barrier and wonder. Their marriage had been the more ideal because of the additional rapport, something that compensated for an inevitable, half-sensed estrangement from the rest of the world.

"How's 'Psychohistory' going?" Moon asked after a while.

"Better than I expected. I've got a new angle on Quayle. If I talk about myself, that seems to draw him out. It gives him enough confidence to let him open his mind to me. We may have those first chapters ready for Oldfield, in spite of everything."

"Good. Just the same, he can't rush us. If we've got to shoot out books that fast, we might as well go back to the days of semantic confusion. Which we won't!"

"Well," Burkhalter said, getting up, "I'll smoosh along. See you."

"About Reilly—"

"Let it lay." Burkhalter went out, heading for the address his visor had listed. He touched the dagger at his belt. Dueling wouldn't do for Baldies, but—

A greeting thought crept into his mind, and, under the arch that led into the campus, he paused to grin at Sam Shane, a New Orleans area Baldy who affected a wig of flaming red. They didn't bother to talk.

Personal question, involving mental, moral and physical well-being.

A satisfied glow. And you, Burkhalter? For an instant Burkhalter half-saw what the symbol of his name meant to Shane.

Shadow of trouble.

A warm willing anxiousness to help. There was a bond between Baldies.

Burkhalter thought: But everywhere I'd go there'd be the same suspicion. We're freaks.

More so elsewhere, Shane thought. There are a lot of us in Modoc Town. People are invariably more suspicious where they're not in daily contact with—Us.

The boy—

I've trouble too, Shane thought. It's worried me. My two girls—

Delinquency?

Yes.

Common denominators?

Don't know. More than one of Us have had the same trouble with our kids.

Secondary characteristic of the mutation? Second generation emergence?

Doubtful, Shane thought, scowling in his mind, shading his concept with a wavering question. We'll think it over later. Must go.

Burkhalter sighed and went on his way. The houses were strung out around the central industry of Modoc, and he cut through a park toward his destination. It was a sprawling curved building, but it wasn't inhabited, so Burkhalter filed Reilly for future reference, and, with a glance at his timer, angled over a hillside toward the school. As he expected, it was recreation time, and he spotted Al lounging under a tree, some distance from his companions, who were involved in a pleasantly murderous game of Blowup.

He sent his thought ahead.

The Green Man had almost reached the top of the mountain. The hairy gnomes were pelting on his trail, most unfairly shooting sizzling light-streaks at their quarry, but the

Green Man was agile enough to dodge. The rocks were leaning—

"Al."

—inward, pushed by the gnomes, ready to—

"*Al!*" Burkhalter sent his thought with the word, jolting into the boy's mind, a trick he very seldom employed, since youth was practically defenseless against such invasion.

"Hello, Dad," Al said, undisturbed. "What's up?"

"A report from your teacher."

"I didn't do anything."

"She told me what it was. Listen, kid. Don't start getting any funny ideas in your head."

"I'm not."

"Do you think a Baldy is better or worse than a non-Baldy?"

Al moved his feet uncomfortably. He didn't answer.

"Well," Burkhalter said, "the answer is both and neither. And here's why. A Baldy can communicate mentally, but he lives in a world where most people can't."

"They're dumb," Al opined.

"Not so dumb, if they're better suited to their world than you are. You might as well say a frog's better than a fish because he's an amphibian." Burkhalter briefly amplified and explained the terms telepathically.

"Well . . . oh, I get it, all right."

"Maybe," Burkhalter said slowly, "What you need is a swift kick in the pants. That thought wasn't so hot. What was it again?"

Al tried to hide it, blanking out. Burkhalter began to lift the barrier, an easy matter for him, but stopped. Al regarded his father in a most unfilial way—in fact, as a sort of boneless fish. That had been clear.

"If you're so egotistical," Burkhalter pointed out, "maybe you can see it this way. Do you know why there aren't any Baldies in key positions?"

"Sure I do," Al said unexpectedly. "They're afraid."

"Of what, then?"

"The—" That picture had been very curious, a commingling of something vaguely familiar to Burkhalter. "The non-Baldies."

"Well, if we took positions where we could take advantage of our telepathic function, non-Baldies would be plenty envious—especially if we were successes. If a Baldy even invented a better mousetrap, plenty of people would say he'd stolen the idea from some non-Baldy's mind. You get the point?"

"Yes, Dad." But he hadn't. Burkhalter sighed and looked up. He recognized one of Shane's girls on a nearby hillside, sitting alone against a boulder. There were other isolated figures here and there. Far to the east the snowy rampart of the Rockies made an irregular pattern against blue sky.

"Al," Burkhalter said, "I don't want you to get a chip on your shoulder. This is a pretty swell world, and the people in it are, on the whole, nice people. There's a law of averages. It isn't sensible for us to get too much wealth or power, because that'd militate against us—and we don't need it anyway. Nobody's poor. We find our work, we do it, and we're reasonably happy. We have some advantages non-Baldies don't have; in marriage, for example. Mental intimacy is quite as important as physical. But I don't want you to feel that being a Baldy makes you a god. It doesn't. I can still," he added thoughtfully, "spank it out of you, in case you care to follow out that concept in your mind at the moment."

Al gulped and beat a hasty retreat. "I'm sorry. I won't do it again."

"And keep your hair on, too. Don't take your wig off in class. Use the stickum stuff in the bathroom closet."

"Yes, but . . . Mr. Venner doesn't wear a wig."

"Remind me to do some historical research with you on zoot-suiters," Burkhalter said. "Mr. Venner's wiglessness is probably his only virtue, if you consider it one."

"He makes money."

"Anybody would, in that general store of his. But people don't buy from him if they can help it, you'll notice. That's what I mean by a chip on your shoulder. He's got one. There are Baldies like Venner, Al, but you might, sometime, ask the guy if he's happy. For your information, I am. More than Venner, anyway. Catch?"

"Yes, Dad." Al seemed submissive, but it was merely that. Burkhalter, still troubled, nodded and walked away. As he passed near the Shane girl's boulder he caught a scrap:—*at the summit of the Glass Mountains, rolling rocks back at the gnomes until*—

He withdrew; it was an unconscious habit, touching minds that were sensitive, but with children it was definitely unfair. With adult Baldies it was simply the instinctive gesture of tipping your hat; one answered or one didn't. The barrier could be erected; there could be a blank-out; or there could be the direct snub of concentration on a single thought, private and not to be intruded on.

A 'copter with a string of gliders was coming in from the south: a freighter laden with frozen foods from South America, to judge by the markings. Burkhalter made a note to pick up an Argentine steak. He'd got a new recipe he wanted to try out, a charcoal broil with barbecue sauce, a welcome change from the short-wave cooked meats they'd been having for a week. Tomatoes, chile, mm-m—what else? Oh, yes. The duel with Reilly. Burkhalter absently touched his dagger's hilt and made a small, mocking sound in his throat. Perhaps he was innately a pacifist. It was rather difficult to think of a duel seriously, even though everyone else did, when the details of a barbecue dinner were prosaic in his mind.

So it went. The tides of civilization rolled in century-long waves across the continents, and each particular wave, though conscious of its participation in the tide, nevertheless was more preoccupied with dinner. And, unless you happened to be a thousand feet tall, had the brain of a god and a god's life-span, what was the difference? People missed a lot—people like Venner, who was certainly a crank, not batty enough to qualify for the asylum, but certainly a potential paranoid type. The man's refusal to wear a wig labeled him as an individualist, but as an exhibitionist, too. If he didn't feel ashamed of his hairlessness, why should he bother to flaunt it? Besides, the man had a bad temper, and if people kicked him around, he asked for it by starting the kicking himself.

But as for Al, the kid was heading for something approaching delinquency. It couldn't be the normal development of childhood, Burkhalter thought. He didn't pretend to be an expert, but he was still young enough to remember his own formative years, and he had had more handicaps than Al had now; in those days, Baldies had been very new and very freakish. There'd been more than one movement to isolate, sterilize, or even exterminate the mutations.

Burkhalter sighed. If he had been born before the Blowup, it might have been different. Impossible to say. One could read history, but one couldn't live it. In the future, perhaps, there might be telepathic libraries in which that would be possible. So many opportunities, in fact—and so few that the world was ready to accept as yet. Eventually Baldies would not be regarded as freaks, and by that time real progress would be possible.

But people don't make history—Burkhalter thought. Peoples do that. Not the individual.

He stopped by Reilly's house again, and this time the man answered, a burly, freckled, squint-eyed fellow with immense hands and, Burkhalter noted, fine muscular co-ordination. He rested those hands on the Dutch door and nodded.

"Who're you, mister?"

"My name's Burkhalter."

Comprehension and wariness leaped into Reilly's eyes. "Oh. I see. You got my call?"

"I did," Burkhalter said. "I want to talk to you about it. May I come in?"

"O.K." He stepped back, opening the way through a hall and into a spacious living room, where diffused light filtered through glassy mosaic walls. "Want to set the time?"

"I want to tell you you're wrong."

"Now wait a minute," Reilly said, patting the air. "My wife's out now, but she gave me the straight of it. I don't like this business of sneaking into a man's mind; it's crooked. You should have told *your* wife to mind her business—or keep her tongue quiet."

Burkhalter said patiently, "I give you my word, Reilly, that Ethel didn't read your wife's mind."

"Does she say so?"

"I . . . well, I haven't asked her."

"Yeah," Reilly said with an air of triumph.

"I don't need to. I know her well enough. And . . . well, I'm a Baldy myself."

"I know you are," Reilly said. "For all I know, you may be reading my mind now." He hesitated. "Get out of my house. I like my privacy. We'll meet at dawn tomorrow, if that's satisfactory with you. Now get out." He seemed to have something on his mind, some ancient memory, perhaps, that he didn't wish exposed.

Burkhalter nobly resisted the temptation. "No Baldy would read—"

"Go on, get out!"

"Listen! You wouldn't have a chance in a duel with me!"

"Do you know how many notches I've got?" Reilly asked.

"Ever dueled a Baldy?"

"I'll cut the notch deeper tomorrow. Get out, d'you hear?"

Burkhalter, biting his lips, said, "Man, don't you realize that in a duel I could read your mind?"

"I don't care . . . what?"

"I'd be half a jump ahead of you. No matter how instinctive your actions would be, you'd know them a split second ahead of time in your mind. And I'd know all your tricks and weaknesses, too. Your technique would be an open book to me. Whatever you thought of—"

"No." Reilly shook his head. "Oh, no. You're smart, but it's a phony set-up."

Burkhalter hesitated, decided, and swung about, pushing a chair out of the way. "Take out your dagger," he said. "Leave the sheath snapped on; I'll show you what I mean."

Reilly's eyes widened. "If you want it now—"

"I don't." Burkhalter shoved another chair away. He unclipped his dagger, sheath and all, from his belt, and made sure the little safety clip was in place. "We've room enough here. Come on."

Scowling, Reilly took out his own dagger, held it awkwardly, baffled by the sheath, and then suddenly feinted forward. But Burkhalter wasn't there; he had anticipated, and his own leather sheath slid up Reilly's belly.

"That," Burkhalter said, "would have ended the fight."

For answer Reilly smashed a hard dagger-blow down, curving at the last moment into a throat-cutting slash. Burkhalter's free hand was already at his throat; his other hand, with the sheathed dagger, tapped Reilly twice over the heart. The freckles stood out boldly against the pallor of the larger man's face. But he was not yet ready to concede. He tried a few more passes, clever, well-trained cuts, and they failed, because Burkhalter had anticipated them. His left hand invariably covered the spot where Reilly had aimed, and which he never struck.

Slowly Reilly let his arm fall. He moistened his lips and swallowed. Burkhalter busied himself reclipping his dagger in place.

"Burkhalter," Reilly said, "you're a devil."

"Far from it. I'm just afraid to take a chance. Do you really think being a Baldy is a snap?"

"But if you can read minds—"

"How long do you think I'd last if I did any dueling? It would be too much of a set-up. Nobody would stand for it, and I'd end up dead. I can't duel, because it'd be murder, and people would know it was murder. I've taken a lot of cracks, swallowed a lot of insults, for just that reason. Now, if you like, I'll swallow another and apologize. I'll admit anything you say. But I can't duel with you, Reilly."

"No, I can see that. And—I'm glad you came over." Reilly was still white. "I'd have walked right into a set-up."

"Not my set-up," Burkhalter said. "I wouldn't have dueled. Baldies aren't so lucky, you know. They've got handicaps—like this. That's why they can't afford to take chances and antagonize people, and why we never read minds, unless we're asked to do so."

"It makes sense. More or less." Reilly hesitated. "Look, I withdraw that challenge. O.K.?"

"Thanks," Burkhalter said, putting out his hand. It was taken rather reluctantly. "We'll leave it at that, eh?"

"Right." But Reilly was still anxious to get his guest out of the house.

Burkhalter walked back to the Publishing Center and whistled tunelessly. He could tell Ethel now; in fact, he had to, for secrets between them would have broken up the completeness of their telepathic intimacy. It was not that their minds lay bare to each other, it was, rather, that any barrier could be sensed by the other, and the perfect *rapport* wouldn't have been so perfect. Curiously, despite this utter intimacy, husband and wife managed to respect one another's privacy.

Ethel might be somewhat distressed, but the trouble had blown over, and, besides, she was a Baldy too. Not that she looked it, with her wig of fluffy chestnut hair and those long, curving lashes. But her parents had lived east of Seattle during the Blowup, and afterward, too, before the hard radiation's effects had been thoroughly studied.

The snow-wind blew down over Modoc and fled southward along the Utah Valley. Burkhalter wished he was in his 'copter, alone in the blue emptiness of the sky. There was a quiet, strange peace up there that no Baldy ever quite achieved on the earth's surface, except in the depths of a wilderness. Stray fragments of thoughts were always flying about, subsensory, but like the almost-unheard whisper of a needle on a phonograph record, never ceasing. That, certainly, was why almost all Baldies loved to fly and were expert pilots. The high waste deserts of the air were their blue hermitages.

Still, he was in Modoc now, and overdue for his interview with Quayle. Burkhalter hastened his steps. In the main hall he met Moon, said briefly and cryptically that he'd taken care of the duel, and passed on, leaving the fat man to stare a question after him. The only visor call was from Ethel; the playback said she was worried about Al, and would Burkhalter check with the school. Well, he had already done so—unless the boy had managed to get into more trouble since then. Burkhalter put in a call and reassured himself. Al was as yet unchanged.

He found Quayle in the same private solarium, and thirsty. Burkhalter ordered a couple of dramzowies sent up, since he had no objection to loosening Quayle's inhibitions. The gray-haired author was immersed in a sectional historical globe-map, illuminating each epochal layer in turn as he searched back through time.

"Watch this," he said, running his hand along the row of buttons. "See how the German border fluctuates?" It fluctuated, finally vanishing entirely as semimodern times were reached. "And Portugal. Notice its zone of influence? Now—" The zone shrank steadily from 1600 on, while other countries shot out radiating lines and assumed sea power.

Burkhalter sipped his dramzowie. "Not much of that now."

"No, since . . . what's the matter?"

"How do you mean?"

"You look shot."

"I didn't know I showed it," Burkhalter said wryly. "I just finagled my way out of a duel."

"That's one custom I never saw much sense to," Quayle said. "What happened? Since when can you finagle out?"

Burkhalter explained, and the writer took a drink and snorted. "What a spot for you. Being a Baldy isn't such an advantage after all, I guess."

"It has distinct disadvantages at times." On impulse Burkhalter mentioned his son. "You see my point, eh? I don't *know*, really, what standards to apply to a young Baldy. He is a mutation, after all. And the telepathic mutation hasn't had time to work out yet. We can't rig up controls, because guinea pigs and rabbits won't breed telepaths. That's been tried, you know. And—well, the child of a Baldy needs very special training so he can cope with his ultimate maturity."

"You seem to have adjusted well enough."

"I've—learned. As most sensible Baldies have. That's why I'm not a wealthy man, or in politics. We're really buying safety for our species by forgoing certain individual advantages. Hostages to destiny—and destiny spares us. But we get paid too, in a way. In the coinage of future benefits—negative benefits, really, for we ask only to be spared and accepted—and so we have to deny ourselves a lot of present, positive benefits. An appeasement to fate."

"Paying the piper." Quayle nodded.

"We are the pipers. The Baldies as a group, I mean. And our children. So it balances; we're really paying ourselves. If I wanted to take unfair advantage of my telepathic power—my son wouldn't live very long. The Baldies would be wiped out. Al's got to learn that, and he's getting pretty antisocial."

"All children are antisocial," Quayle pointed out. "They're utter individualists. I should think the only reason for worrying would be if the boy's deviation from the norm were connected with his telepathic sense."

"There's something in that." Burkhalter reached out left-handedly and probed delicately at Quayle's mind, noting that the antagonism was considerably lessened. He grinned to himself and went on talking about his own troubles. "Just the same, the boy's father to the man. And an adult Baldy has got to be pretty well adjusted, or he's sunk."

"Environment is as important as heredity. One complements the other. If a child's reared correctly, he won't have much trouble—unless heredity is involved."

"As it may be. There's so little known about the telepathic mutation. If baldness is one secondary characteristic, maybe—something else—emerges in the third or fourth generations. I'm wondering if telepathy is really good for the mind."

Quayle said, "Humph. Speaking personally, it makes me nervous—"

"Like Reilly."

"Yes," Quayle said, but he didn't care much for the comparison. "Well—anyhow, if a mutation's a failure, it'll die out. It won't breed true."

"What about hemophilia?"

"How many people have hemophilia?" Quayle asked. "I'm trying to look at it from the angle of psychohistorian. If there'd been telepaths in the past, things might have been different."

"How do you know there weren't?" Burkhalter asked.

Quayle blinked. "Oh. Well. That's true, too. In medieval times they'd have been called wizards—or saints. The Duke-Rhine experiments—but such accidents would have been abortive. Nature fools around trying to hit the . . . ah . . . the jackpot, and she doesn't always do it on the first try."

"She may not have done it now." That was habit speaking, the ingrained caution of modesty. "Telepathy may be merely a semi successful try at something pretty unimaginable. A sort of four-dimensional sensory concept, maybe."

"That's too abstract for me." Quayle was interested, and his own hesitancies had almost vanished; by accepting Burkhalter as a telepath, he had tacitly wiped away his objections to telepathy *per se*. "The old-time Germans always had an idea they were different; so did that Oriental race that had the islands off the China coast—the Japanese. They knew, very definitely, that they were a superior race because they were directly descended from gods. They were short in stature; heredity made them self-conscious when dealing with larger races. But the Chinese aren't tall, the Southern Chinese, and they weren't handicapped in that way."

"Environment, then?"

"Environment, which caused propaganda. The . . . ah . . . the Japanese took Buddhism, and altered it completely into Shinto, to suit their own needs. The samurai, warrior-knights, were the ideals, the code of honor was fascinatingly cockeyed. The principle of Shinto was to worship your superiors and subjugate your inferiors. Ever seen the Japanese jewel-trees?"

"I don't remember them. What are they?"

"Miniature replicas of espaliered trees, made of jewels, with trinkets hanging on the branches. Including a mirror—always. The first jewel-tree was made to lure the Moon-goddess out of a cave where she was sulking. It seems the lady was so intrigued by the trinkets and by her face reflected in the mirror that she came out of her hideout. All the Japanese morals were dressed up in pretty clothes; that was the bait. The old-time Germans did much the same thing. The last German dictator, Hitler, revived the old Siegfried legend. It was racial paranoia. The Germans worshiped the house-tyrant, not the mother, and they had extremely strong family ties. That extended to the state. They symbolized Hitler as their All-Father, and that led to a whole series of complicated events, and eventually we got the Blowup. And, finally, mutations."

"After the deluge, me," Burkhalter murmured, finishing his dramzowie. Quayle was staring at nothing.

"Funny," he said after a while. "This All-Father business—"

"Yes?"

"I wonder if you know how powerfully it can affect a man?"

Burkhalter didn't say anything. Quayle gave him a sharp glance.

"Yes," the writer said quietly. "You're a man, after all. I owe you an apology, you know."

Burkhalter smiled. "You can forget that."

"I'd rather not," Quayle said. "I've just realized, pretty suddenly, that the telepathic sense isn't so important. I mean—it doesn't make you *different*. I've been talking to you—"

"Sometimes it takes people years before they realize what you're finding out," Burkhalter remarked. "Years of living and working with something they think of as a Baldy."

"Do you know what I've been concealing in my mind?" Quayle asked.

"No. I don't."

"You lie like a gentleman. Thanks. Well, here it is, and I'm telling you by choice, because I want to. I don't care if you got the information out of my mind already; I just want to tell you of my own free will. My father . . . I imagine I hated him . . . was a tyrant, and I remember one time, when I was just a kid and we were in the mountains, he beat me and a lot of people were looking on. I've tried to forget that for a long time. Now"—Quayle shrugged—"it doesn't seem quite so important."

"I'm not a psychologist," Burkhalter said. "If you want my personal reaction, I'll just say that it doesn't matter. You're not a little boy any more, and the guy I'm talking to and working with is the adult Quayle."

"Hm-m-m. Ye-es. I suppose I knew that all along—how unimportant it was, really. It was simply having my privacy violated. . . . I think I know you better now, Burkhalter. You can—walk in."

"We'll work better," Burkhalter said, grinning. "Especially with Darius."

Quayle said, "I'll try not to keep any reservation in my mind. Frankly, I won't mind telling you—the answers. Even when they're personal."

"Check on that. D'you want to tackle Darius now?"

"O.K.," Quayle said, and his eyes no longer held suspicious wariness. "Darius I identify with my father—"

It was smooth and successful. That afternoon they accomplished more than they had during the entire previous fortnight. Warm with satisfaction on more than one point, Burkhalter stopped off to tell Dr. Moon that matters were looking up, and then set out toward home, exchanging thoughts with a couple of Baldies, his co-workers, who were knocking off for the day. The Rockies were bloody with the western light, and the coolness of the wind was pleasant on Burkhalter's cheeks, as he hiked homeward.

It was fine to be accepted. It proved that it could be done. And a Baldy often needed reassurance, in a world peopled by suspicious strangers. Quayle had been a hard nut to crack, but—Burkhalter smiled.

Ethel would be pleased. In a way, she'd had a harder time than he'd ever had. A woman would, naturally. Men were desperately anxious to keep their privacy unviolated by a woman, and as for non-Baldy women—well, it spoke highly for Ethel's glowing personal charm that she had finally been accepted by the clubs and feminine groups of Modoc. Only Burkhalter knew Ethel's desperate hurt at being bald, and not even her husband had ever seen her unwigged.

His thought reached out before him into the low, double-winged house on the hillside, and interlocked with hers in a warm intimacy. It was something more than a kiss. And, as always, there was the exciting sense of expectancy, mounting and mounting till the last door swung open and they touched physically. *This*, he thought, *is why I was born a Baldy; this is worth losing worlds for.*

At dinner that rapport spread out to embrace Al, an intangible, deeply-rooted something that made the food taste better and the water like wine. The word *home*, to telepaths, had a meaning that non-Baldies could not entirely comprehend, for it embraced a bond they could not know. There were small, intangible caresses.

Green Man going down the Great Red Slide; the Shaggy Dwarfs trying to harpoon him as he goes.

"Al," Ethel said, "are you still working on your Green Man?"

Then something utterly hateful and cold and deadly quivered silently in the air, like an icicle jaggedly smashing through golden, fragile glass. Burkhalter dropped his napkin and looked up, profoundly shocked. He felt Ethel's thought shrink back, and swiftly reached out to touch and reassure her with mental contact. But across the table the little boy, his cheeks still round with the fat of babyhood, sat silent and wary, realizing he had blundered, and seeking safety in complete immobility. His mind was too weak to resist probing, he knew, and he remained perfectly still, waiting, while the echoes of a thought hung poisonously in silence.

Burkhalter said, "Come on, Al." He stood up. Ethel started to speak.

"Wait, darling. Put up a barrier. Don't listen in." He touched her mind gently and tenderly, and then he took Al's hand and drew the boy after him out into the yard. Al watched his father out of wide, alert eyes.

Burkhalter sat on a bench and put Al beside him. He talked audibly at first, for clarity's sake, and for another reason. It was distinctly unpleasant to trick the boy's feeble guards down, but it was necessary.

"That's a very queer way to think of your mother," he said. "It's a queer way to think of me." Obscenity is more obscene, profanity more profane, to a telepathic mind, but this had been neither one. It had been—cold and malignant.

And this is flesh of my flesh, Burkhalter thought, looking at the boy and remembering the eight years of his growth. *Is the mutation to turn into something devilish?*

Al was silent.

Burkhalter reached into the young mind. Al tried to twist free and escape, but his father's strong hands gripped him. Instinct, not reasoning, on the boy's part, for mind's can touch over long distances.

He did not like to do this, for increased sensibility had gone with sensitivity, and violations are always violations. But ruthlessness was required. Burkhalter searched. Sometimes he threw key words violently at Al, and surges of memory pulsed up in response.

In the end, sick and nauseated, Burkhalter let Al go and sat alone on the bench, watching the red light die on the snowy peaks. The whiteness was red-stained. But it was not too late. The man was a fool, had been a fool from the beginning, or he would have known the impossibility of attempting such a thing as this.

The conditioning had only begun. Al could be reconditioned. Burkhalter's eyes hardened. And would be. *And would be.* But not yet, not until the immediate furious anger had given place to sympathy and understanding.

Not yet.

He went into the house, spoke briefly to Ethel, and televised the dozen Baldies who worked with him in the Publishing Center. Not all of them had families, but none was missing when, half an hour later, they met in the back room of the Pagan Tavern downtown. Sam Shane had caught a fragment of Burkhalter's knowledge, and all of them read his emotions. Welded into a sympathetic unit by their telepathic sense, they waited till Burkhalter was ready.

Then he told them. It didn't take long, via thought. He told them about the Japanese jewel-tree with its glittering gadgets, a shining lure. He told them of racial paranoia and propaganda. And that the most effective propaganda was sugar-coated, disguised so that the motive was hidden.

A Green Man, hairless, heroic—symbolic of a Baldy.

And wild, exciting adventures, the lure to catch the young fish whose plastic minds were impressionable enough to be led along the roads of dangerous madness. Adult Baldies could listen, but they did not; young telepaths had a higher threshold of mental receptivity, and adults do not read the books of their children except to reassure themselves that there is nothing harmful in the pages. And no adult would bother to listen to the Green Man mindcast. Most of them had accepted it as the original daydream of their own children.

"I did," Shane put in. "My girls—"

"Trace it back," Burkhalter said. "I did."

The dozen minds reached out on the higher frequency, the children's wave length, and something jerked away from them, startled and apprehensive.

"He's the one." Shane nodded.

They did not need to speak. They went out of the Pagan Tavern in a compact, ominous group, and crossed the street to the general store. The door was locked. Two of the men burst it open with their shoulders.

They went through the dark store and into a back room where a man was standing beside an overturned chair. His bald skull gleamed in an overhead light. His mouth worked impotently.

His thought pleaded with them—was driven back by an implacable deadly wall.

Burkhalter took out his dagger. Other slivers of steel glittered for a little while—

And were quenched.

Venner's scream had long since stopped, but his dying thought of agony lingered within Burkhalter's mind as he walked homeward. The wigless Baldy had not been insane, no. But he had been paranoidal.

What he had tried to conceal, at the last, was quite shocking. A tremendous, tyrannical egotism, and a furious hatred of nontelepaths. A feeling of self-justification that was, perhaps, insane. *And—we are the Future! The Baldies! God made us to rule lesser men!*

Burkhalter sucked in his breath, shivering. The mutation had not been entirely successful. One group had adjusted, the Baldies who wore wigs and had become fitted to their environment. One group had been insane, and could be discounted; they were in asylums.

But the middle group were merely paranoid. They were not insane, and they were not sane. They wore no wigs.

Like Venner.

And Venner had sought disciples. His attempt had been foredoomed to failure, but he had been one man.

One Baldy—paranoid.

There were others, many others.

Ahead, nestled into the dark hillside, was the pale blotch that marked Burkhalter's home. He sent his thought ahead, and it touched Ethel's and paused very briefly to reassure her.

Then it thrust on, and went into the sleeping mind of a little boy who, confused and miserable, had finally cried himself to sleep. There were only dreams in that mind now, a little discolored, a little stained, but they could be cleansed. And would be.

WANTED—AN ENEMY

by Fritz Leiber (1910-)

ASTOUNDING SCIENCE FICTION
February

The tall and greatly gifted Fritz Leiber received the Grand Master Award of the Science Fiction Writers of America in 1981, and it would be difficult to find a person more worthy. He has been giving pleasure and mental stimulation to sf and fantasy readers for more than forty years, maintaining a very high level of quality while working in areas as far apart as hard-science fiction and sword and sorcery.

The problem of resolving conflict has long captured the attention of sf writers, and they have responded with notions that range from single-combat to placing weapons of mass destruction in the hands of everyone. In "Wanted—An Enemy" (a mysteriously neglected story) he discusses the dangers and opportunities of the "common enemy" solution.

(Marty's mention of Fritz's Grand Master Award in 1981 reminds me of the shock I received in that connection. —No, not that he received it instead of me. I'm not that *self-centered.*

It was just that Norman Spinrad, the soft-spoken president of the Science Fiction Writers of America called me a month or so ahead of time to make sure I'd be at the banquet because he wanted me to make the presentation of the Grand Master Award. He told me Fritz would get it and swore me to secrecy.

I kept the secret. I didn't even tell my wife. The night before the award banquet, Janet and I were in a taxi with Clifford Simak who had won the Grand Master Award on a previous occasion. Cliff said to me, "I think Fritz Leiber ought to get it this time. He's a terribly under-appreciated writer." I maintained an indifferent silence, nearly bursting my shirt buttons in the effort.

Came the banquet! Did I get the reward of my having maintained secrecy under pressure? No! Norman Spinrad, forgetting completely that he had assigned me the honor, handed the Award to Fritz himself. But never mind—as long as Fritz got it. I.A.)

The bright stars of Mars made a glittering roof for a fantastic tableau. A being equipped with retinal vision would have seen an Earthman dressed in the familiar coat and trousers of the twentieth century standing on a boulder that put him a few feet above the rusty sand. His face was bony and puritanic. His eyes gleamed wildly from deep sockets. Occasionally his long hair flopped across them. His lips worked vociferously, showing big yellowed teeth, and there was a cloud of blown spittle in front of them, for he was making a speech—in the English language. He so closely resembled an old-style soapbox orator that one looked around for the lamp-post, the dull-faced listeners overflowing the curb, and the strolling cop.

But the puzzling globe of soft radiance surrounding Mr. Whitlow struck highlights from enamel-black shells and jointed legs a little resembling those of an ant under a microscope. Each individual in the crowd consisted of a yard-long oval body lacking a separate head or any sensory or other orifices in its gleaming black surface except for a small mouth that worked like a sliding door and kept opening and closing at regular intervals. To this body were attached eight of the jointed legs, the inner pairs showing highly manipulative end-organs.

These creatures were ranged in a circle around Mr. Whitlow's boulder. Facing him was one who crouched a little apart from the rest, on a smaller boulder. Flanking this one, were two whose faintly silvered shells suggested weathering and, therefore, age.

Beyond them—black desert to a horizon defined only by the blotting out of the star fields.

Low in the heavens gleamed sky-blue Earth, now Mars' evening star, riding close to the meager crescent of Phobos.

To the Martian coleopteroids this scene presented itself in a very different fashion, since they depended on perception rather than any elaborate sensory set-up. Their internal brains were directly conscious of everything within a radius of about fifty yards. For them the blue earthshine was a diffuse photonic cloud just above the threshold of perception, similar to but distinct from the photonic clouds of the starlight and faint moonshine; they could perceive no image of Earth unless they used lenses to create such an image within their perceptive range. They were conscious of the ground beneath them as a sandy hemisphere tunneled through by various wrigglers and the centipedelike burrowers. They were conscious of each other's armored, neatly-compartmented bodies, and each other's thoughts. But chiefly their attention was focused on that squidgy, uninsulated, wasteful jumble of organs that thought of itself as Mr. Whitlow—an astounding moist suppet of life on dry, miserly Mars.

The physiology of the coleopteroids was typical of a depleted-planet economy. Their shells were double; the space between could be evacuated at night to conserve heat, and flooded by day to absorb it. Their lungs were really oxygen accumulators. They inhaled the rarefied atmosphere about one hundred times for every exhalation, the double-valve mouth, permitting the building up of high internal pressure. They had one hundred percent utilization of inhaled oxygen, and exhaled pure carbon dioxide freighted with other respiratory excretions. Occasional whiffs of this exceedingly bad breath made Mr. Whitlow wrinkle his flaring nostrils.

Just what permitted Mr. Whitlow to go on functioning, even speechifying, in the chill oxygen dearth was by no means so obvious. It constituted as puzzling a question as the source of the soft glow that bathed him.

Communication between him and his audience was purely telepathic. He was speaking vocally at the request of the coleopteroids, because like most nontelepaths he could best organize and clarify his thoughts while talking. His voice died out abruptly in the thin air. It sounded like a phonograph needle scratching along without amplification, and intensified the eerie ludicrousness of his violent gestures and facial contortions.

"And so," Whitlow concluded wheezily, brushing the long hair from his forehead, "I come back to my original proposal; Will you attack Earth?"

"And we, Mr. Whitlow," thought the Chief Coleopteroid, "come back to our original question, which you still have not answered: Why should we?"

Mr. Whitlow made a grimace of frayed patience. "As I have told you several times, I cannot make a fuller explanation. But I assure you of my good faith. I will do my best to provide transportation for you, and facilitate the thing in every way. Understand, it need only be a token invasion. After a short time you can retire to Mars with your spoils. Surely you cannot afford to pass up this opportunity."

"Mr. Whitlow," replied the Chief Coleopteroid with a humor as poisonously dry as his planet, "I cannot read your thoughts unless you vocalize them. They are too confused. But I can sense your biases. You are laboring under a serious misconception as to our psychology. Evidently it is customary in your world to think of alien intelligent beings as evil monsters, whose only desire is to ravage, destroy, tyrannize, and inflict unspeakable cruelties on creatures less advanced than themselves. Nothing could be farther from the truth. We are an ancient and unemotional race. We have outgrown the passions and vanities—even the ambitions—of our youth. We undertake no projects except for sound and sufficient reason."

"But if that's the case, surely you can see the practical advantages of my proposal. At little or no risk to yourselves, you will acquire valuable loot."

The Chief Coleopteroid settled back on his boulder, and his thoughts did the same. "Mr. Whitlow, let me remind you that we have never gone to war lightly. During the whole course of our history, our only intelligent enemies have been the molluscoids of the tideless seas of Venus. In the springtide of their culture they came conquesting in their water-filled spaceships, and we fought several long and bitter wars. But eventually they attained racial maturity and a certain dispassionate wisdom, though not equivalent to our own. A perpetual truce was declared, on condition that each party stick to its own planet and attempt no more forays. For ages we have abided by that truce, living in mutual isolation. So you can see, Mr. Whitlow, that we would be anything but inclined to accept such a rash and mysterious proposal as yours."

"May I make a suggestion?" interjected the Senior Coleopteroid on the Chief's right. His thoughts flicked out subtly toward Whitlow. "You seem, Earthling, to possess powers that are perhaps even in excess of our own. Your arrival on Mars without any perceptible means of transport and your ability to endure its rigors without any obvious insulation, are sufficient proofs. From what you tell us, the other inhabitants of your planet possess no such powers. Why don't you attack them by yourself, like the solitary armored poison-worm? Why do you need our aid?"

"My friend," said Mr. Whitlow solemnly, bending forward and fixing his gaze on the silvery-shelled elder, "I abhor war as the foulest evil, and active participation in it as the greatest crime. Nonetheless, I would sacrifice myself as you suggest, could I attain my ends that way. Unfortunately, I cannot. It would not have the psychological effect I desire. Moreover"—he paused embarrassedly—"I might as well confess that I am not wholly master of my powers. I don't understand them. The workings of an inscrutable providence have put into my hands a device that is probably the handiwork of creatures vastly more intelligent than any in this solar system, perhaps even this cosmos. It enables me to cross space and time. It protects me from danger. It provides me with warmth and illumination. It concentrates your Martian atmosphere in a sphere around me, so that I can breathe normally. But as for using it in any larger way—I'd be mortally afraid of its getting out of control. My one small experiment was disastrous. I wouldn't dare."

The Senior Coleopteroid shot a guarded aside to the Chief. "Shall I try to hypnotize his disordered mind and get this device from him?"

"Do so."

"Very well, though I'm afraid the device will protect his mind as well as his body. Still, it's worth the chance."

"Mr. Whitlow," thought the Chief abruptly, "it is time we got down to cases. Every word you say makes your proposal sound more irrational, and your own motives more unintelligible. If you expect us to take any serious interest, you must give us a clear answer to one question: Why do you want us to attack Earth?"

Whitlow twisted. "But that's the one question I don't want to answer."

"Well, put it this way then," continued the Chief patiently. "What personal advantage do you expect to gain from our attack?"

Whitlow drew himself up and tucked in his necktie. "None! None whatsoever! I seek nothing for myself!"

"Do you want to rule Earth?" the Chief persisted.

"No! No! I detest all tyranny."

"Revenge, then? Has Earth hurt you and are you trying to hurt it back?"

"Absolutely not! I would never stoop to such barbaric behavior. I hate no one. The desire to see anyone injured is farthest from my thoughts."

"Come, come, Mr. Whitlow! You've just begged us to attack Earth. How can you square that with your sentiments?"

Whitlow gnawed his lip baffledly.

The Chief slipped in a quick question to the Senior Coleopteroid. "What progress?"

"None whatsoever. His mind is extraordinarily difficult to grasp. And as I anticipated, there is a shield."

Whitlow rocked uneasily on his shoulder, his eyes fixed on the star-edged horizon.

"I'll tell you this much," he said. "It's solely because I love Earth and mankind so much that I want you to attack her."

"You choose a strange way of showing your affection," the Chief observed.

"Yes," continued Whitlow, warming a bit, his eyes still lost. "I want you to do it in order to end war."

"This gets more and more mysterious. Start war to stop it? That is a paradox which demands explanation. Take care, Mr. Whitlow, or I will fall into your error of looking on alien beings as evil and demented monsters."

Whitlow lowered his gaze until it was fixed on the Chief. He sighed windily. "I guess I'd better tell you," he muttered. "You'd have probably found out in the end. Though it would have been simpler the other way—"

He pushed back the rebellious hair and massaged his forehead, a little wearily. When he spoke again it was in a less oratorical style.

"I am a pacifist. My life is dedicated to the task of preventing war. I love my fellow men. But they are steeped in error and sin. They are victims of their baser passions. Instead of marching on, hand in hand, trustingly, toward the glorious fulfillment of all their dreams, they insist on engaging in constant conflict, in vile war."

"Perhaps there is a reason for that," suggested the Chief mildly. "Some inequalities that require leveling or—"

"Please," said the pacifist reprovingly. "These wars have grown increasingly more violent and terrible. I, and others, have sought to reason with the majority, but in vain. They persist in their delusions. I have racked my brain to find a solution. I have considered every conceivable remedy. Since I came into the possession of . . . er . . . the device, I have sought throughout the cosmos and even in other time streams, for the secret of preventing war. With no success. Such intelligent races as I encountered were either engaged in war, which ruled them out, or had never known war—these were very obliging but obviously could volunteer no helpful information—or else had outgrown war by the painful and horrible process of fighting until there was nothing more to fight about."

"As we have," the Chief thought, in an undertone.

The pacifist spread his hands, palms toward the stars. "So, once more, I was thrown on my own resources. I studied mankind from every angle. Gradually I became convinced that its worst trait—and the one most responsible for war—was its overgrown sense of self-importance. On my planet man is the lord of creation. All the other animals are merely one among many—no species is pre-eminent. The flesh-eaters have their flesh-eating rivals. Each browser or gazer competes with other types for the grass and herbage. Even the fish in the seas and the myriad parasites that swarm in bloodstreams are divided into species of roughly equal ability and competence. This makes for humility and a sense of perspective. No species is inclined to fight among itself when it realizes that by so doing it will merely clear the way for the other species to take over. Man alone has no serious rivals. As a result, he had developed delusions of grandeur—and of persecution and hate. Lacking the restraint that rivalry would provide, he fouls his planetary nest with constant civil war.

"I mulled this idea for some time. I thought wistfully of how different mankind's development might have been had he been compelled to share his planet with some equally intelligent species, say a mechanically minded sea dweller. I considered, how, when great natural catastrophes occur, such as fires and floods and earthquakes and plagues, men temporarily quit squabbling and work hand in hand—rich and poor, friend and enemy alike. Unfortunately such cooperation only lasts until man once more asserts his mastery over his environment. It does not provide a constant sobering threat. And then . . . I had an inspiration."

Mr. Whitlow's gaze swept the black-shelled forms—a jumble of satiny crescent highlights ringing the sphere of light enveloping him. Similarly his mind swept their cryptically armored thoughts.

"I remembered an incident from my childhood. A radio broadcast—we make use of high velocity vibrations to transmit sound—had given an impishly realistic fictional report of an invasion of Earth by beings from Mars, beings of that evil and destructive nature which, as you say, we tend to attribute to alien life. Many believed the report. There were brief scares and panics. It occurred to me how, at the first breath of an actual invasion of that sort, warring peoples would forget their differences and join staunchly together to meet the invader. They would realize that the things they were fighting about were really trifling matters, phantoms of moodiness and fear. Their sense of perspective would be restored. They would see that the all-important fact was that they were men alike, facing a common enemy, and they would rise magnificently to the challenge. Ah my friends, when that vision occurred to me, of warring mankind at one stroke united, and united forever, I stood trembling and speechless. I—"

Even on Mars, emotion choked him.

"Very interesting," thought the Senior Coleopteroid blandly, "but wouldn't the method you propose be a contradiction of that higher morality to which I can perceive you subscribe?"

The pacifist bowed his head. "My friend, you are quite right—in the large and ultimate sense. And let me assure you"—the fire crept back into his hoarse voice—"that when that day comes, when the question of interplanetary relations arises, I will be in the vanguard of the interspecieists, demanding full equality for coleopteroid and man alike. But"—his feverish eyes peered up again through the hair that had once more fallen across his forehead—"that is a matter for the future. The immediate question is: How to stop war on Earth. As I said before, your invasion need only be a token one, and of course the more bloodless, the better. It would only take one taste of an outside menace, one convincing proof that he has equals and even superiors in the cosmos, to restore man's normalcy of outlook, to weld him into a mutually protective brotherhood, to establish peace forever!"

He threw his hands wide and his head back. His hair flipped into its proper place, but his tie popped out again.

"Mr. Whitlow," thought the Chief, with a cold sardonic merriment, "if you have any notion that we are going to invade another planet for the sake of improving the psychology of its inhabitants, disabuse yourself of it at once. Earthlings mean nothing to us. Their rise is such a recent matter that we hardly had taken note of it until you called it to our attention. Let them go on warring, if they want to. Let them kill themselves off. It is no concern of ours."

Whitlow blinked. "Why—" he started angrily. Then he caught himself. "But I wasn't asking you to do it for humanitarian reasons. I pointed out that there would be loot—"

"I very much doubt if your Earthlings have anything that would tempt us."

Whitlow almost backed off his boulder. He started to splutter something, but again abruptly changed his tack. There was a flicker of shrewdness in his expression. "Is it possible you're holding back because you're afraid the Venusian molluscoids will attack you if you violate the perpetual truce by making a foray against another planet?"

"By no means," thought the Chief harshly, revealing for the first time a certain haughtiness and racial pride bred of dry eons of tradition. "As I told you before, the molluscoids are a distinctly inferior race. Mere waterlings. We have seen nothing of them for ages. For all we know they've died out. Certainly we wouldn't be bound by any outworn agreements with them, if there were a sound and profitable reason for breaking them. And we are in no sense—no sense whatever—afraid of them."

Whitlow's thoughts fumbled confusedly, his spatulate-fingered hands making unconsiously appropriate gestures. Driven back to his former argument, he faltered lamely. "But surely then there must be some loot that would make it worth your while to invade Earth. After all, Earth is a planet rich in oxygen and water and minerals and life forms, whereas Mars has to contend with a dearth of all these things."

"Precisely," thought the Chief. "And we have developed a style of life that fits in perfectly with that dearth. By harvesting the interplanetary dust in the neighborhood of Mars, and by a judicious use of transmutation and other techniques, we are assured of a sufficient supply of all necessary raw materials. Earth's bloated abundance would be an embarrassment to us, upsetting our system. An increased oxygen supply would force us to learn a new rhythm of breathing to avoid oxygen-drowning, besides making any invasion of Earth uncomfortable and dangerous. Similar hazards might attend an oversupply of other elements and compounds. And as for Earth's obnoxiously teeming life forms, none of them would be any use to us on Mars—except for the unlucky chance of one of them finding harborage in our bodies and starting an epidemic."

Whitlow winced. Whether he knew it or not, his planetary vanity had been touched. "But you're overlooking the most important things," he argued, "the products of man's industry and ingenuity. He has changed the face of his planet much more fully than you have yours. He has covered it with roads. He does not huddle savagely in the open as you do. He has built vast cities. He has constructed all manner of vehicles. Surely among such a wealth of things you would find many to covet."

"Most unlikely," retorted the Chief. "I cannot see envisaged in your mind any that would awaken even our passing interest. We are adapted to our environment. We have no need of garments and housing and all the other artificialities which your ill-adjusted Earthlings require. Our mastery of our planet is greater than yours, but we do not advertise it so obtrusively. From your picture I can see that your Earthlings are given to a worship of bigness and a crude type of exhibitionism."

"But then there are our machines," Whitlow insisted, seething inwardly, plucking at his collar. "Machines of tremendous complexity, for every purpose. Machines that would be as useful to another species as to us."

"Yes, I can imagine them," commented the Chief cuttingly. "Huge, clumsy, jumbles of wheels and levers, wires and grids. In any case, ours are better."

He shot a swift question to the Senior. "Is his anger making his mind any more vulnerable?"

"Not yet."

Whitlow made one last effort, with great difficulty holding his indignation in check. "Besides all that, there's our art. Cultural treasures of incalculable value. The work of a species more richly creative than your own. Books, music, paintings, sculpture. Surely—"

"Mr. Whitlow, you are becoming ridiculous," said the Chief. "Art is meaningless apart from its cultural environment. What interest could we be expected to take in the fumbling self-expression of an immature species? Moreover, none of the art forms you mention would be adapted to our style of perception, save sculpture—and in that field our efforts are incomparably superior, since we have a direct consciousness of solidity. Your mind is only a shadow-mind, limited to flimsy two-dimensional patterns."

Whitlow drew himself up and folded his arms across his chest. "Very well!" he grated out. "I see I cannot persuade you. But"—he shook his finger at the Chief—"let me tell you something! You're contemptuous of man. You call him crude and childish. You pour scorn on his industry, his science, his art. You refuse to help him in his need. You think you can afford to disregard him. All right. Go ahead. That's my advice to you. Go ahead—and see what happens!" A vindictive light grew in his eyes. "I know my fellow man. From years of study I know him. War has made him a tyrant and exploiter. He has enslaved the beasts of field and forest. He has enslaved his own kind, when he could, and when he couldn't he has bound them with the subtler chains of economic necessity and the awe of prestige. He's wrongheaded, brutal, a tool of his baser impulses—and also he's clever, doggedly persistent, driven by a boundless ambition! He already has atomic power and rocket transport. In a few decades he'll have spaceships and subatomic weapons. Go ahead and wait! Constant warfare will cause him to develop those weapons to undreamed of heights of efficient destructiveness. Wait for that too! Wait until he arrives on Mars in force. Wait until he makes your acquaintance and realizes what marvelous workers you'd be with your armored adaptability to all sorts of environments. Wait until he picks a quarrel with you and defeats you and enslaves you and ships you off, packed in evil-smelling hulls, to labor in Earth's mines and on her ocean bottoms, in her stratosphere and on the planetoids that man will be desirous of exploiting. Yes, go ahead and wait!"

Whitlow broke off, his chest heaving. For a moment he was conscious only of his vicious satisfaction at having told off these exasperating beetle-creatures. Then he looked around.

The coleopteroids had drawn in. The forms of the foremost were defined with a hatefully spiderish distinctness, almost invading his sphere of light. Similarly their thoughts had drawn in, to form a menacing wall blacker than the encircling Martian night. Gone were the supercilious amusement and dispassionate withdrawal that had so irked him. Incredulously he realized that he had somehow broken through their armor and touched them on a vulnerable spot.

He caught one rapid thought, from the Senior to the Chief: "And if the rest of them are anything like this one, they'll behave just as he says. It is an added confirmation."

He looked slowly around, his hair-curtained forehead bent forward, searching for a clue to the coleopteroids' sudden change in attitude. His baffled gaze ended on the Chief.

"We've changed our minds, Mr. Whitlow," the Chief volunteered grimly. "I told you at the beginning that we never hesitate about undertaking projects when given a sound and sufficient reason. What your silly arguments about humanitarianism and loot failed to provide, your recent outburst has furnished us. It is as you say. The Earthlings will eventually attack us, and with some hope of success, if we wait. So logically we must take preventive action, the sooner the better. We will reconnoiter Earth, and if conditions there are as you assert, we will invade her."

From the depths of a confused despondency Whitlow was in an instant catapulted to the heights of feverish joy. His fanatical face beamed. His lanky frame seemed to expand. His hair flipped back.

"Marvelous!" he chortled, and then rattled on excitedly, "Of course, I'll do everything I can to help. I'll provide transport—"

"That will not be necessary," the Chief interrupted flatly. "We have no more trust in your larger powers than you have yourself. We have our own spaceships, quite adequate to any undertaking. We do not make an ostentatious display of them, any more than we make a display of the other mechanical aspects of our culture. We do not use them, as your Earthlings would, to go purposely skittering about. Nevertheless, we have them, stored away in the event of need."

But not even this contemptuous rebuff could spoil Whitlow's exultation. His face was radiant. Half-formed tears made him blink his hectic eyes. His Adam's apple bobbed chokingly.

"Ah my friends . . . my good friends! If only I could express to you . . . what this moment means to me! If I could only tell you how happy I am when I envisage the greater moment that is coming! When men will look up from their trenches and foxholes, from their bombers and fighters, from their observation posts and headquarters, from their factories and homes, to see this new menace in the skies. When all their petty differences of opinion will drop away from them like a soiled and tattered garment. When they will cut the barbed-wire entanglements of an illusory hate, and join together, hand in hand, true brothers at last, to meet the common foe. When, in the accomplishment of a common task, they will at last achieve perfect and enduring peace!"

He paused for breath. His glazed eyes were lovingly fixed on the blue star of Earth, now just topping the horizon.

"Yes," faintly came the Chief's dry thought. "To one of your emotional temperament, it will probably be a very satisfying and touching scene—for a little while."

Whitlow glanced down blankly. It was as if the Chief's last thought had lightly scratched him—a feathery flick from a huge poisoned claw. He did not understand it, but he was conscious of upwelling fear.

"What—" he faltered. "What . . . do you mean?"

"I mean," thought the Chief, "that in our invasion of Earth it probably won't be necessary for us to use the divide-and-rule tactics that would normally be indicated in such a case—you know, joining with one faction on Earth to help defeat the other—warring beings never care who their allies are—and then fomenting further disunities, and so on. No, with our superiority in armament, we can probably do a straight cleanup job and avoid bothersome machinations. So you'll probably have that glimpse of Earthlings united that you set so much store by."

Whitlow stared at him from a face white with dawning horror. He licked his lips. "What did you mean by—'for a little while'?" he whispered huskily. "What did you mean by 'glimpse'?"

"Surely that should be obvious to you, Mr. Whitlow," replied the Chief with offensive good humor. "You don't for one minute suppose we'd make some footling little invasion and, after overawing the Earthlings, retire? That would be the one way to absolutely assure their eventual counterinvasion of Mars. Indeed, it would probably hasten it—and they'd come as already hostile destroyers intent on wiping out a menace. No, Mr. Whitlow, when we invade Earth, it will be to protect ourselves from a potential future danger. Our purpose will be total and complete extermination, accomplished as swiftly and efficiently as possible. Our present military superiority makes our success certain."

Whitlow goggled at the Chief blankly, like a dirty and somewhat yellowed plaster statue of himself. He opened his mouth—and shut it without saying anything.

"You never believed, did you, Mr. Whitlow," continued the Chief kindly, "that we'd ever do anything for your sake? Or for anyone's—except us coleopteroids?"

Whitlow stared at the horrible, black, eight-legged eggs crowding ever closer—living embodiments of the poisonous blackness of their planet.

All he could think to mumble was: "But . . . but I thought you said . . . it was a misconception to think of alien beings as evil monsters intent only on ravaging . . . and destroying—"

"Perhaps I did, Mr. Whitlow. Perhaps I did," was the Chief's only reply.

In that instant Mr. Whitlow realized what an alien being really was.

As in a suffocating nightmare, he watched the coleopteroids edge closer. He heard the Chief's contemptuously unguarded aside to the Senior, "Haven't you got hold of his mind yet?" and the Senior's "No," and the Chief's swift order to the others.

Black eggs invaded his lightsphere, cruel armored claws opening to grab—those were Mr. Whitlow's last impressions of Mars.

Instants later—for the device provided him with instantaneous transportation across any spatial expanse—Mr. Whitlow found himself inside a bubble that miraculously maintained normal atmospheric pressure deep under the tideless Venusian seas. The reverse of a fish in a tank, he peered out at the gently waving luminescent vegetation and the huge mud-girt buildings it half masked. Gleaming ships and tentacled creatures darted about.

The Chief Molluscoid regarded the trespasser on his private gardens with a haughty disfavor that even surprise could not shake.

"What are you?" he thought coldly.

"I . . . I've come to inform you of a threatened breach in an agelong truce."

Five eyes on longish stalks regarded him with a coldness equal to that of the repeated thought: "But what are you?"

A sudden surge of woeful honesty compelled Mr. Whitlow to reply, "I suppose . . . I suppose you'd call me a warmonger."

BLIND ALLEY

by Isaac Asimov (1920-   )

ASTOUNDING SCIENCE FICTION,
March

(I can never judge my own stories. I know which ones I like better than others—there are almost none that I actively dislike—but I can't tell which are better *than others. So Marty decides which of mine, if any, belong in any of these collections.*

I like this story because it reminds me of the one time when I was part of the bureaucracy—during World War II when I worked at the Naval Air Experimental Station in Philadelphia [*along with Robert Heinlein and L. Sprague de Camp.*] *In those years I was constantly faced with red tape and the queerly involuted system of letter-writing that I made use of in the story.*

It was a challenge and I remember once writing a specification in bureaucratese which I deliberately made as complicated and intricate as possible while adhering strictly to all the rules. I have formidable abilities in this respect and I ended up with something that I feared would get me court-martialed and it was only my sense of humor that prodded me into sending it up through the chain of command. I wasn't court-martialed. In fact, I was commended and praised for a sterling piece of work and I think it was that which gave the idea for "Blind Alley." I.A.)

Only once in Galactic History was an intelligent race of non-Humans discovered—

"Essays on History,"
by Ligurn Vier

I.

From: Bureau for the Outer Provinces
To: Loodun Antyok, Chief Public Administrator, A-8
Subject: Civilian Supervisor of Cepheus 18, Administrative Position as,
References:

(a) Act of Council 2515, of the year 971 of the Galactic Empire, entitled, "Appointment of Officials of the Administrative Service, Methods for, Revision of."

(b) Imperial Directive, Ja 2374, dated 243/975 G.E.

1. By authorization of reference (a), you are hereby appointed to the subject position. The authority of said position as Civilian Supervisor of Cepheus 18 will extend over non-Human subjects of the Emperor living upon the planet under the terms of autonomy set forth in reference (b).

2. The duties of the subject position shall comprise the general supervision of all non-Human internal affairs, co-ordination of authorized government investigating and reporting committees, and the preparation of semiannual reports on all phases of non-Human affairs.

C. Morily, Chief, BuOuProv,
12/977 G.E.

Loodun Antyok had listened carefully, and now he shook his round head mildly, "Friend, I'd like to help you, but you've grabbed the wrong dog by the ears. You'd better take this up with the Bureau."

Tomor Zammo flung himself back into his chair, rubbed his beak of a nose fiercely, thought better of whatever he was going to say, and answered quietly, "Logical, but not practical. I can't make a trip to Trantor now. You're the Bureau's representative on Cepheus 18. Are you entirely helpless?"

"Well, even as Civilian Supervisor, I've got to work within the limits of Bureau policy."

"Good," Zammo cried, "then, tell me what Bureau policy is. I head a scientific investigating committee, under direct Imperial authorization with, supposedly, the widest powers; yet at every angle in the road I am pulled up short by the civilian authorities with only the parrot shriek of 'Bureau policy' to justify themselves. What *is* Bureau policy? I haven't received a decent definition yet."

Antyok's gaze was level and unruffled. He said, "As I see it—and this is not official, so you can't hold me to it—Bureau policy consists in treating the non-Humans as decently as possible."

"Then, what authority have they—"

"*Ssh!* No use raising your voice. As a matter of fact, His Imperial Majesty is a humanitarian and a disciple of the philosophy of Aurelion. I can tell you quietly that it is pretty well-known that it is the Emperor himself who first suggested that this world be established. You can bet that Bureau policy will stick pretty close to Imperial notions. And you can bet that I can't paddle my way against *that* sort of current."

"Well, m'boy," the physiologist's fleshy eyelids quivered, "if you take that sort of attitude, you're going to lose your job. No, I won't have you kicked out. That's not what I mean at all. Your job will just fade out from under you, because nothing is going to be accomplished here!"

"Really? Why?" Antyok was short, pink, and pudgy, and his plump-cheeked face usually found it difficult to put on display any expression other than one of bland and cheerful politeness—but it looked grave now.

"You haven't been here long. I have." Zammo scowled. "Mind if I smoke?" The cigar in his hand was gnarled and strong and was puffed to life carelessly.

He continued roughly, "There's no place here for humanitarianism, administrator. You're treating non-Humans as if they were Humans, and it won't work. In fact, I don't like the word 'non-Human.' They're animals."

"They're intelligent," interjected Antyok softly.

"Well, intelligent animals, then. I presume the two terms are not mutually exclusive. Alien intelligences mingling in the same space won't work, anyway."

"Do you propose killing them off?"

"Galaxy, no!" He gestured with his cigar. "I propose we

look upon them as objects for study, and only that. We could learn a good deal from these animals if we were allowed to. Knowledge, I might point out, that would be used for the immediate benefit of the human race. *There's* humanity for you. *There's* the good of the masses, if it's this spineless cult of Aurelion that interests you."

"What, for instance, do you refer to?"

"To take the most obvious—You have heard of their chemistry, I take it?"

"Yes," Antyok admitted. "I have leafed through most of the reports on the non-Humans published in the last ten years. I expect to go through more."

"Hmp. Well— Then, all I need to say is that their chemical therapy is extremely thorough. For instance, I have witnessed personally the healing of a broken bone—what passes for a broken bone with them, I mean—by the use of a pill. The bone was whole in fifteen minutes. Naturally, none of their drugs are any earthly use on Humans. Most would kill quickly. But if we found out how they worked on the non-Humans—on the animals—"

"Yes, yes. I see the significance."

"Oh, you do. Come, that's gratifying. A second point is that these animals communicate in an unknown manner."

"Telepathy!"

The scientist's mouth twisted, as he ground out, "Telepathy! Telepathy! Telepathy! Might as well say by witch brew. Nobody knows anything about telepathy except its name. What is the mechanism of telepathy? What is the physiology and the physics of it? I would like to find out, but I can't. Bureau policy if I listen to you, forbids."

Anytok's little mouth pursed itself. "But— Pardon me, doctor, but I don't follow you. How are you prevented? Surely the Civil Administration has made no attempt to hamper scientific investigation of these non-Humans. I cannot speak for my predecessor entirely, of course, but I myself—"

"No direct interference has occurred. I don't speak of that. But by the Galaxy, administrator, we're hampered by the spirit of the entire set-up. You're making us deal with Humans. You allow them their own leader and internal autonomy. You pamper them and give them what Aurelion's philosophy would call 'rights.' I can't deal with their leader."

"Why not?"

"Because he refuses to allow me a free hand. He refuses to allow experiments on any subject without the subject's own consent. The two or three volunteers we get are not too bright. It's an impossible arrangement."

Antyok shrugged helplessly.

Zammo continued, "In addition, it is obviously impossible to learn anything of value concerning the brains, physiology, and chemistry of these animals without dissection, dietary experiments, and drugs. You know, administrator, scientific investigation is a hard game. Humanity hasn't much place in it."

Loodun Antyok tapped his chin with a doubtful finger, "Must it be quite so hard? These are harmless creatures, these non-Humans. Surely, dissection— Perhaps, if you were to approach them a bit differently—I have the idea that you antagonize them. Your attitude might be somewhat overbearing."

"Overbearing! I am not one of these whining social psychologists who are all the fad these days. I don't believe you can solve a problem that requires dissection by approaching it with what is called the 'correct personal attitude' in the cant of the times."

"I'm sorry you think so. Sociopsychological training is required of all administrators above the grade of A-4."

Zammo withdrew his cud of a cigar from his mouth and replaced it after a suitably contemptuous interval, "Then you'd better use a bit of your technique on the Bureau. You know, I *do* have friends at the Imperial court."

"Well, now, I *can't* take the matter up with them, not baldly. Basic policy does not fall within my cognizance, and such things can only be initiated by the Bureau. But, you know, we might try an indirect approach on this." He smiled faintly, "Strategy."

"What sort?"

Antyok pointed a sudden finger, while his other hand fell lightly on the rows of gray-bound reports upon the floor just next his chair, "Now, look, I've gone through most of these. They're dull, but contain *some* facts. For instance, when was the last non-Human infant born on Cepheus 18?"

Zammo spent little time in consideration. "Don't know. Don't care either."

"But the Bureau would. There's *never* been a non-Human infant born on Cepheus 18—not in the two years the world has been established. Do you know the reason?"

The physiologist shrugged, "Too many possible factors. It would take study."

"All right, then. Suppose you write a report—"

"Reports! I've written twenty."

"Write another. Stress the unsolved problems. Tell them you must change your methods. Harp on the birth-rate problem. The bureau doesn't dare ignore that. If the non-Humans die out, someone will have to answer to the Emperor. You see—"

Zammo stared, his eyes dark, "That will swing it?"

"I've been working for the Bureau for twenty-seven years. I know its way."

"I'll think about it." Zammo rose and stalked out of the office. The door slammed behind him.

It was later that Zammo said to a co-worker, "He's a bureaucrat, in the first place. He won't abandon the orthodoxies of paper work and he won't risk sticking his neck out. He'll accomplish little by himself, yet maybe more than a little if we work through him."

From: Administrative Headquarters, Cepheus 18
To: BuOuProv
Subject: Outer Province Project 2563, Part II—Scientific Investigations of non-Humans of Cepheus 18, Coordination of,

References:

(a) BuOuProv letr. Cep-N-CM/jg, 100132, dated 302/975 G.E.

(b) AdHQ-Ceph18 letr. AA-LA/mn, dated 140/977 G.E.

Enclosure:

1. SciGroup 10, Physical & Biochemical Division, Report, entitled, "Physiologic Characteristics of non-Humans of Cepheus 18, Part XI," dated 172/977 G.E.

1. Enclosure 1, included herewith, is forwarded for the information of the BuOuProv. It is to be noted that Section XII, paragraphs 1–16 of Encl. 1, concern possible changes in present BuOuProv policy with regard to non-Humans with a view to facilitating physical and chemical investigations at present proceeding under authorization of reference (a)

2. It is brought to the attention of the BuOuProv that reference (b) has already discussed possible changes in investigating methods and that it remains the opinion of AdHQ-Ceph18 that such changes are as yet premature.

It is nevertheless suggested that the question of non-Human birth rate be made the subject of a BuOuProv project assigned to AdHQ-Ceph18 in view of the importance attached by SciGroup 10 to the problem, as evidenced in Section V of Enclosure 1.

L. Antyok, Supery, AdHQ-Ceph18,
174/977

From: BuOuProv
To: AdHQ-Ceph18
Subject: Outer Province Project 2563—Scientific Investigations of non-Humans of Cepheus 18, Co-ordination of,
Reference:
(a) AdHQ-Ceph18 letr. AA-LA/mn, dated 174/977 G.E.

1. In response to the suggestion contained in paragraph 2 of reference (a), it is considered that the question of the non-Human birth rate does not fall within the cognizance of AdHQ-Ceph18. In view of the fact that SciGroup 10 has reported said sterility to be probably due to a chemical deficiency in the food supply, all investigations in the field are relegated to SciGroup 10 as the proper authority.

2. Investigating procedures by the various SciGroups shall continue according to current directives on the subject. No changes in policy are envisaged.

C. Morily, Chief, BuOuProv,
186/977 G.E.

II.

There was a loose-jointed gauntness about the news reporter which made him appear somberly tall. He was Gustiv Bannerd, with whose reputation was combined ability—two things which do not invariably go together despite the maxims of elementary morality.

Loodum Antyok took his measure doubtfully and said, "There's no use denying that you're right. But the SciGroup report was confidential. I don't understand how—"

"It leaked," said Bannerd, callously. "Everything leaks."

Antyok was obviously baffled, and his pink face furrowed slightly, "Then I'll just have to plug the leak here. I can't pass your story. All references to SciGroup complaints have to come out. You see that, don't you?"

"No." Bannerd was calm enough. "It's important; and I have my rights under the Imperial directive. I think the Empire should know what's going on."

"But it isn't going on," said Antyok, despairingly. "Your claims are all wrong. The Bureau isn't going to change its policy. I showed you the letters."

"You think you can stand up against Zammo when he puts the pressure on?" the newsman asked derisively.

"I will—if I think he's wrong."

"If!" stated Bannerd flatly. Then, in a sudden fervor, "Antyok, the Empire has something great here; something greater by a good deal than the government apparently realizes. They're destroying it. They're treating these creatures like animals."

"Really—" began Antyok, weakly.

"Don't talk about Cepheus 18. It's a zoo. It's a high-class zoo, with your petrified scientists teasing those poor creatures with their sticks poking through the bars. You throw them chunks of meat, but you cage them up. I know! I've been writing about them for two years now. I've almost been living with them."

"Zammo says—"

"Zammo!" This with hard contempt.

"Zammo says," insisted Antyok with worried firmness, "that we treat them too like Humans as it is."

The newsman's straight, long cheeks were rigid, "Zammo is rather animallike in his own right. He is a science-worshiper. We can do with less of them. Have you read Aurelion's works?" The last was suddenly posed.

"Umm. Yes. I understand the Emperor—"

"The Emperor tends toward us. That is good—better than the hounding of the last reign."

"I don't see where you're heading."

"These aliens have much to teach us. You understand? It is nothing that Zammo and his SciGroup can use; no chemistry, no telepathy. It's a way of life; a way of thinking. The aliens have no crime, no misfits. What effort is being made to study their philosophy? Or to set them up as a problem in social engineering?"

Antyok grew thoughtful, and his plump face smoothed out. "It is an interesting consideration. It would be a matter for psychologists—"

"No good. Most of them are quacks. Psychologists point

out problems, but their solutions are fallacious. We need men of Aurelion. Men of The Philosophy—"

"But look here, we can't turn Cepheus 18 into . . . into a metaphysical study."

"Why not? It can be done easily."

"How?"

"Forget your puny test-tube peerings. Allow the aliens to set up a society free of Humans. Give them an untrammeled independence and allow an intermingling of philosophies—"

Antyok's nervous response came, "That can't be done in a day."

"We can start in a day."

The administrator said slowly, "Well, I can't prevent you from trying to start." He grew confidential, his mild eyes thoughtful, "You'll ruin your own game, though, if you publish SciGroup 10's report and denounce it on humanitarian grounds. The Scientists are powerful."

"And we of The Philosophy as well."

"Yes, but there's an easy way. You needn't rave. Simply point out that the SciGroup is not solving its problems. Do so unemotionally and let the readers think out your point of view for themselves. Take the birth-rate problem, for instance. *There's* something for you. In a generation, the non-Humans might die out, for all science can do. Point out that a more philosophical approach is required. Or pick some other obvious point. Use your judgment, eh?"

Antyok smiled ingratiatingly as he arose, "But, for the Galaxy's sake, don't stir up a bad smell."

Bannerd was stiff and unresponsive, "You may be right."

It was later that Bannerd wrote in a capsule message to a friend, "He is not clever, by any means. He is confused and has no guiding line through life. Certainly utterly incompetent in his job. But he's a cutter and a trimmer, compromises his way around difficulties, and will yield concessions rather than risk a hard stand. He may prove valuable in that. Yours in Aurelion."

From: AdHQ-Ceph18
To: BuOuProv
Subject: Birth rate of non-Humans on Cepheus 18, News Report on.
References:
(a) AdHQ-Ceph18 letr. AA-LA/mn, dated 174/977 G.E.

(b) Imperial Directive, Ja2374, dated 243/975 G.E.
Enclosures:
1-G. Bannerd news report, date-lined Cepheus 18, 201/977 G.E.
2-G. Bannerd news report, date-lined Cepheus 18, 203/977 G.E.

1. The sterility of non-Humans on Cepheus 18, reported to the BuOuProv in reference (a), has become the subject of news reports to the galactic press. The news reports in question are submitted herewith for the information of the BuOuProv as Enclosures 1 and 2. Although said reports are based on material considered confidential and closed to the public, the news reporter in question maintained his rights to free expression under the terms of reference (b).

2. In view of the unavoidable publicity and misunderstanding on the part of the general public now inevitable, it is requested that the BuOuProv direct future policy on the problem of non-Human sterility.

L. Antyok, Superv. AdHQ-Ceph18,
209/977 G.E.

From: BuOuProv
To: AdHQ-Ceph18
Subject: Birth rate of non-Humans on Cepheus 18, Investigation of.
References:
a() AdHQ-Ceph18 letr. AA-LA/mn, dated 209/977 G.E.
(b) AdHQ-Ceph18 letr. AA-LA/mn, dated 174/977 G.E.

1. It is proposed to investigate the causes and the means of precluding the unfavorable birth-rate phenomena mentioned in references (a) and (b). A project is therefore set up, entitled, "Birth rate of non-Humans on Cepheus 18, Investigation of" to which, in view of the crucial importance of the subject, a priority of AA is given.

2. The number assigned to the subject project is 2910, and all expenses incidental to it shall be assigned to Appropriation number 18/78.

C. Morily, Chief, BuOuProv,
223/977 G.E.

III.

If Tomor Zammo's ill-humor lessened within the grounds of SciGroup 10 Experimental Station, his friendliness had not thereby increased. Antyok found himself standing alone at the viewing window into the main field laboratory.

The main field laboratory was a broad court set at the environmental conditions of Cepheus 18 itself for the discomfort of the experimenters and the convenience of the experimentees. Through the burning sand, and the dry, oxygen-rich air, there sparkled the hard brilliance of hot, white sunlight. And under the blaze, the brick-red non-Humans, wrinkled of skin and wiry of build, huddled in their squatting positions of ease, by ones and twos.

Zammo emerged from the laboratory. He paused to drink water thirstily. He looked up, moisture gleaming on his upper lip. "Like to step in there?"

Antyok shook his head definitely. "No, thank you. What's the temperature right now?"

"A hundred twenty, if there were shade. And they complain of the cold. It's drinking time now. Want to watch them drink?"

A spray of water shot upward from the fountain in the center of the court, and the little alien figures swayed to their feet and hopped eagerly forward in a queer, springy half-run. They milled about the water, jostling one another. The centers of their faces were suddenly disfigured by the projection of a long and flexible fleshy tube, which thrust forward into the spray and was withdrawn dripping.

It continued for long minutes. The bodies swelled and the wrinkles disappeared. They retreated slowly, backing away, with the drinking tube flicking in and out, before receding finally into a pink, wrinkled mass above a wide, lipless mouth. They went to sleep in groups in the shaded angles, plump and sated.

"Animals!" said Zammo, with contempt.

"How often do they drink?" asked Antyok.

"As often as they want. They can go a week if they have to. We water them every day. They store it under their skin. They eat in the evenings. Vegetarians, you know."

Antyok smiled chubbily, "It's nice to get a bit of first-hand information occasionally. Can't read reports all the time."

"Yes?"—noncommittally. Then, "What's new? What about the lacy-pants boys on Trantor?"

Antyok shrugged dubiously. "You can't get the Bureau to commit itself, unfortunately. With the Emperor sympathetic to the Aurelionists, humanitarianism is the order of the day. You know that."

There was a pause in which the administrator chewed his lip uncertainly. "But there's this birth-rate problem now. It's finally been assigned to AdHQ, you know—and double A priority, too."

Zammo muttered wordlessly.

Antyok said, "You may not realize it, but that project will now take precedence over all other work proceeding on Cepheus 18. It's important."

He turned back to the viewing window and said thoughtfully with a bald lack of preamble. "Do you think those creatures might be unhappy?"

"Unhappy!" The word was an explosion.

"Well, then," Antyok corrected hastily, "maladjusted. You understand? It's difficult to adjust an environment to a race we know so little of."

"Say—did you ever see the world we took them from?"

"I've read the reports—"

"Reports!"—infinite contempt. "I've *seen* it. This may look like desert out there to you, but it's a watery paradise to those devils. They have all the food and water they can get. They have a world to themselves with vegetation and natural water flow, instead of a lump of silica and granite where fungi were force-grown in caves and water had to be steamed out of gypsum rock. In ten years, they would have been dead to the last beast, and we saved them. Unhappy? Ga-a-ah, if they are, they haven't the decency of most animals."

"Well, perhaps. Yet I have a notion."

"A notion? What is your notion?" Zammo reached for one of his cigars.

"It's something that might help you. Why not study the creatures in a more integrated fashion? Let them use their initiative. After all, they did have a highly developed science. Your reports speak of it continually. Give them problems to solve."

"Such as?"

"Oh . . . oh," Antyok waved his hands helplessly. "Whatever you think might help most. For instance, spaceships. Get them into the control room and study their reactions."

"Why?" asked Zammo with dry bluntness.

"Because the reaction of their minds to tools and controls adjusted to the human temperament can teach you a lot. In addition, it will make a more effective bribe, it seems to me, than anything you've yet tried. You'll get more volunteers if they think they'll be doing something interesting."

"That's your psychology coming out. Hm-m-m. Sounds better than it probably is. I'll sleep on it. And where would I get permission, in any case, to let them handle spaceships? I've none at *my* disposal, and it would take a good deal longer than it was worth to follow down the line of red tape to get one assigned to us."

Antyok pondered, and his forehead creased lightly, "It doesn't *have* to be spaceships. But even so—If you would write up another report and make the suggestion yourself—strongly, you understand—I might figure out some way of tying it up with my birth-rate project. A double-A priority can get practically anything, you know, without questions."

Zammo's interest lacked a bit even of mildness, "Well, maybe. Meanwhile, I've some basal metabolism tests in progress, and it's getting late. I'll think about it. It's got its points."

From: AdHQ-Ceph18

To: BuOuProv

Subject: Outer Province Project 2910, Part I—Birth rate of non-Humans on Cepheus 18, Investigation of,

Reference:

(a) BuOuProv letr. Ceph-N-CM/car, 115097, 223/977 G.E.

Enclosure:

1. SciGroup 10, Physical & Biochemical Division report, Part XV, dated 220/977 G.E.

1. Enclosure 1 is forwarded herewith for the information of the BuOuProv.

2. Special attention is directed to Section V, Paragraph 3 of Enclosure 1 in which it is requested that a spaceship be assigned SciGroup 10 for use in expediting investigations authorized by the BuOuProv. It is considered by AdHQ-Ceph18 that such investigation may be of material use in aiding work now in progress on the subject project, authorized by reference (a). It is suggested, in view of the high priority placed by the BuOuProv upon

the subject project, that immediate consideration be given the SciGroup's request.

L. Antyok, Superv. AdHQ-Ceph18,
240/977 G.E.

From: BuOuProv
To: AdHQ-Ceph18
Subject: Outer Province Project 2910—Birth rate of non-Humans on Cepheus 18, Investigation of.
Reference:
(a) AdHQ-Ceph18 letr. AA-LA/mn, dated 240/977 G.E.

1. Training Ship *AN-R-2055* is being placed at the disposal of AdHQ-Ceph18 for use in investigation of non-Humans on Cepheus 18 with respect to the subject project and other authorized OuProv projects, as requested in Enclosure 1 to reference (a).
2. It is urgently requested that work on the subject project be expedited by all available means.

C. Morily, Head, BuOuProv,
251/977 G.E.

IV.

The little bricky creature must have been more uncomfortable than his bearing would admit to. He was carefully wrapped in a temperature already adjusted to the point where his human companions steamed in their open shirts.

His speech was high-pitched and careful, "I find it damp, but not unbearably so at this low temperature."

Antyok smiled, "It was nice of you to come. I had planned to visit you, but a trial run in your atmosphere out there—" The smile had become rueful.

"It doesn't matter. You other worldlings have done more for us than ever we were able to do for ourselves. It is an obligation that is but imperfectly returned by the endurance on my part of a trifling discomfort." His speech seemed always indirect, as if he approached his thoughts sidelong, or as if it were against all etiquette to be blunt.

Gustiv Bannerd, seated in an angle of the room, with one long leg crossing the other, scrawled nimbly and said, "You don't mind if I record all this?"

The Cepheid non-Human glanced briefly at the journalist, "I have no objection."

Antyok's apologetics persisted, "This is not a purely social affair, sir. I would not have forced discomfort on you for that. There are important questions to be considered, and you are the leader of your people."

The Cepheid nodded, "I am satisfied your purposes are kindly. Please proceed."

The administrator almost wriggled in his difficulty in putting thoughts into words. "It is a subject," he said, "of delicacy, and one I would never bring up if it weren't for the overwhelming importance of the . . . uh . . . question. I am only the spokesman of my government—"

"My people consider the otherworld government a kindly one."

"Well, yes, they are kindly. For that reason, they are disturbed over the fact that your people no longer breed."

Antyok paused, and waited with worry for a reaction that did not come. The Cepheid's face was motionless except for the soft, trembling motion of the wrinkled area that was his deflated drinking tube.

Antyok continued, "It is a question we have hesitated to bring up because of its extremely personal angles. Noninterference is my government's prime aim, and we have done our best to investigate the problem quietly and without disturbing your people. But, frankly, we—"

"Have failed?" finished the Cepheid, at the other's pause.

"Yes. Or at least, we have not discovered a concrete failure to reproduce the exact environment of your original world; with, of course, the necessary modification to make it more livable. Naturally, it is thought there is some chemical shortcoming. And so I ask your voluntary help in the matter. Your people are advanced in the study of your own biochemistry. If you do not choose, or would rather not—"

"No, no, I can help." The Cepheid seemed cheerful about it. The smooth flat planes of his loose-skinned, hairless skull wrinkled in an alien response to an uncertain emotion. "It is not a matter that any of us would have thought would have disturbed you other-worldlings. That it does is but another indication of your well-meaning kindness. This world we find congenial, a paradise in comparison to our old. It lacks in nothing. Conditions such as now prevail belong in our legends of the Golden Age."

"Well—"

"But there is a something; a something you may not understand. We cannot expect different intelligences to think alike."

"I shall try to understand."

The Cepheid's voice had grown soft, its liquid undertones more pronounced, "We were dying on our native world; but we were fighting. Our science, developed through a history older than yours, was losing; but it had not yet lost. Perhaps it was because our science was fundamentally biological, rather than physical as yours is. Your people discovered new forms of energy and reached the stars. Our people discovered new truths of psychology and psychiatry and built up a working society free of disease and crime.

"There is no need to question which of the two angles of approach was the more laudable, but there is no uncertainty as to which proved more successful in the end. In our dying world, without the means of life or sources of power, our biological science could but make the dying easier.

"And yet we fought. For centuries past, we had been groping toward the elements of atomic power, and slowly the spark of hope had glimmered that we might break through the two-dimensional limits of our planetary surface and reach the stars. There were no other planets in our system to serve as stepping stones. Nothing but some twenty light-years to the nearest star, without the knowledge of the possibility of the existence of other planetary systems, but rather of the contrary.

"But there is something in all life that insists on striving; even on useless striving. There were only five thousand of us left in the last days. Only five thousand. And our first ship was ready. It was experimental. It would probably have been a failure. But already we had all the principles of propulsion and navigation correctly worked out."

There was a long pause, and the Cepheid's small black eyes seemed glazed in recollection.

The newspaperman put in suddenly, from his corner, "And then we came?"

"And then you came," the Cepheid agreed simply. "It changed everything. Energy was ours for the asking. A new world, congenial and, indeed, ideal, was ours even without asking. If our problems of society had long been solved by ourselves, our more difficult problems of environment were suddenly solved for us, no less completely."

"Well?" urged Antyok.

"Well—it was somehow not well. For centuries, our ancestors had fought toward the stars, and now the stars suddenly proved to be the property of others. We had fought for life, and it had become a present handed to us by others. There is no longer any reason to fight. There is no longer anything to attain. All the universe is the property of your race."

"This world is yours," said Antyok gently.

"By sufferance. It is a gift. It is not ours by right."

"You have earned it, in my opinion."

And now the Cepheid's eyes were sharply fixed on the other's countenance, "You mean well, but I doubt that you understand. We have nowhere to go, save this gift of a world. We are in a blind alley. The function of life is striving, and that is taken from us. Life can no longer interest us. We have no offspring—voluntarily. It is our way of removing ourselves from your way."

Absent-mindedly, Antyok had removed the fluoroglobe from the window seat, and spun it on its base. Its gaudy surface reflected light as it spun, and its three-foot-high bulk floated with incongruous grace and lightness in the air.

Antyok said, "Is that your only solution? Sterility?"

"We might escape still," whispered the Cepheid, "but where in the Galaxy is there place for us? It is all yours."

"Yes, there is no place for you nearer than the Magellanic Clouds if you wished independence. The Magellanic Clouds—"

"And you would not let us go of yourselves. You mean kindly, I know."

"Yes, we mean kindly—but we could not let you go."

"It is a mistaken kindness."

"Perhaps, but could you not reconcile yourselves? You have a world."

"It is something past complete explanations. Your mind is different. We could not reconcile ourselves, I believe, administrator, that you have thought of all this before. The concept of the blind alley we find ourselves trapped in is not new to you."

Antyok looked up, startled, and one hand steadied the fluoroglobe, "Can you read my mind?"

"It is just a guess. A good one, I think."

"Yes—but *can* you read my mind? The minds of Humans

in general, I mean. It is an interesting point. The scientists say you cannot, but sometimes I wonder if it is that you simply will not. Could you answer that? I am detaining you, unduly, perhaps."

"No . . . no—" But the little Cepheid drew his enveloping robe closer, and buried his face in the electrically heated pad at the collar for a moment. "You other-worldlings speak of reading minds. It is not so at all, but it is assuredly hopeless to explain."

Antyok mumbled the old proverb, "One cannot explain sight to a man blind from birth."

"Yes, just so. This sense which you call 'mind reading,' quite erroneously, cannot be applied to us. It is not that we cannot receive the proper sensations, it is that your people do not transmit them, and we have no way of explaining to you how to go about it."

"Hm-m-m."

"There are times, of course, of great concentration or emotional tension on the part of an other-worldling when some of us who are more expert in this sense; more sharp-eyed, so to speak; detect vaguely *something*. It is uncertain; yet I myself have at times wondered—"

Carefully, Antyok began spinning the fluoroglobe once more. His pink face was set in thought, and his eyes were fixed upon the Cepheid. Gustiv Bannerd stretched his fingers and reread his notes, his lips moving silently.

The fluoroglobe spun, and slowly the Cepheid seemed to grow tense as well, as his eyes shifted to the colorful sheen of the globe's fragile surface.

The Cepheid said, "What is that?"

Antyok started, and his face smoothed into an almost chuckling placidity, "This? A Galactic fad of three years ago; which means that it is a hopelessly old-fashioned relic this year. It is a useless device but it looks pretty. Bannerd, could you adjust the windows to nontransmission?"

There was a soft click of a contact, and the windows became curved regions of darkness, while in the center of the room, the fluoroglobe was suddenly the focus of a rosy effulgence that seemed to leap outward in streamers. Antyok, a scarlet figure in a scarlet room, placed it upon the table and spun it with a hand that dripped red. As it spun, the colors changed with a slowly increasing rapidity, blended and fell apart into more extreme contrasts.

Antyok was speaking in an eerie atmosphere of molten, shifting rainbow, "The surface is of a material that exhibits variable fluorescence. It is almost weightless, extremely fragile, but gyroscopically balanced so that it rarely falls, with ordinary care. It is rather pretty, don't you think?"

From somewhere the Cepheid's voice came, "Extremely pretty."

"But it has outworn its welcome; outlived its fashionable existence."

The Cepheid's voice was abstracted, "It is very pretty."

Bannerd restored the light at a gesture, and the colors faded.

The Cepheid said, "That is something my people would enjoy." He stared at the globe with fascination.

And now Antyok rose. "You had better go. If you stay longer, the atmosphere may have bad effects. I thank you humbly for your kindness."

"I thank you humbly for yours." The Cepheid had also risen.

Antyok said, "Most of your people, by the way, have accepted our offers to them to study the make-up of our modern spaceships. You understand, I suppose, that the purpose was to study the reactions of your people to our technology. I trust that conforms with your sense of propriety."

"You need not apologize. I, myself, have not the makings of a human pilot. It was most interesting. It recalls our own efforts—and reminds us of how nearly on the right track we were."

The Cepheid left, and Antyok sat, frowning.

"Well," he said to Bannerd, a little sharply. "You remember our agreement, I hope. This interview can't be published."

"Bannerd shrugged, "Very well."

Antyok was at his seat, and his fingers fumbled with the small metal figurine upon his desk, "What do you think of all this, Bannerd?"

"I am sorry for them. I think I understand how they feel. We must educate them out of it. The Philosophy can do it."

"You think so?"

"Yes."

"We can't let them go, of course."

"Oh, no. Out of the question. We have too much to learn from them. This feeling of theirs is only a passing stage. They'll think differently, especially when we allow them the completest independence."

"Maybe. What do you think of the fluoroglobes, Bannerd? He liked them. It might be a gesture of the right sort to order several thousand of them. The Galaxy knows, they're a drug on the market right now, and cheap enough."

"Sounds like a good idea," said Bannerd.

"The Bureau would never agree, though. I know them."

The newsman's eyes narrowed, "But it might be just the thing. They need new interests."

"Yes? Well, we *could* do something. I could include your transcript of the interview as part of a report and just emphasize the matter of the globes a bit. After all, you're a member of The Philosophy and might have influence with important people, whose word with the Bureau might carry much more weight than mine. You understand—?"

"Yes," mused Bannerd. "Yes."

From: AdHQ-Ceph18
To: BuOuProv
Subject: OuProv Project 2910, Part II; Birth rate of non-Humans on Cepheus 18, Investigation of.
Reference:
(a) BuOuProv letr. Cep-N-CM/car, 115097, dated 223/977 G.E.
Enclosure:
1. Transcript of conversation between L. Antyok of AdHQ-Ceph18, and Ni-San, High Judge of the non-Humans on Cepheus 18.

1. Enclosure 1 is forwarded herewith for the information of the BuOuProv.

2. The investigation of the subject undertaken in response to the authorization of reference (a) is being pursued along the new lines indicated in Enclosure 1. The BuOuProv is assured that every means will be used to combat the harmful psychological attitude at present prevalent among the non-Humans.

3. It is to be noted that the High Judge of the non-Humans on Cepheus 18 expressed interest in fluoroglobes. A preliminary investigation into this fact of non-Human psychology has been initiated.

L. Antyok, Superv. AdHQ-Ceph18,
272/977 G.E.

From: BuOuProv
To: AdHQ-Ceph18
Subject: OuProv Project 2910; Birth rate of non-Humans on Cepheus 18, Investigation of.
Reference:
(a) AdHQ-Ceph18 letr. AA-LA/mn, dated 272/977 G.E.

1. With reference to Enclosure 1 of reference (a), five thousand fluoroglobes have been allocated for shipment to Cepheus 18, by the Department of Trade.

2. It is instructed that AdHQ-Ceph18 make use of all methods of appeasing non-Human's dissatisfaction, consistent with the necessities of obedience to Imperial proclamations.

C. Morily, Chief, BuOuProv,
283/977 G.E.

V.

The dinner was over, the wine had been brought in, and the cigars were out. The groups of talkers had formed, and the captain of the merchant fleet was the center of the largest. His brilliant white uniform quite outsparkled his listeners.

He was almost complacent in his speech: "The trip was nothing. I've had more than three hundred ships under me before this. Still, I've never had a cargo quite like this. What do you want with five thousand fluoroglobes on this desert, by the Galaxy!"

Loodun Antyok laughed gently. He shrugged. "For the non-Humans. It wasn't a difficult cargo, I hope."

"No, not difficult. But bulky. They're fragile, and I couldn't carry more than twenty to a ship, with all the government regulations concerning packing and precautions against breakage. But it's the government's money, I suppose."

Zammo smiled grimly. "Is this your first experience with government methods, captain?"

"Galaxy, no," exploded the spaceman. "I try to avoid it, of course, but you can't help getting entangled on occasion. And it's an abhorrent thing when you are, and that's the truth. The red tape! The paper work! It's enough to stunt your growth and curdle your circulation. It's a tumor, a cancerous growth on the Galaxy. I'd wipe out the whole mess."

Antyok said, "You're unfair, captain. You don't understand."

"Yes? Well, now, as one of these bureaucrats," and he smiled amiably at the word, "suppose you explain your side of the situation, administrator."

"Well, now," Antyok seemed confused, "government is a serious and complicated business. We've got thousands of planets to worry about in this Empire of ours and billions of people. It's almost past human ability to supervise the business of governing without the tightest sort of organization. I think there are something like four hundred million men today in the Imperial Administrative Service alone, and in order to co-ordinate their efforts and to pool their knowledge, you *must* have what you call red tape and paper work. Every bit of it, senseless though it may seem, annoying though it may be, has its uses. Every piece of paper is a thread binding the labors of four hundred million Humans. Abolish the Administrative Service and you abolish the Empire; and with it, interstellar peace, order, and civilization."

"Come—" said the captain.

"No. I mean it." Antyok was earnestly breathless. "The rules and system of the Administrative set-up must be sufficiently all-embracing and rigid so that in case of incompetent officials, and sometimes one *is* appointed—you may laugh, but there are incompetent scientists, and newsmen, and captains, too—in case of incompetent officials, I say, little harm will be done. For, at the worst, the system can move by itself."

"Yes," grunted the captain, sourly, "and if a capable administrator should be appointed? He is then caught by the same rigid web and is forced into mediocrity."

"Not at all," replied Antyok warmly. "A capable man can work within the limits of the rules and accomplish what he wishes."

"How?" asked Bannerd.

"Well . . . well—" Antyok was suddenly ill at ease. "One method is to get yourself an A-priority project, or double-A, if possible."

The captain leaned his head back for laughter, but never quite made it, for the door was flung open and frightened men were pouring in. The shouts made no sense at first. Then:

"Sir, the ships are gone. These non-Humans have taken them by force."

"What? All?"

"Every one. Ships and creatures—"

It was two hours later that the four were together again, alone in Antyok's office now.

Antyok said coldly, "They've made no mistakes. There's not a ship left behind, not even your training ship, Zammo. And there isn't a government ship available in this entire half of the Sector. By the time we organize a pursuit they'll be out of the Galaxy and halfway to the Magellanic Clouds. Captain, it was your responsibility to maintain an adequate guard."

The captain cried, "It was our first day out of space. Who could have known—"

Zammo interrupted fiercely, "Wait a while, captain. I'm beginning to understand. Antyok," his voice was hard, "you engineered this."

"I?" Antyok's expression was strangely cool, almost indifferent.

"You told us this evening that a clever administrator got an A-priority project assigned to accomplish what he wished. You got such a project in order to help the non-Humans escape."

"I did? I beg your pardon, but how could that be? It was you yourself in one of your reports that brought up the problem of the failing birth rate. It was Bannerd, here, whose sensational articles frightened the Bureau into making a double A-priority project out of it. I had nothing to do with it."

"*You* suggested that I mention the birth rate," said Zammo, violently.

"Did I?" said Antyok, composedly.

"And for that matter," roared Bannerd suddenly, "you suggested that I mention the birth rate in my articles."

The three ringed him now and hemmed him in. Antyok leaned back in his chair and said easily, "I don't know what you mean by suggestions. If you are accusing me, please stick to evidence—legal evidence. The laws of the Empire go by written, filmed, or transcribed material, or by witnessed statements. All my letters as administrator are on file here, at the Bureau, and at other places. I never asked for an A-priority project. The Bureau assigned it to me, and Zammo and Bannerd are responsible for that. In print, at any rate."

Zammo's voice was an almost inarticulate growl, "You hoodwinked me into teaching the creatures how to handle a spaceship."

"It was *your* suggestion. I have your report proposing they be studied in their reaction to human tools on file. So has the Bureau. The evidence—the *legal* evidence, is plain. I had nothing to do with it."

"Nor with globes?" demanded Bannerd.

The captain howled suddenly, "You had my ships brought here purposely. Five thousand globes! You knew it would require hundreds of craft."

"I never asked for globes," said Antyok coldly. "That was the Bureau's idea, although I think Bannerd's friends of The Philosophy helped that along."

Bannerd fairly choked. He spat out, "You were asking that Cepheid leader if he could read minds. You were telling him to express interest in the globes."

"Come, now. You prepared the transcript of the conversation yourself, and that, too, is on file. You can't prove it." He stood up, "You'll have to excuse me. I must prepare a report for the Bureau."

At the door, Antyok turned, "In a way, the problem of the non-Humans is solved, even if only to their own satisfaction. They'll breed now, and have a world they've earned themselves. It's what they wanted.

"Another thing. Don't accuse me of silly things. I've been in the Service for twenty-seven years, and I assure you that my paper work is proof enough that I have been thoroughly correct in everything I have done. And captain, I'll be glad to continue our discussion of earlier this evening at your convenience and explain how a capable administrator can work through red tape and still get what he wants."

It was remarkable that such a round, smooth baby-face could wear a smile quite so sardonic.

From: BuOuProv
To: Loodun Antyok, Chief Public Administrator, A-8
Subject: Administrative Service, Standing in.
Reference:
(a) AdServ Court Decision 22874-Q, dated 1/978 G.E.

1. In view of the favorable opinion handed down in reference (a) you are hereby absolved of all responsibility for the flight of non-Humans on Cepheus 18. It is requested that you hold yourself in readiness for your next appointment.

R. Horpritt, Chief, AdServ,
15/978 G.E.

CORRESPONDENCE COURSE

by Raymond F. Jones (1915-)

ASTOUNDING SCIENCE FICTION,
April

Raymond F. Jones was an interesting and relatively neglected science fiction writer, mostly appearing in Astounding *with his "Peace Engineer" series and many others. His two best works are the novel* Renaissance *(1951, serialized in* Astounding *in 1944) and the brilliant "Noise Level" (1947), but he published some fifteen books in the field, including* This Island Earth *(1952) which was made into one of the better sf films of the 1950s. His particular strength was in the area of ideas, not in execution, but he produced considerable work of interest.*

"Correspondence Course" has strong ideas and a powerful message.

(One of the inevitable tricks tried by any writer is the double-double-cross. In other words you work toward a surprise ending which you make just apparent enough for the reader to see dimly. And as that reader congratulates himself on having outsmarted the writer, that same writer pulls a rabbit out of his hat and reveals the real surprise ending.

Usually, this is the case with events, with matters such as the identity of the villain or the motive of the hero.

It is far less common to have this surprise come in the matter of the theme of the story; or the "moral," if you prefer. Here is a story in which you may prepare to be surprised at the nature and purpose of the "correspondence course" of the title, and then find out that's not at all what Jones had most in mind. Don't worry; I'm not giving away anything, for even with this hint I doubt you'll get it. I.A.)

The old lane from the farmhouse to the letter box down by the road was the same dusty trail that he remembered from eons before. The deep summer dust stirred as his feet moved slowly and haltingly. The marks of his left foot were deep and firm as when he had last walked the lane, but where his right foot moved there was a ragged, continuous line with irregular depressions and there was the sharp imprint of a cane beside the dragging footprints.

He looked up to the sky a moment as an echelon of planes from the advanced trainer base fifty miles away wheeled overhead. A nostalgia seized him, an overwhelming longing for the men he had known—and for Ruth.

He was home; he had come back alive, but with so many gone who would never come back, what good was it?

With Ruth gone it was no good at all. For an instant his mind burned with pain and his eyes ached as if a bomb-burst had blinded him as he remembered that day in the little field hospital where he had watched her die and heard the enemy planes overhead.

Afterwards, he had gone up alone, against orders, determined to die with her, but take along as many Nazis as he could.

But he hadn't died. He had come out of it with a bullet-shattered leg and sent home to rust and die slowly over many years.

He shook his head and tried to fling the thoughts out of his mind. It was wrong. The doctors had warned him—

He resumed his slow march, half dragging the all but useless leg behind him. This was the same lane down which he had run so fast those summer days so long ago. There was a swimming hole and a fishing pond a quarter of a mile away. He tried to dim his vision with half-shut eyes and remember those pleasant days and wipe out all fear and bitterness from his mind.

It was ten o'clock in the morning and Mr. McAfee, the rural postman, was late, but Jim Ward could see his struggling, antique Ford raising a low cloud of dust a mile down the road.

Jim leaned heavily upon the stout cedar post that supported the mailbox and when Mr. McAfee rattled up he managed to wave and smile cheerily.

Mr. McAfee adjusted his spectacles on the bridge of his nose with a rapid trombone manipulation.

"Bless me, Jim, it's good to see you up and around!"

"Pretty good to be up." Jim managed to force enthusiasm into his voice. But he knew he couldn't stand talking very long to old Charles McAfee as if everything had not changed since the last time.

"Any mail for the Wards, today?"

The postman shuffled the fistful of mail. "Only one."

Jim glanced at the return address block and shrugged. "I'm on the sucker lists already. They don't lose any time when they find out there's still bones left to pick on. You keep it."

He turned painfully and faced toward the house. "I've got to be getting back. Glad to have seen you, Mr. McAfee."

"Yeah, sure, Jim. Glad to have seen you. But I . . . er . . . got to deliver the mail—" He held the letter out hopefully.

"O.K." Jim laughed sharply and grasped the circular.

He went only as far as the giant oak whose branches extended far enough to overshadow the mailbox. He sat down in the shade with his back against the great bole and tried to watch the echelon still soaring above the valley through the rifts in the leaf coverage above him. After a time he glanced down at the circular letter from which his fingers were peeling little fragments of paper. Idly, he ripped open the envelope and glanced at the contents. In cheap, garish typograph with splatterings of red and purple ink the words seemed to be trying to jump at him.

SERVICEMAN—WHAT OF THE FUTURE?

You have come back from the wars. You have found life different than you knew it before, and much that was familiar is gone. But new things have come, new things that are here to stay and are a part of the world you are going to live in.

Have you thought of the place you will occupy? Are you prepared to resume life in the ways of peace?

WE CAN HELP YOU

Have you heard of the POWER CO-ORDINATOR? No, of course you haven't because it has been a hush-hush secret source of power that has been turning the wheels of war industries for many months. But now the secret of this vast source of new power can be told, and the need for hundreds, yes, thousands of trained technicians—such as you, yourself, may become—will be tremendous in the next decade.

LET US PROVE TO YOU

Let us prove to you that we know what we are talking about. We are so certain that you, as a soldier trained in intricate operations of the machines of war, will be interested in this almost miraculous new source of power and the technique of handling it that we are willing to send you absolutely FREE the first three lessons of our twenty-five lesson course that will train you to be a POWER CO-ORDINATOR technician.

Let us prove it to you. Fill out the enclosed coupon and mail it today!

Don't just shrug and throw this circular away as just another advertisement. MAIL THE COUPON NOW!

Jim Ward smiled reminiscently at the style of the circular. It reminded him of Billy Hensley and the time when they were thirteen. They sent in all the clipped and filled-out coupons they could find in magazines. They had samples of soap and magic tricks and catalogues and even a live bird came as the result of one. They kept all the stuff in Hensley's attic until Billy's dad finally threw it all out.

Impulsively, in whimsical tribute to the gone-forever happiness of those days, Jim Ward scratched his name and address in pencil and told the power co-ordinators to send him their three free lessons.

Mr. McAfee had only another mile to go up the road before he came to the end and returned past the Ward farm to Kramer's Forks. Jim waited and hailed him.

"Want to take another letter?"

The postman halted the clattering Ford and jumped down. "What's that?"

Jim repeated his request and held up the stamped reply card. "Take this with you?"

Mr. McAfee turned it over and read every word on the back of the card. "Good thing," he grunted. "So you're going to take a correspondence course in this new power what-is-it? I think that's mighty fine, Jim. Give you new interests—sort of take your mind off things."

"Yeah, sure." Jim struggled up with the aid of his cane and the bole of the oak tree. "Better see if I can make it back to the house now."

All the whimsy and humor had suddenly gone out of the situation.

It was a fantastically short time—three days later—that Mr. McAfee stopped again at the Ward farm. He glanced at the thick envelope in his pack and the return address block it bore. He could see Jim Ward on the farmhouse porch and turned the Ford up the lane. Its rattle made Jim turn his head and open his eyes from the thoughtless blankness into which he had been trying to sink. He removed the pipe from his mouth and watched the car approach.

"Here's your course," shouted Mr. McAfee. "Here's your first lesson!"

"What lesson?"

"The correspondence course you sent for. The power what-is-it? Don't you remember?"

"No," said Jim. "I'd forgotten all about it. Take the thing away. I don't want it. It was just a silly joke."

"You hadn't ought to feel that way, Jim. After all, your leg is going to be all right. I heard the Doc say so down in the drugstore last night. And everything is going to be all right. There's no use of letting it get you down. Besides—I got to deliver the mail."

He tossed the brown envelope on the porch beside Jim. "Brought it up special because I thought you'd be in a hurry to get it."

Jim smiled in apology. "I'm sorry, Mac. Didn't mean to

take it out on you. Thanks for bringing it up. I'll study it good and hard this morning right here on the porch."

Mr. McAfee beamed and nodded and rattled away. Jim closed his eyes again, but he couldn't find the pleasing blankness he'd found before. Now the screen of his mind showed only the sky with thundering, plummeting engines—and the face of a girl lying still and white with closed eyes.

Jim opened his eyes and his hands slipped to his sides and touched the envelope. He ripped it open and scanned the pages. It was the sort of stuff he had collected as a boy, all right. He glanced at the paragraph headings and tossed the first lesson aside. A lot of obvious stuff about comparisons between steam power and waterfalls and electricity. It seemed all jumbled up like a high school student's essay on the development of power from the time of Archimedes.

The mimeographed pages were poorly done. They looked as if the stencils had been cut on a typrwriter that had been hit on the type faces with a hammer.

He tossed the second lesson aside and glanced at the top sheet of the third. His hand arrested itself midway in the act of tossing this lesson beside the other two. He caught a glimpse of the calculations on an inside page and opened up the booklet.

There was no high school stuff there. His brain struggled to remember the long unused methods of the integral calculus and the manipulation of partial differential equations.

There were pages of the stuff. It was like a sort of beacon light, dim and far off, but pointing a sure pathway to his mind and getting brighter as he progressed. One by one, he followed the intricate steps of the math and the short paragraphs of description between. When at last he reached the final page and turned the book over and scowled heavily the sun was halfway down the afternoon sky.

He looked away over the fields and pondered. This was no elementary stuff. Such math as this didn't belong in a home study correspondence course. He picked up the envelope and concentrated on the return address block.

All it said was: M. H. Quilcon Schools, Henderson, Iowa. The lessons were signed at the bottom with the mimeographed reproductions of M. H. Quilcon's ponderous signature.

Jim picked up lesson one again and began reading slowly and carefully, as if hidden between the lines he might find some mystic message.

By the end of July his leg was strong enough for him to walk without the cane. He walked slowly and with a limp and once in a while the leg gave way as if he had a trick knee. But he learned quickly to catch himself before he fell and he reveled in the thrill of walking again.

By the end of July the tenth lesson of the correspondence course had arrived and Jim knew that he had gone as far as he could alone. He was lost in amazement as he moved in the new scientific wonderland that opened up before him. He had known that great strides had been made in techniques and production, but it seemed incredible that such a basic discovery as power co-ordination had been producing war machines these many months. He wondered why the principle had not been applied more directly as a weapon itself—but he didn't understand enough about it to know whether it could or not. He didn't even understand yet from where the basic energy of the system was derived.

The tenth lesson was as poorly produced as the rest of them had been, but it was practically a book in its thickness. When he had finished it Jim knew that he had to know more of the background of the new science. He had to talk to someone who knew something about it. But he knew of no one who had ever heard of it. He had seen no advertisements of the M. H. Quilcon Schools. Only the first circular and these lessons.

As soon as he had finished the homework on lesson ten and had given it into Mr. McAfee's care, Jim Ward made up his mind to go down to Henderson, Iowa, and visit the Quilcon School.

He wished he had retained the lesson material because he could have taken it there faster than it would arrive via the local mail channels.

The streamliner barely stopped at Henderson, Iowa, long enough to allow him to disembark. Then it was gone and Jim Ward stared about him.

The sleepy looking ticket seller, dispatcher, and janitor eyed him wonderingly and spat a huge amber stream across his desk and out the window.

"Looking for somebody, mister?"

"I'm looking for Henderson, Iowa. Is this it?" Jim asked dubiously.

"You're here, mister. But don't walk too fast or you'll be

out of it. The city limits only go a block past Smith's Drugstore."

Jim noticed the sign over the door and glanced at the inscription that he had not seen before: Henderson, Iowa. Pop. 806.

"I'm looking for a Mr. M. H. Quilcon. He runs a correspondence school here somewhere. Do you know of him?"

The depot staff shifted its cud again and spat thoughtfully. "Been here twenty-nine years next October. Never heard a name like that around here, and I know 'em all."

"Are there any correspondence schools here?"

"Miss Marybell Anne Simmons gives beauty operator lessons once in a while, but that's all the school of that kind that I know of."

Disconcerted, Jim Ward murmured his thanks and moved slowly out of the station. The sight before him was dismaying. He wondered if the population hadn't declined since the estimate on the sign in the station was made.

A small mercantile store that sagged in the middle faced him from across the street. Farther along was a tiny frame building labeled Sheriff's Office. On his side Jim saw Smith's drugstore a couple of hundred feet down from the station with a riding saddle and a patented fertilizer displayed in the window. In the other direction was the combined post office, bank and what was advertised as a newspaper and printing office.

Jim strode toward this last building while curious watchers on the porch of the mercantile store stared at him trudging through the dust.

The postmistress glanced up from the armful of mail that she was sorting into boxes as Jim entered. She offered a cheery hello that seemed to tinkle from the buxom figure.

"I'm looking for a man named Quilcon. I thought you might be able to give me some information concerning him."

"*Kweelcon?*" She furrowed her brow. "There's no one here by that name. How do you spell it?"

Before he could answer, the woman dropped a handful of letters on the floor. Jim was certain that he saw the one he had mailed to the school before he left.

As the woman stooped to recover the letters a dark brown shadow streaked across the floor. Jim got the momentary impression of an enormous brown slug moving with lightning speed.

The postmistress gave a scream of anger and scuffled her feet to the door. She returned in a moment.

"Armadillo," she explained. "Darn thing's been hanging around here for months and nobody seems to be able to kill it." She resumed putting the mail in the boxes.

"I think you missed one," said Jim. She did not have the one that he recognized as the one he'd mailed.

The woman looked about her on the floor. "I got them all, thank you. Now what did you say this man's name was?"

Jim leaned over the counter and looked at the floor. He was sure—But there was obviously no other letter in sight and there was no place it could have gone.

"Quilcon," said Jim slowly. "I'm not sure of the pronunciation myself, but that's the way it seemed it should be."

"There's no one in Henderson by that name. Wait a minute now. That's a funny thing—you know it was about a month ago that I saw an envelope going out of here with a name something like that in the upper left corner. I thought at the time it was a funny name and wondered who put it in, but I never did find out and I thought I'd been dreaming. How's you know to come here looking for him?"

"I guess I must have received the mail you saw."

"Well, you might ask Mr. Herald. He's in the newspaper office next door. But I'm sure there's no one in this town by that name."

"You publish a newspaper here?"

The woman laughed. "We call it that. Mr. Herald owns the bank and a big farm and puts this out free as a hobby. It's not much, but everybody in town reads it. On Saturday he puts out a regular printed edition. This is the daily."

She held up a small mimeographed sheet that was moderately legible. Jim glanced at it and moved towards the door. "Thanks, anyway."

As he went out into the summer sun there was something gnawing at his brain, an intense you-forgot-something-in-there sort of feeling. He couldn't place it and tried to ignore it.

Then as he stepped across the threshold of the printing office he got it. That mimeographed newssheet he had seen—it bore a startling resemblance to the lessons he had received from M. H. Quilcon. The same purple ink. Slightly crooked sheets. But that was foolish to try to make a connection there. All mimeographed jobs looked about alike.

Mr. Herald was a portly little man with a fringe around his baldness. Jim repeated his inquiry.

"Quilcon?" Mr. Herald pinched his lips thoughtfully. "No, can't say as I ever heard the name. Odd name—I'm sure I'd know it if I'd ever heard it."

Jim Ward knew that further investigation here would be a waste of time. There was something wrong somewhere. The information in his correspondence course could not be coming out of this half dead little town.

He glanced at a copy of the newssheet lying on the man's littered desk beside an ancient Woodstock. "Nice little sheet you put out there," said Jim.

Mr. Herald laughed. "Well, it's not much, but I get a kick out of it, and the people enjoy reading about Mrs. Kelly's lost hogs and the Dorius kid's whooping cough. It livens things up."

"Ever do any work for anybody else—printing or mimeographing?"

"If anybody wants it, but I haven't had an outside customer in three years."

Jim glanced about searchingly. The old Woodstock seemed to be the only typewriter in the room.

"I might as well go on," he said. "But I wonder if you'd mind letting me use your typewriter to write a note and leave in the postoffice for Quilcon if he ever shows up."

"Sure, go ahead. Help yourself."

Jim sat down before the clanking machine and hammered out a brief paragraph while Mr. Herald wandered to the back of the shop. Then Jim rose and shoved the paper in his pocket. He wished he had brought a sheet from one of the lessons with him.

"Thanks," he called to Mr. Herald. He picked up a copy of the latest edition of the newspaper and shoved it in his pocket with the typed sheet.

On the trip homeward he studied the mimeographed sheet until he had memorized every line, but he withheld conclusions until he reached home.

From the station he called the farm and Hank, the hired man, came to pick him up. The ten miles out to the farm seemed like a hundred. But at last in his own room Jim spread out the two sheets of paper he'd brought with him and opened up lesson one of the correspondence course.

There was no mistake. The stencils of the course manuals had been cut on Mr. Herald's ancient machine. There was the same nick out of the side of the o, and the b was flattened on the bulge. The r was minus half its base.

Mr. Herald had prepared the course.

Mr. Herald must then be M. H. Quilcon. But why had he denied any knowledge of the name? Why had he refused to see Jim and admit his authorship of the course?

At ten o'clock that night Mr. McAfee arrived with a special delivery letter for Jim.

"I don't ordinarily deliver these way out here this time of night," he said. "But I thought you might like to have it. Might be something important. A job or something, maybe. It's from Mr. Quilcon."

"Thanks. Thanks for bringing it, Mac."

Jim hurried into his room and ripped open the letter. It read:

Dear Mr. Ward:

Your progress in understanding the principles of power co-ordination are exceptional and I am very pleased to note your progress in connection with the tenth lesson which I have just received from you.

An unusual opportunity has arisen which I am moved to offer you. There is a large installation of a power co-ordination engine in need of vital repairs some distance from here. I believe that you are fully qualified to work on this machine under supervision which will be provided and you would gain some valuable experience. The installation is located some distance from the city of Henderson. It is about two miles out on the Balmer Road. You will find there the Hortan Machine Works at which the installation is located. Repairs are urgently needed and you are the closest qualified student able to take advantage of this opportunity which might lead to a valuable permanent connection. Therefore, I request that you come at once. I will meet you there.

Sincerely,
M. H. Quilcon

For a long time Jim Ward sat on the bed with the letter and the sheets of paper spread out before him. What had begun as a simple quest for information was rapidly becoming an intricate puzzle.

Who was M. H. Quilcon?

It seemed obvious that Mr. Herald, the banker and part-time newspaper publisher, must be Quilcon. The correspondence course manuals had certainly been produced on his typewriter. The chances of any two typewriters having exactly the same four or five disfigurements in type approached the infinitesimal.

And Herald—if he were Quilcon—must have written this letter just before or shortly after Jim's visit. The letter was certainly a product of the ancient Woodstock.

There was a fascination in the puzzle and a sense of something sinister, Jim thought. Then he laughed aloud at his own melodrama and began repacking the suitcase. There was a midnight train he could get back to Henderson.

It was hot afternoon when he arrived in the town for the second time. The station staff looked up in surprise as he got off the train.

"Back again? I thought you'd given up."

"I've found out where Mr. Quilcon is. He's at the Hortan Machine Works. Can you tell me exactly where that is?"

"Never heard of it."

"It's supposed to be about two miles out of town on Balmer Road."

"That's just the main street of town going on down through the Willow Creek district. There's no machine works out there. You must be in the wrong state, mister. Or somebody's kidding you."

"Do you think Mr. Herald could tell me anything about such a machine shop. I mean, does he know anything about machinery or things related to it?"

"Man, no! Old man Herald don't care about nothing but money and that little fool paper of his. Machinery! He can't hook up anything more complicated than his suspenders."

Jim started down the main street toward the Willow Creek district. Balmer Road rapidly narrowed and turned, leaving the town out of sight behind a low rise. Willow Creek was a glistening thread in the midst of meadow land.

There was no more unlikely spot in the world for a machine works of any kind, Jim thought. Someone must be playing an utterly fantastic joke on him. But how or why they had picked on him was mystifying.

At the same time he knew within him that it was no joke. There was a deadly seriousness about it all. The principles of power co-ordination were right. He had slaved and dug through them enough to be sure of that. He felt that he could almost build a power co-ordinating engine now with the proper means—except that he didn't understand from where the power was derived!

In the timelessness of the bright air about him, with the only sound coming from the brook and the leaves on the willow trees beside it, Jim found it impossible to judge time or distance.

He paced his steps and counted until he was certain that at least two miles had been covered. He halted and looked about almost determined to go back and re-examine the way he had come.

He glanced ahead, his eyes scanning every minute detail of the meadowland. And then he saw it.

The sunlight glistened as if on a metal surface. And above the bright spot in the distance was the faintly readable legend:

HORTAN MACHINE WORKS

Thrusting aside all judgment concerning the incredibility of a machine shop in such a locale, he crossed the stream and made his way over the meadow toward the small rise.

As he approached, the machine works appeared to be merely a dome-shaped structure about thirty feet in diameter and with an open door in one side. He came up to it with a mind ready for anything. The crudely painted sign above the door looked as if it had been drawn by an inexpert barn painter in a state of intoxication.

Jim entered the dimly lit interior of the shop and set his case upon the floor beside a narrow bench that extended about the room.

Tools and instruments of unfamiliar design were upon the bench and upon the walls. But no one appeared.

Then he noticed an open door and a steep, spiral ramp that led down to a basement room. He stepped through and half slid, half walked down to the next level.

There was artificial lighting by fluorescent tubes of unusual construction, Jim noticed. But still no sign of anyone. And there was not an object in the room that appeared familiar to him. Articles that vaguely resembled furniture were against the walls.

He felt uneasy amid the strangeness of the room and he was about to go back up the steep ramp when a voice came to him.

"This is Mr. Quilcon. Is that you, Mr. Ward?"

"Yes. Where are you?"

"I am in the next room, unable to come out until I finish a bit of work I have started. Will you please go on down to the room below? You will find the damaged machinery there. Please go right to work on it. I'm sure that you have a complete understanding of what is necessary. I will join you in a moment."

Hesitantly, Jim turned to the other side of the room where he saw a second ramp leading down to a brilliantly lighted room. He glanced about once more, then moved down the ramp.

The room was high-ceilinged and somewhat larger in diameter than the others he had seen and it was almost completely occupied by the machine.

A series of close fitting towers with regular bulbous swellings on their columns formed the main structure of the engine. These were grouped in a solid circle with narrow walkways at right angles to each other passing through them.

Jim Ward stood for a long time examining their surfaces that rose twenty feet from the floor. All that he had learned from the curious correspondence course seemed to fall into place. Diagrams and drawings of such machines had seemed incomprehensible. Now he knew exactly what each part was for and how the machine operated.

He squeezed his body into the narrow walkway between the towers and wormed his way to the center of the engine. His bad leg made it difficult, but he at last came to the damaged structure.

One of the tubes had cracked open under some tremendous strain and through the slit he could see the marvelously intricate wiring with which it was filled. Wiring that was burned now and fused to a mass. It was in a control circuit that rendered the whole machine functionless, but its repair would not be difficult, Jim knew.

He went back to the periphery of the engine and found the controls of a cranelike device which he lowered and seized the cracked sleeve and drew off the damaged part.

From the drawers and bins in the walls he selected parts and tools and returned to the damaged spot.

In the cramped space he began tearing away the fused parts and wiring. He was lost and utterly unconscious of anything but the fascination of the mighty engine. Here within this room was machine capacity to power a great city.

Its basic function rested upon the principle of magnetic currents in contrast to electric currents. The discovery of magnetic currents had been announced only a few months before he came home from the war. The application of the discovery had been swift.

And he began to glimpse the fundamental source of the energy supplying the machine. It was in the great currents of gravitational and magnetic force flowing between the planets and the suns of the universe. As great as atomic energy and as boundless in its resources, this required no fantastically dangerous machinery to harness. The principle of the power co-ordinator was simple.

The pain of his cramped position forced Jim to move out to rest his leg. As he stood beside the engine he resumed his pondering on the purpose it had in this strange location. Why was it built there and what use was made of its power?

He moved about to restore the circulation in his legs and sought to trace the flow of energy through the engine, determine where and what kind of a load was placed upon it.

His search led him below into a third sub-basement of the building and there he found the thing he was searching for, the load into which the tremendous drive of the engine was coupled.

But here he was unable to comprehend fully, for the load was itself a machine of strange design, and none of its features had been covered in the correspondence course.

The machine upstairs seized upon the magnetic currents of space and selected and concentrated those flowing in a given direction.

The force of these currents was then fed into the machines in this room, but there was no point of reaction against which the energy could be applied.

Unless—

The logical, inevitable conclusion forced itself upon his mind. There was only one conceivable point of reaction.

He stood very still and a tremor went through him. He looked up at the smooth walls about him. Metal, all of them.

And this room—it was narrower than the one above—as if the entire building were tapered from the dome protruding out of the earth to the basement floor.

The only possible point of reaction was the building itself.

But it wasn't a building. It was a vessel.

Jim clawed and stumbled his way up the incline into the engine room, then beyond into the chamber above. He was halfway up the top ramp when he heard the voice again.

"Is that you, Mr. Ward? I have almost finished and will be with you in a moment. Have you completed the repairs. Was it very difficult?"

He hesitated, but didn't answer. Something about the quality of that voice gave him a chill. He hadn't noticed it before because of his curiosity and his interest in the place. Now he detected its unearthly, inhuman quality.

He detected the fact that it wasn't a voice at all, but that the words had been formed in his brain as if he himself had spoken them.

He was nearly at the top of the ramp and drew himself on hands and knees to the floor level when he saw the shadow of the closing door sweep across the room and heard the metallic clang of the door. It was sealed tight. Only the small windows—or ports—admitted light.

He rose and straightened and calmed himself with the thought that the vessel could not fly. It could not rise with the remainder of the repair task unfinished—and he was not going to finish it; that much was certain.

"Quilcon!" he called. "Show yourself! Who are you and what do you want of me?"

"I want you to finish the repair job and do it quickly," the voice replied instantly. "And quickly—it must be finished quickly."

There was a note of desperation and despair that seemed to cut into Jim. Then he caught sight of the slight motion against the wall beside him.

In a small, transparent hemisphere that was fastened to the side of the wall lay the slug that Jim had seen at the post office, the thing the woman had called an "armadillo." He had not even noticed it when he first entered the room. The thing was moving now with slow pulsations that swelled its surface and great welts like dark veins stood out upon it.

From the golden-hued hemisphere a maze of cable ran to

instruments and junction boxes around the room and a hundred tiny pseudopods grasped terminals inside the hemisphere.

It was a vessel—and this slug within the hemisphere was its alien, incredible pilot. Jim knew it with startling cold reality that came to him in waves of thought that emanated from the slug called Quilcon and broke over Jim's mind. It was a ship and a pilot from beyond Earth—from out of the reaches of space.

"What do you want of me? Who are you?" said Jim Ward.

"I am Quilcon. You are a good student. You learn well."

"What do you want?"

"I want you to repair the damaged engine."

There was something wrong with the creature. Intangibly, Jim sensed it. An aura of sickness, a desperate urgency came to his mind.

But something else was in the foreground of Jim's mind. The horror of the alien creature diminshed and Jim contemplated the miracle that had come to mankind.

"I'll bargain with you," he said quietly. "Tell me how to build a ship like this for my people and I will fix the engines for you."

"No! No—there is no time for that. I must hurry—"

"Then I shall leave without any repairs."

He moved toward the door and instantly a paralyzing wave took hold of him as if he had seized a pair of charged electrodes. It relaxed only as he stumbled back from the door.

"My power is weak," said Quilcon, "but it is strong enough for many days yet—many of your days. Too many for you to live without food and water. Repair the engine and then I shall let you go."

"Is what I ask too much to pay for my help?"

"You have had pay enough. You can teach your people to build power co-ordinator machines. Is that not enough?"

"My people want to build ships like this one and move through space."

"I cannot teach you that. I do not know. I did not build this ship."

There were surging waves of troubled thought that washed over his mind, but Jim Ward's tenseness eased. The first fear of totally alien life drifted from his mind and he felt a strange affinity for the creature. It was injured and sick, he knew, but he could not believe that it did not know how the ship was built.

"Those who built this ship come often to trade upon my world," said Quilcon. "But we have no such ships of our own. Most of us have no desire to see anything but the damp caves and sunny shores of our own world. But I longed to see the worlds from which these ships came.

"When this one landed near my cave I crept in and hid myself. The ship took off then and we traveled an endless time. Then an accident to the engine killed all three of those who manned the ship and I was left alone.

"I was injured, too, but I was not killed. Only the other of me died."

Jim did not understand the queer phrase, but he did not break into Quilcon's story.

"I was able to arrange means to control the flight of the ship, to prevent its destruction as it landed upon this planet, but I could not repair it because of the nature of my body."

Jim saw then that the creature's story must be true. It was obvious that the ship had been built to be manned by beings utterly unlike Quilcon.

"I investigated the city of yours near by and learned of your ways and customs. I needed the help of one of you to repair the ship. By force I could persuade one of you to do simple tasks, but none so complex as this requires.

"Then I discovered the peculiar customs of learning among you. I forced the man Herald to prepare the materials and send them to you. I received them before the person at the post office could see them. I got your name from the newspapers along with several others who were unsatisfactory.

"I had to teach you to understand the power co-ordinator because only by voluntary operation of your highest faculties will you be able to understand and repair the machine. I can assist but not force you to do that."

The creature began pleading again. "And now will you repair the engine quickly. I am dying—but shall live longer than you—it is a long journey to my home planet, but I must get there and I need every instant of time that is left to me."

Jim caught a glimpse of the dream vision that was the creature's home world. It was a place of securty and peace—in Quilcon's terms. But even its alienness did not block out the sense of quiet beauty that Quilcon's mind transmitted to Jim's. They were a species of high intelligence. Exceptionally developed in the laws of mathematics and theory of logic, they were handicapped in bodily development from inquiring into other fields of science whose existence was demonstrated by their logic and their mathematics. The more intellectual among them were frustrated creatures whose lives were made tolerable only by an infinite capacity for stoicism and adaptation.

But of them all, Quilcon was among the most restless and rebellious and ambitious. No one of them had ever dared such a journey as he had taken. A swelling pity and understanding came over Jim Ward.

"I'll bargain with you," he said desperately. "I'll repair the engine if you'll let me have its principles. If you don't have them, you can get them to me with little trouble. My people must have such a ship as this."

He tried to visualize what it would mean to Earth to have space flight a century or perhaps five centuries before the slow plodding of science and research might reveal it.

But the creature was silent.

"Quilcon—" Jim repeated. He hoped it hadn't died.

"I'll bargain with you," said Quilcon at last. "Let me be the other of you, and I'll give you what you want."

"The other of me? What are you talking about?"

"It is hard for you to understand. It is union—such as we make upon our world. When two or more of us want to be together we go together in the same brain, the same body. I am alone now, and it is an unendurable existence because I have known what it is to have another of me.

"Let me come into your brain, into your mind and live there with you. We will teach your people and mine. We will take this ship to all the universes of which living creatures can dream. It is either this or we both die together, for too much time has gone for me to return. This body dies."

Stunned by Quilcon's ultimatum, Jim Ward stared at the ugly slug on the wall. Its brown body was heaving with violent pulsations of pain and a sense of delirium and terror came from it to Jim.

"Hurry! Let me come!" it pleaded.

He could feel sensations as if fingers were probing his cranium looking, pleading for entrance. It turned him cold.

He looked into the years and thought of an existence with this alien mind in his. Would they battle for eventual possession of his body and he perhaps be subjected to slavery in his own living corpse?

He tried to probe Quilcon's thoughts, but he could find no sense or intent of conquest. There were almost human amenities intermingled with a world of new science and thought.

He knew Quilcon would keep his promise to give the secrets of the ship to the men of Earth. That alone would be worth the price of his sacrifice—if it should be sacrifice.

"Come!" he said quietly.

It was as if a torrent of liquid light were flowing into his brain. It was blinding and excruciating in its flaming intensity. He thought he sensed rather than saw the brown husk of Quilcon quiver in the hemisphere and shrivel like a brown nut.

But in his mind there was union and he paused and trembled with the sudden great reality of what he knew. He knew what Quilcon was and gladness flowed into him like light. A thought soared through his brain: Is sex only in the difference of bodily function and the texture of skin and the tone of voice?

He thought of another day when there was death in the sky and on the Earth below, and in a little field hospital. A figure on a white cot had murmured, "You'll be all right, Jim. I'm going on, I guess, but you'll be all right. I know it. Don't miss me too much."

He had known there would be no peace for him ever, but now there was peace and the voice of Quilcon was like that voice from long ago, for as the creature probed into his thoughts its inherent adaptability matched its feelings and thought to his and said, "Everything *is* all right, isn't it, Jim Ward?"

"Yes . . . yes it is." The intensity of his feelings almost blinded him. "And I want to call you Ruth, after another Ruth—"

"I like that name." There was shyness and appreciation in the tones, and it was not strange to Jim that he could not see the speaker, for there was a vision in his mind far lovelier than any Earthly vision could have been.

"We'll have everything," he said. "Everything that your world and mine can offer. We'll see them all."

But like the other Ruth who had been so practical, this one

was, too. "First we have to repair the engine. Shall we do it, now?"

The solitary figure of Jim Ward moved toward the ramp and disappeared into the depths of the ship.

FIRST CONTACT

by Murray Leinster (Will F. Jenkins, 1896-1975)

ASTOUNDING SCIENCE FICTION,
May

Murray Leinster was the Dean of Science Fiction Writers, a man whose career spanned almost half a century, from "The Runaway Skyscraper" in 1919 to the end of the 1960s. Very few of his mostly pedestrian novels are in print, but as a short story writer he could be very good indeed, particularly during the second half of the 40s and the 1950s. He was one of the very few Gernsback era writers who could successfully make the transition to modern sf, and he won a Hugo Award as late as 1956 (for "Exploration Team"). His finest work can be found in The Best of Murray Leinster *(1978).*

"First Contact" is a genuine classic, a story that imaginatively addressed questions that are still on the minds of sf readers and the general public—what will it be like when earthlings meet aliens? How will they know if the other can be trusted?

(Unquestionably, "First Contact" is Leinster's most famous and most referred-to story. It was so famous, in fact, that it called for a response from a Soviet science fiction writer, Ivan Yefremov. Yefremov wrote "The Heart of the Serpent," which also dealt with the first meeting in space of Earthmen and aliens but from a different viewpoint. Whereas in Leinster's story the central motif is that of fear and distrust; that in Yefremov's story is that of the

uniting bond of reason. Naturally, the Soviets made much of the fact that this showed the superior nature, both intellectually and morally, of communist philosophy versus capitalist philosophy—but even so I found myself sympathizing with Yefremov. I want *the uniting band of reason to triumph over fear and mistrust.*

The question of first-contact remains important in science fiction, by the way. Indeed, as our expertise in space flight advances and as we remain uncertain as to the possibility of life elsewhere, the question ought to grow ever more important. Carl Sagan has recently undertaken to do his first piece of fiction for an advance of two million dollars [a record for science fiction] and the subject?—First Contact. I. A.)

Tommy Dort went into the captain's room with his last pair of stereophotos and said:

"I'm through, sir. These are the last two pictures I can take."

He handed over the photographs and looked with professional interest at the visiplates, which showed all space outside the ship. Subdued, deep-red lighting indicated the controls and such instruments as the quartermaster on duty needed for navigation of the spaceship *Llanvabon*. There was a deeply cushioned control chair. There was the little gadget of oddly angled mirrors—remote descendant of the back-view mirrors of twentieth-century motorists—which allowed a view of all the visiplates without turning the head. And there were the huge plates which were so much more satisfaction for a direct view of space.

The *Llanvabon* was a long way from home. The plates, which showed every star of visual magnitude and could be stepped up to any desired magnification, portrayed stars of every imaginable degree of brilliance, in the startlingly different colors they show outside of atmosphere. But every one was unfamiliar. Only two constellations could be recognized as seen from Earth, and they were shrunken and distorted.

The Milky Way seemed vaguely out of place. But even such oddities were minor compared to a sight in the forward plates.

There was a vast, vast mistiness ahead. A luminous mist. It seemed motionless. It took a long time for any appreciable nearing to appear in the vision plates, though the spaceship's velocity indicator showed an incredible speed. The mist was the Crab Nebula, six light-years long, three and a half light-years thick, with outward-reaching members that in the telescopes of Earth gave it some resemblance to the creature for which it was named. It was a cloud of gas, infinitely tenuous, reaching half again as far as from Sol to its nearest neighbor-sun. Deep within it burned two stars; a double star; one component the familiar yellow of the sun of Earth, the other an unholy white.

Tommy Dort said meditatively:

"We're heading into a deep, sir?"

The skipper studied the last two plates of Tommy's taking, and put them aside. He went back to his uneasy contemplation of the vision plates ahead. The *Llanvabon* was decelerating at full force. She was a bare half light-year from the nebula. Tommy's work was guiding the ship's course, now, but the work was done. During all the stay of the exploring ship in the nebula, Tommy Dort would loaf. But he'd more than paid his way so far.

He had just completed a quite unique first—a complete photographic record of the movement of a nebula during a period of four thousand years, taken by one individual with the same apparatus and with control exposures to detect and record any systematic errors. It was an achivement in itself worth the journey from Earth. But in addition, he had also recorded four thousand years of the history of a double star, and four thousand years of the history of a star in the act of degenerating into a white dwarf.

It was not that Tommy Dort was four thousand years old. He was, actually, in his twenties. But the Crab Nebula is four thousand light-years from Earth, and the last two pictures had been taken by light which would not reach Earth until the sixth millennium A.D. On the way here—at speeds incredible multiples of the speed of light—Tommy Dort had recorded each aspect of the nebula by the light which had left it from forty centuries since to a bare six months ago.

The *Llanvabon* bored on through space. Slowly, slowly,

slowly, the incredible luminosity crept across the vision plates. It blotted out half the universe from view. Before was glowing mist, and behind was a star-studded emptiness. The mist shut off three-fourths of all the stars. Some few of the brightest shone dimly through it near its edge, but only a few. Then there was only an irregularly shaped patch of darkness astern, against which stars shone unwinking. The *Llanvabon* dived into the nebula, and it seemed as if it bored into a tunnel of darkness with walls of shining fog.

Which was exactly what the spaceship was doing. The most distant photographs of all had disclosed structural features in the nebula. It was not amorphous. It had form. As the *Llanvabon* drew nearer, indications of structure grew more distinct, and Tommy Dort had argued for a curved approach for photographic reasons. So the spaceship had come up to the nebula on a vast logarithmic curve, and Tommy had been able to take successive photographs from slightly different angles and get stereopairs which showed the nebula in three dimensions; which disclosed billowings and hollows and an actually complicated shape. In places, the nebula displayed convolutions like those of a human brain. It was into one of those hollows that the spaceship now plunged. They had been called "deeps" by analogy with crevasses in the ocean floor. And they promised to be useful.

The skipper relaxed. One of the skipper's functions, nowadays, is to think of things to worry about, and then to worry about them. The skipper of the *Llanvabon* was conscientious. Only after a certain instrument remained definitely nonregistering did he ease himself back in his seat.

"It was just hardly possible," he said heavily, "that those deeps might be nonluminous gas. But they're empty. So we'll be able to use overdrive as long as we're in them."

It was a light-year-and-a-half from the edge of the nebula to the neighborhood of the double star which was its heart. That was the problem. A nebula is a gas. It is so thin that a comet's tail is solid by comparison, but a ship traveling on overdrive—above the speed of light—does not want to hit even a merely hard vacuum. It needs pure emptiness, such as exists between the stars. But the *Llanvabon* could not do much in this expanse of mist if it was limited to speeds a merely hard vacuum would permit.

The luminosity seemed to close in behind the spaceship, which slowed and slowed and slowed. The overdrive went off with the sudden *pinging* sensation which goes all over a person when the overdrive field is released.

Then, almost instantly, bells burst into clanging, strident uproar all through the ship. Tommy was almost deafened by the alarm bell which rang in the captain's room before the quartermaster shut it off with a flip of his hand. But other bells could be heard ringing throughout the rest of the ship, to be cut off as automatic doors closed one by one.

Tommy Dort stared at the skipper. The skipper's hands clenched. He was up and staring over the quartermaster's shoulder. One indicator was apparently having convulsions. Others strained to record their findings. A spot on the diffusedly bright mistiness of a bow-quartering visiplate grew brighter as the automatic scanner focused on it. That was the direction of the object which had sounded collision-alarm. But the object locator itself—according to its reading, there was one solid object some eighty thousand miles away—an object of no great size. But there was another object whose distance varied from extreme range to zero, and whose size shared its impossible advance and retreat.

"Step up the scanner," snapped the skipper.

The extra-bright spot on the scanner rolled outward, obliterating the undifferentiated image behind it. Magnification increased. But nothing appeared. Absolutely nothing. Yet the radio locator insisted that something monstrous and invisible made lunatic dashes toward the *Llanvabon*, at speeds which inevitably implied collision, and then fled coyly away at the same rate.

The visiplate went up to maximum magnification. Still nothing. The skipper ground his teeth. Tommy Dort said meditatively:

"D'you know, sir, I saw something like this on a liner of the Earth-Mars run once, when we were being located by another ship. Their locator beam was the same frequency as ours, and every time it hit, it registered like something monstrous, and solid."

"That," said the skipper savagely, "is just what's happening now. There's something like a locator beam on us. We're getting that beam and our own echo besides. But the other ship's invisible! Who is out here in an invisible ship with locator devices? Not men, certainly!"

He pressed the button in his sleeve communicator and snapped:

"Action stations! Man all weapons! Condition of extreme alert in all departments immediately!"

His hands closed and unclosed. He stared again at the visiplate which showed nothing but a formless brightness.

"Not men?" Tommy Dort straightened sharply. "You mean—"

"How many solar systems in our galaxy?" demanded the skipper bitterly. "How many plants fit for life? And how many kinds of life could there be? If this ship isn't from Earth—and it isn't—it has a crew that isn't human. And things that aren't human but are up to the level of deepspace travel in their civilization could mean anything!"

The skipper's hands were actually shaking. He would not have talked so freely before a member of his own crew, but Tommy Dort was of the observation staff. And even a skipper whose duties include worrying may sometimes need desperately to unload his worries. Sometimes, too, it helps to think aloud.

"Something like this has been talked about and speculated about for years," he said softly. "Mathematically, it's been an odds-on bet that somewhere in our galaxy there'd be another race with a civilization equal to or further advanced than ours. Nobody could ever guess where or when we'd meet them. But it looks like we've done it now!"

Tommy's eyes were very bright.

"D'you suppose they'll be friendly, sir?"

The skipper glanced at the distance indicator. The phantom object still made its insane, nonexistent swoops toward and away from the *Llanvabon*. The secondary indication of an object at eighty thousand miles stirred ever so slightly.

"It's moving," he said curtly. "Heading for us. Just what we'd do if a strange spaceship appeared in our hunting grounds! Friendly? Maybe! We're going to try to contact them. We have to. But I suspect this is the end of this expedition. Thank God for the blasters!"

The blasters are those beams of ravening destruction which take care of recalcitrant meteorites in a spaceship's course when the deflectors can't handle them. They are not designed as weapons, but they can serve as pretty good ones. They can go into action at five thousand miles, and draw on the entire power output of a whole ship. With automatic aim and a traverse of five degrees, a ship like the *Llanvabon* can come very close to blasting a hole through a small-sized asteroid which gets in its way. But not on overdrive, of course.

Tommy Dort had approached the bow-quartering visiplate. Now he jerked his head around.

"Blasters, sir? What for?"

The skipper grimaced at the empty visiplate.

"Because we don't know what they're like and can't take a chance! I know!" he added bitterly. "We're going to make contacts and try to find out all we can about them—especially where they come from. I suppose we'll try to make friends—but we haven't much chance. We can't trust them a fraction of an inch. We daren't! They've locators. Maybe they've tracers better than any we have. Maybe they could trace us all the way home without our knowing it! We can't risk a nonhuman race knowing where Earth is unless we're sure of them! And how can we be sure? They could come to trade, of course—or they could swoop down on overdrive with a battle fleet that could wipe us out before we knew what happened. We wouldn't know which to expect, or when!"

Tommy's face was startled.

"It's all been thrashed out over and over, in theory," said the skipper. "Nobody's ever been able to find a sound answer, even on paper. But you know, in all their theorizing, no one considered the crazy, rank impossibility of a deep-space contact, with neither side knowing the other's home world! But we've got to find an answer in fact! What are we going to do about them? Maybe these creatures will be aesthetic marvels, nice and friendly and polite—and underneath with the sneaking brutal ferocity of a Japanese. Or maybe they'll be crude and gruff as a Swedish farmer—and just as decent underneath. Maybe they're something in between. But am I going to risk the possible future of the human race on a guess that it's safe to trust them? God knows it would be worthwhile to make friends with a new civilization! It would be bound to stimulate our own, and maybe we'd gain enormously. But I can't take chances. The one thing I won't risk is having them know how to find Earth! Either I know they can't follow me, or I don't go home! And they'll probably feel the same way!"

He pressed the sleeve-communicator button again.

"Navigation officers, attention! Every star map on this ship is to be prepared for instant destruction. This includes photographs and diagrams from which our course or starting point could be deduced. I want all astronomical data gathered and arranged to be destroyed in a split second, on order. Make it fast and report when ready!"

He released the button. He looked suddenly old. The first contact of humanity with an alien race was a situation which had been foreseen in many fashions, but never one quite so hopeless of solution as this. A solitary Earth-ship and a solitary alien, meeting in a nebula which must be remote from the home planet of each. They might wish peace, but the line of conduct which best prepared a treacherous attack was just the seeming of friendliness. Failure to be suspicious might doom the human race—and a peaceful exchange of the fruits of civilization would be the greatest benefit imaginable. Any mistake would be irreparable, but a failure to be on guard would be fatal.

The captain's room was very, very quiet. The bow-quartering visiplate was filled with the image of a very small section of the nebula. A very small second indeed. It was all diffused, featureless, luminous mist. But suddenly Tommy Dort pointed.

"There, sir!"

There was a small shape in the mist. It was far away. It was a black shape, not polished to mirror-reflection like the hull of the *Llanvabon*. It was bulbous—roughly pear-shaped. There was much thin luminosity between, and no details could be observed, but it was surely no natural object. Then Tommy looked at the distance indicator and said quietly: "It's headed for us at very high acceleration, sir. The odds are that they're thinking the same thing, sir, that neither of us will dare let the other go home. Do you think they'll try a contact with us, or let loose with their weapons as soon as they're in range?"

The *Llanvabon* was no longer in a crevasse of emptiness in the nebula's thin substance. She swam in luminescence. There were no stars save the two fierce glows in the nebula's heart. There was nothing but an all-enveloping light, curiously like one's imagining of underwater in the tropics of Earth.

The alien ship had made one sign of less than lethal intention. As it drew near the *Llanvabon*, it decelerated. The *Llanvabon* itself had advanced for a meeting and then come to a dead stop. Its movement had been a recognition of the nearness of the other ship. Its pausing was both a friendly sign and a precaution against attack. Relatively still, it could swivel on its own axis to present the least target to a slashing assault, and it would have a longer firing-time than if the two ships flashed past each other at their combined speeds.

The moment of actual approach, however, was tenseness itself. The *Llanvabon*'s needle-pointed bow aimed unwaveringly at the alien bulk. A relay to the captain's room put a key under his hand which would fire the blasters with maximum power. Tommy Dort watched, his brow wrinkled. The aliens must be of a high degree of civilization if they had spaceships, and civilization does not develop without the development of foresight. These aliens must recognize all the implications of this first contact of two civilized races as fully as did the humans on the *Llanvabon.*

The possibility of an enormous spurt in the development of both, by peaceful contact and exchange of their separate technologies, would probably appeal to them as to man. But when dissimilar human cultures are in contact, one must usually be subordinate or there is war. But subordination between races arising on separate planets could not be peacefully arranged. Men, at least, would never consent to subordination, nor was it likely that any highly developed race would agree. The benefits to be derived from commerce could never make up for a condition of inferiority. Some races—men, perhaps—would prefer commerce to conquest. Perhaps—perhaps!—these aliens would also. But some types even of human beings would have craved red war. If the alien ship now approaching the *Llanvabon* returned to its home base with news of humanity's existence and of ships like the *Llanvabon*, it would give its race the choice of trade or battle. They might want trade, or they might want war. But it takes two to make trade, and only one to make war. They could not be sure of men's peacefulness, or could men be sure of theirs. The only safety for either civilization would lie in the destruction of one or both of the two ships here and now.

But even victory would not be really enough. Men would need to know where this alien race was to be found, for avoidance if not for battle. They would need to know its weapons, and its resources, and if it could be a menace and how it could be eliminated in case of need. The aliens would feel the same necessities concerning humanity.

So the skipper of the *Llanvabon* did not press the key which might possibly have blasted the other ship to nothingness. He dared not. But he dared not not fire either. Sweat came out on his face.

A speaker muttered. Someone from the range room.

"The other ship's stopped, sir. Quite stationary. Blasters are centered on it, sir."

It was an urging to fire. But the skipper shook his head, to himself. The alien ship was no more than twenty miles away. It was dead-black. Every bit of its exterior was an abysmal, nonreflecting sable. No details could be seen except by minor variations in its outline against the misty nebula.

"It's stopped dead, sir," said another voice. "They've sent a modulated short wave at us, sir. Frequency modulated. Apparently a signal. Not enough power to do any harm."

The skipper said through tight-locked teeth:

"They're doing something now. There's movement on the outside of their hull. Watch what comes out. Put the auxiliary blasters on it."

Something small and round came smoothly out of the oval outline of the black ship. The bulbous hulk moved.

"Moving away, sir," said the speaker. "The object they let out is stationary in the place they've left."

Another voice cut in:

"More frequency modulated stuff, sir. Unintelligible."

Tommy Dort's eyes brightened. The skipper watched the visiplate, with sweat-droplets on his forehead.

"Rather pretty, sir," said Tommy, meditatively. "If they sent anything toward us, it might seem a projectile or a bomb. So they came close, let out a lifeboat, and went away again. They figure we can send a boat or a man to make contact without risking our ship. They must think pretty much as we do."

The skipper said, without moving his eyes from the plate:

"Mr. Dort would you care to go out and look the thing over? I can't order you, but I need all my operating crew for emergencies. The observation staff—"

"Is expendable. Very well, sir," said Tommy briskly. "I won't take a lifeboat, sir. Just a suit with a drive in it. It's smaller and the arms and legs will look unsuitable for a bomb. I think I should carry a scanner, sir."

The alien ship continued to retreat. Forty, eighty, four hundred miles. It came to a stop and hung there, waiting. Climbing into his atomic-driven spacesuit just within the

Llanvabon's air lock, Tommy heard the reports as they went over the speakers throughout the ship. That the other ship had stopped its retreat at four hundred miles was encouraging. It might not have weapons effective at a greater distance than that, and so felt safe. But just as the thought formed itself in his mind, the alien retreated precipitately still farther. Which, as Tommy reflected as he emerged from the lock, might be because the aliens had realized they were giving themselves away, or might be because they wanted to give the impression that they had done so.

He swooped away from the silvery-mirror *Llanvabon*, through a brightly glowing emptiness which was past any previous experience of the human race. Behind him, the *Llanvabon* swung about and darted away. The skipper's voice came in Tommy's helmet phones.

"We're pulling back, too, Mr. Dort. There is a bare possibility that they've some explosive atomic reaction they can't use from their own ship, but which might be destructive even as far as this. We'll draw back. Keep your scanner on the object."

The reasoning was sound, if not very comforting. An explosive which would destroy anything within twenty miles was theoretically possible, but humans didn't have it yet. It was decidedly safest for the *Llanvabon* to draw back.

But Tommy Dort felt very lonely. He sped through emptiness toward the tiny black speck which hung in incredible brightness. The *Llanvabon* vanished. Its polished hull would merge with the glowing mist at a relatively short distance, anyhow. The alien ship was not visible to the naked eye, either. Tommy swam in nothingness, four thousand light-years from home, toward a tiny black spot which was the only solid object to be seen in all of space.

It was a slightly distorted sphere, not much over six feet in diameter. It bounced away when Tommy landed on it, feet-first. There were small tentacles, or horns, which projected in every direction. They looked rather like the detonating horns of a submarine mine, but there was a glint of crystal at the tip-end of each.

"I'm here," said Tommy into his helmet phone.

He caught hold of a horn and drew himself to the object. It was all metal, dead-black. He could feel no texture through his space gloves, of course, but he went over and over it, trying to discover its purpose.

"Deadlock, sir," he said presently. "Nothing to report that the scanner hasn't shown you."

Then, through his suit, he felt vibrations. They translated themselves as clankings. A section of the rounded hull of the object opened out. Two sections. He worked his way around to look in and see the first nonhuman civilized beings that any man had ever looked upon.

But what he saw was simply a flat plate on which dim red glows crawled here and there in seeming aimlessness. His helmet phones emitted a startled exclamation. The skipper's voice:

"Very good, Mr. Dort. Fix your scanner to look into that plate. They dumped out a robot with an infrared visiplate for communication. Not risking any personnel. Whatever we might do would damage only machinery. Maybe they expect us to bring it on board—and it may have a bomb charge that can be detonated when they're ready to start for home. I'll send a plate to face one of its scanners. You return to the ship."

"Yes, sir," said Tommy. "But which way is the ship, sir?"

There were no stars. The nebula obscured them with its light. The only thing visible from the robot was the double star at the nebula's center. Tommy was no longer oriented. He had but one reference point.

"Head straight away from the double star," came the order in his helmet phone. "We'll pick you up."

He passed another lonely figure, a little later, headed for the alien sphere with a vision plate to set up. The two spaceships, each knowing that it dared not risk its own race by the slightest lack of caution, would communicate with each other through this small round robot. Their separate vision systems would enable them to exchange all the information they dared give, while they debated the most practical way of making sure that their own civilization would not be endangered by this first contact with another. The truly most practical method would be the destruction of the other ship in a swift and deadly attack—in self-defense.

The *Llanvabon*, thereafter, was a ship in which there were two separate enterprises on hand at the same time. She had come out from Earth to make close-range observations on the smaller component of the double star at the nebula's center. The nebula itself was the result of the most titanic explosion of which men have any knowledge. The explosion took place some time in the year 2946 B.C., before the first of the seven cities of long-dead Ilium was even thought of. The light of that explosion reached Earth in the year 1054 A.D., and was duly recorded in ecclesiastical annals and somewhat more reliably by Chinese court astronomers. It was bright enough to be seen in daylight for twenty-three successive days. Its light—and it was four thousand light-years away—was brighter than that of Venus.

From these facts, astronomers could calculate nine hundred years later the violence of the detonation. Matter blown away from the center of the explosion would have traveled outward at the rate of two million three hundred thousand miles an hour; more than thirty-eight thousand miles a minute; something over six hundred thirty-eight miles per second. When twentieth-century telescopes were turned upon the scene of this vast explosion, only a double star remained—and the nebula. The brighter star of the doublet was almost unique in having so high a surface temperature that it showed no spectrum lines at all. It had a continuous spectrum. Sol's surface temperature is about 7,000° Absolute. That of the hot white star is 500,000 degrees. It has nearly the mass of the sun, but only one fifth its diameter, so that its density is one hundred seventy-three times that of water, sixteen times that of lead, and eight times that of iridium—the heaviest substance known on Earth. But even this density is not that of a dwarf white star like the companion of Sirius. The white star in the Crab Nebula is an incomplete dwarf; it is a star still in the act of collapsing. Examination—including the survey of a four-thousand-year column of its light—was worthwhile. The *Llanvabon* had come to make that examination. But the finding of an alien spaceship upon a similar errand had implications which overshadowed the original purpose of the expedition.

A tiny bulbous robot floated in the tenuous nebular gas. The normal operating crew of the *Llanvabon* stood at their posts with a sharp alertness which was productive of tense nerves. The observation staff divided itself, and a part went half-heartedly about the making of the observations for which the *Llanvabon* had come. The other half applied itself to the problem the spaceship offered.

It represented a culture which was up to space travel on an interstellar scale. The explosion of a mere five thousand years since must have blasted every trace of life out of existence in the area now filled by the nebula. So the aliens of the black spaceship came from another solar system. Their trip must have been, like that of the Earth ship, for purely scientific purposes. There was nothing to be extracted from the nebula.

They were, then, at least near the level of human civilization, which meant that they had or could develop arts and articles of commerce which men would want to trade for, in friendship. But they would necessarily realize that the existence and civilization of humanity was a potential menace to their own race. The two races could be friends, but also they could be deadly enemies. Each, even if unwillingly, was a monstrous menace to the other. And the only safe thing to do with a menace is to destroy it.

In the Crab Nebula the problem was acute and immediate. The future relationship of the two races would be settled here and now. If a process for friendship could be established, one race, otherwise doomed, would survive and both would benefit immensely. But that process had to be established, and confidence built up, without the most minute risk of danger from treachery. Confidence would need to be established upon a foundation of necessarily complete distrust. Neither dared return to its own base if the other could do harm to its race. Neither dared risk any of the necessities to trust. The only safe thing for either to do was destroy the other or be destroyed.

But even for war, more was needed than mere destruction of the other. With interstellar traffic, the aliens must have atomic power and some form of overdrive for travel above the speed of light. With radio location and visiplates and short-wave communication they had, of course, many other devices. What weapons did they have? How widely extended was their culture? What were their resources? Could there be a development of trade and friendship, or were the two races so unlike that only war could exist between them? If peace was possible, how could it be begun?

The men on the *Llanvabon* needed facts—and so did the crew of the other ship. They must take back every morsel of information they could. The most important information of all would be of the location of the other civilization, just in case of war. That one bit of information might be the decisive factor in an interstellar war. But other facts would be enormously valuable.

The tragic thing was that there could be no possible information which could lead to peace. Neither ship could stake its own race's existence upon any conviction of the good will or the honor of the other.

So there was a strange truce between the two ships. The alien went about its work of making observations, as did the *Llanvabon.* The tiny robot floated in bright emptiness. A scanner from the *Llanvabon* was focused upon a vision plate from the alien. A scanner from the alien regarded a vision plate from the *Llanvabon.* Communication began.

It progressed rapidly. Tommy Dort was one of those who made the first progress report. His special task on the expedition was over. He had now been assigned to work on the problem of communication with the alien entities. He went with the ship's solitary psychologist to the captain's room to convey the news of success. The captain's room, as usual, was a place of silence and dull-red indicator lights and the great bright visiplates on every wall and on the ceiling.

"We've established fairly satisfactory communication, sir," said the psychologist. He looked tired. His work on the trip was supposed to be that of measuring personal factors of error in the observation staff, for the reduction of all observations to the nearest possible decimal to the absolute. He had been pressed into service for which he was not especially fitted, and it told upon him. "That is, we can say almost anything we wish to them, and can understand what they say in return. But of course we don't know how much of what they say is the truth."

The skipper's eyes turned to Tommy Dort.

"We've hooked up some machinery," said Tommy, "that amounts to a mechanical translator. We have vision plates, of course, and then shortwave beams direct. They use frequency-modulation plus what is probably variation in wave forms—like our vowel and consonant sounds in speech. We've never had any use for anything like that before, so our coils won't handle it, but we've developed a sort of code which isn't the language of either set of us. They shoot over short-wave stuff with frequency-modulation, and we record it as sound. When we shoot it back, it's reconverted into frequency-modulation."

The skipper said, frowning:

"Why wave-form changes in short waves? How do you know?"

"We showed them our recorder in the vision plates, and they showed us theirs. They record the frequency-modulation direct. I think," said Tommy carefully, "they don't use sound at all, even in speech. They've set up a communication room, and we've watched them in the act of communicating with us. They made no perceptible movement of anything that corresponds to a speech organ. Instead of a microphone, they simply stand near something that would work as a pick-up antenna. My guess, sir, is that they use microwaves for what you might call person-to-person conversation. I think they make short-wave trains as we make sounds."

The skipper stared at him:

"That means they have telepathy?"

"M-m-m. Yes, sir," said Tommy. "Also it means that we have telepathy too, as far as they are concerned. They're probably deaf. They've certainly no idea of using sound waves in air for communication. They simply don't use noises for any purpose."

The skipper stored the information away.

"What else?"

"Well, sir," said Tommy doubtfully, "I think we're all set. We agreed on arbitrary symbols for objects, sir, by the way of the visiplates, and worked out relationships and verbs and so on with diagrams and pictures. We've a couple of thousand words that have mutual meanings. We set up an analyzer to sort out their short-wave groups, which we feed into a decoding machine. And then the coding end of the machine picks out recordings to make the wave groups we want to send back. When you're ready to talk to the skipper of the other ship, sir, I think we're ready."

"H-m-m. What's your impression of their psychology?" The skipper asked the question of the psychologist.

"I don't know, sir," said the psychologist, harassed. "They seem to be completely direct. But they haven't let slip even a hint of the tenseness we know exists. They act as if they were simply setting up a means of communication for friendly conversation. But there is . . . well . . . an overtone—"

The psychologist was a good man at psychological mensuration, which is a good and useful field. But he was not equipped to analyze a completely alien thought-pattern.

"If I may say so, sir—" said Tommy uncomfortably.

"What?"

"They're oxygen brothers," said Tommy, "and they're not

too dissimilar to us in other ways. It seems to me, sir, that parallel evolution has been at work. Perhaps intelligence evolves in parallel lines, just as . . . well . . . basic bodily functions. I mean," he added conscientiously, "any living being of any sort must ingest, metabolize, and excrete. Perhaps any intelligent brain must perceive, apperceive, and find a personal reaction. I'm sure I've detected irony. That implies humor, too. In short, sir, I think they could be likable."

The skipper heaved himself to his feet.

"H-m-m," he said profoundly, "we'll see what they have to say."

He walked to the communications room. The scanner for the vision plate in the robot was in readiness. The skipper walked in front of it. Tommy Dort sat down at the coding machine and tapped at the keys. Highly improbable noises came from it, went into a microphone, and governed the frequency-modulation of a signal sent through space to the other spaceship. Almost instantly the vision screen which with one relay—in the robot—showed the interior of the other ship lighted up. An alien came before the scanner and seemed to look inquisitively out of the plate. He was extraordinarily manlike, but he was not human. The impression he gave was of extreme baldness and a somehow humorous frankness.

"I'd like to say," said the skipper heavily, "the appropriate things about this first contact of two dissimilar civilized races, and of my hopes that a friendly intercourse between the two people will result."

Tommy Dort hesitated. Then he shrugged and tapped expertly upon the coder. More improbable noises.

The alien skipper seemed to receive the message. He made a gesture which was wryly assenting. The decoder on the *Llanvabon* hummed to itself and word-cards dropped into the message frame. Tommy said dispassionately:

"He says, sir, 'That is all very well, but is there any way for us to let each other go home alive? I would be happy to hear of such a way if you can contrive it. At the moment it seems to me that one of us must be killed.' "

The atmosphere was of confusion. There were too many questions to be answered all at once. Nobody could answer any of them. And all of them had to be answered.

The *Llanvabon* could start for home. The alien ship might or might not be able to multiply the speed of light by one more unit than the Earth vessel. If it could, the *Llanvabon* would get close enough to Earth to reveal its destination—and then have to fight. It might or might not win. Even if it did win, the aliens might have a communication system by which the *Llanvabon*'s destination might have been reported to the aliens' home planet before battle was joined. But the *Llanvabon* might lose in such a fight. If she were to be destroyed, it would be better to be destroyed here, without giving any clue to where human beings might be found by a forewarned, forearmed alien battle fleet.

The black ship was in exactly the same predicament. It too, could start for home. But the *Llanvabon* might be faster, and an overdrive field can be trailed, if you set to work on it soon enough. The aliens, also, would not know whether the *Llanvabon* could report to its home base without returning. If the alien were to be destroyed, it also would prefer to fight it out here, so that it could not lead a probable enemy to its own civilization.

Neither ship, then, could think of flight. The course of the *Llanvabon* into the nebula might be known to the black ship, but it had been the end of a logarithmic curve, and the aliens could not know its properties. They could not tell from that from what direction the Earth ship had started. As of the moment, then, the two ships were even. But the question was and remained, "What now?"

There was no specific answer. The aliens traded information for information—and did not always realize what information they gave. The humans traded information for information—and Tommy Dort sweated blood in his anxiety not to give any clue to the whereabouts of Earth.

The aliens saw by infrared light, and the vision plates and scanners in the robot communication-exchange had to adapt their respective images up and down an optical octave each, for them to have any meaning at all. It did not occur to the aliens that their eyesight told that their sun was a red dwarf, yielding light of greatest energy just below the part of the spectrum visible to human eyes. But after that fact was realized on the *Llanvabon*, it was realized that the aliens, also, should be able to deduce the Sun's spectral type by the light to which men's eyes were best adapted.

There was a gadget for the recording of short-wave trains which was as casually in use among the aliens as a sound-recorder is among men. The humans wanted that badly. And the aliens were fascinated by the mystery of sound. They were able to perceive noise, of course, just as a man's palm will perceive infrared light by the sensation of heat it produces, but they could no more differentiate pitch or tone-quality than a man is able to distinguish between two frequencies of heat-radiation even half an octave apart. To them, the human science of sound was a remarkable discovery. They would find uses for noises which humans had never imagined—if they lived.

But that was another question. Neither ship could leave without first destroying the other. But while the flood of information was in passage, neither ship could afford to destroy the other. There was the matter of the outer coloring of the two ships. The *Llanvabon* was mirror-bright exteriorly. The alien ship was dead-black by visible light. It absorbed heat to perfection, and should radiate it away again as readily. But it did not. The black coating was not a "black body" color or lack of color. It was a perfect reflector of certain infrared wave lengths while simultaneously it fluoresced in just those wave bands. In practice, it absorbed the higher frequencies of heat, converted them to lower frequencies it did not radiate—and stayed at the desired temperature even in empty space.

Tommy Dort labored over his task of communications. He found the alien thought-processes not so alien that he could not follow them. The discussion of technics reached the matter of interstellar navigation. A star map was needed to illustrate the process. It would not have been logical to use a star map from the chart room—but from a star map one could guess the point from which the map was projected. Tommy had a map made specially, with imaginary but convincing star images upon it. He translated directions for its use by the coder and decoder. In return, the aliens presented a star map of their own before the visiplate. Copied instantly by photograph, the Nav officers labored over it, trying to figure out from what spot in the galaxy the stars and Milky Way would show at such an angle. It baffled them.

It was Tommy who realized finally that the aliens had made a special star map for their demonstration too, and that it was a mirror-image of the faked map Tommy had shown them previously.

Tommy could grin, at that. He began to like these aliens.

They were not humans, but they had a very human sense of the ridiculous. In course of time Tommy essayed a mild joke. It had to be translated into code numerals, these into quite cryptic groups of short-wave, frequency-modulated impulses, and these went to the other ship and into heaven knew what to become intelligible. A joke which went through such formalities would not seem likely to be funny. But the alien did see the point.

There was one of the aliens to whom communication became as normal a function as Tommy's own code-handlings. The two of them developed a quite insane friendship, conversing by coder, decoder, and short-wave trains. When technicalities in the official messages grew too involved, that alien sometimes threw in strictly nontechnical interpolations akin to slang. Often, they cleared up the confusion. Tommy, for no reason whatever, had filed a code-name of "Buck" which the decoder picked out regularly when this particular one signed his own symbol to a message.

In the third week of communication, the decoder suddenly presented Tommy with a message in the message frame:

You are a good guy. It is too bad we have to kill each other.—BUCK.

Tommy had been thinking much the same thing. He tapped off the rueful reply:

We can't see any way out of it. Can you?

There was a pause, and the message frame filled up again:

If we could believe each other, yes. Our skipper would like it. But we can't believe you, and you can't believe us. We'd trail you home if we got a chance, and you'd trail us. But we feel sorry about it.—BUCK.

Tommy Dort took the messages to the skipper.

"Look here, sir!" he said urgently. "These people are almost human, and they're likable cusses."

The skipper was busy about his important task of thinking things to worry about, and worrying about them. He said tiredly:

"They're oxygen breathers. Their air is twenty-eight percent oxygen instead of twenty, but they could do very well on Earth. It would be a highly desirable conquest for them. And we still don't know what weapons they've got or what they can develop. Would you tell them how to find Earth?"

"N-no," said Tommy, unhappily.

"They probably feel the same way," said the skipper dryly. "And if we did manage to make a friendly contact, how long would it stay friendly? If their weapons were inferior to ours, they'd feel that for their own safety they had to improve them. And we, knowing they were planning to revolt, would crush them while we could—for our own safety! If it happened to be the other way about, they'd have to smash us before we could catch up to them."

Tommy was silent, but he moved restlessly.

"If we smash this black ship and get home," said the skipper, "Earth Government will be annoyed if we don't tell them where it came from. But what can we do? We'll be lucky enough to get back alive with our warning. It isn't possible to get out of those creatures any more information than we give them, and we surely won't give them our address! We've run into them by accident. Maybe—if we smash this ship—there won't be another contact for thousands of years. And it's a pity, because trade could mean so much! But it takes two to make a peace, and we can't risk trusting them. The only answer is to kill them if we can, and if we can't, to make sure that when they kill us they'll find out nothing that will lead them to Earth. I don't like it," added the skipper tiredly, "but there simply isn't anything else to do!"

On the *Llanvabon*, the technicians worked frantically in two divisions. One prepared for victory, and the other for defeat. The ones working for victory could do little. The main blasters were the only weapons with any promise. Their mountings were cautiously altered so that they were no longer fixed nearly dead ahead, with only a 5° traverse. Electronic controls which followed a radiolocator master-finder would keep them trained with absolute precision upon a given target regardless of its maneuverings. More, a hitherto unsung genius in the engine room devised a capacity-storage system by which the normal full-output of the ship's engines could be momentarily accumulated and released in surges of stored power far above normal. In theory, the range of the blasters should be multiplied and their destructive power considerably stepped up. But there was not much more that could be done.

The defeat crew had more leeway. Star charts, navigational instruments carrying telltale notations, the photographic record Tommy Dort had made on the six-months' journey from Earth, and every other memorandum offering clues to Earth's position, were prepared for destruction. They were put in sealed files, and if any one of them was opened by one who did not know the exact, complicated process, the contents of all the files would flash into ashes and the ash be churned past any hope of restoration. Of course, if the *Llanvabon* should be victorious, a carefully not-indicated method of reopening them in safety would remain.

There were atomic bombs placed all over the hull of the ship. If its human crew should be killed without complete destruction of the ship, the atomic-power bombs should detonate if the *Llanvabon* was brought alongside the alien vessel. There were no ready-made atomic bombs on board, but there were small spare atomic-power units on board. It was not hard to trick them so that when they were turned on, instead of yielding a smooth flow of power they would explode. And four men of the earth ship's crew remained always in spacesuits with closed helmets, to fight the ship should it be punctured in many compartments by an unwarned attack.

Such an attack, however, would not be treacherous. The alien skipper had spoken frankly. His manner was that of one who wryly admits the uselessness of lies. The skipper and the *Llanvabon,* in turn, heavily admitted the virtue of frankness. Each insisted—perhaps truthfully—that he wished for friendship between the two races. But neither could trust the other not to make every conceivable effort to find out the one thing he needed most desperately to conceal—the location of his home planet. And neither dared believe that the other was unable to trail him and find out. Because each felt it his own duty to accomplish that unbearable—to the other—act, neither could risk the possible existence of his race by trusting the other. They must fight because they could not do anything else.

They could raise the stakes of the battle by an exchange of information beforehand. But there was a limit to the stake either would put up. No information on weapons, population, or resources would be given by either. Not even the distance of their home bases from the Crab Nebula would be told. They exchanged information, to be sure, but they knew a battle to the death must follow, and each strove to represent his own civilization as powerful enough to give pause to the other's ideas of possible conquest—and thereby increased its appearance of menace to the other, and made battle more unavoidable.

It was curious how completely such alien brains could mesh, however. Tommy Dort, sweating over the coding and decoding machines, found a personal equation emerging from the at first stilted arrays of word-cards which arranged themselves. He had seen the aliens only in the vision screen, and then only in light at least one octave removed from the light they saw by. They, in turn, saw him very strangely, by transposed illumination from what to them would be the far ultra-violet. But their brains worked alike. Amazingly alike. Tommy Dort felt an actual sympathy and even something close to friendship for the gill-breathing, bald, and dryly ironic creatures of the black space vessel.

Because of that mental kinship he set up—though hopelessly—a sort of table of the aspects of the problem before them. He did not believe that the ailens had any instinctive desire to destroy man. In fact, the study of communications from the aliens had produced on the *Llanvabon* a feeling of tolerance not unlike that between enemy soldiers during a truce on Earth. The men felt no enmity, and probably neither did the aliens. But they had to kill or be killed for strictly logical reasons.

Tommy's table was specific. He made a list of objectives the men must try to achieve, in the order of their importance. The first was the carrying back of news of the existence of the alien culture. The second was the location of that alien culture in the galaxy. The third was the carrying back of as much information as possible about that culture. The third was being worked on, but the second was probably impossible. The first—and all—would depend on the result of the fight which must take place.

The aliens' objectives would be exactly similar, so that the men must prevent, first, news of the existence of Earth's culture from being taken back by the aliens, second, alien discovery of the location of Earth, and third, the acquiring by the aliens of information which would help them or encourage them to attack humanity. And again the third was in train, and the second was probably taken care of, and the first must await the battle.

There was no possible way to avoid the grim necessity of the destruction of the black ship. The aliens would see no solution to their problems but the destruction of the *Llanvabon.* But Tommy Dort, regarding his tabulation ruefully, realized that even complete victory would not be a perfect solution. The ideal would be for the *Llanvabon* to take back the alien ship for study. Nothing less would be a complete attainment of the third objective. But Tommy realized that he hated the idea of so complete a victory, even if it could be accomplished. He would hate the idea of killing even nonhuman creatures who understood a human fitting out a fleet of fighting ships to destroy an alien culture because its existence was dangerous. The pure accident of this encounter, between peoples who could like each other, had created a situation which could only result in wholesale destruction.

Tommy Dort soured on his own brain which could find no answer which would work. But there had to be an answer! The gamble was too big! It was too absurd that two spaceships should fight—neither one primarily designed for fighting—so that the survivor could carry back news which would set one race to frenzied preparation for war against the unwarned other.

If both races could be warned, though, and each knew that the other did not want to fight, and if they could communicate with each other but not locate each other until some grounds for mutual trust could be reached—

It was impossible. It was chimerical. It was a daydream. It was nonsense. But it was such luring nonsense that Tommy Dort ruefully put it into the coder to his gill-breathing friend Buck, then some hundred thousand miles off in the misty brightness of the nebula.

"Sure," said Buck, in the decoder's word-card's flicking into place in the message frame. "That is a good dream. But I like you and still won't believe you. If I said that first, you would like me but not believe me, either. I tell you the truth more than you believe, and maybe you tell me the truth more than I believe. But there is no way to know. I am sorry."

Tommy Dort stared gloomily at the message. He felt a very horrible sense of responsibility. Everyone did, on the *Llanvabon.* If they failed in this encounter, the human race would run a very good chance of being exterminated in time to come. If they succeeded, the race of the aliens would be the one to face destruction, most likely. Millions or billions of lives hung upon the actions of a few men.

Then Tommy Dort saw the answer.

It would be amazingly simple, if it worked. At worst it might give a partial victory to humanity and the *Llanvabon.* He sat quite still, not daring to move lest he break the chain of thought that followed the first tenuous idea. He went over and over it, excitedly finding objections here and meeting them, and overcoming impossibilities there. It was the answer! He felt sure of it.

He felt almost dizzy with relief when he found his way to the captain's room and asked leave to speak.

It is the function of a skipper, among others, to find things to worry about. But the *Llanvabon*'s skipper did not have to look. In the three weeks and four days since the first contact with the alien black ship, the skipper's face had grown lined and old. He had not only the *Llanvabon* to worry about. He had all of humanity.

"Sir," said Tommy Dort, his mouth rather dry because of his enormous earnestness, "may I offer a method of attack on the black ship? I'll undertake it myself, sir, and if it doesn't work our ship won't be weakened."

The skipper looked at him unseeingly.

"The tactics are all worked out, Mr. Dort," he said heavily. "They're being cut on tape now, for the ship's handling. It's a terrible gamble, but it has to be done."

"I think," said Tommy carefully, "I've worked out a way to take the gamble out. Suppose, sir, we send a message to the other ship, offering—"

His voice went on in the utterly quiet captain's room, with the visiplates showing only a vast mistiness outside and the two fiercely burning stars in the nebula's heart.

The skipper himself went through the air lock with Tommy. For one reason, the action Tommy had suggested would need his authority behind it. For another, the skipper had worried more intensely than anybody else on the *Llanvabon*, and he was tired of it. If he went with Tommy, he would do the thing himself, and if he failed he would be the first one killed—and the tape for the Earth ship's maneuvering was already fed into the control board and correlated with the master-timer. If Tommy and the skipper were killed, a single control pushed home would throw the *Llanvabon* into the most furious possible all-out attack, which would end in the complete destruction of one ship or the other—or both. So the skipper was not deserting his post.

The outer air lock door swung wide. It opened upon that shining emptiness which was the nebula. Twenty miles away, the little round robot hung in space, drifting in an incredible orbit about the twin central suns, and floating ever nearer and nearer. It would never reach either of them, of course. The white star alone was so much hotter than Earth's sun that its heat-effect would produce Earth's temperature on an object five times as far from it as Neptune is from Sol. Even removed to the distance of Pluto, the little robot would be raised to cherry-red heat by the blazing white dwarf. And it could not possibly approach to the ninety-odd million miles which is the Earth's distance from the sun. So near, its metal would melt and boil away as vapor. But, half a light-year out, the bulbous object bobbed in emptiness.

The two spacesuited figures soared away from the *Llanvabon*. The small atomic drives which made them minute spaceships on their own had been subtly altered, but the change did not interfere with their functioning. They headed for the communication robot. The skipper, out in space, said gruffly:

"Mr. Dort, all my life I have longed for adventure. This is the first time I could ever justify it to myself."

His voice came through Tommy's space-phone receivers. Tommy wet his lips and said:

"It doesn't seem like adventure to me, sir. I want terribly for the plan to go through. I thought adventure was when you didn't care."

"Oh, no," said the skipper. "Adventure is when you toss your life on the scales of chance and wait for the pointer to stop."

They reached the round object. They clung to its short, scanner-tipped horns.

"Intelligent, those creatures," said the skipper heavily. "They must want desperately to see more of our ship than the communication room, to agree to this exchange of visits before the fight."

"Yes, sir," said Tommy. But privately, he suspected that Buck—his gill-breathing friend—would like to see him in the flesh before one or both of them died. And it seemed to him that between the two ships had grown up an odd tradition of courtesy, like that between two ancient knights before a tourney, when they admired each other wholeheartedly before hacking at each other with all the contents of their respective armories.

They waited.

Then, out of the mist, came two other figures. The alien spacesuits were also power-driven. The aliens themselves were shorter than men, and their helmet openings were coated with a filtering material to cut off visible and ultraviolet rays which to them would be lethal. It was not possible to see more than the outline of the heads within.

Tommy's helmet phone said, from the communication room on the *Llanvabon*:

"They say that their ship is waiting for you, sir. The air lock door will be open."

The skipper's voice said heavily:

"Mr. Dort, have you seen their spacesuits before? If so, are you sure they're not carrying anything extra, such as bombs?"

"Yes, sir," said Tommy. "We've showed each other our space equipment. They've nothing but regular stuff in view, sir."

The skipper made a gesture to the two aliens. He and Tommy Dort plunged on for the black vessel. They could not make out the ship very clearly with the naked eye, but directions for change of course came from the communication room.

The black ship loomed up. It was huge, as long as the *Llanvabon* and vastly thicker. The air lock did stand open. The two spacesuited men moved in and anchored themselves with magnetic-soled boots. The outer door closed. There was a rush of air and simultaneously the sharp quick tug of artificial gravity. Then the inner door opened.

All was darkness. Tommy switched on his helmet light at the same instant as the skipper. Since the aliens saw by infrared, a white light would have been intolerable to them. The men's helmet lights were, therefore, of the deep-red tint used to illuminate instrument panels so there will be no dazzling of eyes that must be able to detect the minutest specks of white light on a navigating vision plate. There were aliens waiting to receive them. They blinked at the brightness of the helmet lights. The space-phone receivers said in Tommy's ear:

"They say, sir, their skipper is waiting for you."

Tommy and the skipper were in a long corridor with a soft flooring underfoot. Their lights showed details of which every one was exotic.

"I think I'll crack my helmet, sir," said Tommy.

He did. The air was good. By analysis it was thirty percent oxygen instead of twenty for normal air on Earth, but the pressure was less. It felt just right. The artificial gravity, too, was less than that maintained on the *Llanvabon*. The home planet of the aliens would be smaller than Earth, and—by the infrared data—circling close to a nearly dead, dull-red sun. The air had smells in it. They were utterly strange, but not unpleasant.

An arched opening. A ramp with the same soft stuff underfoot. Lights which actually shed a dim, dull-red glow about. The aliens had stepped up some of their illuminating equipment as an act of courtesy. The light might hurt their eyes, but it was a gesture of consideration which made Tommy even more anxious for his plan to go through.

The alien skipper faced them with what seemed to Tommy a gesture of wryly humorous deprecation. The helmet phones said:

"He says, sir, that he greets you with pleasure, but he has been able to think of only one way in which the problem created by the meeting of these two ships can be solved."

"He means a fight," said the skipper. "Tell him I'm here to offer another choice."

The *Llanvabon*'s skipper and the skipper of the alien ship were face to face, but their communication was weirdly indirect. The aliens used no sound in communication. Their talk, in fact, took place on microwaves and approximated telepathy. But they could not hear, in any ordinary sense of the word, so the skipper's and Tommy's speech approached telepathy, too, as far as they were concerned. When the skipper spoke, his space phone sent his words back to the *Llanvabon*, where the words were fed into the coder and short-wave equivalents sent back to the black ship. The alien skipper's reply went to the *Llanvabon* and through the decoder, and was retransmitted by space phone in words read from the message frame. It was awkward, but it worked.

The short and stocky alien skipper paused. The helmet phones relayed his translated, soundless reply.

"He is anxious to hear, sir."

The skipper took off his helmet. He put his hands at his belt in a belligerent pose.

"Look here!" he said truculently to the bald, strange creature in the unearthly red glow before him. "It looks like we have to fight and one batch of us get killed. We're ready to do it if we have to. But if you win, we've got it fixed so you'll never find out where Earth is, and there's a good chance we'll get you anyhow! If we win, we'll be in the same fix. And if we win and go back home, our government will fit out a fleet and start hunting your planet. And if we find it we'll be ready to blast it to hell! If you win, the same thing will happen to us! And it's all foolishness! We've stayed here a month, and we've swapped information, and we don't hate each other. There's no reason for us to fight except for the rest of our respective races!"

The skipper stopped for breath, scowling. Tommy Dort inconspicuously put his own hands on the belt of his spacesuit. He waited, hoping desperately that the trick would work.

"He says, sir," reported the helmet phones, "that all you say is true. But that his race has to be protected, just as you feel that yours must be."

"Naturally," said the skipper angrily, "but the sensible thing to do is to figure out how to protect it! Putting its future up as a gamble in a fight is not sensible. Our races have to be warned of each other's existence. That's true. But each should have proof that the other doesn't want to fight, but wants to be friendly. And we shouldn't be able to find each other, but we should be able to communicate with each other to work out grounds for a common trust. If our governments want to be fools, let them! But we should give them the chance to make friends, instead of starting a space war out of mutual funk!"

Briefly, the space phone said:

"He says that the difficulty is that of trusting each other now. With the possible existence of his race at stake, he cannot take any chance, and neither can you, of yielding an advantage."

"But my race," boomed the skipper, glaring at the alien captain, "my race has an advantage now. We came here to your ship in atom-powered spacesuits! Before we left, we altered the drives! We can set off ten pounds of sensitized fuel apiece, right here in this ship, or it can be set off by remote control from our ship! It will be rather remarkable if your fuel store doesn't blow up with us! In other words, if you don't accept my proposal for a commonsense approach to this predicament, Dort and I blow up in an atomic explosion, and your ship will be wrecked if not destroyed—and the *Llanvabon* will be attacking with everything it's got within two seconds after the blast goes off!"

The captain's room of the alien ship was a strange scene, with its dull-red illumination and the strange, bald, gill-breathing aliens watching the skipper and waiting for the inaudible translation of the harangue they could not hear. But a sudden tension appeared in the air. A sharp, savage feeling of strain. The alien skipper made a gesture. The helmet phones hummed.

"He says, sir, what is your proposal?"

"Swap ships!" roared the skipper. "Swap ships and go on home! We can fix our instruments so they'll do no trailing, he can do the same with his. We'll each remove our star maps and records. We'll each dismantle our weapons. The air will serve, and we'll take their ship and they'll take ours, and neither one can harm or trail the other, and each will carry home more information than can be taken otherwise! We can agree on this same Crab Nebula as a rendezvous when the double-star has made another circuit, and if our people want to meet them they can do it, and if they are scared they can duck it! That's my proposal! And he'll take it, or Dort and I blow up their ship and the *Llanvabon* blasts what's left!"

He glared about him while he waited for the translation to reach the tense small stocky figures about him. He could tell when it came because the tenseness changed. The figures stirred. They made gestures. One of them made convulsive movements. It lay down on the soft floor and kicked. Others leaned against its walls and shook.

The voice in Tommy Dort's helmet phones had been strictly crisp and professional, before, but now it sounded blankly amazed.

"He says, sir, that it is a good joke. Because the two crew members he sent to our ship, and that you passed on the way, have their spacesuits stuffed with atomic explosive too, sir, and he intended to make the very same offer and threat! Of course he accepts, sir. Your ship is worth more to him than his own, and his is worth more to you than the *Llanvabon*. It appears, sir, to be a deal."

Then Tommy Dort realized what the convulsive movements of the aliens were. They were laughter.

It wasn't quite as simple as the skipper had outlined it. The actual working out of the proposal was complicated. For three days the crews of the two ships were intermingled, the aliens learning the workings of the *Llanvabon*'s engines, and the men learning the controls of the black spaceship. It was a good joke—but it wasn't all a joke. There were men on the black ship, and aliens on the *Llanvabon*, ready at an instant's notice to blow up the vessels in question. And they would have done it in case of need, for which reason the need did not appear. But it was, actually, a better arrangement to have two expeditions return to two civilizations, under the current arrangement, than for either to return alone.

There were differences, though. There was some dispute about the removal of records. In most cases the dispute was settled by the destruction of the records. There was more trouble caused by the *Llanvabon*'s books, and the alien equivalent of a ship's library, containing works which approximated the novels of Earth. But those items were valuable to possible friendship, because they would show the two cultures, each to the other, from the viewpoint of normal citizens and without propaganda.

But nerves were tense during those three days. Aliens unloaded and inspected the foodstuffs intended for the men on the black ship. Men transshipped the foodstuffs the aliens would need to return to their home. There were endless details, from the exchange of lighting equipment to suit the eyesight of the exchanging crews, to a final check-up of apparatus. A joint inspection party of both races verified that all detector devices had been smashed but not removed, so that they could not be used for trailing and had not been smuggled away. And of course, the aliens were anxious not to leave any useful weapon on the black ship, nor the men upon the *Llanvabon*. It was a curious fact that each crew was best qualified to take exactly the measures which made an evasion of the agreement impossible.

There was a final conference before the two ships parted, back in the communication room of the *Llanvabon*.

"Tell the little runt," rumbled the *Llanvabon*'s former skipper, "that he's got a good ship and he'd better treat her right."

The message frame flicked word-cards into position.

"I believe," it said on the alien skipper's behalf, "that your ship is just as good. I will hope to meet you here when the double star has turned one turn."

The last man left the *Llanvabon*. It moved away into the misty nebula before they had returned to the black ship. The vision plates in that vessel had been altered for human eyes, and human crewmen watched jealously for any trace of their former ship as their new craft took a crazy, evading course to a remote part of the nebula. It came to a crevasse of nothingness, leading to the stars. It rose swiftly to clear space. There was the instant of breathlessness which the overdrive field produces as it goes on, and then the black ship whipped away into the void at many times the speed of light.

Many days later, the skipper saw Tommy Dort poring over one of the strange objects which were the equivalent of books. It was fascinating to puzzle over. The skipper was pleased with himself. The technicians of the *Llanvabon*'s former crew were finding out desirable things about the ship almost momently. Doubtless the aliens were as pleased with their discoveries in the *Llanvabon*. But the black ship would be enormously worthwhile—and the solution that had been found was by any standard much superior even to combat in which the Earthmen had been overwhelmingly victorious.

"Hm-m-m. Mr. Dort," said the skipper profoundly. "You've no equipment to make another photographic record on the way back. It was left on the *Llanvabon*. But fortunately, we have your record taken on the way out, and I shall report most favorably on your suggestion and your assistance in carrying it out. I think very well of you, sir."

"Thank you, sir," said Tomy Dort.

He waited. The skipper cleared his throat.

"You . . . ah . . . first realized the close similarity of mental processes between the aliens and ourselves," he observed. "What do you think of the prospects of a friendly arrangement if we keep a rendezvous with them at the nebula as agreed?"

"Oh, we'll get along all right, sir," said Tommy. "We've got a good start toward friendship. After all, since they see by infrared, the planets they'd want to make use of wouldn't suit us. There's no reason why we shouldn't get along. We're almost alike in psychology."

"Hm-m-m. Now just what do you mean by that?" demanded the skipper.

"Why, they're just like us, sir!" said Tommy. "Of course they breathe through gills and they see by heat waves, and their blood has a copper base instead of iron and a few little details like that. But otherwise we're just alike! There were only men in their crew, sir, but they have two sexes as we have, and they have families, and . . . er . . . their sense of humor— In fact—"

Tommy hesitated.

"Go on, sir," said the skipper.

"Well— There was the one I call Buck, sir, because he hasn't any name that goes into sound waves," said Tommy. "We got along very well. I'd really call him my friend, sir. And we were together for a couple of hours just before the two ships separated and we'd nothing in particular to do. So I became convinced that humans and aliens are bound to be good friends if they have only half a chance. You see, sir, we spent those two hours telling dirty jokes."

THE VANISHING VENUSIANS

by Leigh Brackett (1915-1978)

PLANET STORIES,
Spring

One reason why much pulp science fiction is unreadable today is that discoveries in science have invalidated some of the basic assumptions upon which these stories rest. This is particularly true in the case of astronomy—we now know what is on the other side of the moon and we have set mechanical feet and eyes on the planet Mars. We also know a great deal about Venus, enough to invalidate the entire setting of "The Vanishing Venusians"—no bodies of water and no Venusians swimming in them.

But "The Vanishing Venusians" belongs in this book because of its color, its strong characterizations, and its adventure; all characteristics of the work of its author, the late and lamented Leigh Brackett, a star of and the essence of the best of Planet Stories *in the 1940s.*

(Marty mentioned the fact that Venus has no bodies of water [or any liquid] and no Venusians swimming in them.

Actually Venus is even worse than that. It has a temperature considerably higher than that required to melt lead on every part of its surface from its poles to its equator by day and by night. It has an atmosphere ninety times as dense as that of Earth, consisting almost entirely of carbon dioxide. And its clouds are composed of droplets of sulfuric acid.

Unless our technology advances to the point where we can alter the essential properties of Venus's atmosphere and import water, human beings will never colonize the planet and, in fact, never set foot upon it. —And that's too bad. Of all the planets of pre-space-age astronomy, Venus was the most interesting. What stories it gave us of a lush, primitive world overflowing with life. And it's gone—all gone—and we are left with a hot, utterly barren ball of rock.

And yet while the science fiction stories of the past are still with us, as Leigh's is, the memory will remain. I.A.)

The breeze was steady enough, but it was not in a hurry. It filled the lug sail just hard enough to push the dirty weed-grown hull through the water, and no harder. Matt Harker lay alongside the tiller and counted the trickles of sweat crawling over his nakedness, and stared with sullen, opaque eyes into the indigo night. Anger, leashed and impotent, rose in his throat like bitter vomit.

The sea—Rory McLaren's Venusian wife called it the Sea of Morning Opals—lay unstirring, black, streaked with phosphorescence. The sky hung low over it, the thick cloud blanket of Venus that had made the Sun a half-remembered legend to the exiles from Earth. Riding lights burned in the blue gloom, strung out in line. Twelve ships, thirty-eight hundred people, going no place, trapped in the interval between birth and death and not knowing what to do about it.

Matt Harker glanced upward at the sail and then at the stern lantern of the ship ahead. His face, in the dim glow that lights Venus even at inght, was a gaunt oblong of shadows and hard bone, reamed and scarred with living, with wanting and not having, with dying and not being dead. He was a lean man, wiry and not tall, with a snakelike surety of motion.

Somebody came scrambling quietly aft along the deck, avoiding the sleeping bodies crowded everywhere. Harker said, without emotion, "Hi, Rory."

Rory McLaren said, "Hi, Matt." He sat down. He was young, perhaps half Harker's age. There was still hope in his face, but it was growing tired. He sat for a while without speaking, looking at nothing, and then said, "Honest to God, Matt, how much longer can we last?"

"What's the matter, kid? Starting to crack?"

"I don't know. Maybe. When are we going to stop somewhere?"

"When we find a place to stop."

"Is there a place to stop? Seems like ever since I was born we've been hunting. There's always something wrong. Hostile natives, or fever, or bad soil, always something, and we go on again. It's not right. It's not any way to try to live."

Harker said, "I told you not to go having kids."

"What's that got to do with it?"

"You start worrying. The kid isn't even here yet, and already you're worrying."

"Sure I am." McLaren put his head in his hands suddenly and swore. Harker knew he did that to keep from crying. "I'm worried," McLaren said, "that maybe the same thing'll happen to my wife and kid that happened to yours. We got fever aboard."

Harker's eyes were like blown coals for an instant. Then he glanced up at the sail and said, "They'd be better off if it didn't live."

"That's no kind of a thing to say."

"It's the truth. Like you asked me, when are we going to stop somewhere? Maybe never. You bellyache about it ever since you were born. Well, I've been at it longer than that. Before you were born I saw our first settlement burned by the Cloud People, and my mother and father crucified in their own vineyard. I was there when this trek to the Promised Land began, back on Earth, and I'm still waiting for the promise."

The sinews in Harker's face were drawn like knots of wire. His voice had a terrible quietness.

"Your wife and kid would be better off to die now, while Viki's still young and has hope, and before the child ever opens its eyes."

Sim, the big black man, relieved Harker before dawn. He started singing, softly—something mournful and slow as the breeze, and beautiful. Harker cursed him and went up into the bow to sleep, but the song stayed with him. *Oh, I looked over Jordan, and what did I see, comin' for to carry me home. . . .*

Harker slept. Presently he began to moan and twitch, and then cry out. People around him woke up. They watched with interest. Harker was a lone wolf awake, ill-tempered and violent. When, at long intervals, he would have one of his spells, no one was anxious to help him out of it. They liked peeping inside of Harker when he wasn't looking.

Harker didn't care. He was playing in the snow again. He was seven years old, and the drifts were high and white, and above them the sky was so blue and clean that he wondered if God mopped it every few days like Mom did the kitchen floor. The sun was shining. It was like a great gold coin, and it made the snow burn like crushed diamonds. He put his arms up to the sun, and the cold air slapped him with clean hands, and he laughed. And then it was all gone. . . .

"By gawd," somebody said. "Ain't them tears on his face?"

"Bawling. Bawling like a little kid. Listen at him."

"Hey," said the first one sheepishly. "Reckon we oughta wake him up?"

"Hell with him, the old sour-puss. Hey, listen to that . . . !"

"Dad," Harker whispered. "Dad, I want to go home."

The dawn came like a sifting of fire-opals through the layers of pearl-gray cloud. Harker heard the yelling dimly in his sleep. He felt dull and tired, and his eyelids stuck together. The yelling gradually took shape and became the word "Land!" repeated over and over. Harker kicked himself awake and got up.

The tideless sea glimmered with opaline colors under the mist. Flocks of little jewel-scaled sea-dragons rose up from the ever-present floating islands of weed, and the weed itself, part of it, writhed and stretched with sentient life.

Ahead there was a long low hummock of muddy ground fading into tangled swamp. Beyond it, rising sheer into the clouds, was a granite cliff, a sweeping escarpment that stood like a wall against the hopeful gaze of the exiles.

Harker found Rory McLaren standing beside him, his arm around Viki, his wife. Viki was one of several Venusians who had married into the Earth colony. Her skin was clear white, her hair a glowing silver, her lips vividly red. Her eyes were like the sea, changeable, full of hidden life. Just now they had that special look that the eyes of women get when they're thinking about creation. Harker looked away.

McLaren said, "It's land."

Harker said, "It's mud. It's swamp. It's fever. It's like the rest."

Viki said, "Can we stop here, just a little while?"

Harker shrugged. "That's up to Gibbons." He wanted to ask what the hell difference it made where the kid was born, but for once he held his tongue. He turned away. Somewhere in the waist a woman was screaming in delirium. There were three shapes wrapped in ragged blankets and laid on planks by the port scuppers. Harker's mouth twitched in a crooked smile.

"We'll probably stop long enough to bury them," he said. "Maybe that'll be time enough."

He caught a glimpse of McLaren's face. The hope in it was not tired any more. It was dead. Dead, like the rest of Venus.

Gibbons called the chief men together aboard his ship—the leaders, the fighters and hunters and seamen, the tough leathery men who were the armor around the soft body of the colony. Harker was there, and McLaren. McLaren was young, but up until lately he had had a quality of optimism that cheered his shipmates, a natural leadership.

Gibbons was an old man. He was the original guiding spirit of the five thousand colonists who had come out from Earth to a new start on a new world. Time and tragedy, disappointment and betrayal had marked him cruelly, but his head was still high. Harker admired his guts while cursing him for an idealistic fool.

The inevitable discussion started as to whether they should try a permanent settlement on this mud flat or go on wandering over the endless, chartless seas. Harker said impatiently:

"For cripesake, look at the place. Remember the last time. Remember the time before that, and stop bleating."

Sim, the big black, said quietly, "The people are getting awful tired. A man was meant to have roots some place. There's going to be trouble pretty soon if we don't find land."

Harker said, "You think you can find some, pal, go to it."

Gibbons said heavily, "But he's right. There's hysteria, fever, dysentery and boredom, and the boredom's worst of all."

McLaren said, "I vote to settle."

Harker laughed. He was leaning by the cabin port, looking out at the cliffs. The gray granite looked clean above the swamp. Harker tried to pierce the clouds that hid the top, but couldn't. His dark eyes narrowed. The heated voices behind him faded into distance. Suddenly he turned and said, "Sir, I'd like permission to see what's at the top of those cliffs."

There was complete silence. Then Gibbons said slowly, "We've lost too many men on journeys like that before, only to find the plateau uninhabitable."

"There's always the chance. Our first settlement was in the high plateaus, remember. Clean air, good soil, no fever."

"I remember," Gibbons said. "I remember." He was silent for a while, then he gave Harker a shrewd glance. "I know you, Matt. I might as well give permission."

Harker grinned. "You won't miss me much anyhow. I'm not a good influence anymore." He started for the door. "Give me three weeks. You'll take that long to careen and scrape the bottoms anyhow. Maybe I'll come back with something."

McLaren said, "I'm going with you, Matt."

Harker gave him a level-eyed stare. "You better stay with Viki."

"If there's good land up there, and anything happens to you so you can't come back and tell us. . . ."

"Like not bothering to come back, maybe?"

"I didn't say that. Like we both won't come back. But two is better than one."

Harker smiled. The smile was enigmatic and not very nice. Gibbons said, "He's right, Matt." Harker shrugged. Then Sim stood up.

"Two is good," he said, "but three is better." He turned to Gibbons. "There's nearly five hundred of us, sir. If there's new land up there, we ought to share the burden of finding it."

Gibbons nodded. Harker said, "You're crazy, Sim. Why you want to do all that climbing, maybe to no place?"

Sim smiled. His teeth were unbelievably white in the sweat-polished blackness of his face. "But that's what my people always done, Matt. A lot of climbing, to no place."

They made their preparations and had a last night's sleep. McLaren said good-bye to Viki. She didn't cry. She knew why he was going. She kissed him, and all she said was, "Be careful." All he said was, "I'll be back before he's born."

They started at dawn, carrying dried fish and sea-berries made into pemmican, and their long knives and ropes for climbing. They had long ago run out of ammunition for their few blasters, and they had no equipment for making more.

All were adept at throwing spears, and carried three short ones barbed with bone across their backs.

It was raining when they crossed the mud flat, wading thigh-deep in heavy mist. Harker led the way through the belt of swamp. He was an old hand at it, with an uncanny quickness in spotting vegetation that was as independently alive and hungry as he was. Venus is one vast hothouse, and the plants have developed into species as varied and marvelous as the reptiles or the mammals, crawling out of the pre-Cambrian seas as primitive flagellates and growing wills of their own, with appetites and motive power to match. The children of the colony learned at an early age not to pick flowers. The blossoms too often bit back.

The swamp was narrow, and they came out of it safely. A great swamp-dragon, a *leshen*, screamed not far off, but they hunt by night, and it was too sleepy to chase them. Harker stood finally on firm ground and studied the cliff.

The rock was roughened by weather, hacked at by ages of erosion, savaged by earthquake. There were stretches of loose shale and great slabs that looked as though they would peel off at a touch, but Harker nodded.

"We can climb it," he said. "Question is, how high is up?"

Sim laughed. "High enough for the Golden City, maybe. Have we all got a clear conscience? Can't carry no load of sin that far!"

Rory McLaren looked at Harker.

Harker said, "All right, I confess. I don't care if there's land up there or not. All I wanted was to get the hell out of that damn boat before I went clean nuts. So now you know."

McLaren nodded. He didn't seem surprised. "Let's climb."

By morning of the second day they were in the clouds. They crawled upward through opal-tinted steam, half liquid, hot and unbearable. They crawled for two more days. The first night or two Sim sang during his watch, while they rested on some ledge. After that he was too tired. McLaren began to give out, though he wouldn't say so. Matt Harker grew more taciturn and ill-tempered, if possible, but otherwise there was no change. The clouds continued to hide the top of the cliff.

During one rest break McLaren said hoarsely, "Don't these cliffs ever end?" His skin was yellowish, his eyes glazed with fever.

"Maybe," said Harker, "they go right up beyond the sky."

The fever was on him again, too. It lived in the marrow of the exiles, coming out at intervals to shake and sear them, and then retreating. Sometimes it did not retreat, and after nine days there was no need.

McLaren said, "You wouldn't care if they did, would you?"

"I didn't ask you to come."

"But you wouldn't care."

"Ah, shut up."

McLaren went for Harker's throat.

Harker hit him, with great care and accuracy. McLaren sagged down and took his head in his hands and wept. Sim stayed out of it. He shook his head, and after a while he began to sing to himself, or someone beyond himself. "Oh, nobody knows the trouble I see. . . ."

Harker pulled himself up. His ears rang and he shivered uncontrollably, but he could still take some of McLaren's weight on himself. They were climbing a steep ledge, fairly wide and not difficult.

"Let's get on," said Harker.

About two hundred feet beyond that point the ledge dipped and began to go down again in a series of broken steps. Overhead the cliff face bulged outward. Only a fly could have climbed it. They stopped. Harker cursed with vicious slowness. Sim closed his eyes and smiled. He was a little crazy with fever himself.

"Golden City's at the top. That's where I'm going."

He started off along the ledge, following its decline toward a jutting shoulder, around which it vanished. Harker laughed sardonically. McLaren pulled free of him and went doggedly after Sim. Harker shrugged and followed.

Around the shoulder the ledge washed out completely.

They stood still. The steaming clouds shut them in before, and behind was a granite wall hung within thick fleshy creepers. Dead end.

"Well?" said Harker.

McLaren sat down. He didn't cry, or say anything. He just sat. Sim stood with his arms hanging and his chin on his huge black chest. Harker said, "See what I meant, about the Promised Land? Venus is a fixed wheel, and you can't win."

It was then that he noticed the cool air. He had thought it was just a fever chill, but it lifted his hair, and it had a definite pattern on his body. It even had a cool, clean smell to it. It was blowing out through the creepers.

Harker began ripping with his knife. He broke through into a cave mouth, a jagged rip worn smooth at the bottom by what must once have been a river.

"That draft is coming from the top of the plateau," Harker said. "Wind must be blowing up there and pushing it down. There may be a way through."

McLaren and Sim both showed a slow, terrible growth of hope. The three of them went without speaking into the tunnel.

2

They made good time. The clean air acted as a tonic, and hope spurred them on. The tunnel sloped upward rather sharply, and presently Harker heard water, a low thunderous murmur as of an underground river up ahead. It was utterly dark, but the smooth channel of stone was easy to follow.

Sim said, "Isn't that light up ahead?"

"Yeah," said Harker. "Some kind of phosphorescence. I don't like that river. It may stop us."

They went on in silence. The glow grew stronger, the air more damp. Patches of phosphorescent lichen appeared on the walls, glimmering with dim jewel tones like an unhealthy rainbow. The roar of the water was very loud.

They came upon it suddenly. It flowed across the course of their tunnel in a broad channel worn deep into the rock, so that its level had fallen below its old place and left the tunnel dry. It was a wide river, slow and majestic. Lichen spangled the roof and walls, reflecting in dull glints of color from the water.

Overhead there was a black chimney going up through the rock, and the cool draft came from there with almost hurricane force, much of which was dissipated in the main river tunnel. Harker judged there was a cliff formation on the surface that siphoned the wind downward. The chimney was completely inaccessible.

Harker said, "I guess we'll have to go upstream, along the side." The rock was eroded enough to make that possible, showing wide ledges at different levels.

McLaren said, "What if this river doesn't come from the surface? What if it starts from an underground source?"

"You stuck your neck out," Harker said. "Come on."

They started. After a while, tumbling like porpoises in the black water, the golden creatures swam by, and saw the men, and stopped, and swam back again.

They were not very large, the largest about the size of a twelve-year-old child. Their bodies were anthropoid, but adapted to swimming with shimmering webs. They glowed with a golden light, phosphorescent like the lichen, and their eyes were lidless and black, like one huge spreading pupil. Their faces were incredible. Harker could remember, faintly, the golden dandelions that grew on the lawn in summer. The heads and faces of the swimmers were like that, covered with streaming petals that seemed to have independent movements, as though they were sensory organs as well as decoration.

Harker said, "For cripesake, what are they?"

"They look like flowers," McLaren said.

"They look more like fish," the black man said.

Harker laughed. "I'll bet they're both. I'll bet they're plannies that grew where they had to be amphibious." The colonists had shortened plant-animal to planimal, and then just planny. "I've seen gimmicks in the swamps that weren't so far away from these. But jeez, get the eyes on 'em! They look human."

"The shape's human, too, almost." McLaren shivered. "I wish they wouldn't look at us that way."

Sim said, "As long as they just look. I'm not gonna worry. . . ."

They didn't. They started to close in below the men, swimming effortlessly against the current. Some of them began to clamber out on the low ledge behind them. They were agile and graceful. There was something unpleasantly childlike about them. There were fifteen or twenty of them, and they reminded Harker of a gang of mischievous kids—only the mischief had a queer soulless quality of malevolence.

Harker led the way faster along the ledge. His knife was drawn and he carried a short spear in his right hand.

The tone of the river changed. The channel broadened, and up ahead Harker saw that the cavern ended in a vast shadowy place, the water spreading into a dark lake, spilling slowly out over a low wide lip of rock. More of the shining child-things were playing there. They joined their fellows, closing the ring tighter around the three men.

"I don't like this," McLaren said. "If they'd only make a noise!"

They did, suddenly—a shrill tittering like a blasphemy of childish laughter. Their eyes shone. They rushed in, running wetly along the ledge, reaching up out of the water to claw at ankles, laughing. Inside his tough flat belly Harker's guts turned over.

McLaren yelled and kicked. Claws raked his ankle, spiny needle-sharp things like thorns. Sim ran his spear clean through a golden breast. There were no bones in it. The body was light and membranous, and the blood that ran out was sticky and greenish, like sap. Harker kicked two of the things back in the river, swung his spear like a ball bat and knocked two more off the ledge—they were unbelievably light—and shouted, "Up there, that high ledge. I don't think they can climb that."

He thrust McLaren bodily past him and helped Sim fight a rear-guard action while they all climbed a rotten and difficult transit. McLaren crouched at the top and hurled chunks of stone at the attackers. There was a great crack running up and clear across the cavern roof, scar of some ancient earthquake. Presently a small slide started.

"Okay," Harker panted. "Quit before you bring the roof down. They can't follow us." The plannies were equipped for swimming, not climbing. They clawed angrily and slipped back, and then retreated sullenly to the water. Abruptly they seized the body with Sim's spear through it and devoured it, quarreling fiercely over it. McLaren leaned over the edge and was sick.

Harker didn't feel so good himself. He got up and went on. Sim helped McLaren, whose ankle was bleeding badly.

This higher ledge angled up and around the wall of the great lake-cavern. It was cooler and drier here, and the lichens thinned out, and vanished, leaving total darkness. Harker yelled once. From the echo of his voice the place was enormous.

Down below in the black water golden bodies streaked like comets in an ebon universe, going somewhere, going fast. Harker felt his way carefully along. His skin twitched with a nervous impulse of danger, a sense of something unseen, unnatural, and wicked.

Sim said, "I hear something."

They stopped. The blind air lay heavy with a subtle

fragrance, spicy and pleasant, yet somehow unclean. The water sighed lazily far below. Somewhere ahead was a smooth rushing noise which Harker guessed was the river inlet. But none of that was what Sim meant.

He meant the rippling, rustling sound that came from everywhere in the cavern. The black surface of the lake was dotted now with spots of burning phosphorescent color, trailing fiery wakes. The spots grew swiftly, coming nearer, and became carpets of flowers, scarlet and blue and gold and purple. Floating fields of them, and towed by shining swimmers.

"My God," said Harker softly. "How big are they?"

"Enough to make three of me." Sim was a big man. "Those little ones were children, all right. They went and got their papas. Oh, Lord!"

The swimmers were very like the smaller ones that attacked them by the river, except for their giant size. They were not cumbersome. They were magnificent, supple-limbed and light. Their membranes had spread into great shining wings, each rib tipped with fire. Only the golden dandelion heads had changed.

They had shed their petals. Their adult heads were crowned with flat, coiled growths having the poisonous and filthy beauty of fungus. And their faces were the faces of men.

For the first time since childhood Harker was cold.

The fields of burning flowers were swirled together at the base of the cliff. The golden giants cried out suddenly, a sonorous belling note, and the water was churned to blazing foam as thousands of flowerlike bodies broke away and started up the cliff on suckered, spidery legs.

It didn't look as though it was worth trying, but Harker said, "Let's get the hell on!" There was a faint light now, from the army below. He began to run along the ledge, the others close on his heels. The flower-hounds coursed swiftly upward, and their masters swam easily below, watching.

The ledge dropped. Harker shot along it like a deer. Beyond the lowest dip it plunged into the tunnel whence the river came. A short tunnel, and at the far end . . .

"Daylight!" Harker shouted. "Daylight!"

McLaren's bleeding leg gave out and he fell.

Harker caught him. They were at the lowest part of the dip. The flower-beasts were just below, rushing higher.

McLaren's foot was swollen, the calf of his leg discolored. Some swift infection from the planny's claws. He fought Harker. "Go on," he said. "Go on!"

Harker slapped him hard across the temple. He started on, half carrying McLaren, but he saw it wasn't going to work. McLaren weighed more than he did. He thrust McLaren into Sim's powerful arms. The big black nodded and ran, carrying the half-conscious man like a child. Harker saw the first of the flower-things flow up onto the ledge in front of them.

Sim hurdled them. They were not large, and there were only three of them. They rushed to follow and Harker speared them, slashing and striking with the sharp bone tip. Behind him the full tide rushed up. He ran, but they were faster. He drove them back with spear and knife, and ran again, and turned and fought again, and by the time they had reached the tunnel Harker was staggering with weariness.

Sim stopped. He said, "There's no way out."

Harker glanced over his shoulder. The river fell sheer down a high face of rock—too high and with too much force in the water even for the giant water-plannies to think of attempting. Daylight poured through overhead, warm and welcoming, and it might as well have been on Mars.

Dead end.

Then Harker saw the little eroded channel twisting up at the side. Little more than a drainpipe, and long dry, leading to a passage beside the top of the falls—a crack barely large enough for a small man to crawl through. It was a hell of a ragged hope, but. . . .

Harker pointed, between jabs at the swarming flowers. Sim yelled, "You first." Because Harker was the best climber, he obeyed, helping the gasping McLaren up behind him. Sim wielded his spear like a lightning brand, guarding the rear, creeping up inch by inch.

He reached a fairly secure perch, and stopped. His huge chest pumped like a bellows, his arm rose and fell like a polished bar of ebony. Harker shouted to him to come on. He and McLaren were almost at the top.

Sim laughed. "How you going to get me through that little bitty hole?"

"Come on, you fool!"

"You better hurry. I'm about finished."

"Sim! Sim, damn you!"

"Crawl out through that hole, runt, and pull that stringbean with you! I'm a man-sized man, and I got to stay." Then, furiously, "Hurry up or they'll drag you back before you're through."

He was right. Harker knew he was right. He went to work pushing and jamming McLaren through the narrow opening. McLaren was groggy and not much help, but he was thin and small-boned, and he made it. He rolled out on a slope covered with green grass, the first Harker had seen since he was a child. He began to struggle after McLaren. He did not look back at Sim.

The black man was singing, about the glory of the coming of the Lord.

Harker put his head back into the darkness of the creek. "Sim!"

"Yeah?" Faintly, hoarse, echoing.

"There's land here, Sim. Good land."

"Yeah."

"Sim, we'll find a way. . . ."

Sim was singing again. The sound grew fainter, diminishing downward into distance. The words were lost, but not what lay behind them. Matt Harker buried his face in the green grass, and Sim's voice went with him into the dark.

The clouds were turning color with the sinking of the hidden sun. They hung like a canopy of hot gold washed in blood. It was utterly silent, except for the birds. You never heard birds like that down in the low places. Matt Harker rolled over and sat up slowly. He felt as though he had been beaten. There was a sickness in him, and a shame, and the old dark anger lying coiled and deadly above his heart.

Before him lay the long slope of grass to the river, which bent away to the left out of sight behind a spur of granite. Beyond the slope was a broad plain and then a forest of gigantic trees. They seemed to float in the coppery haze, their dark branches outspread like wings and starred with flowers. The air was cool, with no taint of mud or rot. The grass was rich, the soil beneath it clean and sweet.

Rory McLaren moaned softly and Harker turned. His leg looked bad. He was in a sort of stupor, his skin flushed and dry. Harker swore softly, wondering what he was going to do.

He looked back toward the plain, and he saw the girl.

He didn't know how she got there. Perhaps out of the bushes that grew in thick clumps on the slope. She could have been there a long time, watching. She was watching now, standing quite still about forty feet away. A great scarlet butterfly clung to her shoulder, moving its wings with lazy delight.

She seemed more like a child than a woman. She was naked, small and slender and exquisite. Her skin had a faint translucent hint of green under its whiteness. Her hair, curled short to her head, was deep blue, and her eyes were blue also, and very strange.

Harker stared at her, and she at him, neither of them moving. A bright bird swooped down and hovered by her lips for a moment, caressing her with its beak. She touched it and smiled, but she did not take her eyes from Harker.

Harker got to his feet, slowly, easily. He said, "Hello."

She did not move, or make a sound, but quite suddenly a pair of enormous birds, beaked and clawed like eagles and black as sin, made a whistling rush down past Harker's head and returned, circling. Harker sat down again.

The girl's strange eyes moved from him, upward to the crack in the hillside whence he had come. Her lips didn't move, but her voice—or something—spoke clearly inside Harker's head.

"You came from—There." *There* had tremendous feeling in it, and none of it nice.

Harker said, "Yes. A telepath, huh?"

"But you're not. . . ." A picture of the golden swimmers formed in Harker's mind. It was recognizable, but hatred and fear had washed out all the beauty, leaving only horror.

Harker said, "No." He explained about himself and McLaren. He told about Sim. He knew she was listening carefully to his mind, testing it for truth. He was not worried about what she would find. "My friend is hurt," he said. "We need food and shelter."

For some time there was no answer. The girl was looking at Harker again. His face, the shape and texture of his body, his hair, and then his eyes. He had never been looked at quite that way before. He began to grin. A provocative, be-damned-to-you grin that injected a surprising amount of light and charm into his sardonic personality.

"Honey," he said, "you are terrific. Animal, mineral, or vegetable?"

She tipped her small round head in surprise, and asked his own question right back. Harker laughed. She smiled, her mouth making a small inviting V, and her eyes had sparkles in them. Harker started toward her.

Instantly the birds warned him back. The girl laughed, a mischievous ripple of merriment. "Come," she said, and turned away.

Harker frowned. He leaned over and spoke to McLaren, with peculiar gentleness. He managed to get the boy erect, and then swung him across his shoulders, staggering slightly under the weight. McLaren said distinctly, "I'll be back before he's born."

Harker waited until the girl had started, keeping his distance. The two black birds followed watchfully. They walked out across the thick grass of the plain, toward the trees. The sky was now the color of blood.

A light breeze caught the girl's hair and played with it. Matt Harker saw that the short curled strands were broad and flat, like blue petals.

3

It was a long walk to the forest. The top of the plateau seemed to be bowl-shaped, protected by encircling cliffs. Harker, thinking back to that first settlement long ago, decided that this place was infinitely better. It was like the visions he had seen in fever dreams—the Promised Land. The coolness and cleanness of it were like having weights removed from your lungs and heart and body.

The rejuvenating air didn't make up for McLaren's weight, however. Presently Harker said, "Hold it," and sat down, tumbling McLaren gently onto the grass. The girl stopped. She came back a little way and watched Harker, who was blowing like a spent horse. He grinned up at her.

"I'm shot," he said. "I've been too busy for a man of my age. Can't you get hold of somebody to help me carry him?"

Again she studied him with puzzled fascination. Night was closing in, a clear indigo, less dark than at sea level. Her eyes had a curious luminosity in the gloom.

"Why do you do that?" she asked.

"Do what?"

"Carry it."

By "it" Harker guessed she meant McLaren. He was suddenly, coldly conscious of a chasm between them that no amount of explanation could bridge. "He's my friend. He's . . . I have to."

She studied his thought and then shook her head. "I don't understand. It's spoiled—" her thought-image was a combination of "broken," "finished," and "useless"—"Why carry it around?"

"McLaren's not an 'it.' He's a man like me, my friend. He's hurt, and I have to help him."

"I don't understand." Her shrug said it was his funeral, also that he was crazy. She started on again, paying no attention to Harker's call for her to wait. Perforce, Harker picked up McLaren and staggered on again. He wished Sim were here, and immediately wished he hadn't thought of Sim. He hoped Sim had died quickly before—before what? *Oh God, it's dark and I'm scared and my belly's all gone to cold water, and that thing trotting ahead of me through the blue haze . . .*

The thing was beautiful, though. Beautifully formed, fascinating, a curved slender gleam of moonlight, a chaliced flower holding the mystic, scented nectar of the unreal, the unknown, the undiscovered. Harker's blood began, in spite of himself, to throb with a deep excitement.

They came under the fragrant shadows of the trees. The forest was open, with broad mossy ridges and clearings. There were flowers underfoot, but no brush, and clumps of ferns. The girl stopped and stretched up her hand. A feathery branch, high out of her reach, bent and brushed her face, and she plucked a great pale blossom and set it in her hair.

She turned and smiled at Harker. He began to tremble, partly with weariness, partly with something else.

"How do you do that?" he asked.

She was puzzled. "The branch, you mean? Oh, that!" She laughed. It was the first sound he had heard her make, and it shot through him like warm silver. "I just think I would like a flower, and it comes."

Teleportation, telekinetic energy—what did the books call it? Back on Earth they knew something about that, but the colony hadn't had much time to study even its own meager library. There had been some religious sect that could make roses bend into their hands. Old wisdom, the force behind the Biblical miracles, just the infinite power of thought. Very simple. Yeah. Harker wondered uneasily whether she could work it on him, too. But then, he had a brain of his own. Or did he?

"What's your name?" he asked.

She gave a clear, trilled sound. Harker tried to whistle it and gave up. Some sort of tone-language, he guessed, without words as he knew them. It sounded as though they—her people, whatever they were—had copied the birds.

"I'll call you Button," he said. "Bachelor Button—but you wouldn't know."

She picked the image out of his mind and sent it back to him. Blue fringe-topped flowers nodding in his mother's china bowl. She laughed again and sent her black birds away and led on into the forest, calling out like an oriole. Other voices answered her, and presently, racing the light wind between the trees, her people came.

They were like her. There were males, slender little creatures like young boys, and girls like Button. There were several hundred of them, all naked, all laughing and curious, their lithe pliant bodies flitting moth-fashion through the indigo shadows. They were topped with petals—Harker called them that, though he still wasn't sure—of all colors from blood-scarlet to pure white.

They trilled back and forth. Apparently Button was telling them all about how she found Harker and McLaren. The whole mob pushed on slowly through the forest and ended finally in a huge clearing where there were only scattered trees. A spring rose and made a little lake, and then a stream that wandered off among the ferns.

More of the little people came, and now he saw the young ones. All sizes, from tiny thin creatures on up, replicas of their elders. There were no old ones. There were none with imperfect or injured bodies. Harker, exhausted and on the thin edge of a fever-bout, was not encouraged.

He set McLaren down by the spring. He drank, gasping like an animal, and bathed his head and shoulders. The forest people stood in a circle, watching. They were silent now. Harker felt coarse and bestial, somehow, as though he had belched loudly in church.

He turned to McLaren. He bathed him, helped him drink, and set about fixing the leg. He needed light, and he needed flame.

There were dry leaves, and mats of dead moss in the rocks around the spring. He gathered a pile of these. The forest people watched. Their silent luminous stare got on Harker's nerves. His hands were shaking so that he made four tries with his flint and steel before he got a spark.

The tiny flicker made the silent ranks stir sharply. He blew on it. The flames licked up, small and pale at first, then taking hold, growing, crackling. He saw their faces in the springing light, their eyes stretched with terror. A shrill crying broke from them and then they were gone, like rustling leaves before a wind.

Harker drew his knife. The forest was quiet now. Quiet but not at rest. The skin crawled on Harker's back, over his scalp, drew tight on his cheekbones. He passed the blade through the flame. McLaren looked up at him. Harker said, "It's okay, Rory," and hit him carefully on the point of the jaw. McLaren lay still. Harker stretched out the swollen leg and went to work.

It was dawn again. He lay by the spring in the cool grass, the ashes of his fire gray and dead beside the dark stains. He felt rested, relaxed, and the fever seemed to have gone out of him. The air was like wine.

He rolled over on his back. There was a wind blowing. It was a live, strong wind, with a certain smell to it. The trees were rollicking, almost shouting with pleasure. Harker breathed deeply. The smell, the pure clean edge . . .

Suddenly he realized that the clouds were high, higher than he had ever known them to be. The wind swept them up, and the daylight was bright, so bright that . . .

Harker sprang up. The blood rushed in him. There was a stinging blur in his eyes. He began to run, toward a tall tree, and he flung himself upward into the branches and climbed, recklessly, into the swaying top.

The bowl of the valley lay below him, green, rich, and lovely. The gray granite cliffs rose around it, grew higher in the direction from which the wind blew. Higher and higher, and beyond them, far beyond, were mountains, flung towering against the sky.

On the mountains, showing through the whipping veils of cloud, there was snow, white and cold and blindingly pure, and as Harker watched there was a gleam, so quick and fleeting that he saw it more with his heart than with his eyes. . . .

Sunlight. Snowfields, and above them, the sun.

After a long time he clambered down again into the silence

of the glade. He stood there, not moving, seeing what he had not had time to see before.

Rory McLaren was gone. Both packs, with food and climbing ropes and bandages and flint and steel were gone. The short spears were gone. Feeling on his hip, Harker found nothing but bare flesh. His knife and even his breechclout had been taken.

A slender, exquisite body moved forward from the shadows of the trees. Huge white blossoms gleamed against the curly blue that crowned the head. Luminous eyes glanced at Harker, full of mockery and a subtle animation. Button smiled.

Matt Harker walked toward Button, not hurrying, his hard sinewy face blank of expression. He tried to keep his mind that way, too. "Where is the other one, my friend?"

"In the finish-place." She nodded vaguely toward the cliffs near where Harker and McLaren had escaped from the caves. Her thought-image was somewhere between rubbish-heap and cemetery, as nearly as Harker could translate it. It was also completely casual, a little annoyed that time should be wasted on such trifles.

"Did you . . . is he still alive?"

"It was when we put it there. It will be all right, it will just wait until it—stops. Like all of them."

"Why was he moved? Why did you . . ."

"It was ugly." Button shrugged. "It was broken, anyway." She stretched her arms upward and lifted her head to the wind. A shiver of delight ran through her. She smiled again at Harker, sidelong.

He tried to keep his anger hidden. He started walking again, not as though he had any purpose in mind, bearing toward the cliffs. His way lay past a bush with yellow flowers and thorny, pliant branches. Suddenly it writhed and whipped him across the belly. He stopped short and doubled over, hearing Button's laughter.

When he straightened up she was in front of him. "It's red," she said, surprised, and laid little pointed fingers on the scratches left by the thorns. She seemed thrilled and fascinated by the color and feel of his blood. Her fingers moved, probing the shape of his muscles, the texture of his skin and the dark hair on his chest. They drew small lines of fire along his neck, along the ridge of his jaw, touching his features one by one, his eyelids, his black brows.

"What are you?" whispered her mind to his.

"This." Harker put his arms around her, slowly. Her flesh slid cool and strange under his hands, sending an indescribable shudder through him, partly pleasure, partly revulsion. He bent his head. Her eyes deepened, lakes of blue fire, and then he found her lips. They were cool and strange like the rest of her, pliant, scented with spice, the same perfume that came with sudden overpowering sweetness from her curling petals.

Harker saw movement in the forest aisles, a clustering of bright flower-heads. Button drew back. She took his hand and led him away, off toward the river and the quiet ferny places along its banks. Glancing up, Harker saw that the two black birds were following overhead.

"You are really plants, then? Flowers, like those?" He touched the white blossoms on her head.

"You are really a beast, then? Like the furry, snarling things that climb up through the pass sometimes?"

They both laughed. The sky above them was the color of clean fleece. The warm earth and crushed ferns were sweet beneath them. "What pass?" asked Harker.

"Over there." She pointed off toward the rim of the valley. "It goes down to the sea, I think. Long ago we used to go down there but there's no need, and the beasts make it dangerous."

"Do they," said Harker, and kissed her in the hollow below her chin, "What happens when the beasts come?"

Button laughed. Before he could stir, Harker was trapped fast in a web of creepers and tough fern, and the black birds were screeching and clashing their sharp beaks in his face.

"That happens," Button said. She stroked the ferns. "Our cousins understand us, even better than the birds."

Harker lay sweating, even after he was free again. Finally he said, "Those creatures in the underground lake. Are they your cousins?"

Button's fear-thought thrust against his mind like hands pushing away. "No, don't. . . . Long, long ago the legend is that this valley was a huge lake, and the Swimmers lived in it. They were a different species from us, entirely. We came from the high gorges, where there are only barren cliffs now. This was long ago. As the lake receded, we grew more numerous and began to come down, and finally there was a battle and we drove the Swimmers over the falls into the black lake. They have tried and tried to get out, to get back to the light, but they can't. They send their thoughts through to us sometimes. They . . ." She broke off. "I don't want to talk about them anymore."

"How would you fight them if they did get out?" asked Harker easily. "Just with the birds and the growing things?"

Button was slow in answering. Then she said, "I will show you one way." She laid her hand across his eyes. For a moment there was only darkness. Then a picture began to form—people, his own people, seen as reflections in a dim and distorted mirror but recognizable. They poured into the valley through a notch in the cliffs, and instantly every bush and tree and blade of grass was bent against them. They fought, slashing with their knives, making headway, but slowly. And then, across the plain, came a sort of fog, a thin drifting curtain of soft white.

It came closer, moving with force of its own, not heeding the wind. Harker saw that it was thistledown. Seeds, borne on silky wings. It settled over the people trapped in the brush. It was endless and unhurrying, covering them all with a fine fleece. They began to writhe and cry out with pain, with a terrible fear. They struggled, but they couldn't get away.

The white down dropped away from them. Their bodies were covered with countless tiny green shoots, sucking the chemicals from the living flesh and already beginning to grow.

Button's spoken thought cut across the image. "I have seen your thoughts, some of them, since the moment you came out of the caves. I can't understand them, but I can see our plains gashed to the raw earth and our trees cut down and everything made ugly. If your kind came here, we would have to go. And the valley belongs to us."

Matt Harker's brain lay still in the darkness of his skull, wary, drawn in upon itself. "It belonged to the Swimmers first."

"They couldn't hold it. We can."

"Why did you save me, Button? What do you want of me?"

"There was no danger from you. You were strange. I wanted to play with you."

"Do you love me, Button?" His fingers touched a large smooth stone among the fern roots.

"Love? What is that?"

"It's tomorrow and yesterday. It's hoping and happiness and pain, the complete self because it's selfless, the chain that binds you to life and makes living it worthwhile. Do you understand?"

"No. I grow, I take from the soil and the light, I play with the others, with the birds and the wind and flowers. When the time comes I am ripe with seed, and after that I go to the finish-place and wait. That's all I understand. That's all there is."

He looked up into her eyes. A shudder crept over him. "You have no soul, Button. That's the difference between us. You live, but you have no soul."

After that it was not so hard to do what he had to do. To do quickly, very quickly, the thing that was his only faint chance of justifying Sim's death. The thing that Button may have glimpsed in his mind but could not guard against, because there was no understanding in her of the thought of murder.

4

The black birds darted at Harker, but the compulsion that sent them flickered out too soon. The ferns and creepers shook, and then were still, and the birds flew heavily away. Matt Harker stood up.

He thought he might have a little time. The flower-people probably kept in pretty close touch mentally, but perhaps they wouldn't notice Button's absence for a while. Perhaps they weren't prying into his own thoughts, because he was Button's toy. Perhaps. . . .

He began to run, toward the cliffs where the finish-place was. He kept as much as possible in the open, away from shrubs. He did not look again, before he left, at what lay by his feet.

He was close to his desination when he knew that he was spotted. The birds returned, rushing down at him on black whistling wings. He picked up a dead branch to beat them off and it crumbled in his hands. Telekinesis, the power of mind over matter. Harker had read once that if you knew how you could always make your point by thinking the dice into position. He wished he could think himself up a blaster. Curved beaks ripped his arms. He covered his face and grabbed one of the birds by the neck and killed it. The other one screamed and this time Harker wasn't so lucky. By the time he had killed the second one he'd felt claws in him and his face was laid open along the cheekbones. He began to run again.

Bushes swayed toward him as he passed. Thorny branches stretched. Creepers rose like snakes from the grass, and every green blade was turned knifelike against his feet. But he had already reached the cliffs and there were open rocky spaces and the undergrowth was thin.

He knew he was near the finish-place because he could smell it. The gentle withered fragrance of flowers past their prime, and under that a dead, sour decay. He shouted McLaren's name, sick with dread that there might not be an answer, weak with relief when there was one. He raced over tumbled rocks toward the sound. A small creeper tangled his foot and brought him down. He wrenched it by the roots from its shallow crevice and went on. As he glanced back over his shoulder he saw a thin white veil, a tiny patch in the distant air, drifting toward him.

He came to the finish-place.

It was a box canyon, quite deep, with high sheer walls, so that it was almost like a wide well. In the bottom of it bodies were thrown in a dry, spongy heap. Colorless flower-bodies, withered and gray, an incredible compost pile.

Rory McLaren lay on top of it, apparently unhurt. The two packs were beside him, with the weapons. Strewn over the heap, sitting, lying, moving feebly about, were the ones who waited, as Button had put it, to stop. Here were the aged, the faded and worn out, the imperfect and injured, where their ugliness could not offend. They seemed already dead mentally. They paid no attention to the men, nor to each other. Sheer blind vitality kept them going a little longer, as a geranium will bloom long after its cut stalk is desiccated.

"Matt," McLaren said. "Oh, God, Matt, I'm glad to see you!"

"Are you all right?"

"Sure. My leg even feels pretty good. Can you get me out?"

"Throw those packs up here."

McLaren obeyed. He began to catch Harker's feverish mood, warned by Harker's bleeding, ugly face that something nasty was afoot. Harker explained rapidly while he got out one of the ropes and half hauled McLaren out of the pit. The white veil was close now. Very close.

"Can you walk?" Harker asked.

McLaren glanced at the fleecy cloud. Harker had told him about it. "I can walk," he said. "I can run like hell."

Harker handed him the rope. "Get around the other side of the canyon. Clear across, see?" He helped McClaren on with his pack. "Stand by with the rope to pull me up. And keep to the bare rocks."

McLaren went off. He limped badly, his face twisted with pain. Harker swore. The cloud was so close that now he could see the millions of tiny seeds floating on their silken fibers, thistledown guided by the minds of the flower-people in the valley. He shrugged into his pack straps and began winding bandages and tufts of dead grass around the bone tip of a recovered spear. The edge of the cloud was almost on him when he got a spark into the improvised torch and sprang down onto the heap of dead flower-things in the pit.

He sank and floundered on the treacherous surface, struggling across it while he applied the torch. The dry, withered substance caught. He raced the flames to the far wall and glanced back. The dying creatures had not stirred, even when the fire engulfed them. Overhead, the edges of the seed-cloud flared and crisped. It moved on blindly over the fire. There was a pale flash of light and the cloud vanished in a puff of smoke.

"Rory!" Harker yelled. "Rory!"

For a long minute he stood there, coughing, strangling in thick smoke, feeling the rushing heat crisp his skin. Then, when it was almost too late, McLaren's sweating face appeared above him and the rope snaked down. Tongues of flame flicked his backside angrily as he ran monkey-fashion up the wall.

They got away from there, higher on the rocky ground, slashing occasionally with their knives at brush and creepers they could not avoid. McLaren shuddered.

"It's impossible," he said. "How do they do it?"

"They're blood cousins. Or should I say sap. Anyhow, I suppose it's like radio control—a matter of transmitting the right frequencies. Here, take it easy a minute."

McLaren sank down gratefully. Blood was seeping through

the tight bandages where Harker had incised his wound. Harker looked back into the valley.

The flower-people were spread out in a long crescent, their bright multicolored heads clear against the green plain. Harker guessed that they would be guarding the pass. He guessed that they had known what was going on in his mind as well as Button had. New form of communism, one mind for all and all for one mind. He could see that even without McLaren's disability they couldn't make it to the pass. Not a mouse could have made it.

He wondered how soon the next seed-cloud would come.

"What are we going to do, Matt? Is there any way . . ." McLaren wasn't thinking about himself. He was looking at the valley like Lucifer yearning at Paradise, and he was thinking of Viki. Not just Viki alone, but Viki as a symbol of thirty-eight hundred wanderers on the face of Venus.

"I don't know," said Harker. "The pass is out, and the caves are out . . . . hey! Remember when we were fighting off those critters by the river and you nearly started a cave-in throwing rocks? There was a fault there, right over the edge of the lake. An earthquake split. If we could get at it from the top and shake it down . . ."

It was a minute before McLaren caught on. His eyes widened. "A slide would dam up the lake. . . ."

"If the level rose enough, the Swimmers could get out." Harker gazed with sultry eyes at the bobbing flower-heads below.

"But if the valley's flooded, Matt, and those critters take over, where does that leave our people?"

"There wouldn't be too much of a slide, I don't think. The rock's solid on both sides of the fault. And anyway, the weight of the water backed up there would push through anything, even a concrete dam, in a couple of weeks." Harker studied the valley floor intently. "See the way that slopes there? Even if the slide didn't wash out, a little digging would drain the flood off down the pass. We'd just be making a new river."

"Maybe." McLaren nodded. "I guess so. But that still leaves the Swimmers. I don't think they'd be any nicer than these babies about giving up their land." His tone said he would rather fight Button's people any day.

Harker's mouth twisted in a slow grin. "The Swimmers are

water creatures, Rory. Amphibious. Also, they've lived underground, in total darkness, for God knows how long. You know what happens to angleworms when you get 'em out in the light. You know what happens to fungus that grows in the dark." He ran his fingers over his skin, almost with reverence. "Noticed anything about yourself, Rory? Or have you been too busy?"

McLaren stared. He rubbed his own skin, and winced, and rubbed again, watching his fingers leave streaks of livid white that faded instantly. "Sunburn," he said wonderingly. "My God. Sunburn!"

Harker stood up. "Let's go take a look." Down below the flower-heads were agitated. "They don't like that thought, Rory. Maybe it can be done, and they know it."

McLaren rose, leaning on a short spear like a cane. "Matt. They won't let us get away with it."

Harker frowned. "Button said there were other ways beside the seed. . . ." He turned away. "No use standing here worrying about it."

They started climbing again, very slowly on account of McLaren. Harker tried to gauge where they were in relation to the cavern beneath. The river made a good guide. The rocks were almost barren of growth here, which was a godsend. He watched, but he couldn't see anything threatening approaching from the valley. The flower-people were mere dots now, perfectly motionless.

The rock formation changed abruptly. Ancient quakes had left scars in the shape of twisted strata, great leaning slabs of granite poised like dancers, and cracks that vanished into darkness.

Harker stopped. "This is it. Listen, Rory. I want you to go off up there, out of the danger area. . . ."

"Matt, I. . . ."

"Shut up. One of us has got to be alive to take word back to the ships as soon as he can get through the valley. There's no great rush and you'll be able to travel in three—four days. You. . . ."

"But why me? You're a better mountain man. . . ."

"You're married," said Harker curtly. "It'll only take one of us to shove a couple of those big slabs down. They're practically ready to fall of their own weight. Maybe nothing will happen. Maybe I'll get out all right. But it's a little silly if both of us take the risk, isn't it?"

"Yeah. But Matt. . . ."

"Listen, kid." Harker's voice was oddly gentle. "I know what I'm doing. Give my regards to Viki and the. . . ."

He broke off with a sharp cry of pain. Looking down incredulously, he saw his body covered with little tentative flames, feeble, flickering, gone, but leaving their red footprints behind them.

McLaren had the same thing.

They stared at each other. A helpless terror took Harker by the throat. Telekinesis again. The flower-people turning his own weapon against them. They had seen fire, and what it did, and they were copying the process in their own minds, concentrating, all of them together, the whole mental force of the colony centered on the two men. He could even understand why they focused on the skin. They had taken the sunburn-thought and applied it literally.

Fire. Spontaneous combustion. A simple, easy reaction, if you knew the trick. There was something about a burning bush . . .

The attack came again, stronger this time. The flower-people were getting the feel of it now. It hurt. Oh God, it hurt. McLaren screamed. His loincloth and bandages began to smoulder.

What to do, thought Harker, *quick, tell me what to do. . . .*

The flower-people focus on us through our minds, our conscious minds. Maybe they can't get the subconscious so easily, because the thoughts are not directed, they're images, symbols, vague things. Maybe if Rory couldn't think consciously they couldn't find him. . . .

Another flare of burning, agonizing pain. In a minute they'll have the feel of it. They can keep it going. . . .

Without warning, Harker slugged McLaren heavily on the jaw and dragged him away to where the rock was firm. He did it all with astonishing strength and quickness. There was no need to save himself. He wasn't going to need himself much longer.

He went away a hundred feet or so, watching McLaren. A third attack struck him, sickened and dazed him so that he nearly fell. Rory McLaren was not touched.

Harker smiled. He turned and ran back toward the rotten place in the cliffs. A part of his conscious thought was so strongly formed that his body obeyed it automatically, not stopping even when the flames appeared again and again on his flesh, brightening, growing, strengthening as the thought-energies of Button's people meshed together. He flung down one teetering giant of stone, and the shock jarred another loose. Harker stumbled on to a third, based on a sliding bed of shale, and thrust with all his strength and beyond it, and it went too, with crashing thunder.

Harker fell. The universe dissolved into shuddering, roaring chaos beyond a bright veil of flame and a smell of burning flesh. By that time there was only one thing clear in Matt Harker's understanding—the second part of his conscious mind, linked to and even stronger than the first.

The image he carried with him into death was a tall mountain with snow on its shoulders, blazing in the sun.

It was night. Rory McLaren lay prone on a jutting shelf above the valley. Below him the valley was lost in indigo shadows, but there was a new sound in it—the swirl of water angry and swift.

There was new life in it, too. It rode the crest of the flood waters, burning gold in the blue night, shining giants returning in vengeance to their own place. Great patches of blazing jewel-toned phosphorescence dotted the water—the flower-hounds, turned loose to hunt. And in between them, rolling and leaping in deadly play, the young of the Swimmers went.

McLaren watched them hunt the forest people. He watched all night, shivering with dread, while the golden titans exacted payment for the ages they had lived in darkness. By dawn it was all over. And then, through the day, he watched the Swimmers die.

The river, turned back on itself, barred them from the caves. The strong bright light beat down. The Swimmers turned at first to greet it with a pathetic joy. And then they realized. . . .

McLaren turned away. He waited, resting, until, as Harker had predicted, the block washed away and the backed-up water could flow normally again. The valley was already draining when he found the pass. He looked up at the mountains and breathed the sweet wind, and felt a great shame and humility that he was here to do it.

He looked back toward the caves where Sim had died, and the cliffs above where he had buried what remained of Matt Harker. It seemed to him that he should say something, but no words came, only that his chest was so full he could hardly breathe. He turned mutely down the rocky pass, toward the Sea of Morning Opals and the thirty-eight hundred wanderers who had found a home.

INTO THY HANDS

by Lester del Rey (1915-   )

ASTOUNDING SCIENCE FICTION,
August

Lester del Rey is a veteran of this series ("The Day is Done," 1939; "Dark Mission," 1940; "Hereafter, Inc.," 1941; "The Wings of Night" and "Nerves," 1942; "Kindness," 1944), who published one of the first hardcover single-author collections in science fiction, the now-rare And Some Were Human *(Prime Press, 1948). He has served science fiction in just about every possible capacity—magazine editor, book editor, book reviewer, and author—a vivid example of the tremendous overlap in functions that characterizes the field.*

Although he had considerable competition from one of your editors, one of his specialties was excellent stories about robots, and "Into Thy Hands" is one of his best on the subject.

(I mentioned in an earlier introduction that Cliff Simak had felt Fritz Leiber to have been "under-appreciated." My feeling is that Lester is. He is a most remarkable writer, always clear and always interesting, whatever it is he does. Whether he writes a history of science fiction, or a eulogy, or an obituary, there are always insights within them that I don't think you'll find anywhere else.

I always listen carefully to whatever he says for I know that I will come across sparkles of thought that I can adopt and treat as my own. Lester doesn't mind; there are plenty of other sparkles where those came from.

One of my own fictional characters is modeled on Lester. That is Emmanuel Rubin of my mystery series concerning the Black Widowers. Lester denies the similarity but I can prove it. Manny Rubin is always engaged in controversy in those stories and, no matter how I try, he manages to win every argument. If that isn't Lester, nothing is. I.A.)

Simon Ames was old, and his face was bitter as only that of a confirmed idealist can be. Now a queer mixture of emotions crossed it momentarily, as he watched the workmen begin pouring cement to fill the small opening of the domelike structure, but his eyes returned again to the barely visible robot within.

"The last Ames' Model 10," he said ruefully to his son. "And even then I couldn't put in full memory coils! Only the physical sciences here; biologicals in the other male form, humanities in the female. I had to fall back on books and equipment to cover the rest. We're already totally converted to soldier robots, and no more humanoid experiments. Dan, is there no way conceivable war can be avoided?"

The young Rocket Force captain shrugged, and his mouth twitched unhappily. "None, Dad. They've fed their people on the glories of carnage and loot so long they have to find some pretext to use their hordes of warrior robots."

"The stupid, blind idiots!" The old man shuddered. "Dan, it sounds like old wives' fears, but this time it's true; unless we somehow avoid or win this war quickly, there'll be no one left to wage another. I've spent my life on robots, I know what they can do—and should never be made to do! Do you think I'd waste a fortune on these storehouses on a mere whim?"

"I'm not arguing, Dad. God knows, I feel the same!" Dan watched the workmen pour the last concrete, to leave no break in the twenty-foot thick walls. "Well, at least if anyone does survive, you've done all you can for them. Now it's in the hands of God!"

Simon Ames nodded, but there was no satisfaction on his face as he turned back with his son. "All we could—and never enough! And God? I wouldn't even know which of the three to pray survives—science, life, culture." The words sighed into silence, and his eyes went back to the filled-in tunnel.

Behind them, the ugly dome hugged the ground while the rains of God and of man's destruction washed over it. Snow covered it and melted, and other things built up that no summer sun could disperse, until the ground was level with its top. The forest crept forward, and the seasons flicked by in unchanging changes that pyramided decade upon century. Inside, the shining case of SA-10 waited immovably.

And at last the lightning struck, blasting through a tree, downward into the dome, to course through a cable, short-circuit a ruined timing switch, and spend itself on the ground below.

Above the robot, a cardinal burst into song, and he looked up, his stolid face somehow set in a look of wonder. For a moment, he listened, but the bird had flown away at the sight of his lumbering figure. With a tired little sigh, he went on, crashing through the brush of the forest until he came back near the entrance to his cave.

The sun was bright above, and he studied it thoughtfully; the word he knew, and even the complex carbon-chain atomic breakdown that went on within it. But he did not know how he knew, or why.

For a second longer he stood there silently, then opened his mouth for a long wailing cry. "Adam! Adam, come forth!" But there were doubts in the oft-repeated call now and the pose of his head as he waited. And again only the busy sounds of the forest came back to him.

"Or God? God, do you hear me?"

But the answer was the same. A field mouse slipped out from among the grass and a hawk soared over the woods. The wind rustled among the trees, but there was no sign from the Creator. With a lingering backward look, he turned slowly to the tunnel he had made and wriggled back down it into his cave.

Inside, light still came from a single unbroken bulb, and he let his eyes wander, from the jagged breech in the thick wall, across to where some ancient blast had tossed crumpled concrete against the opposite side. Between lay only ruin and dirt. Once, apparently, that half had been filled with books and films, but now there were only rotted fragments of bindings and scraps of useless plastic tape mixed with broken glass in the filth of the floor.

Only on the side where he had been was the ruin less than complete. There stood the instruments of a small laboratory, many still useful, and he named them one by one, from the purring atomic generator to the projector and screen set up on one table.

Here, and in his mind, were order and logic, and the world above had conformed to an understandable pattern. He alone seemed to be without purpose. How had he come here, and why had he no memory of himself? If there was no purpose, why was he sentient at all? The questions held no discoverable answers.

There were only the cryptic words on the scrap of plastic tape preserved inside the projector. But what little of them was understandable was all he had; he snapped off the light and squatted down behind the projector, staring intently at the screen as he flicked the machine on.

There was a brief fragment of some dark swirling, and then dots and bright spheres, becoming suns and planets that spun out of nothing into a celestial pattern. "In the beginning," said a voice quietly, "God created the heavens and the earth." And the screen filled with that, and the beginnings of life.

"Symbolism?" the robot muttered. Geology and astronomy were part of his knowledge, at least; and yet, in a mystic beauty, this was true enough. Even the life-forms above had fitted with those being created on the screen.

Then a new voice, not unlike his own resonant power, filled the speaker. "Let us go down and create man in our image!" And a mist of light that symbolized God appeared, shaping man from the dust of the ground and breathing life into him. Adam grew lonely, and Eve was made from his rib, to be shown Eden and tempted by the serpentine mist of darkness; and she tempted the weak Adam, until God discovered their sin and banished them. But the banishment ended in a blur of ruined film as the speaker went dead.

The robot shut it off, trying to read its meaning. It *must* concern him, since he alone was here to see it. And how could that be unless he were one of its characters? Not Eve or Satan, but perhaps Adam; but then God should have answered him. On the other hand, if he were God, then perhaps the record was unfulfilled and Adam not yet formed, so that no answer could be given.

He nodded slowly to himself. Why should he not have rested here with this film to remind him of his plan, while the world readied itself for Adam? And now, awake again, he must go forth and create man in his own image! But first, the danger of which the film had warned must be removed.

He straightened, determination coming into his steps as he squirmed purposefully upwards. Outside the sun was still shining, and he headed toward it into the grossly unkempt Eden forest. Now stealth came to him as he moved silently through the undergrowth, like a great metal wraith, with eyes that darted about and hands ready to snap forward at lightning speed.

And at last he saw it, curled up near a large rock. It was smaller than he had expected, a mere six feet of black, scaly suppleness, but the shape and forked tongue were unmistakable. He was on it with a blur of motion and a cry of elation; and when he moved away, the lifeless object on the rock was forever past corrupting the most naïve Eve.

The morning sun found the robot bent over what had once been a wild pig, a knife moving precisely in his hand. Delicately he opened the heart and manipulated it, studying the valve action. Life, he was deciding, was highly complex, and a momentary doubt struck him. It had seemed easy on the film! And at times he wondered why he should know the complex order of the heavens but nothing of this other creation of his.

But at last he buried the pig's remains, and settled down among the varicolored clays he had collected, his fingers moving deftly as he rolled a white type into bones for the skeleton, followed by a red clay heart. The tiny nerves and blood vessels were beyond his means, but that could not be helped; and surely if he had created the gigantic sun from nothing, Adam could rise from the crudeness of his sculpturing.

The sun climbed higher, and the details multiplied. Inside the last organ was complete, including the grayish lump that was the brain, and he began the red sheathing of muscles. Here more thought was required to adapt the arrangement of the pig to the longer limbs and different structure of this new body; but his mind pushed grimly on with the mathematics involved, and at last it was finished.

Unconsciously he began a crooning imitation of the bird songs as his fingers molded the colored clays to hide the muscles and give smooth symmetry to the body. He had been forced to guess at the color, though the dark lips on the film had obviously been red from blood below them.

Twilight found him standing back, nodding approval of the work. It was a faithful copy of the film Adam, waiting only the breath of life; and that must come from him, be a part of the forces that flowed through his own metal nerves and brain.

Gently he fastened wires to the head and feet of the clay body; then he threw back his chest plate to fasten the other ends to his generator terminals, willing the current out into the figure lying before him. Weakness flooded through him instantly, threatening to black out his consciousness, but he did not begrudge the energy. Steam was spurting up and covering the figure as a mist had covered Adam, but it slowly subsided, and he stopped the current, stealing a second for relief as the full current coursed back through him. Then softly he unhooked the wires and drew them back.

"Adam!" The command rang through the forest, vibrant with his urgency. "Adam, rise up! I, your creator, command it!"

But the figure lay still, and now he saw great cracks in it, while the noble smile had baked into a gaping leer. There was no sign of life! It was dead, as the ground from which it came.

He squatted over it, moaning, weaving from side to side, and his fingers tried to draw the ugly cracks together, only to cause greater ruin. And at last he stood up, stamping his legs until all that was left was a varicolored smear on the rock. Still he stamped and moaned as he destroyed the symbol of his failure. The moon mocked down at him with a wise and cynical face, and he howled at it in rage and anguish, to be answered by a lonely owl, querying his identity.

A powerless God, or a Godless Adam! Things had gone so well in the film as Adam rose from the dust of the ground——

But the film was symbolism, and he had taken it literally! Of course he had failed. The pigs were not dust, but colloidal jelly complexes. And they knew more than he, for there had been little ones that proved they could somehow pass the breath of life along.

Suddenly he squared his shoulders and headed into the forest again. Adam should yet rise to ease his loneliness. The pigs knew the secret, and he could learn it; what he needed now were more pigs, and they should not be too hard to obtain.

But two weeks later it was a worried robot who sat watching his pigs munch contentedly at their food. Life, instead of growing simpler, had become more complicated. The fluoroscope and repaired electron microscope had shown him much, but always something was lacking. Life seemed to begin only with life; for even the two basic cells were alive in some manner strangely different from his own. Of course God-life might differ from animal-life, but——

With a shrug he dismissed his metaphysics and turned back to the laboratory, avoiding the piglets that ambled trustingly under his feet. Slowly he drew out the last ovum from the nutrient fluid in which he kept it, placing it on a slide and under the optical microscope. Then, with a little platinum filament, he brought a few male spermatozoa toward the ovum, his fingers moving surely through the thousandths of an inch needed to place it.

His technique had grown from failures, and now the sperm cell found and pierced the ovum. As he watched, the round single cell began to lengthen and divide across the middle. This was going to be one of his successes! There were two, then four cells, and his hands made lightning, infinitesimal gestures, keeping it within the microscope field while he changed the slide for a thin membrane, lined with thinner tubes to carry oxygen, food, and tiny amounts of the stimulating and controlling hormones with which he hoped to shape its formation.

Now there were eight cells, and he waited feverishly for them to reach toward the membrane. But they did not! As he watched, another division began, but stopped; the cells had died again. All his labor and thought had been futile, as always.

He stood there silently, relinquishing all pretensions to godhood. His mind abdicated, letting the dream vanish into nothingness; and there was nothing to take its place and give him purpose and reason—only a vacuum instead of a design.

Dully he unbarred the rude cage and began chasing the

grumbling, reluctant pigs out and up the tunnel, into the forest and away. It was a dull morning, with no sun apparent, and it matched his mood as the last one disappeared, leaving him doubly lonely. They had been poor companions, but they had occupied his time, and the little ones had appealed to him. Now even they were gone.

Wearily he dropped his six hundred pounds onto the turf, staring at the black clouds over him. An ant climbed up his body inquisitively, and he watched it without interest. Then it, too, was gone.

"Adam!" The cry came from the woods, ringing and compelling. "Adam, come forth!"

"God!" With metal limbs that were awkward and unsteady, he jerked upright. In the dark hour of his greatest need, God had finally come! "God, here I am!"

"Come forth, Adam, Adam! Come forth, Adam!"

With a wild cry, the robot dashed forward toward the woods, an electric tingling suffusing him. He was no longer unwanted, no longer a lost chip in the storm. God had come for him. He stumbled on, tripping over branches, crashing through bushes, heedless of his noise; let God know his eagerness. Again the call came, now farther aside, and he turned a bit, lumbering forward. "Here I am, I'm coming!"

God would ease his troubles and explain why he was so different from the pigs; God would know all that. And then there'd be Eve, and no more loneliness! He'd have trouble keeping her from the Tree of Knowledge, but he wouldn't mind that!

And from still a different direction the call reached him. Perhaps God was not pleased with his noise. The robot quieted his steps and went forward reverently. Around him the birds sang, and now the call came again, ringing and close. He hastened on, striving to blend speed with quiet in spite of his weight.

The pause was longer this time, but when the call came it was almost overhead. He bowed lower and crept to the ancient oak from which it came, uncertain, half-afraid, but burning with anticipation.

"Come forth, Adam, Adam!" The sound was directly above, but God did not manifest Himself visibly. Slowly the robot looked up through the boughs of the tree. Only a bird was there—and from its open beak the call came forth again. "Adam, Adam!"

A mockingbird he'd heard imitating the other birds, now mimicking his own voice and words! And he'd followed that through the forest, hoping to find God! He screeched suddenly at the bird, his rage so shrill that it leaped from the branch in hasty flight, to perch in another tree and cock its head at him. "God?" it asked in his voice, and changed to the raucous call of a jay.

The robot slumped back against the tree, refusing to let hope ebb wholly from him. He knew so little of God; might not He have used the bird to call him here? At least the tree was not unlike the one under which God had put Adam to sleep before creating Eve.

First sleep, *then* the coming of God! He stretched out determinedly, trying to imitate the pigs' torpor, fighting back his mind's silly attempts at speculation as to where his rib might be. It was slow and hard, but he persisted grimly, hypnotizing himself into mental numbness; and bit by bit, the sounds of the forest faded to only a trickle in his head. Then that, too, was stilled.

He had no way of knowing how long it lasted, but suddenly he sat up groggily, to the rumble of thunder, while a torrent of lashing rain washed in blinding sheets over his eyes. For a second, he glanced quickly at his side, but there was no scar.

Fire forked downward into a nearby tree, throwing splinters of it against him. This was definitely not according to the film! He groped to his feet, flinging some of the rain from his face, to stumble forward toward his cave. Again lightning struck, nearer, and he increased his pace to a driving run. The wind lashed the trees, snapping some with wild ferocity, and it took the full power of his magnets to forge ahead at ten miles an hour instead of his normal fifty. Once it caught him unaware, and crashed him down over a rock with a wild clang of metal, but it could not harm him, and he stumbled on until he reached the banked-up entrance of his muddy tunnel.

Safe inside, he dried himself with the infrared lamp, sitting beside the hole and studying the wild fury of the gale. Surely its furor held no place for Eden, where dew dampened the leaves in the evening under caressing, musical breezes!

He nodded slowly, his clenched jaws relaxing. This could

not be Eden, and God expected him there. Whatever evil knowledge of Satan had lured him here and stolen his memory did not matter; all that counted was to return, and that should be simple, since the Garden lay among rivers. Tonight he'd prepare here out of the storm, and tomorrow he'd follow the stream in the woods until it led him where God waited.

With the faith of a child, he turned back and began tearing the thin berylite panels from his laboratory tables and cabinets, picturing his homecoming and Eve. Outside the storm raged and tore, but he no longer heard it. Tomorrow he would start for home! The word was misty in his mind, as all the nicer words were, but it had a good sound, free of loneliness, and he liked it.

Six hundred long endless years had dragged their slow way into eternity, and even the tough concrete floor was pitted by those centuries of pacing and waiting. Time had eroded all hopes and plans and wonder, and now there was only numb despair, too old to vent itself in rage, or madness, even.

The female robot slumped motionlessly on the atomic excavator, her eyes centered aimlessly across the dome, beyond the tiers of books and films and the hulking machines that squatted eternally on the floor. There a pickax lay, and her eyes rested on it listlessly; once, when the dictionary revealed its picture and purpose, she had thought it the key to escape, but now it was only another symbol of futility.

She wandered over aimlessly, picking it up by its two metal handles and striking the wooden blade against the wall; another splinter chipped from the wood, and century-old dust dropped to the floor, but that offered no escape. Nothing did. Mankind and her fellow robots must have perished long ago, leaving her neither hope for freedom nor use for it if it were achieved.

Once she had planned and schemed with all her remarkable knowledge of psychology to restore man's heritage, but now the note-littered table was only a mockery; she thrust out a weary hand—

And froze into a metal statue! Faintly, through all the metal mesh and concrete, a dim, weak signal trickled into the radio that was part of her!

With all her straining energy, she sent out an answering call; but there was no response. As she stood rigidly for long minutes, the signals grew stronger, but remained utterly aloof and unaware of her. Now some sudden shock seemed to cut through them, raising their power until the thoughts of another robot mind were abruptly clear—thoughts without sense, clothed in madness! And even as the lunacy registered, they began to fade; second by second, they dimmed into the distance and left her alone again and hopeless!

With a wild, clanging yell, she threw the useless pickax at the wall, watching it rebound in echoing din. But she was no longer aimless; her eyes had noted chipped concrete breaking away with the sharp metal point, and she caught the pick before it could touch the floor, seizing the nub of wood in small, strong hands. The full force of her magnet lifted and swung, while her feet kicked aside the rubble that came cascading down from the force of her blows.

Beyond that rapidly crumbling wall lay freedom and—madness! Surely there could be no human life in a world that could drive a robot mad, but if there were— She thrust back the picture and went savagely on attacking the massive wall.

The sun shone on a drenched forest filled with havoc from the storm, to reveal the male robot pacing tirelessly along the banks of the shallow stream. In spite of the heavy burden he carried, his legs moved swiftly now, and when he came to sandy stretches, or clear land that bore only turf, his great strides lengthened still farther; already he had dallied too long with delusions in this unfriendly land.

Now the stream joined a larger one, and he stopped, dropping his ungainly bundle and ripping it apart. Scant minutes later, he was pushing an assembled berylite boat out and climbing in. The little generator from the electron microscope purred softly and a stream jet began hissing underneath; it was crude, but efficient, as the boiling wake behind him testified, and while slower than his fastest pace, there would be no detours or impassable barriers to bother him.

The hours sped by and the shadows lengthened again, but now the stream was wider, and his hopes increased, though he watched the banks idly, not yet expecting Eden. Then he rounded a bend to jerk upright and head toward shore, observing something totally foreign to the landscape. As he beached the boat, and drew nearer, he saw a great gaping hole bored into the earth for a hundred feet in depth and a quarter mile in diameter, surrounded by obviously artificial ruins. Tall bent shafts stuck up haphazardly, amid jumbles of concrete and bits of artifacts damaged beyond recognition. Nearby a pole leaned at a silly angle, bearing a sign.

He scratched the corrosion off and made out dim words:

WELCOME TO HOGANVILLE. POP. 1,876.

It meant nothing to him, but the ruins fascinated him. This must be some old trick of Satan; such ugliness could be nothing else.

Shaking his head, he turned back to the boat, to speed on while the stars came out. Again he came to ruins, larger and harder to see, since the damage was more complete and the forest had claimed most of it. He was only sure because of the jagged pits in which not even a blade of grass would grow. And sometimes as the night passed there were smaller pits, as if some single object had been blasted out of existence. He gave up the riddle of such things, finally; it was no concern of his.

When morning came again, the worst ruins were behind, and the river was wide and strong, suggesting that the trip must be near its end. Then the faint salty tang of the ocean reached him, and he whooped loudly, scanning the country for an observation point.

Ahead, a low hill broke the flat country, topped by a rounded bowl of green, and he made toward it. The boat crunched on gravel, and he was springing off over the turf to the hill, up it, and onto the bowl-shaped top that was covered with vines. Here the whole lower course of the river was visible, with no more large branches in the twenty-five miles to the sea. The land was pleasant and gentle, and it was not hard to imagine Eden out there.

But now for the first time, as he started down, he noticed that the mound was not part of the hill as it had seemed. It was of the same gray-green concrete as the walls of the cave from which he had broken, like a bird from an egg.

And here was another such thing, like an egg unhatched yet but already cracking, as the gouged-out pit on its surface near him testified. For a moment, the idea contained in the figure of speech staggered him, and then he was ripping away the concealing vines and dropping into the hole, reaching for a small plate pinned to an unharmed section nearby. It was a poor tool, but if Eve were trapped inside, needing help to break the shell, it would do.

"To you who may survive the holocaust, I, Simon Ames——" The words caught his eyes, drawing his attention to the plate in spite of his will, their tense strangeness pulling his gaze across them. "—dedicate this. There is no easy entrance, but you will expect no easy heritage. Force your way, take what is within, use it! To you who need it and will work for it, I have left all knowledge that was——"

Knowledge! Knowledge, forbidden by God! Satan had put before his path the unquestioned thing meant by the Tree of Knowledge symbol, concealed as a false egg, and he had almost been caught! A few minutes more——! He shuddered, and backed out, but optimism was freshening inside him again. Let it be the Tree! That meant this was really part of Eden, and being forewarned by God's marker, he had no fear for the wiles of Satan, alive or dead.

With long, loping strides he headed down the hill toward the meadows and woods, leaving the now useless boat behind. He would enter Eden on his own feet, as God had made him!

Half an hour later he was humming happily to himself as he passed beside lush fields, rich with growing things, along a little woodland path. Here was order and logic, as they should be. This was surely Eden!

And to confirm it came Eve! She was coming down the trail ahead, her hair floating behind, and some loose stuff draped over her hips and breasts, but the form underneath was Woman, beautiful and unmistakable. He drew back out of sight, suddenly timid and uncertain, only vaguely wondering how she came here before him. Then she was beside him, and he moved impulsively, his voice a whisper of ecstasy!

"Eve!"

"Oh, Dan! Dan!" It was a wild shriek that cut the air, and she was rushing away in panic, into the deeper woods. He shook his head in bewilderment, while his own legs began a more forceful pumping after her. He was almost upon her when he saw the serpent, alive and stronger than before!

But not for long! As a single gasp broke from her, one of his arms lifted her aside, while the other snapped out to pinch the fanged head completely off the body. His voice was gently reproving as he put her down. "You shouldn't have fled to the serpent, Eve!"

"To—— Ugh! But—— You could have killed me before it

struck!" The taut whiteness of fear was fading from her face, replaced by defiance and doubt.

"Killed you?"

"You're a robot! Dan!" Her words cut off as a brawny figure emerged from the underbrush, an ax in one hand and a magnificent dog at his heels. "Dan, he saved me . . . but he's a robot!"

"I saw, Syl. Steady! Edge this way, if you can. Good! They sometimes get passive streaks, I've heard. Shep!"

The dog's thick growl answered, but his eyes remained glued to the robot. "Yeah, Dan?"

"Get the people; just yell robot and hike back. O.K., scram! You . . . what do you want?"

SA-IO grunted harshly, hunching his shoulders. "Things that don't exist! Companionship and a chance to see my strength and the science I know. Maybe I'm not supposed to have such things, but that's what I wanted!"

"Hm-m-m. There are fairy stories about friendly robots hidden somewhere to help us, at that. We could use help. What's your name, and where from?"

Bitterness crept into the robot's voice as he pointed up river. "From the sunward side. So far, I've only found who I'm not!"

"So? Meant to get up there myself when the colony got settled." Dan paused, eyeing the metal figure speculatively. "We lost our books in the hell-years, mostly, and the survivors weren't exactly technicians. So while we do all right with animals, agriculture, medicine and such, we're pretty primitive otherwise. If you really do know the sciences, why not stick around?"

The robot had seen too many hopes shattered like his clay man to believe wholly in this promise of purpose and companionship, but his voice caught as he answered. "You . . . want me?"

"Why not? You're a storehouse of knowledge, Say-Ten, and we——"

"Satan?"

"Your name; there on your chest." Dan pointed with his left hand, his body suddenly tense. "See? Right there!"

And now, as SA-IO craned his neck, the foul letters were visible, high on his chest! Ess, aye—

His first warning was the ax that crashed against his chest, to rock him back on his heels, and come driving down again, powered by muscles that seemed almost equal to his own. It struck again, and something snapped inside him. All the strength vanished, and he collapsed to the ground with a jarring crash, knocking his eyelids closed. Then he lay there, unable even to open them.

He did not try, but lay waiting almost eagerly for the final blows that would finish him. Satan, the storehouse of knowledge, the tempter of men—the one person he had learned to hate! He'd come all this way to find a name and a purpose; now he had them! No Wonder God had locked him away in a cave to keep him from men.

"Dead! That little fairy story threw him off guard." There was a tense chuckle from the man. "Hope his generator's still O.K. We could heat every house in the settlement with that. Wonder where his hideout was?"

"Like the one up north with all the weapons hidden? Oh, Dan!" A strange smacking sound accompanied that, and then her voice sobered. "We'd better get back for help in hauling him."

Their feet moved away, leaving the robot still motionless but no longer passive. The Tree of Knowledge, so easily seen without the vine covering over the hole, was barely twenty miles away, and no casual search could miss it! He had to destroy it first!

But the little battery barely could maintain his consciousness, and the generator no longer served him. Delicate detectors were sending their messages through his nerves, assuring him it was functioning properly under automatic check, but beyond his control. Part of the senseless signaling device within him must have been defective, unless the baking of the clay man had somehow overloaded a part of it, and now it was completely wrecked, shorting aside all the generator control impulses, leaving him unable to move a finger.

Even when he blanked his mind almost completely out, the battery could not power his hands. His evil work was done; now he would heat their house, while they sought the temptation he had offered them. And he could do nothing to stop it. God denied him the chance to right the wrong he had done, even.

Bitterly he prayed on, while strange noises sounded near him and he felt himself lifted and carried bumpily at a rapid rate. God would not hear him! And at last he stopped, while the bumping went on to whatever end he was destined. Finally even that stopped, and there were a few moments of absolute quiet.

"Listen! I know you still live!" It was a gentle, soothing voice, hypnotically compelling, that broke in on the dark swirls of his thoughts. Brief thoughts of God crossed his mind, but it was a female voice, which must mean one of the settlement women who must have believed him and be trying to save him in secret. It came again. "Listen and believe me! You *can* move—a very very little, but enough for me to see. Try to repair yourself, and let me be the strength in your hands. Try! Ah, your arm!"

It was inconceivable that she could follow his imperceptible movements, and yet he felt his arm lifted and placed on his chest as the thought crossed his mind. But it was none of his business to question how or why. All his energy must be devoted to getting his strength before the men could find the Tree!

"So . . . I turn this . . . this nut. And the other— There, the plate is off. What do I do now?"

That stopped him. His life force had been fatal to a pig, and probably would kill a woman. Yet she trusted him. He dared not move—but the idea must have been father to the act, for his fingers were brushed aside and her arms scraped over his chest, to be followed by an instant flood of strength pouring through him.

Her fingers had slipped over his eyes, but he did not need them as he ripped the damaged receiver from its welds and tossed it aside. Now there was worry in her voice, over the crooning cadence she tried to maintain. "Don't be too surprised at what you may see. Everything's all right!"

"Everything's all right!" he repeated dutifully, lingering over the words as his voice sounded again in his ears. For a moment more, while he reaffixed his plate, he let her hold his eyes closed. "Woman, who are you?"

"Eve. Or at least, Adam, those names will do for us." And the fingers withdrew, though she remained out of sight behind him.

But there was enough for the first glance before him. In spite of the tiers of bookcases and film magazines, the machines, and the size of the laboratory, this was plainly the double of his own cave, circled with the same concrete walls! That could only mean the Tree!

With a savage lurch, he was facing the rescuer, seeing another robot, smaller, more graceful, and female in form, calling to all the hunger and loneliness he had known! But those emotions had betrayed him before, and he forced them back bitterly. There could be no doubt while the damning letters spelled out her name. Satan was male and female, and Evil had gone forth to rescue its kind!

Some of the warring hell of emotions must have shown in his movements, for she was retreating before him, her hands fumbling up to cover the marks at which he stared. "Adam, no! The man read it wrong—dreadfully wrong. It's not a name. We're machines, and all machines have model numbers, like these. Satan wouldn't advertise his name. And I never had evil intentions!"

"Neither did I!" He bit the words out, stumbling over the objects on the floor as he edged her back slowly into a blind alley, while striving to master his own rebellious emotions at what he must do. "Evil must be destroyed! Knowledge is forbidden to men!"

"Not all knowledge! Wait, let me finish! Any condemned person has a right to a few last words—— It was the Tree of Knowledge of *Good and Evil.* God called it that! And He had to forbid them to eat, because they couldn't know which was the good; don't you see, He was only protecting them until they were older and able to choose for themselves! Only Satan gave them evil fruit—hate and *murder*—to ruin them. Would you call healing the sick, good government, or improving other animals evil? That's knowledge, Adam, glorious knowledge God wants man to have. Can't you see?"

For a second as she read his answer, she turned to flee; then, with a little sobbing cry, she was facing him again, unresisting. "All right, murder me! Do you think death frightens me after being imprisoned here for six hundred years with no way to break free? Only get it over with!"

Surprise and the sheer audacity of the lie held his hands as his eyes darted from the atomic excavator to a huge drill, and a drum marked as explosives. And yet—even that cursory glance could not overlook the worn floor and thousand marks of age-long occupation, though the surface of the dome had been unbroken a few hours before. Reluctantly, his eyes swung back to the excavator, and hers followed.

"Useless! The directions printed on it say to move the

thing marked 'Orifice Control' to zero before starting. It can't be moved!"

She stopped, abruptly speechless, as his fingers lifted the handle from its ratchet and spun it easily back to zero! Then she was shaking her head in defeat and lifting listless hands to help him with the unfastening of her chest plate. There was no color left in her voice.

"Six hundred years because I didn't lift a handle! Just because I have absolutely no conception of mechanics, where all men have some instinct they take for granted. They'd have mastered these machines in time and learned to read meaning into the books I memorized without even understanding the titles. But I'm like a dog tearing at a door, with a simple latch over his nose. Well, that's that. Good-bye, Adam!"

But perversely, now that the terminals lay before him, he hesitated. After all, the instructions had not mentioned the ratchet; it was too obvious to need mention, but—— He tried to picture such ignorance, starting at one of the Elementary Radio books above him. "Application of a Cavity Resonator." Mentally, he could realize that a nonscience translation was meaningless: Use of a sound producer or strengthener in a hole! And then the overlooked factor struck him.

"But you did get out!"

"Because I lost my temper and threw the pickax. That's how I found the metal was the blade, not the wood. The only machines I could use were the projector and typer I was meant to use—and the typer broke!"

"Um-m-m." He picked the little machine up, noting the yellowed incomplete page still in it, even as he slipped the carriage tension cord back on its hook. But his real attention was devoted to the cement dust ground into the splintered handle of the pick.

No man or robot could be such a complete and hopeless dope, and yet he no longer doubted. She was a robot moron! And if knowledge were evil, then surely she belonegd to God! All the horror of his contemplated murder vanished, leaving his mind clean and weak before the relief that flooded him as he motioned her out.

"All right, you're not evil. You can go."

"And you?"

And himself? Before, as Satan, her arguments would have

been plausible, and he had discounted them. But now—it *had* been the Tree of Knowledge of Good and Evil! And yet——

"Dogs!" She caught at him, dragging him to the entrance where the baying sound was louder. "They're hunting you, Adam—dozens of them!"

He nodded, studying the distant forms of men on horseback, while his fingers busied themselves with a pencil and scrap of paper. "And they'll be here in twenty minutes. Good or evil, they must not find what's here. Eve, there's a boat by the river; pull the red handle the way you want to go, hard for fast, a light pull for slow. Here's a map to my cave, and you'll be safe there."

Almost instantly, he was back at the excavator and in its saddle, his fingers flashing across its panel; its heavy generator bellowed gustily, and the squat, heavy machine began twisting through the narrow aisles and ramming obstructions aside. Once outside, where he could use its full force without danger of backwash, ten minutes would leave only a barren hill; and the generator could be overdriven by adjustment to melt itself and the machine into useless slag.

"Adam!" She was spraddling into the saddle behind him, shouting over the roar of the thin blade of energy that was enlarging the tunnel.

"Go on, get away, Eve! You can't stop me!"

"I don't want to—they're not ready for such machines as this, yet! And between us, we can rebuild everything here, anyhow. Adam?"

He grunted uneasily, unable to turn away from the needle beam. It was hard enough trying to think without her distraction, knowing that he dared not take chances and must destroy himself, while her words and the instincts within him fought against his resolution. "You talk too much!"

"And I'll talk a lot more, until you behave sensibly! You'll make your mind sick, trying to decide now; come up the river for six months with me. You can't do any harm there, even if you are Satan! Then, when you've thought it over, Adam, you can do what you like. But not now!"

"For the last time, will you go?" He dared not think now, while he was testing his way through the flawed, cracked cement, and yet he could not quiet his mind to her words, that went on and on. "GO!"

"Not without you! Adam, my receiver isn't defective; I

knew you'd try to kill me when I rescued you! Do you think I'll give up so easily now?"

He snapped the power to silence with a rude hand, flinging around to face her. "You knew—and still saved me? Why?"

"Because I needed you, and the world needs you. You had to live, even if you killed me!"

Then the generator roared again, knifing its way through the last few inches, and he swung out of the dome and began turning it about. As the savage bellow of full power poured out of the main orifice, he turned his head to her and nodded.

She might be the dumbest robot in creation, but she was also the sweetest. It was wonderful to be needed and wanted!

And behind him, Eve nodded to herself, blessing Simon Ames for listing psychology as a humanity. In six months, she could complete his re-education and still have time to recite the whole of the Book he knew as a snatch of film. But not yet! Most certainly not Leviticus yet; Genesis would give her trouble enough.

It was wonderful to be needed and wanted!

Spring had come again, and Adam sat under one of the budding trees, idly feeding one of the new crop of piglets as Eve's hands moved swiftly, finishing what were to be his clothes, carefully copied from those of Dan.

They were almost ready to go south and mingle with men in the task of leading the race back to its heritage. Already the yielding plastic he had synthesized and she had molded over them was a normal part of them, and the tiny magnetic muscles he had installed no longer needed thought to reveal their emotions in human expressions. He might have been only an uncommonly handsome man as he stood up and went over to her.

"Still hunting God?" she asked lightly, but there was no worry on her face. The metaphysical binge was long since cured.

A thoughtful smile grew on his face as he began donning the clothes. "He is still where I found Him—— Something inside us that needs no hunting. No, Eve, I was wishing the other robot had survived. Even though we found no trace of his dome where your records indicated, I still feel he should be with us."

"Perhaps he is, in spirit, since you insist robots have souls. Where's your faith, Adam?"

But there was no mockery inside her. Souls or not, Adam's God had been very good to them.

And far to the south, an aged figure limped over rubble to the face of a cliff. Under his hands, a cleverly concealed door swung open, and he pushed inward, closing and barring it behind him, and heading down the narrow tunnel to a rounded cavern at its end. It had been years since he had been there, but the place was still home to him as he creaked down onto a bench and began removing tattered, travel-stained clothes. Last of all, he pulled a mask and gray wig from his head, to reveal the dented and worn body of the third robot.

He sighed wearily as he glanced at the few tattered books and papers he had salvaged from the ruinous growth of stalagmites and stalactites within the chamber, and at the corroded switch the unplanned dampness had shorted seven hundred years before. And finally, his gaze rested on his greatest treasure. It was faded, even under the plastic cover, but the bitter face of Simon Ames still gazed out in recognizable form.

The third robot nodded toward it with a strange mixture of old familiarity and ever-new awe. "Over two thousand miles in my condition, Simon Ames, to check on a story I heard in one of the colonies, and months of searching for them. But I had to know. But they're good for the world. They'll bring all the things I couldn't, and their thoughts are young and strong, as the race is young and strong."

For a moment, he stared about the chamber and to the tunnel his adapted bacteria had eaten toward the outside world, resting his eyes again on the picture. Then he cut off the main generator and settled down in the darkness.

"Seven hundred years since I came out to find man extinct on the earth," he muttered to the picture. "Four hundred since I learned enough to dare attempt his re-creation, and over three hundred since the last of my superfrozen human ova grew to success. Now I've done my part. Man has an unbroken tradition back to your race, with no knowledge of the break. He's strong and young and fruitful, and he has new leaders, better than I could ever be alone. I can do no more for him!"

For a moment there was only the sound of his hands sliding against metal, and then a faint sigh. "Into my hands, Simon Ames, you gave your race. Now, into Thy Hands, God of that race, if you exist as my brother believes, I commend him—and my spirit."

Then there was a click as his hands found the switch to his generator, and final silence.

CAMOUFLAGE

by Henry Kuttner

ASTOUNDING SCIENCE FICTION,
September

"Camouflage" is about a cyborg, a person who is part human and part machine. Of course, cyborgs are now commonplace, especially in a technical sense, since an artificial limb with moving parts or a pacemaker would meet the definition. Cyborgs have been common in science fiction since the Gernsback era, one early example being E. V. Odle's The Clockwork Man *of 1923. The general trend toward biological extrapolation in recent sf has produced several outstanding novels in the last few years, including Frederik Pohl's award-winning* Man Plus *(1976). An excellent anthology on the subject is* Human-Machines *(1975), edited by Thomas N. Scortia and George Zebrowski. The Kuttners employed cyborgs in a number of their stories, and C. L. Moore's "No Woman Born" (see Volume 6 of this series) is justly considered a classic treatment of the theme.*

(Ever since I was quite young, I have thought considerably about the possibility of being reduced to a simple brain with everything else just prosthetic attachments. I read about it in the Hawk Carse stories of the early 1930s to say nothing of the popular Professor Jameson series. It seemed the one sure route to immortality without giving up anything that was really essential to humanity. Your consciousness, your intelligence, your memory, your ca-

pacity to learn would all be untouched and as for physical sensations and even sex—well, they were not essential.

Yet come to think of it, evolution has done its best to produce just such a situation. The brain is tightly enclosed in a bony cranium so that it is the best protected part of the body. It is wired by way of nerves to the best prosthetic attachments evolution could manage—made of flesh and blood, to be sure. And to top it off, the brain is long-lived. Although its cells are too specialized to multiply they nevertheless can endure, and work, for over a hundred years.

But then, after many a summer, they die. And they would die even if they were protected by metal rather than bone, and no matter how efficiently they were fed. Of course, we might construct an artificial brain of material more durable and just as compact and versatile as the cells of the human brain, but that would be a whole other ball game. I.A.)

Talman was sweating by the time he reached 16 Knobhill Road. He had to force himself to touch the annunciator plate. There was a low whirring as photoelectrics checked and okayed his fingerprints; then the door opened and Talman walked into the dim hallway. He glanced behind him to where, beyond the hills, the spaceport's lights made a pulsating, wan nimbus.

Then he went on, down a ramp, into a comfortably furnished room where a fat, gray-haired man was sitting in an easy chair, fingering a highball glass. Tension was in Talman's voice as he said, "Hello, Brown. Everything all right?"

A grin stretched Brown's sagging cheeks. "Sure," he said. "Why not? The police weren't after you, were they?"

Talman sat down and began mixing himself a drink from the server nearby. His thin, sensitive face was shadowed.

"You can't argue with your glands. Space does that to me anyway. All the way from Venus I kept expecting somebody to walk up to me and say, 'You're wanted for questioning.' "

"Nobody did."

"I didn't know what I'd find here."

"The police didn't expect us to head for Earth," Brown said, rumpling his gray hair with a shapeless paw. "And that was your idea."

"Yeah. Consulting psychologist to—"

"—to criminals. Want to step out?"

"No," Talman said frankly, "not with the profits we've got in sight already. This thing's big."

Brown grinned. "Sure it is. Nobody ever organized crime before, in just this way. There wasn't any crime worth a row of pins until we started."

"Where are we now, though? On the run."

"Fern's found a foolproof hideout."

"Where?"

"In the Asteroid Belt. We need one thing, though."

"What's that?"

"An atomic power plant."

Talman looked startled. But he saw that Brown wasn't kidding. After a moment, he put down his glass and scowled.

"I'd say it's impossible. A power plant's too big."

"Yeah," Brown said, "except that this one's going by space to Callisto."

"Hijacking? We haven't enough men—"

"The ship's under Transplant-control."

Talman cocked his head to one side. "Uh. That's out of my line—"

"There'll be a skeleton crew, of course. But we'll take care of them—and take their places. Then it'll simply be a matter of unhitching the Transplant and rigging up manuals. It isn't out of your line at all. Fern and Cunningham can do the technical stuff, but we've got to find out first just how dangerous a Transplant can be."

"I'm no engineer."

Brown went on, ignoring the comment. "The Transplant who's handling this Callisto shipment used to be Bart Quentin. You knew him, didn't you?"

Talman, startled, nodded. "Sure. Years ago. Before—"

"You're in the clear, as far as the police are concerned. Go to see Quentin. Pump him. Find out . . . Cunningham will tell you what to find out. After that, we can go ahead. I hope."

"I don't know. I'm not—"

Brown's brows came down. *"We've got to find a hideout!* That's absolutely vital right now. Otherwise, we might as well walk into the nearest police station and hold out our hands for cuffs. We've been clever, but now—we've got to hide. Fast!"

"Well . . . I get that. But do you know what a Transplant really is?"

"A free brain. One that can use artificial gadgets."

"Technically, yeah. Ever seen a Transplant working a power-digger? Or a Venusian sea-dredge? Enormously complicated controls it'd normally take a dozen men to handle?"

"Implying a Transplant's a superman?"

"No," Talman said slowly, "I don't mean that. But I've got an idea it'd be safer to tangle with a dozen men than with one Transplant."

"Well," Brown said, "go up to Quebec and see Quentin. He's there now, I found out. Talk to Cunningham first. We'll work out the details. What we've got to know are Quentin's powers and his vulnerable points. And whether or not he's telepathic. You're an old friend of Quentin, and you're a psychologist, so you're the guy for the job."

"Yeah."

"We've got to get that power plant. *We've got to hide, now!"*

Talman thought that Brown had probably planned this from the beginning. The fat man was shrewd enough; he'd been sufficiently clever to realize that ordinary criminals would stand no chance in a highly technical, carefully specialized world. Police forces could call on the sciences to aid them. Communication was excellent and fast, even between the planets. There were gadgets—The only chance of bringing off a successful crime was to do it fast and then make an almost instantaneous get-away.

But the crime had to be planned. When competing against an organized social unit, as any crook does, it's wise to create a similar unit. A blackjack has no chance against a rifle. A strong-arm bandit was doomed to quick failure, for a similar reason. The traces he left would be analyzed; chemistry, psychology and criminology would track him down; he'd be made to confess. Made to, without any third-degree methods. So—

So Cunningham was an electronics engineer. Fern was an

astrophysicist. Talman himself was a psychologist. Big, blond Dalquist was a hunter, by choice and profession, beautifully integrated and tremendously fast with a gun. Cotton was a mathematician—and Brown himself was the coordinator. For three months the combination had worked successfully on Venus. Then, inevitably, the net closed, and the unit filtered back to Earth, ready to take the next step in the long-range plan. What it was, Talman hadn't known till now. But he could readily see its logical necessity.

In the vast wilderness of the Asteroid Belt they could hide forever, if necessary, emerging to pull off a coup whenever opportunity offered. Safe, they could build up an underground criminal organization, with a spy-system flung broadcast among the planets—yes, it was the inevitable way. Just the same, he felt hesitant about matching wits with Bart Quentin. The man wasn't—human—anymore—

He was worried on the way to Quebec. Cosmopolitan though he was, he couldn't help anticipating tension, embarrassment, when he saw Quent. To pretend to ignore that—accident—would be too obvious. Still—He remembered that, seven years ago, Quentin had possessed a fine, muscular physique, and had been proud of his skill as a dancer. As for Linda, he wondered what had happened on that score. She couldn't still be Mrs. Bart Quentin, under the circumstances. Or could she?

He watched the St. Lawrence, a dull silver bar, below the plane as it slanted down. Robot pilots—a narrow beam. Only during violent storms did standard pilots take over. In space it was a different matter. And there were other jobs, enormously complicated, that only human brains could handle. A very special type of brain, at that.

A brain like Quentin's.

Talman rubbed his narrow jaw and smiled wanly, trying to locate the source of his worry. Then he had the answer. Did Quent, in this new incarnation, possess more than five senses? Could he detect reactions a normal man could not appreciate? If so, Van Talman was definitely sunk.

He glanced at his seatmate, Dan Summers of Wyoming Engineers, through whom he had made the contact with Quentin. Summers, a blond young man with sun-wrinkles around his eyes, grinned casually.

"Nervous?"

"Could be that," Talman said. "I was wondering how much he'll have changed."

"Results are different in every case."

The plane, beam-controlled, slid down the slopes of sunset air toward the port. Quebec's lighted towers made an irregular backdrop.

"They do change, then?"

"I suppose, psychically, they've got to. You're a psychologist, Mr. Talman. How'd you feel, if—"

"There might be compensations."

Summers laughed. "That's an understatement. Compensations . . . why, immortality's only one such . . . compensation!"

"You consider that a blessing?" Talman asked.

"Yes, I do. He'll remain at the peak of his powers for God knows how long. There'll be no deterioration. Fatigue poisons are automatically eliminated by irradiation. Brain cells can't replace themselves, of course, the way . . . say . . . muscular tissue can; but Quent's brain can't be injured, in its specially built case. Arteriosclerosis isn't any problem, with the plasmic solution we use—no calcium's deposited on the artery walls. The physical condition of his brain is automatically and perfectly controlled. The only ailments Quent can ever get are mental."

"Claustrophobia? No. You say he's got eye lenses. There'd be an automatic feeling of extension."

Summers said, "If you notice any change—outside of the perfectly normal one of mental growth in seven years—I'll be interested. With me—well, I grew up with the Transplants. I'm no more conscious of their mechnical, interchangeable bodies than a physician would think of a friend as a bundle of nerves and veins. It's the reasoning faculty that counts, and that hasn't altered."

Talman said thoughtfully, "You're a sort of physician, to the Transplants, anyway. A layman might get another sort of reaction. Especially if he were used to seeing . . . a face."

"I'm never conscious of that lack."

"Is Quent?"

Summers hesitated. "No," he said finally, "I'm sure he isn't. He's beautifully adjusted. The reconditioning to Transplant life takes about a year. After that it's all velvet."

"I've seen Transplants working, on Venus, from a distance. But there aren't many spotted away from Earth."

"We haven't enough trained technicians. It takes literally half a lifetime to train a man to handle Transplantation. A man has to be a qualified electronic engineer before he even starts." Summers laughed. "The insurance companies cover a lot of the initial expense, though."

Talman was puzzled. "How's that?"

"They underwrite. Occupational risk, immortality. Working in atomic research is dangerous, my friend!"

They emerged from the plane into the cool night air. Talman said, as they walked toward a waiting car, "We grew up together, Quentin and I. But his accident happened two years after I left Earth, and I never saw him since."

"As a Transplant? Uh-huh. Well, it's an unfortunate name. Some jackass tagged the label on, whereas propaganda experts should have worked it out. Unfortunately it stuck. Eventually we hope to popularize the—Transplants. Not yet. We're only starting. We've only two hundred and thirty of them so far, the successful ones."

"Many failures?"

"Not now. In the early days—It's *complicated*. From the first trephining to the final energizing and reconditioning, it's the most nerve-racking, brain-straining, difficult technical task the human mind's ever worked out. Reconciling a colloid mechanism with an electronic hookup—but the result's worth it."

"Technologically. I wonder about the human values."

"Psychologically? We-ell . . . Quentin will tell you about that angle. And technologically you don't know the half of it. No colloid machine, like the brain, has ever been developed—till now. And this isn't purely mechanical. It's merely a miracle, the synthesis of intelligent living tissue with delicate, responsive machinery."

"But handicapped by the limitation of the machine—and the brain."

"You'll see. Here we are. We're dining with Quent—"

Talman stared. *"Dining?"*

"Yeah." Summers' eyes showed quizzical amusement. "No, he doesn't eat steel shavings. In fact—"

The shock of meeting Linda again took Talman by surprise. He had not expected to see her. Not now, under these altered conditions. But she hadn't changed much; she was still the same warm, friendly woman he remembered, a little older now, yet very lovely and very gracious. She had always had charm. She was slim and tall, her head crowned by a bizarre coiffure of honey-amber coils, her brown eyes without the strain Talman might have expected.

He took her hands. "Don't say it," he said. "I know how long it's been."

"We won't count the years, Van." She laughed up at him. "We'll pick up right where we left off. With a drink, eh?"

"I could use one," Summers said, "but I've got to report back to headquarters. I'll just see Quent for a minute. Where is he?"

"In there." Linda nodded toward a door and turned back to Talman. "So you've been on Venus? You look bleached enough. Tell me how it's been."

"All right." He took the shaker from her hands and swirled the Martinis carefully. He felt embarrassment. Linda lifted an eyebrow.

"Yes, we're still married, Bart and I. You're surprised."

"A little."

"He's still Bart," she said quietly. "He may not look it, but he's the man I married, all right. So you can relax, Van."

He poured the Martinis. Without looking at her, he said, "As long as you're satisfied—"

"I know what you're thinking. That it'd be like having a machine for a husband. At first . . . well, I got over that feeling. We both did, after a while. There was constraint; I suppose you'll feel it when you see him. Only that isn't important, really. He's—Bart." She pushed a third glass toward Talman, and he looked at it in surprise.

"Not—"

She nodded.

The three of them dined together. Talman watched the two-foot-by-two cylinder resting on the table opposite him and tried to read personality and intelligence into the double lenses. He couldn't help imagining Linda as a priestess, serving some sort of alien god-image, and the concept was disturbing. Now Linda was forking chilled, sauce-daubed shrimps into the metallic compartment and spooning them out when the amplifier signaled.

Talman had expected a flat, toneless voice, but the sonovox gave depth and timbre whenever Quentin spoke.

"Those shrimps are perfectly usable, Van. It's only habit that makes us throw chow out after I've had it in my food-box. I taste the stuff, all right—but I haven't any salivary juices."

"You—taste 'em."

Quentin laughed a little. "Look, Van. Don't try to pretend this seems natural to you. You'll have to get used to it."

"It took me a long time," Linda said. "But after a while I found myself thinking it was just the sort of silly thing Bart always used to do. Remember the time you put on that suit of armor for the Chicago board meeting?"

"Well, I made my point," Quentin said. "I forget what it was now, but—we were talking about taste. I can taste these shrimps, Van. Certain nuances are lacking, yeah. Very delicate sensations are lost on me. But there's more to it than sweet and sour, salt and bitter. Machines could taste years ago."

"There's no digestion—"

"And there's no pylorospasm. What I lose in refinements of taste I make up for in freedom from gastrointestinal disorders."

"You don't burp any more, either," Linda said. "Thank God."

"I can talk with my mouth full, too," Quentin said. "But I'm not the super-machine-bodied-brain you're subconsciously thinking I am, chum. I don't spit death rays."

Talman grinned uneasily. "Was I thinking that?"

"I'll bet you were. But—" The timbre of the voice changed. "I'm not super. I'm plenty human, inside, and don't think I don't miss the old days sometimes. Lying on the beach and feeling the sun on my skin, little things like that. Dancing in rhythm to music, and—"

"Darling," Linda said.

The voice changed again. "Yeah. It's the small, trivial factors that make up a complete life. But I've got substitutes now—parallel factors. Reactions quite impossible to describe, because they're . . . let's say . . . electronic vibrations instead of the familiar neural ones. I *do* have senses, but through mechanical organs. When impulses reach my brain, they're automatically translated into familiar symbols. Or—" He hesitated. "Not so much now, though."

Linda laid a bit of planked fish in the food-compartment. "Delusions of grandeur, eh?"

"Delusions of alteration—but no delusion, my love. You see, Van, when I first turned into a Transplant, I had no standard of comparison except the arbitrary one I already knew. That was suited to a human body—only. When, later, I felt an impulse from a digger gadget, I'd automatically feel as if I had my foot on a car accelerator. Now those old symbols are fading. I . . . feel . . . more directly now, without translating the impulses into the old-time images."

"That would be faster," Talman said.

"It is. I don't have to think of the value of pi when I get a pi signal. I don't have to break down the equation. I'm beginning to sense what the equation means."

"Synthesis with a machine?"

"Yet I'm not robot. It doesn't affect the identity, the personal essence of Bart Quentin." There was a brief silence, and Talman saw Linda look sharply toward the cylinder. Then Quentin continued in the same tone. "I get a tremendous bang out of solving problems. I always did. And now it's not just on paper. I carry out the whole task myself, from conception to finish. I dope out the application, and . . . Van, I *am* the machine!"

"Machine?" Talman said.

"Ever noticed, when you're driving or piloting, how you identify yourself with the machine? It's an extension of you. I go one step farther. And it's satisfying. Suppose you could carry empathy to the limit and *be* one of your patients while you were solving his problem? It's an—ecstasy."

Talman watched Linda pour sauterne into a separate chamber. "Do you ever get drunk any more?" he asked.

Linda gurgled. "Not on liquor—but Bart gets high, all right!"

"How?"

"Figure it out," Quentin said, a little smugly.

"Alcohol's absorbed into the bloodstream, thence reaching the brain—the equivalent of intravenous shots, maybe?"

"I'd rather put cobra venom in my circulatory system," the Transplant said. "My metabolic balance is too delicate, too perfectly organized, too upset by introducing foreign substances. No, I use electrical stimulus—an induced high-frequency current that gets me high as a kite."

Talman stared. "And that's a substitute?"

"It is. Smoking and drinking are irritants, Van. So's thinking, for that matter! When I feel the psychic need for a binge, I've a gadget that provides stimulating irritation—and I'll bet you'd get more of a bang out of it than you would out of a quart of mescal."

"He quotes Housman," Linda said. "And does animal imitations. With his tonal control, Bart's a wonder." She stood up. "If you'll excuse me for a bit, I've got some K.P. Automatic as the kitchen is, there are still buttons to push."

"Can I help?" Talman offered.

"Thanks, no. Stay here with Bart. Want me to hitch up your arms, darling?"

"Nope," Quentin said. "Van can take care of my liquid diet. Step it up, Linda—Summers and I've got to get back on the job soon."

"The ship's ready?"

"Almost."

Linda paused in the doorway, biting her lips. "I'll never get used to your handling a spaceship all by yourself. Especially that thing."

"It may be jury-rigged, but it'll get to Callisto."

"Well . . . there's a skeleton crew, isn't there?"

"There is," Quentin said, "but it isn't needed. The insurance companies demand an emergency crew. Summers did a good job, rigging the ship in six weeks."

"With chewing gum and paper clips," Linda remarked. "I only hope it holds." She went out as Quentin laughed softly. There was a silence. Then, as never before, Talman felt that his companion was . . . was . . . had changed. For he felt Quentin gazing at him, and—Quentin wasn't there.

"Brandy, Van," the voice said. "Pour a little in my box."

Talman started to obey, but Quentin checked him. "Not out of the bottle. It's been a long time since I mixed rum and coke in my mouth. Use the inhaler. That's it. Now. Have a drink yourself and tell me how you feel."

"About—?"

"Don't you know?"

Talman went to the window and stood looking down at the reflected fluorescent shining in the St. Lawrence. "Seven years, Quent. It's hard to get used to you in this—form."

"I haven't lost anything."

"Not even Linda," Talman said. "You're lucky."

Quentin said steadily, "She stuck with me. The accident, five years ago, wrecked me. I was fooling around with atomic research, and there were chances that had to be taken. I was mangled, butchered, in the explosion. Don't think Linda and I hadn't planned in advance. We knew the occupational risk."

"And yet you—"

"We figured the marriage could last, even if—But afterward I almost insisted on a divorce. She convinced me we could still make a go of it. And we have."

Talman nodded. "I'd say so."

"That . . . kept . . . me going, for quite a while," Quentin said softly. "You know how I felt about Linda. It's always been just about a perfect equation. Even though the factors have changed, we've adjusted." Suddenly Quentin's laugh made the psychologist swing around. "I'm no monster, Van. Try and get over that idea!"

"I never thought that," Talman protested. "You're—"

"What?"

Silence again. Quentin grunted.

"In five years I've learned to notice how people react to me. Give me some more brandy. I still imagine I taste it with my palate. Odd how associations hang on."

Talman poured liquor from the inhaler. "So you figure you haven't changed, except physically."

"And you figure me as a raw brain in a metal cylinder. Not as the guy you used to get drunk with on Third Avenue. Oh, I've changed—sure. But it's a normal change. There's nothing innately alien about limbs that are metal extensions. It's one step beyond driving a car. If I were the sort of super-gadget you subconsciously think I am, I'd be an utter introvert and spend my time working out cosmic equations." Quentin used a vulgar expletive. "And if I did that, I'd go nuts. Because I'm no superman. I'm an ordinary guy, a physicist, and I've had to adjust to a new body. Which, of course, has its handicaps."

"What, for example?"

"The senses. Or the lack of them. I helped develop a lot of compensatory apparatus. I read escapist fiction, I get drunk by electrical irritation, I taste even if I can't eat. I watch teleshows. I try to get the equivalent of all the purely human sensory pleasures I can. It makes a balance that's very necessary."

"It would be. Does it work, though?"

"Look. I've got eyes that are delicately sensitive to shades and gradations of color. I've got arm attachments that can be refined down until they can handle microscopic apparatus. I can draw pictures—and, under a pseudonym, I'm a pretty popular cartoonist. I do that as a sideline. My real job is still physics. And it's still a good job. You know the feeling of pure pleasure you get when you've worked out a problem, in geometry or electronics or psychology—or anything? Now I work out questions infinitely more complicated, requiring split-second reaction as well as calculation. Like handling a spaceship. More brandy. It's volatile stuff in a hot room."

"You're still Bart Quentin," Talman said, "but I feel surer of that when I keep my eyes shut. Handling a spaceship—"

"I've lost nothing human," Quentin insisted. "The emotional basics haven't changed. It . . . isn't really pleasant to have you come in and look at me with plain horror, but I can understand the reason. We've been friends for a long time, Van. You may forget that before I do."

Sweat was suddenly cold on Talman's stomach. But despite Quentin's words, he felt certain by now that he had part of the answer for which he had come to Quebec. The Transplant had no abnormal powers—there were no telepathic functions.

There were more questions to be asked, of course.

He poured more brandy and smiled at the dully shining cylinder across the table. He could hear Linda singing softly from the kitchen.

The spaceship had no name, for two reasons. One was that she would make only a single trip, to Callisto; the other was odder. She was not, essentially, a ship with a cargo. She was a cargo with a ship.

Atomic power plants are not ordinary dynamos that can be dismantled and crated on a freight car. They were tremendously big, powerful, bulky, and behemothic. It takes two years to complete an atomic setup, and even after that the initial energizing must take place on Earth, at the enormous standards control plant that covers seven counties of Pennsylvania. The Department of Weights, Measures, and Power has a chunk of metal in a thermostatically controlled glass case in Washington; it's the standard meter. Similarly, in Pennsylvania, there is, under fantastic precautionary conditions, the one key atomic-disrupter in the Solar System.

There was only one requirement for fuel; it was best to filter it through a wire screen with, approximately, a one-inch gauge. And that was an arbitrary matter, for convenience in setting up a standard of fuels. For the rest, atomic power ate anything.

Few people played with atomic power; the stuff's violent. The research engineers worked on a stagger system. Even so, only the immortality insurance—the Transplantidae—kept neuroses from developing into psychoses.

The Callisto-bound power plant was too big to be loaded on the largest ship of any commercial line, but it had to get to Callisto. So the technicians built a ship around the power plant. It was not exactly jury-rigged, but it was definitely unstandardized. It occasionally, in matters of design, departed wildly from the norm. The special requirements were met deftly, often unorthodoxly, as they came up. Since the complete control would be in the hands of the Transplant Quentin, only casual accommodations were provided for the comfort of the small emergency crew. They weren't intended to wander through the entire ship unless a breakdown made it necessary, and a breakdown was nearly impossible. In fact, the vessel was practically a living entity. But not quite.

The Transplant had extensions—tools—throughout various sections of the great craft. Yet they were specialized to deal with the job in hand. There were no sensory attachments, except auditory and ocular. Quentin was, for the nonce, simply a super spaceship drive control. The brain cylinder was carried into the craft by Summers, who inserted it—somewhere!—plugged it in, and that finished the construction job.

At 2400 the mobile power plant took off for Callisto.

A third of the way to the Martian orbit, six spacesuited men came into an enormous chamber that was a technician's nightmare.

From a wall amplifier, Quentin's voice said, "What are you doing here, Van?"

"Okay," Brown said. "This is it. We'll work fast now. Cunningham, locate the connection. Dalquist, keep your gun ready."

"What'll I look for?" the big blond man asked.

Brown glanced at Talman. "You're certain there's no mobility?"

"I'm certain," Talman said, his eyes moving. He felt naked exposed to Quentin's gaze, and didn't like it.

Cunningham, gaunt, wrinkled and scowling, said, "The

only mobility's in the drive itself. I was sure of that before Talman double-checked. When a Transplant's plugged in for one job, it's limited to the tools it needs for that job."

"Well, don't waste time talking. Break the circuit."

Cunningham stared through his vision plate. "Wait a minute. This isn't standardized equipment. It's experimental . . . casual. I've got to trace a few . . . um."

Talman was surreptitiously trying to spot the Transplant's eye lenses, and failing. From somewhere in that maze of tubes, coils, wires, grids and engineering hash, he knew, Quentin was looking at him. From several places, undoubtedly—there'd be overall vision, with eyes spotted strategically around the room.

And it was a big room, this central control chamber. The light was misty yellow. It was like some strange, unearthly cathedral in its empty, towering height, a hugeness that dwarfed the six men. Bare grids, abnormally large, hummed and sparked; great vacuum tubes flamed eerily. Around the walls above their heads ran a metal platform, twenty feet up, a metal guard rail casually precautionary. It was reached by two ladders, on opposite walls of the room. Overhead hung a celestial globe, and the dim throbbing of tremendous power murmured in the chlorinated atmosphere.

The amplifier said, "What is this, piracy?"

Brown said casually, "Call it that. And relax. You won't be harmed. We may even send you back to Earth, when we can figure out a safe way to do it."

Cunningham was investigating lucite mesh, taking care to touch nothing. Quentin said, "This cargo isn't worth hijacking. It isn't radium I'm carrying, you know."

"I need a power plant," Brown remarked curtly.

"How did you get aboard?"

Brown lifted a hand to mop sweat from his face, and then, grimacing, refrained. "Find anything yet, Cunningham?"

"Give me time. I'm only an electronics man. This setup's screwy. Fern, give me a hand here."

Talman's discomfort was growing. He realized that Quentin, after the first surprised comment, had ignored him. Some indefinable compulsion made him tilt back his head and say Quentin's name.

"Yeah," Quentin said. "Well? So you're in with this gang?"

"Yes."

"And you were pumping me, up in Quebec. To make sure I was harmless."

Talman made his voice expressionless. "We had to be certain."

"I see. How'd you get aboard? The radar automatically dodges approaching masses. You couldn't have brought your own ship alongside in space."

"We didn't. We got rid of the emergency crew and took their suits."

"Got rid of them?"

Talman moved his eyes toward Brown. "What else could we do? We can't afford half measures in a gamble as big as this. Later on, they'd have been a danger to us, after our plans started moving. Nobody's going to know anything about it except us. And you." Again Talman looked at Brown. "I think, Quent, you'd better throw in with us."

The amplifier ignored whatever implied threat lay in the suggestion.

"What do you want the power plant for?"

"We've got an asteroid picked out," Talman said, tilting his head back to search the great crowded hollow of the ship, swimming a little in the haze of its poisonous atmosphere. He half expected Brown to cut him short, but the fat man didn't speak. It was, he thought, curiously difficult to talk persuasively to someone whose location you didn't know. "The only trouble is, it's airless. With the plant, we can manufacture our own air. It'd be a miracle if anybody ever found us in the Asteroid Belt."

"And then what? Piracy?"

Talman did not answer. The voicebox said thoughtfully, "It might make a good racket, at that. For a while, anyhow. Long enough to clean up quite a lot. Nobody will expect anything like it. Yeah, you might get away with the idea."

"Well," Talman said, "if you think that, what's the next logical step?"

"Not what you think. I wouldn't play along with you. Not for moral reasons, especially, but for motives of self-preservation. I'd be useless to you. Only in a highly intricate, widespread civilization is there any need for Transplants. I'd be excess baggage."

"If I gave you my word—"

"You're not the big shot," Quentin told him. Talman instinctively sent another questioning look at Brown. And from the voicebox on the wall came a curious sound like a smothered laugh.

"All right," Talman said, shrugging. "Naturally you won't decide in our favor right away. Think it over. Remember you're not Bart Quentin anymore—you've got certain mechanical handicaps. While we haven't got too much time, we can spare a little—say ten minutes—while Cunningham looks things over. Then . . . well, we aren't playing for marbles, Quent." His lips thinned. "If you'll throw in with us and guide the ship under our orders, we can afford to let you live. But you've got to make up your mind fast. Cunningham is going to trace you down and take over the controls. After that—"

"What makes you so sure I can be traced down?" Quentin asked calmly. "I know just how much my life would be worth once I'd landed you where you want to go. You don't need me. You couldn't give me the right maintenance even if you wanted to. No, I'd simply join the crewmen you've disposed of. I'll give you an ultimatum of my own."

"You'll—what?"

"Keep quiet and don't monkey with anything, and I'll land in an isolated part of Callisto and let you all escape," Quentin said. "If you don't, God help you."

For the first time Brown showed he had been conscious of that distant voice. He turned to Talman.

"Bluff?"

Talman nodded slowly. "Must be. He's harmless."

"Bluff," Cunningham said, without looking up from his task.

"No," the amplifier told him quietly, "I'm not bluffing. And be careful with that board. It's part of the atomic hookup. If you fool with the wrong connections, you're apt to blast us all out of space."

Cunningham jerked back from the maze of wires snaking out of the bakelite before him. Fern, some distance away, turned a swarthy face to watch. "Easy," he said. "We've got to be sure what we're doing."

"Shut up," Cunningham grunted. "I *do* know. Maybe that's what the Transplant's afraid of. I'll be plenty careful to stay clear of atomic connections, but—" He paused to study the tangled wires. "No. This isn't atomic—I think. Not the control leads, anyway. Suppose I break this connection—" His gloved hand came up with a rubber-sheathed cutter.

The voicebox said, "Cunningham—don't." Cunningham poised the cutter. The amplifier sighed.

"You first, then. Here it is!"

Talman felt the transparent faceplate slap painfully against his nose. The immense room bucked dizzily as he went reeling forward, unable to check himself. All around him he saw grotesque spacesuited figures reeling and stumbling. Brown lost his balance and fell heavily.

Cunningham had been slammed forward into the wires as the ship abruptly decelerated. Now he hung like a trapped fly in the tangle, his limbs, his head, his whole body jerking and twitching with spasmodic violence. The devil's dance increased in fury.

"Get him out of there!" Dalquist yelled.

"Hold it!" Fern shouted. "I'll cut the power—" But he didn't know how. Talman, dry-throated, watched Cunningham's body sprawling, arching, shaking in spastic agony. Bones cracked suddenly.

Cunningham jerked more limpy now, his head flopping grotesquely.

"Get him down," Brown snapped, but Fern shook his head. "Cunningham's dead. And that hookup's dangerous."

"How? Dead?"

Under his thin mustache Fern's lips parted in a humorless smile. "A guy in an epileptic fit can break his own neck."

"Yeah," Dalquist said, obviously shaken. "His neck's broken, all right. Look at the way his head goes."

"Put a twenty-cycle alternating current through yourself and you'd go into convulsions too," Fern advised.

"We can't just leave him there!"

"We can," Brown said, scowling. "Stay away from the walls, all of you." He glared at Talman. "Why didn't you—"

"Sure, I know. But Cunningham should have had sense enough to stay away from bare wires."

"Few wires are insulated around here," the fat man growled. "You said the Transplant was harmless."

"I said he had no mobility. And that he wasn't a telepath." Talman realized that his voice sounded defensive.

Fern said, "A signal's supposed to sound whenever the ship accelerates or decelerates. It didn't go off that time. The Transplant must have cut it out himself, so we wouldn't be warned."

They looked up into that humming, vast, yellow emptiness.

Claustrophobia gripped Talman. The walls looked ready to topple in—to fold down, as though he stood in the cupped hand of a titan.

"We can smash his eye cells," Brown suggested.

"Find 'em." Fern indicated the maze of equipment.

"All we have to do is unhitch the Transplant. Break his connection. Then he goes dead."

"Unfortunately," Fern said, "Cunningham was the only electronic engineer among us. I'm only an astrophysicist!"

"Never mind. We pull one plug and the Transplant blacks out. You can do that much!"

Anger flared. But Cotton, a little man with blinking blue eyes, broke the tension.

"Mathematics—geometry—ought to help us. We want to locate the Transplant, and——" He glanced up and was frozen. "We're off our course!" he said finally, licking dry lips. "See that telltale?"

Far above, Talman could see the enormous celestial globe. On its dark surface a point of red light was clearly marked.

Fern's swarthy face showed a sneer. "Sure. The Transplant's running to cover. Earth's the nearest place where he can get help. But we've plenty of time left. I'm not the technician Cunningham was, but I'm not a complete dope." He didn't look at the rhythmically moving body on the wires. "We don't have to test every connection in the ship."

"Okay, take it, then," Brown grunted.

Awkward in his suit, Fern walked to a square opening in the floor and peered down at a mesh-metal grating eighty feet below. "Right. Here's the fuel feed. We don't need to trace connections through the whole ship. The fuel's dumped out of that leader tube overhead there. Now look. Everything connected with the atomic power is apparently marked with red wax crayon. See?"

They saw. Here and there, on bare plates and boards, were cryptic red markings. Other symbols were in blue, green, black and white.

"Go on that assumption," Fern said. "Temporarily, anyhow. Red's atomic power. Blue . . . green . . . um."

Talman said suddenly, "I don't see anything here that looks like Quentin's brain case."

"Did you expect to?" the astrophysicist asked sardonically. "It's slid into a padded socket somewhere. The brain can stand more gravs than the body, but seven's about tops in any case. Which, incidentally, is fine for us. There'd be no use putting high-speed potential in this ship. The Transplant couldn't stand it, any more than we could."

"Seven G's," Brown said thoughtfully.

"Which would black out the Transplant too. He'll have to remain conscious to pilot the ship through Earth atmosphere. We've got plenty of time."

"We're going pretty slow now," Dalquist put in.

Fern gave the celestial globe a sharp glance. "Looks like it. Let me work on this." He paid out a coil from his belt and hitched himself to one of the central pillars. "That'll guard against any more accidents."

"Tracing a circuit shouldn't be so hard," Brown said.

"Ordinarily it isn't. But you've got everything in this chamber—atomic control, radar, the kitchen sink. And these labels are only for construction convenience. There wasn't any blueprint in this ship. It's a single-shot model. I can find the Transplant, but it'll take time. So shut up and let me work."

Brown scowled but didn't say anything. Cotton's bald head was sweating. Dalquist wrapped his arm about a metal pillar and waited. Talman looked up again at the balcony that hung from the walls. The celestial globe showed a crawling disk of red light.

"Quent," he said.

"Yes, Van." Quentin's voice was quietly distant. Brown put one hand casually to the blaster at his belt.

"Why don't you give up?"

"Why don't you?"

"You can't fight us. Your getting Cunningham was a fluke. We're on guard now—you can't hurt us. It's only a matter of time until we trace you down. Don't look for mercy then, Quent. You can save us trouble by telling us where you are. We're willing to pay for that. After we find you—on our own initiative—you can't bargain. How about it?"

Quentin said simply, "No."

There was silence for a few minutes. Talman was watching Fern, who, very cautiously paying out his coil, was investigating the tangle where Cunningham's body still hung.

Quentin said, "He won't find the answer there. I'm pretty well camouflaged."

"But helpless," Talman said quickly.

"So are you. Ask Fern. If he monkeys with the wrong connections, he's apt to destroy the ship. Look at your own problem. We're heading back toward Earth. I'm swinging into a new course that'll end at the home berth. If you give up now—"

Brown said, "The old statutes never were altered. The punishment for piracy is death."

"There's been no piracy for a hundred years. If an actual case came to trial, it might be a different matter."

"Imprisonment? Reconditioning?" Talman asked. "I'd a lot rather be dead."

"We're decelerating," Dalquist called, getting a firmer grip on his pillar.

Looking at Brown, Talman thought the fat man knew what he had in mind. If technical knowledge failed, psychology might not. And Quentin, after all, was a human brain.

First get the subject off guard.

"Quent."

But Quentin didn't answer. Brown grimaced and turned to watch Fern. Sweat was pouring down the physicist's swarthy face as he concentrated on the hookups, drawing diagrams on the stylo pad he wore attached to his forearm.

After a while Talman began to feel dizzy. He shook his head, realizing that the ship had decelerated almost to zero, and got a firmer grip on the nearest pillar. Fern cursed. He was having a difficult time keeping his footing.

Presently he lost it altogether as the ship went free. Five spacesuited figures clung to convenient handgrips. Fern snarled, "This may be deadlock, but it doesn't help the Transplant. I can't work without gravity—he can't get to Earth without acceleration."

The voicebox said, "I've sent out an S.O.S."

Fern laugehd. "I worked that out with Cunningham—and you talked too much to Talman, too. With a radar meteor-avoider, you don't need signaling apparatus, and you haven't got it." He eyed the apparatus he had just left. "Maybe I was getting too close to the right answer, though, eh? Is that why——"

"You weren't even near it," Quentin said.

"Just the same——" Fern kicked himself away from the pillar, playing out the line behind him. He made a loop about his left wrist, and, hanging in midair, fell to studying the hookup.

Brown lost his grip on the slippery column and floated free like some overinflated balloon. Talman kicked himself across to the railed balcony. He caught the metal bar in gloved hands, swung himself in like an acrobat, and looked down—though it wasn't really *down*—at the control chamber.

"I think you'd better give up," Quentin said.

Brown was floating across to join Fern. "Never," he said, and simultaneously four G's hit the ship with the impact of a pile driver. It wasn't forward acceleration. It was in another, foreplanned direction. Fern saved himself at the cost of an almost dislocated wrist—but the looped line rescued him from a fatal dive into uninsulated wiring.

Talman was slammed down on the balcony. He could see the others plummet to hard impacts on unyielding surfaces. Brown wasn't stopped by the floor plate, though.

He had been hovering over the fuel-feed hole when the acceleration was slammed on.

Talman saw the bulky body pop out of sight down the opening. There was an indescribable sound.

Dalquist, Fern, and Cotton struggled to their feet. They cautiously went toward the hole and peered down.

Talman called, "Is he—"

Cotton had turned away. Dalquist remained where he was, apparently fascinated, Talman thought, until he saw the man's shoulders heaving. Fern looked up toward the balcony.

"He went through the filter screen," he said. "It's a one-inch gauge metal mesh."

"Broke through?"

"No," Fern said deliberately. "He didn't break through. He *went* through."

Four gravities and a fall of eighty feet add up to something slightly terrific. Talman shut his eyes and said, "Quent!"

"Do you give up?"

Fern snarled, "Not on your life! Our unit's not that interdependent. We can do without Brown."

Talman sat on the balcony, held on to the rail, and let his feet hang down into emptiness. He stared across to the celestial globe, forty feet to his left. The red spot that marked the ship stood motionless.

"I don't think you're human anymore, Quent," he said.

"Because I don't use a blaster? I've different weapons to fight with now. I'm not kidding myself, Van. I'm fighting for my life."

"We can still bargain."

Quentin said, "I told you you'd forget our friendship before I did. You must have known this hijacking could only end in my death. But apparently you didn't care about that."

"I didn't expect you to—"

"Yeah," the voicebox said. "I wonder if you'd have been as ready to go through with the plan if I'd still had human form? As for friendship—use your own tricks of psychology, Van. You look on my mechanical body as an enemy, a barrier between you and the real Bart Quentin. Subconsciously, maybe, you hate it, and you're therefore willing to destroy it. Even though you'll be destroying me with it. I don't know—perhaps you rationalize that you'd thus be rescuing me from the thing that's erected the barrier. And you forget that I haven't changed, basically."

"We used to play chess together," Talman said, "but we didn't smash the pawns."

"I'm in check," Quentin countered. "All I've got to fight with are knights. You've still got castles and bishops. You can move straight for your goal. Do you give up?"

"No!" Talman snapped. His eyes were on the red light. He saw a tremor move it, and gripped the metal rail with a frantic clutch. His body swung out as the ship jumped. One gloved hand was torn from its grip. But the other held. The celestial globe was swinging violently. Talman threw a leg over the rail, clambered back to his precarious perch, and looked down.

Fern was still braced by his emergency line. Dalquist and little Cotton were sliding across the floor, to bring up with a crash against a pillar. Someone screamed.

Sweating, Talman warily descended. But by the time he had reached Cotton the man was dead. Radiating cracks in his faceplate and contorted, discolored features gave the answer.

"He slammed right into me," Dalquist gulped. "His plate cracked into the back of my helmet—"

The chlorinated atmosphere within the sealed ship had ended Cotton's life, not easily, but rapidly. Dalquist, Fern and Talman matched glances.

The blond giant said, "Three of us left. I don't like this. I don't like it at all."

Fern showed his teeth. "So we're still underestimating that thing. From now on, hitch yourselves to pillars. Don't move without sound anchorage. Stay clear of everything that might cause trouble."

"We're still heading back toward Earth," Talman said.

"Yeah." Fern nodded. "We could open a port and walk out into free space. But then what? We figured we'd be using this ship. Now we've *got* to."

Dalquist said, "If we gave up—"

"Execution," Fern said flatly. "We've still got time. I've traced some of the connections. I've elminated a lot of hook-ups."

"Still think you can do it?"

"I think so. But don't let go of your handgrips for a second. I'll find the answer before we hit atmosphere."

Talman had a suggestion. "Brains send out recognizable vibration patterns. A directional finder, maybe?"

"If we were in the middle of the Mojave, that would work. Not here. This ship's lousy with currents and radiations. How could we unscramble them without apparatus?"

"We brought some apparatus with us. And there's plenty all around the walls."

"Hooked up. I'm going to be plenty careful about upsetting the *status quo.* I wish Cunningham hadn't gone down the drain."

"Quentin's no fool," Talman said. "He got the electronic engineer first and Brown second. He was trying for you then, too. Bishop and queen."

"Which makes me what?"

"Castle. He'll get you if he can." Talman frowned, trying to remember something. Then he had it. He went over the stylopad on Fern's arm, shielding the writing with his own body from any photoelectrics that might be spotted around the walls or ceiling. He wrote: "He gets drunk on high frequency. Can do?"

Fern crumpled the tissue slip and tore it awkwardly into fragments with his gloved fingers. He winked at Talman and nodded briefly.

"Well, I'll keep trying," he said, and paid out his line to the kit of apparatus he and Cunningham had brought aboard.

Left alone, Dalquist and Talman hitched themselves to pillars and waited. There was nothing else they could do. Talman had already mentioned this high-frequency irritation angle to Fern and Cunningham; they had seen no value to the knowledge then. Now it might be the answer, with applied practical psychology to supplement technology.

Meanwhile, Talman longed for a cigarette. All he could

do, sweating in the uncomfortable suit, was to manipulate a built-in gadget so that he managed to swallow a salt tablet and a few gulps of tepid water. His heart was pounding, and there was a dull ache in his temples. The spacesuit was uncomfortable; he wasn't used to such personal confinement.

Through the built-in receiving gadget he could hear the humming silence, broken by the padding rustle of sheathed boots as Fern moved about. Talman blinked at the chaos of equipment and closed his eyes; the relentless yellow light, not intended for human vision, made little pulses beat nervously somewhere in his eye sockets. Somewhere in this ship, he thought, probably in this very chamber, was Quentin. But camouflaged. How?

Purloined letter stuff? Scarcely. Quentin would have had no reason to expect hijackers. It was pure accident that had intervened to protect the Transplant with such an excellent hiding place. That, and the slapdash methods of technicians, constructing a one-job piece of equipment with the casual convenience of a slipstick.

But, Talman thought, if Quentin could be made to reveal his location—

How? Via induced cerebral irritation—intoxication?

Appeal to basics? But a brain couldn't propagate the species. Self-preservation remained the only constant. Talman wished he'd brought Linda along. He'd have had a lever then.

If only Quentin had had a human body, the answer would not be so difficult to find. And not necessarily by torture. Automatic muscular reactions, the old stand-by of professional magicians, could have led Talman to his goal. Unfortunately, Quentin himself was the goal—a bodiless brain in a padded, insulated metal cylinder. And his spinal cord was a wire.

If Fern could rig up a high-frequency device, the radiations would weaken Quentin's defenses—in one way, if not another. At present the Transplant was a very, very dangerous opponent. And he was perfectly camouflaged.

Well, not perfectly. Definitely no. Because, Talman realized with a sudden glow of excitement, Quentin wasn't simply sitting back, ignoring the pirates, and taking the quickest route back to Earth. The very fact that he was retracing his course instead of going on to Callisto indicated that Quentin wanted to get help. And, meanwhile, via murder, he was doing his utmost to distract his unwelcome guests.

Because, obviously, Quentin *could* be found.

Given time.

Cunningham could have done it. And even Fern was a menace to the Transplant. That meant that Quentin—was afraid.

Talman sucked in his breath. "Quent," he said, "I've a proposition. You listening?"

"Yes," the distant, terribly familiar voice said.

"I've an answer for all of us. You want to stay alive. We want this ship. Right?"

"Correct."

"Suppose we drop you by parachute when we hit Earth atmosphere. Then we can take over the controls and head out again. That way—"

"And Brutus is an honorable man," Quentin remarked. "But of course he wasn't. I can't trust you anymore, Van. Psychopaths and criminals are too amoral. They're ruthless, because they feel the end justifies the means. You're a psychopathic psychologist, Van, and that's exactly why I'd never take your word for anything."

"You're taking a long chance. If we do find the right hookup in time, there'll be no bargaining, you know."

"If."

"It's a long way back to Earth. We're taking precautions now. You can't kill any more of us. We'll simply keep working steadily till we find you. Now—what about it?"

After a pause Quentin said, "I'd rather take my chances. I know technological values better than I do human ones. As long as I depend on my own field of knowledge, I'm safer than if I tried to deal in psychology. I know coefficients and cosines, but I don't know much about the colloid machine in your skull."

Talman lowered his head; sweat dripped from his nose to the interior of the faceplate. He felt a sudden claustrophobia; fear of the cramped quarters of the suit, and fear of the larger dungeon that was the room and the ship itself.

"You're restricted, Quent," he said, too loudly. "You're limited in your weapons. You can't adjust atmospheric pressure in here, or you'd have compressed already and crushed us."

"Crushing vital equipment at the same time. Besides, those suits can take a lot of pressure."

"Your king's still in check."

"So is yours," Quentin said calmly.

Fern gave Talman a slow look that held approval and faint triumph. Under the clumsy gloves, manipulating delicate instruments, the hookup was beginning to take shape. Luckily, it was a job of conversion rather than construction, or time would have been too short.

"Enjoy yourself," Quentin said. "I'm slamming on all the G's we can take."

"I don't feel it," Talman said.

"All we can take, not all I could give out. Go ahead and amuse yourselves. You can't win."

"No?"

"Well—figure it out. As long as you stay hitched in one place, you're reasonably safe. But if you start moving around, I can destroy you."

"Which means we'll have to move—somewhere—in order to reach you, eh?"

Quentin laughed. "I didn't say so. I'm well camouflaged. *Turn that thing off!*"

The shout echoed and re-echoed against the vaulted roof, shaking the amber air. Talman jerked nervously. He met Fern's eye and saw the astrophysicist grin.

"It's hitting him," Fern said. Then there was silence, for many minutes.

The ship abruptly jumped. But the frequency inductor was securely moored, and the men, too, were anchored by their lines.

"Turn it off," Quentin said again. His voice wasn't quite under control.

"Where are you?" Talman asked.

No answer.

"We can wait, Quent."

"Keep waiting, then! I'm . . . I'm not distracted by personal fear. That's one advantage of being a Transplant."

"High irritant value," Fern murmured. "It works fast."

"Come on, Quent," Talman said persuasively. "You've still got the instinct of self-preservation. This can't be pleasant for you."

"It's . . . too pleasant," Quentin said unevenly. "But it won't work. I could always stand my liquor."

"This isn't liquor," Fern countered. He touched a dial.

The Transplant laughed; Talman noted with satisfaction that oral control was slipping. "It won't work, I say. I'm too . . . smart for you."

"Yeah?"

"Yeah. You're not morons—none of you are. Fern's a good technician, maybe, but he isn't good enough. Remember, Van, you asked me in Quebec if there'd been any . . . change? I said there hadn't. I'm finding out now that I was wrong."

"How?"

"Lack of distraction." Quentin was talking too much; a symptom of intoxication. "A brain in a body can never concentrate fully. It's too conscious of the body itself. Which is an imperfect mechanism. Too specialized to be efficient. Respiratory, circulatory—all the systems intrude. Even the habit of breathing's a distraction. Now the ship's my body—at the moment—but it's a perfect mechanism. It functions with absolute efficiency. So my brain's correspondingly better."

"Superman."

"Superefficient. The better mind generally wins at chess, because it can foresee the possible gambits. I can foresee everything you might do. And you're badly handicapped."

"Why?"

"You're human."

Egotism, Talman thought. Was this the Achillean heel? A taste of success had apparently done its psychological work, and the electronic equivalent of drunkenness had released inhibitions. Logical enough. After five years of routine work, no matter how novel that work might be, this suddenly altered situation—this change from active to passive, from machine to protagonist—might have been the catalyst. Ego. And cloudy thinking.

For Quentin wasn't a superbrain. Very definitely he was not. The higher an I.Q., the less need there is for self-justification, direct or indirect. And, oddly, Talman suddenly felt absolved of any lingering compunctions. The real Bart Quentin would never have been guilty of paranoid thought patterns.

So—

Quentin's articulation was clear; there was no slurring. But he no longer spoke with soft palate, tongue and lips, by means of a column of air. Tonal control was noticeably altered now, however, and the Transplant's voice varied from a carrying whisper to almost a shout.

Talman grinned. He was feeling better, somehow.

"We're human," he said, "but we're still sober."

"Nuts. Look at the telltale. We're getting close to Earth."

"Come off it, Quent," Talman said wearily. "You're bluffing, and we both know you're bluffing. You can't stand an indefinite amount of high frequency. Save time and give up now."

"You give up," Quentin said, "I can see everything you do. The ship's a mass of traps anyway. From up here all I have to do is watch until you get close to one. I'm planning my game ahead, every gambit worked out to checkmate for one of you. You haven't got a chance. You haven't got a chance. You haven't got a chance."

From up here, Talman thought. Up where? He remembered little Cotton's remark that geometry could be used to locate the Transplant. Sure. Geometry and psychology. Halve the ship, quarter it, keep bisecting the remainders—

Not necessary. *Up* was the key word. Talman seized upon it with an eagerness that didn't show on his face. *Up*, presumably, reduced by half the area they'd have to search. The lower parts of the ship could be ruled out. Now he'd have to halve the upper section, using the celestial globe, say, as the dividing line.

The Transplant had eye cells spotted all over the ship, of course, but Talman tentatively decided that Quentin thought of himself as situated in one particular spot, not scattered over the whole ship, localized wherever an eye was built in. A man's head is his locus, to his own mind.

Thus Quentin could see the red spot on the celestial globe, but that didn't necessarily mean that he was located in a wall facing that hemisphere of the sphere. The Transplant had to be trapped into references to his actual physical relation to objects in the ship—which would be hard, because this could be done best by references to sight, the normal individual's most important link with his surroundings. And Quentin's sight was almost omnipotent. He could see everything.

There had to be a localization—somehow.

A word-association test would do it. But that implied cooperation. Quentin wasn't that drunk!

Nothing could be gauged by learning what Quentin could *see*—for his brain was not necessarily near any one of his eyes. There would be a subtle, intrinsic realization of location on the Transplant's part; the knowledge that *he*—blind, deaf, dumb except through his distant extensor sensory mechanisms—was in a certain place. And how, except by too obviously direct questioning, could Quentin be made to give the right answers?

It was impossible, Talman thought, with a hopeless sense of frustrated anger. The anger grew stronger. It brought sweat to his face, rousing him to a dull, aching hatred of Quentin. All this was Quentin's fault, the fact that Talman was prisoned here in this hateful spacesuit and this enormous deathtrap of a ship. The fault of a machine—

Suddenly he saw the way.

It would, of course, depend on how drunk Quentin was. He glanced at Fern, questioned the man with his eyes, and in response Fern manipulated a dial and nodded.

"Damn you," Quentin said in a whisper.

"Nuts," Talman said. "You implied you haven't any instinct for self-preservation anymore."

"I . . . didn't—"

"It's true, isn't it?"

"No," Quentin said loudly.

"You forget I'm a psychologist, Quent. I should have seen the angles before. The book was open, ready to read, even before I saw you. When I saw Linda."

"Shut up about Linda!"

Talman had a momentary, sick vision of the drunken, tortured brain somewhere hidden in the walls, a surrealistic nightmare. "Sure," he said. "You don't want to think about her yourself."

"Shut up."

"You don't want to think about yourself, either, do you?"

"What are you trying to do, Van? Get me mad?"

"No," Talman said, "I'm simply fed up, sick and disgusted with the whole business. Pretending that you're Bart Quentin, that you're still human, that we can deal with you on equal terms."

"There'll be no dealing—"

"That's not what I meant, and you know it. I've just realized what you are." He let the words hang in the dim air. He imagined he could hear Quentin's heavy breathing, though he knew it was merely an illusion.

"Please shut up, Van," Quentin said.

"Who's asking me to shut up?"

"I am."

"And what's that?"

The ship jumped. Talman almost lost his balance. The line hitched to the pillar saved him. He laughed.

"I'd be sorry for you, Quent, if you were—you. But you're not."

"I'm not falling for any trick."

"It may be a trick, but it's the truth too. And you've wondered about it yourself. I'm dead certain of that."

"Wondered about what?"

"You're not human any more," Talman said gently. "You're a thing. A machine. A gadget. A spongy gray hunk of meat in a box. Did you really think I could get used to you—now? That I could identify you with the old Quent? You haven't any face!"

The soundbox made noises. They sounded mechanical. Then——"Shut up," Quentin said again, almost plaintively. "I know what you're trying to do."

"And you don't want to face it. Only you've got to face it, sooner or later, whether you kill us now or not. This . . . business . . . is an incident. But the thoughts in your brain will keep growing and growing. And you'll keep changing and changing. You've changed plenty already."

"You're crazy," Quentin said. "I'm no . . . monster."

"You hope, eh? Look at it logically. You haven't dared to do that, have you?" Talman held up his gloved hand and ticked off points on his sheathed fingers. "You're trying very desperately to keep your grip on something that's slipping away—humanity, the heritage you were born to. You hang on to the symbols, hoping they'll mean the reality. Why do you pretend to eat? Why do you insist on drinking brandy out of a glass? You know it might just as well be squirted into you out of an oil can."

"No. No! It's an aesthetic—"

"Garbage. You go to teleshows. You read. You pretend you're human enough to be a cartoonist. It's a desperate, hopeless clinging to something that's already gone from you, all these pretenses. Why do you feel the need for binges? You're maladjusted, because you're pretending you're still human, and you're not, anymore."

"I'm . . . well, something better—"

"Maybe . . . if you'd been born a machine. But you *were* human. You had a human body. You had eyes and hair and lips. Linda must remember that, Quent.

"You should have insisted on a divorce. Look—if you'd

only been crippled by the explosion, she could have taken care of you. You'd have needed her. As it is, you're a self-sufficient, self-contained unit. She does a good job of pretending. I'll admit that. She tries not to think of you as a hopped-up helicopter. A gadget. A blob of wet cellular tissue. It must be tough on her. She remembers you as you used to be."

"She loves me."

"She pities you," Talman said relentlessly.

In the humming stillness the red telltale crept across the globe. Fern's tongue stole out and circled his lips. Dalquist stood quietly watching, his eyes narrowed.

"Yeah," Talman said, "face it. And look at the future. There are compensations. You'll get quite a bang out of meshing your gears. Eventually you'll even stop remembering you ever were human. You'll be happier then. For you can't hang on to it, Quent. It's going away. You can keep on pretending for a while, but in the end it won't matter anymore. You'll be satisfied to be a gadget. You'll see beauty in a machine and not in Linda. Maybe that's happened already. Maybe Linda knows it's happened. You don't have to be honest with yourself yet, you know. You're immortal. But I wouldn't take that kind of immortality as a gift."

"Van——"

"I'm still Van. But you're a machine. Go ahead and kill us, if you want, and if you can do it. Then go back to Earth and, when you see Linda again, look at her face. Look at it when she doesn't know you're watching. You can do that easily. Rig up a photoelectric cell in a lamp or something."

"Van . . . *Van!*"

Talman let his hands drop to his sides. "All right. Where are you?"

The silence grew, while an inaudible question hummed through the yellow vastness. The question, perhaps, in the mind of every Transplant. The question of—a price.

What price?

Utter loneliness, the sick knowledge that the old ties were snapping one by one, and that in place of living, warm humanity there would remain—a mental monster?

Yes, he had wondered—this Transplant who had been Bart Quentin. He had wondered, while the proud, tremendous machines that were his body stood ready to spring into vibrant life.

Am I changing? Am I still Bart Quentin?

Or do they—the humans—look on me as—How does Linda really feel about me now? Am I—

Am I—It?

"Go up on the balcony," Quentin said. His voice was curiously faded and dead.

Talman made a quick gesture. Fern and Dalquist sprang to life. They climbed, each to a ladder, on opposite sides of the room, but carefully, hitching their lines to each rung.

"Where is it?" Talman asked gently.

"The south wall—Use the celestial sphere for orientation. You can reach me—" The voice failed.

"Yes?"

Silence. Fern called down, "Has he passed out?"

"Quent!"

"Yes— About the center of the balcony. I'll tell you when you reach it."

"Easy," Fern warned Dalquist. He took a turn of his line about the balcony rail and edged forward, searching the wall with his eyes.

Talman used one arm to scrub his fogged faceplate. Sweat was trickling down his face and flanks. The crawling yellow light, the humming stillness from machines that should be roaring thunderously, stung his nerves to unendurable tension.

"Here?" Fern called.

"Where is it, Quent?" Talman asked. "Where are you?"

"Van," Quentin said, a horrible, urgent agony in his tone. "You can't mean what you've been saying. You can't. This is—I've got to know. I'm thinking of Linda!"

Talman shivered. He moistened his lips.

"You're a machine, Quent," he said steadily. "You're a gadget. You know I'd never have tried to kill you if you were still Bart Quentin."

And then, with shocking abruptness, Quentin laughed.

"Here it comes, Fern!" he shouted, and the echoes crashed and roared through the vaulted chamber. Fern clawed for the balcony rail.

That was a fatal mistake. The line hitching him to the rail proved a trap—because he didn't see the danger in time to unhook himself.

The ship jumped.

It was beautifully gauged. Fern was jerked toward the wall

and halted by the line. Simultaneously the great celestial globe swung from its support, in a pendulum arc like the drive of a Gargantuan fly swatter. The impact snapped Fern's line instantly.

Vibration boomed through the walls.

Talman hung on to a pillar and kept his eyes on the globe. It swung back and forth in a diminishing arc as inertia overcame momentum. Liquid spattered and dripped from it.

He saw Dalquist's helmet appear over the rail. The man yelled, "Fern!"

There was no answer.

"Fern! Talman!"

"I'm here," Talman said.

"Where's—" Dalquist turned his head to stare at the wall. He screamed.

Obscene gibberish tumbled from his mouth. He yanked the blaster from his maze of apparatus below.

"Dalquist!" Talman shouted. "Hold it!"

Dalquist didn't hear.

"I'll smash the ship," he screamed. "I'll—"

Talman drew his own blaster, steadied the muzzle against the pillar, and shot Dalquist in the head. He watched the body lean over the rail, topple, and crash down on the floor plates. Then he rolled over on his face and lay there, making sick, miserable sounds.

"Van," Quentin said.

Talman didn't answer.

"Van!"

"Yeah!"

"Turn off the inductor."

Talman got up, walked unsteadily to the device, and ripped wires loose. He didn't bother to search for an easier method.

After a long while the ship grounded. The humming vibration of currents died. The dim, huge control chamber seemed oddly empty now.

"I've opened a port," Quentin said. "Denver's about fifty miles north. There's a highway four miles or so in the same direction."

Talman stood up, staring around. His face looked ravaged.

"You tricked us," he mumbled. "All along, you were playing us like fish. My psychology—"

"No," Quentin said. "You almost succeeded."

"What—"

"You don't think of me as a gadget, really. You pretended to, but a little matter of semantics saved me. When I realized what you'd said, I came to my senses."

"What I said?"

"Yeah. That you'd never have tried to kill me if I'd still been Bart Quentin."

Talman was struggilng slowly out of his spacesuit. Fresh, clean air had already replaced the poison atmosphere of the ship. He shook his head dazedly.

"I don't see it."

Quentin's laughter rang out, filling the chamber with its warm, human vibrancy.

"A machine can be stopped or destroyed, Van," he said. "But it can't be—*killed*."

Talman didn't say anything. He was free of the bulky suit now, and he turned hesitantly toward a doorway. He looked back.

"The door's open," Quentin said.

"You're letting me go?"

"I told you in Quebec that you'd forget our friendship before I did. Better step it up, Van, while there's still time. Denver's probably sent out helicopters already."

Talman swept one questioning look around the vast chamber. Somewhere, perfectly camouflaged among those mighty machines, was a small metal cylinder, cradled and shielded in its hidden socket. Bart Quentin——

His throat felt dry. He swallowed, opened his mouth, and closed it again.

He turned on his heel and went out. The muffled sound of his footsteps faded.

Alone in the silent ship, Bart Quentin waited for the technicians who would refit his body for the Callisto flight.

THE POWER

by Murray Leinster

ASTOUNDING SCIENCE FICTION,
September

One of the more unique aspects of science fiction is the number of stories in the field that are structured in the form of letters, memos and diary entries. These can be done in the form of a conventional story, with an address at the beginning and a signature at the end, but they can also consist of exchanges between parties, and this is much more difficult—the wrietr has to build in background information, concern him or herself with plot and characters, and not every writer can do this successfully within the confines of the letter/memo form. While these types of stories can be found outside of sf, they are much more common within the genre.

"The Power" is a brilliant example of the form.

(One of the arguments against the existence of any intelligent civilizations outside the Earth is that if they were there, *they would be* here. *In other words, why haven't they reached us, even if we couldn't reach them?*

Some of the counter-arguments are that the speed of light is truly an unbreakable limit and the time it would take to go from one civilization to another has defeated all attempts so that all of us are eternally isolated. Or that they have indeed reached us, but refuse to interfere with us till we are sufficiently advanced and meanwhile keep us under their pro-

tection. Or that they have reached us in the form of flying saucers and we are just too stodgy to accept the fact.

My own notion of the most interesting counter-argument is that they have indeed reached us but it has been useless. They would clearly be at a level of technology far beyond ours and, if so, we simply would not understand either the technology or them. All our tales of angels and demons might be our failure to understand extraterrestrial visitors.

No, I don't believe this, but it is the stuff good sf can be made of. I.A.)

Memorandum from Professor Charles, Latin Department, Haverford University, to Professor McFarland, the same faculty:

Dear Professor McFarland:

In a recent batch of fifteenth-century Latin documents from abroad, we found three which seem to fit together. Our interest is in the Latin of the period, but their contents seem to bear upon your line. I send them to you with a free translation. Would you let me know your reaction?

Charles.

To Johannus Hartmannus, Licentiate in Philosophy,
Living at the house of the goldsmith Grote,
Lane of the Dyed Flee,
Leyden, the Low Countries

Friend Johannus:

I write this from the Goth's Head Inn, in Padua, the second day after Michaelmas, Anno Domini 1482. I write in haste because a worthy Hollander here journeys homeward and has promised to carry mails for me. He is an amiable lout, but ignorant. Do not speak to him of mysteries. He knows nothing. Less than nothing. Thank him, give him to drink, and speak of me as a pious and worthy student. Then forget him.

I leave Padua tomorrow for the realisation of all my hopes and yours. This time I am sure. I came here to purchase perfumes and mandragora and the other necessities for an Operation of the utmost imaginable importance, which I will conduct five nights hence upon a certain hilltop near the village of Montevecchio. I have found a Word and a Name of incalculable power, which in the place that I know of must open to me knowledge of all mysteries. When you read this, I shall possess powers at which Hermes Trismegistos only guessed, and which Albertus Magnus could speak of only by hearsay. I have been deceived before, but this time I am sure. I have seen proofs!

I tremble with agitation as I write to you. I will be brief. I came upon these proofs and the Word and the Name in the village of Montevecchio. I rode into the village at nightfall, disconsolate because I had wasted a month searching for a learned man of whom I had heard great things. Then I found him—and he was but a silly antiquary with no knowledge of mysteries! So, riding upon my way I came to Montevecchio, and there they told me of a man dying even then because he had worked wonders. He had entered the village on foot only the day before. He was clad in rich garments, yet he spoke like a peasant. At first he was mild and humble, but he paid for food and wine with a gold piece, and villagers fawned upon him and asked for alms. He flung them a handful of gold pieces and when the news spread the whole village went mad with greed. They clustered about him, shrieking pleas, and thronging ever the more ugently as he strove to satisfy them. It is said that he grew frightened and would have fled because of their thrusting against him. But they plucked at his garments, screaming of their poverty, until suddenly his rich clothing vanished in the twinkling of an eye and he was but another ragged peasant like themselves and the purse from which he had scattered gold became a mere coarse bag filled with ashes.

This had happened but the day before my arrival, and the man was yet alive, though barely so because the villagers had cried witchcraft and beset him with flails and stones and then dragged him to the village priest to be exorcised.

I saw the man and spoke to him, Johannus, by representing

myself to the priest as a pious student of the snares Satan has set in the form of witchcraft. He barely breathed, what with broken bones and pitchfork wounds. He was a native of the district, who until now had seemed a simple ordinary soul. To secure my intercession with the priest to shrive him ere he died, the man told me all. And it was much!

Upon this certain hillside where I shall perform the Operation five nights hence, he had dozed at midday. Then a Power appeared to him and offered to instruct him in mysteries. The peasant was stupid. He asked for riches instead. So the Power gave him rich garments and a purse which would never empty so long—said the Power—as it came not near a certain metal which destroys all things of mystery. And the Power warned that this was payment that he might send a learned man to learn what he had offered the peasant, because he saw that peasants had no understanding. Thereupon I told the peasant that I would go and greet this Power and fulfil his desires, and he told me the Name and the Word which would call him, and also the Place, begging me to intercede for him with the priest.

The priest showed me a single gold piece which remained of that which the peasant had distributed. It was of the age of Antonius Pius, yet bright and new as if fresh minted. It had the weight and feel of true gold. But the priest, wryly, laid upon it the crucifix he wears upon a small iron chain about his waist. Instantly it vanished, leaving behind a speck of glowing coal which cooled and was a morsel of ash.

This I saw, Johannus! So I came speedily here to Padua, to purchase perfumes and mandragora and the other necessities for an Operation to pay great honour to this Power whom I shall call up five nights hence. He offered wisdom to the peasant, who desired only gold. But I desire wisdom more than gold, and surely I am learned concerning mysteries and Powers! I do not know any but yourself who surpasses me in true knowledge of secret things. And when you read this, Johannus, I shall surpass even you! But it may be that I will gain knowledge so that I can transport myself by a mystery to your attic, and there inform you myself, in advance of this letter, of the results of this surpassing good fortune which causes me to shake with agitation whenever I think of it.

Your friend Carolus,
at the Goth's Head Inn in Padua.

. . . fortunate, perhaps, that an opportunity has come to send a second missive to you, through a crippled man-at-arms who has been discharged from a mercenary band and travels homeward to sit in the sun henceforth. I have given him one gold piece and promised that you would give him another on receipt of this message. You will keep that promise or not, as pleases you, but there is at least the value of a gold piece in a bit of parchment with strange symbols upon it which I enclose for you."

Item: I am in daily communication with the Power of which I wrote you, and daily learn great mysteries.

Item: Already I perform marvels such as men have never before accomplished by means of certain sigils or talismans the Power has prepared for me.

Item: Resolutely the Power refuses to yield to me the Names or the incantations by which these things are done so that I can prepare such sigils for myself. Instead, he instructs me in divers subjects which have no bearing on the accomplishment of wonders, to my bitter impatience which I yet dissemble.

Item: Within this packet there is a bit of parchment. Go to a remote place and there tear it and throw it upon the ground. Instantly, all about you, there will appear a fair garden with marvellous fruits, statuary, and pavilion. You may use this garden as you will, save that if any person enter it, or you yourself, carrying a sword or dagger or any object however small made of iron, the said garden will disappear immediately and nevermore return.

This you may verify when you please. For the rest, I am like a prisoner trembling at the very door of Paradise, barred from entering beyond the antechamber by the fact of the Power withholding from me the true essentials of mystery, and granting me only crumbs—which, however, are greater marvels than any known certainly to have been practised before. For example, the parchment I send you. This art I have proven many times. I have in my scrip many such sigils, made for me by the Power at my entreaty. But when I have secretly taken other parchments and copied upon them the very symbols to the utmost exactitude, they are valueless. There are words or formulas to be spoken over them or—I think more likely—a greater sigil which gives the parchments their magic property. I begin to make a plan—a very daring plan—to acquire even this sigil.

But you will wish to know of the Operation and its results. I return to Montevecchio from Padua, reaching it in three days. The peasant who had worked wonders was dead, the villagers having grown more fearful and beat out his brains with hammers. This pleased me, because I had feared he would tell another the Word and Name he had told me. I spoke to the priest and told him that I had been to Padua and secured advice from high dignitaries concerning the wonder-working, and had been sent back with special commands to seek out and exorcise the foul fiend who had taught the peasant such marvels.

The next day—the priest himself aiding me!—I took up to the hilltop the perfumes and wax tapers and other things needed for the Operation. The priest trembled, but he would have remained had I not sent him away. And night fell, and I drew the magic circle and the pentacle, with the Signs in their proper places. And when the new moon rose, I lighted the perfumes and the fine candles and began the Operation. I have had many failures, as you know, but this time I knew confidence and perfect certainty. When it came time to use the Name and the Word I called them both loudly, thrice, and waited.

Upon this hilltop there are many greyish stones. At the third calling of the Name, one of the stones shivered and was not. Then a voice said dryly:

'Ah! So that is the reason for this stinking stuff! My messenger sent you here?'

There was a shadow where the stone had been and I could not see clearly. But I bowed low in that direction:

'Most Potent Power,' I said, my voice trembling because the Operation was a success, 'a peasant working wonders told me that you desired speech with a learned man. Beside your Potency I am ignorant indeed, but I have given my whole life to the study of mysteries. Therefore I have come to offer worship or such other compact as you may desire in exchange for wisdom.'

There was a stirring in the shadow, and the Power came forth. His appearance was that of a creature not more than an ell and a half in height, and his expression in the moonlight was that of sardonic impatience. The fragrant smoke seemed to cling about him, to make a cloudiness close about his form.

'I think,' said the dry voice, 'that you are as great a fool as the peasant I spoke to. What do you think I am?'

'A Prince of Celestial race, your Potency,' I said, my voice shaking.

There was a pause. The Power said as if wearily:

'Men! Fools forever! Oh man, I am simply the last of a number of my kind who traveled in a fleet from another star. This small planet of yours has a core of the accursed metal, which is fatal to the devices of my race. A few of our ships came too close. Others strove to aid them, and shared their fate. Many, many years since, we descended from the skies and could never rise again. Now I alone am left.'

Speaking of the world as a planet was an absurdity, of course. The planets are wanderers among the stars, travelling in their cycles and epicycles as explained by Ptolemy a thousand years since. But I saw at once that he would test me. So I grew bold and said:

'Lord, I am not fearful. It is not needful to cozen me. Do I not know of those who were cast out of Heaven for rebellion? Shall I write the name of your leader?'

He said 'Eh?' for all the world like an elderly man. So, smiling, I wrote on the earth the true name of Him whom the vulgar call Lucifer. He regarded the markings on the earth and said:

'Bah! It is meaningless. More of your legendary! Look you, man, soon I shall die. For more years than you are like to believe I have hid from your race and its accursed metal. I have watched men, and despised them. But—I die. And it is not good that knowledge should perish. It is my desire to impart to men the knowledge which else would die with me. It can do no harm to my own kind, and may bring the race of men to some degree of civilisation in the course of ages.'

I bowed to the earth before him. I was aflame with eagerness.

'Most Potent One,' I said joyfully. 'I am to be trusted. I will guard your secrets fully. Not one jot or tittle shall ever be divulged!'

Again his voice was annoyed and dry.

'I desire that this knowledge be spread so that all may learn it. But—' Then he made a sound which I do not understand, save that it seemed to be derisive—'What I have to say may serve, even garbled and twisted. And I do not think you will keep secrets inviolate. Have you pen and parchment?'

'Nay, Lord!'

'You will come again, then, prepared to write what I shall tell you.'

But he remained, regarding me. He asked me questions, and I answered eagerly. Presently he spoke in a meditative voice, and I listened eagerly. His speech bore an odd similarity to that of a lonely man who dwelt much on the past, but soon I realised that he spoke in ciphers, in allegory, from which now and again the truth peered out. As one who speaks for the sake of remembering, he spoke of the home of his race upon what he said was a fair planet so far distant that to speak of leagues and even the span of continents would be useless to convey the distance. He told of cities in which his fellows dwelt—here, of course, I understood his meaning perfectly—and told of great fleets of flying things rising from those cities to go to other fair cities, and of music which was in the very air so that any person, anywhere upon the planet, could hear sweet sounds or wise discourse at will. In this matter there was no metaphor, because the perpetual sweet sounds in Heaven are matters of common knowledge. But he added a metaphor immediately after, because he smiled at me and observed that the music was not created by a mystery, but by waves like those of light, only longer. And this was plainly a cipher, because light is an impalpable fluid without length and surely without waves!

Then he spoke of flying through the emptiness of the empyrean, which again is not clear, because all can see that the heavens are fairly crowded with stars, and he spoke of many suns and other worlds, some frozen and some merely barren rock. The obscurity of such things is patent. And he spoke of drawing near to this world which is ours, and of an error made as if it were in mathematics—instead of in rebellion—so that they drew close to Earth as Icarus to the sun. Then again he spoke in metaphors, because he referred to engines, which are things to cast stones against walls, and in a larger sense for grinding corn and pumping water. But he spoke of engines growing hot because of the accursed metal in the core of Earth, and of the inability of his kind to resist Earth's pull—more metaphor—and then he spoke of a screaming descent from the skies. And all of this, plainly, is a metaphorical account of the casting of the Rebels out of

Heaven, and an acknowledgement that he is one of the said Rebels.

When he paused, I begged humbly that he would show me a mystery and of his grace give me protection in case my converse with him became known.

'What happened to my messenger?' asked the Power.

I told him, and he listened without stirring. I was careful to tell him exactly, because of course he would know that—as all else—by his powers of mystery, and the question was but another test. Indeed, I felt sure that the messenger and all that had taken place had been contrived by him to bring me, a learned student of mysteries, to converse with him in this place.

'Men!' he said bitterly at last. Then he added coldly. 'Nay! I can give you no protection. My kind is without protection upon this earth. If you would learn what I can teach you, you must risk the fury of your fellow countrymen.'

But then, abruptly, he wrote upon parchment and pressed the parchment to some object at his side. He threw it upon the ground.

'If men beset you,' he said scornfully, 'tear this parchment and cast it from you. If you have none of the accursed metal about you, it may distract them while you flee. But a dagger will cause it all to come to naught!'

Then he walked away. He vanished. And I stood shivering for a very long time before I remembered me of the formula given by Apollonius of Tyana for the dismissal of evil spirits. I ventured from the magic circle. No evil befell me. I picked up the parchment and examined it in the moonlight. The symbols upon it were meaningless, even to one like myself who has studied all that is known of mysteries. I returned to the village, pondering.

I have told you so much at length, because you will observe that this Power did not speak with the pride or the menace of which most authors on mysteries and Operations speak. It is often said that an adept must conduct himself with great firmness during an Operation, lest the Powers he has called up overawe him. Yet this Power spoke wearily, with irony, like one approaching death. And he had spoken of death, also. Which was of course a test and a deception, because are not the Principalities and Powers of Darkness immortal? He had some design it was not his will that I should know. So I saw that I must walk warily in this priceless opportunity.

In the village I told the priest that I had had encounter with a foul fiend, who begged that I not exorcise him, promising to reveal certain hidden treasures once belonging to the Church, which he could not touch or reveal to evil men because they were holy, but could describe the location of to me. And I procured parchment, and pens, and ink, and the next day I went alone to the hilltop. It was empty, and I made sure I was unwatched and—leaving my dagger behind me—I tore the parchment and flung it to the ground.

As it touched, there appeared such a treasure of gold and jewels as truly would have driven any man mad with greed. There were bags and chests and boxes filled with gold and precious stones, which had burst with the weight and spilled out upon the ground. There were gems glittering in the late sunlight, and rings and necklaces set with brilliants, and such monstrous hoards of golden coins of every antique pattern . . .

Johannus, even I went almost mad! I leaped forward like one dreaming to plunge my hands into the gold. Slavering, I filled my garments with rubies and ropes of pearls, and stuffed my scrip with gold pieces, laughing crazily to myself. I rolled in the riches. I wallowed in them, flinging the golden coins into the air and letting them fall upon me. I laughed and sang to myself.

Then I heard a sound. On the instant I was filled with terror for the treasure. I leaped to my dagger and snarled, ready to defend my riches to the death.

Then a dry voice said: 'Truly you care naught for riches!'

It was savage mockery. The Power stood regarding me. I saw him clearly now, yet not clearly because there was a cloudiness which clung closely to his body. He was, as I said, an ell and a half in height, and from his forehead there protruded knobby feelers which were not horns but had somewhat the look save for bulbs upon their ends. His head was large and—But I will not attempt to describe him, because he could assume any of a thousand forms, no doubt, so what does it matter?

Then I grew terrified because I had no Circle or Pentacle to protect me. But the Power made no menacing move.

'It is real, that riches,' he said dryly. 'It has colour and weight and the feel of substance. But your dagger will destroy it all.'

Didyas of Corinth has said that treasure of mystery must be fixed by a special Operation before it becomes permanent and free of the power of Those who brought it. They can transmute it back to leaves or other rubbish, if it be not fixed.

'Touch it with your dagger,' said the Power.

I obeyed, sweating in fear. And as the metal iron touched a great pile heap of gold, there was a sudden shifting and then a little flare about me. And the treasure—all, to the veriest crumb of a seed-pearl!—vanished before my eyes. The bit of parchment reappeared, smoking. It turned to ashes. My dagger scorched my fingers. It had grown hot.

'Ah, yes,' said the Power, nodding. 'The force-field has energy. When the iron absorbs it, there is heat.' Then he looked at me in a not unfriendly way. 'You have brought pens and parchment,' he said, 'and at least you did not use the sigil to astonish your fellows. Also you had the good sense to make no more perfumish stinks. It may be that there is a grain of wisdom in you. I will bear with you yet a while. Be seated and take parchment and pen—Stay! Let us be comfortable. Sheathe your dagger, or better, cast it from you.'

I put it in my bosom. And it was as if he thought, and touched something at his side, and instantly there was a fair pavilion about us, with soft cushions and a gently playing fountain.

'Sit,' said the Power. 'I learned that men like such things as this from a man I once befriended. He had been wounded and stripped by robbers, so that he had not so much as a scrap of accursed metal about him, and I could aid him. I learned to speak the language men use nowadays from him. But to the end he believed me an evil spirit and tried valorously to hate me.'

My hands shook with my agitation that the treasure had departed from me. Truly it was a treasure of such riches as no King has ever possessed, Johannus! My very soul lusted after that treasure! The golden coins alone would fill your attic solidly, but the floor would break under their weight, and the jewels would fill hogsheads. Ah, Johannus! That treasure!

'What I will have you write,' said the Power, 'at first will mean little. I shall give facts and theories first, because they are easiest to remember. Then I will give the applications of the theories. Then you men will have the beginning of such civilisation as can exist in the neighbourhood of the accursed metal.'

'Your Potency!' I begged abjectly. 'You will give me another sigil of treasure?'

'Write!' he commanded.

I wrote. And, Johannus, I cannot tell you myself what it is that I wrote. He spoke words, and they were in such obscure cipher that they have no meaning as I con them over. Hark you to this, and seek wisdom for the performance of mysteries in it! 'The civilisation of my race is based upon fields of force which have the property of acting in all essentials as substance. A lodestone is surrounded by a field of force which is invisible and impalpable. But the fields used by my people for dwellings, tools, vehicles, and even machinery are perceptible to the senses and act physically as solids. More, we are able to form these fields in latent fashions; and to fix them to organic objects as permanent fields which require no energy for their maintenance, just as magnetic fields require no energy supply to continue. Our fields, too, may be projected as three-dimensional solids which assume any desired form and have every property of substance except chemical affinity.'

Johannus! Is it not unbelievable that words could be put together, dealing with mysteries, which are so devoid of any clue to their true mystic meaning? I write and I write in desperate hope that he will eventually give me the key, but my brain reels at the difficulty of extracting the directions for Operations which such ciphers must conceal! I give you another instance: 'When a force-field generator has been built as above, it will be found that the pulsatory fields which are consciousness serve perfectly as controls. One has but to visualise the object desired, turn on the generator's auxiliary control, and the generator will pattern its output upon the pulsatory consciousness-field . . .'

Upon this first day of writing, the Power spoke for hours, and I wrote until my hand ached. From time to time, resting, I read back to him the words that I had written. He listened, satisfied.

'Lord!' I said shakily. 'Mighty Lord! Your Potency! These mysteries you bid me write—they are beyond comprehension!'

But he said scornfully:

'Write! Some will be clear to someone. And I will explain it little by little until even you can comprehend the beginning.' Then he added. 'You grow weary. You wish a toy. Well! I will make you a sigil which will make again that treasure you played with. I will add a sigil which will make a boat for you, with an engine drawing power from the sea to carry you wheresoever you wish without need of wind or tide. I will make others so you may create a palace where you will, and fair gardens as you please . . .'

These things he has done, Johannus. It seems to amuse him to write upon scraps of parchment, and think, and then press them against his side before he lays them upon the ground for me to pick up. He has explained amusedly that the wonder in the sigil is complete, yet latent, and is released by the tearing of the parchment, but absorbed and destroyed by iron. In such fashion he speaks in ciphers, but otherwise sometimes he jests!

It is strange to think of it, that I have come little by little to accept this Power as a person. It is not in accord with the laws of mystery. I feel that he is lonely. He seems to find satisfaction in speech with me. Yet he is a Power, one of the Rebels who was flung to earth from Heaven! He speaks of that only in vague, metaphorical terms, as if he had come from another world like *the* world, save much larger. He refers to himself as a voyager of space, and speaks of his race with affection, and of Heaven—at any rate the city from which he comes, because there must be great cities there—with a strange and prideful affection. If it were not for his powers, which are of mystery, I would find it possible to believe that he was a lonely member of a strange race, exiled forever in a strange place, and grown friendly with a man because of his loneliness. But how could there be such as he and not a Power? How could there be another world?

This strange converse has now gone on for ten days or more. I have filled sheets upon sheets of parchment with writing. The same metaphors occur again and again. 'Force-fields' —a term without literal meaning—occurs often. There are other metaphors such as 'coils' and 'primary' and 'secondary' which are placed in context with mention of wires of copper metal. There are careful descriptions, as if in the plainest of language, of sheets of dissimilar metals which are to be placed in acid, and other descriptions of plates of similar metal which are to be separated by layers of air or wax of certain thicknesses, with the plates of certain areas! And there is an explanation of the means by which he lives. 'I, being accustomed to an atmosphere much more dense than that on Earth, am forced to keep about myself a field of force which maintains an air density near that of my home planet for my breathing. This field is transparent, but because it must shift constantly to change and refresh the air I breathe, it causes a certain cloudiness of outline next my body. It is maintained by the generator I wear at my side, which at the same time provides energy for such other force-field artifacts as I may find convenient.'—Ah, Johannes! I grow mad with impatience! Did I not anticipate that he would some day give me the key to this metaphorical speech, so that from it may be extracted the Names and the Words which cause his wonders. I would give over in despair.

Yet he has grown genial with me. He has given me such sigils as I have asked him, and I have tried them many times. The sigil which will make you a fair garden is one of many. He says that he desires to give to man the knowledge he possesses, and then bids we write ciphered speech without meaning, such as: 'The drive of a ship for flight beyond the speed of light is adapted from the simple drive generator already described simply by altering its constants so that it cannot generate in normal space and must create an abnormal space by tension. The process is—' Or else—I choose at random, Johannus—'The accursed metal, iron, must be eliminated not only from all circuits but from nearness to apparatus using high-frequency oscillations, since it absorbs their energy and prevents the functioning . . ."

I am like a man trembling upon the threshold of Paradise, yet unable to enter because the key is withheld. 'Speed of light!' What could it mean in metaphor? In common parlance, as well speak of the speed of weather or of granite! Daily I beg him for the key to his speech. Yet even now, in the sigils he makes for me is greater power than any man has ever known before!

But it is not enough. The Power speaks as if he were lonely beyond compare; the last member of a strange race upon earth; as if he took a strange, companion-like pleasure in merely talking to me. When I beg him for a Name or a Word which would give me power beyond such as he doles out in sigils, he is amused and calls me fool, yet kindly. And he speaks more of his metaphorical speech about forces of nature and fields of force—and gives me a sigil which should I use it will create a palace with walls of gold and pillars of emerald! And then he amusedly reminds me that one greedy looter with an axe or hoe of iron would case it to vanish utterly!

I go almost mad, Johannus! But there is certainly wisdom unutterable to be had from him. Gradually, cautiously, I have come to act as if we were merely friends, of different race and he vastly the wiser, but friends rather than Prince and subject. Yet I remember the warnings of the most authoritative authors that one must be ever on guard against Powers called up in an Operation.

I have a plan. It is dangerous, I well know, but I grow desperate. To stand quivering upon the threshold of such wisdom and power as no man has ever dreamed of before, and then be denied . . .

The mercenary who will carry this to you, leaves tomorrow. He is a cripple, and may be months upon the way. All will be decided ere you receive this. I know you wish me well.

Was there ever a student of mystery in so saddening a predicament, with all knowledge in his grasp yet not quite his?

Your friend
Carolus.

Written in the very bad inn in Montevecchio.

Johannus! A courier goes to Ghent for My Lord of Brabant and I have opportunity to send you mail. I think I go mad, Johannus! I have power such as no man ever possessed before, and I am fevered with bitterness. Hear me!

For three weeks I did repair daily to the hilltop beyond Montevecchio and take down the ciphered speech of which I wrote you. My script was stuffed with sigils, but I had not one word of Power or Name of Authority. The Power grew mocking, yet it seemed sadly mocking. He insisted that his words held no cipher and needed but to be read. Some of them he phrased over and over again until they were but instructions for putting bits of metal together, mechanicwise. Then he made me follow those instructions. But there was no Word, no Name—nothing save bits of metal put together cunningly. And how could inanimate metal, not imbued with power of mystery by Names or Words or incantations, have power to work mystery?

At long last I became convinced that he would never reveal the wisdom he had promised. And I had come to such familiarity with this Power that I could dare to rebel, and even to believe that I had chance of success. There was the cloudiness about his form, which was maintained by a sigil he wore at his side and called a 'generator.' Were that cloudiness destroyed, he could not live, or so he had told me. It was for that reason that he, in person, dared not touch anything of iron. This was the basis of my plan.

I feigned illness, and said that I would rest at a peasant's thatched hut, no longer inhabited, at the foot of the hill on which the Power lived. There was surely no nail of iron in so crude a dwelling. If he felt for me the affection he protested, he would grant me leave to be absent in my illness. If his affection was great, he might even come and speak to me there. I would be alone in the hope that his friendship might go so far.

Strange words for a man to use to a Power! But I had talked daily with him for three weeks. I lay groaning in the hut, alone. On the second day he came. I affected great rejoicing, and made shift to light a fire from a taper I had kept burning. He thought it a mark of honour, but it was actually a signal. And then, as he talked to me in what he thought my illness, there came a cry from without the hut. It was the village priest, a simple man but very brave in his fashion. On the signal of smoke from the peasant's hut, he had crept near and drawn all about it an iron chain that we had muffled with cloth so that it would make no sound. And now he stood before the hut door with his crucifix upraised, chanting exorcisms. A very brave man, that priest, because I had pictured the Power as a foul fiend indeed.

The Power turned and looked at me, and I held my dagger firmly.

'I hold the accursed metal,' I told him fiercely. 'There is a ring of it about this house. Tell me now, quickly, the Words and the Names which make the sigils operate! Tell me the secret of the cipher you had me write! Do this and I will slay this priest and draw away the chain and you may go hence unharmed. But be quick, or—'

The Power cast a sigil upon the ground. When the parchment struck earth, there was an instant's cloudiness as if some dread thing had begun to form. But then the parchment smoked and turned to ash. The ring of iron about the hut had destroyed its power when it was used. The Power knew that I spoke truth.

'Ah!' said the Power dryly. 'Men! And I thought one was my friend!' He put his hand to his side. 'To be sure! I should have known. Iron rings me about. My engine heats . . .'

He looked at me. I held up the dagger, fiercely unyielding.

'The Names!' I cried. 'The Words! Give me power of my own and I will slay the priest!'

'I tried,' said the Power quietly, 'to give you wisdom. And you will stab me with the accursed metal if I do not tell you things which do not exist. But you need not. I cannot live long in a ring of iron. My engine will burn out; my force-field will fail. I will stifle in the thin air which is dense enough for you. Will not that satisfy you? Must you stab me, also?'

I sprang from my pallet of straw to threaten him more fiercely. It was madness, was it not? But I was mad, Johannus!

'Forbear,' said the Power. 'I could kill you now, with me! But I thought you my friend. I will go out and see your priest. I would prefer to die at his hand. He is perhaps only a fool.'

He walked steadily toward the doorway. As he stepped over the iron chain, I thougth I saw a wisp of smoke begin, but he touched the thing at his side. The cloudiness about his person vanished. There was a puffing sound, and his garments jerked as if in a gust of wind. He staggered. But he went on, and touched his side again and the cloudiness returned and he walked more strongly. He did not try to turn aside. He walked directly toward the priest, and even I could see that he walked with a bitter dignity.

And—I saw the priest's eyes grow wide with horror. Because he saw the Power for the first time, and the Power was an ell and a half high, with a large head and knobbed feelers projecting from his forehead, and the priest knew instantly that he was not of any race of men but was a Power and one of those Rebels who were flung out from Heaven.

I heard the Power speak to the priest, with dignity. I did not hear what he said. I raged in my disappointment. But the priest did not waver. As the Power moved toward him, the priest moved toward the Power. His face was filled with horror, but it was resolute. He reached forward with the crucifix he wore always attached to an iron chain about his waist. He thrust it to touch the Power, crying, '*In nomine Patri*—'

Then there was smoke. It came from a spot at the Power's

side where was the engine to which he touched the sigils he had made, to imbue them with the power of mystery. And then—

I was blinded. There was a flare of monstrous, bluish light, like a lightning stroke from heaven. After, there was a ball of fierce yellow flame which gave off a cloud of black smoke. There was a monstrous, outraged bellow of thunder.

Then there was nothing save the priest standing there, his face ashen, his eyes resolute, his eyebrows singed, chanting psalms in a shaking voice.

I have come to Venice. My script is filled with sigils with which I can work wonders. No men can work such wonders as I can. But I use them not. I labour daily, nightly, hourly, minute by minute, trying to find the key to the cipher which will yield the wisdom the Power possessed and desired to give to men. Ah, Johannus! I have those sigils and I can work wonders, but when I have used them they will be gone and I shall be powerless. I had such a chance at wisdom as never man possessed before, and it is gone! Yet I shall spend years—aye!—all the rest of my life, seeking the true meaning of what the Power spoke! I am the only man in all the world who ever spoke daily, for weeks on end, with a Prince of Powers of Darkness, and was accepted by him as a friend to such a degree as to encompass his own destruction. It must be true that I have wisdom written down! But how shall I find instructions for mystery in such metaphors as—to choose a fragment by chance—'plates of two dissimilar metals, immersed in an acid, generate a force for which men have not yet a name, yet which is the basis of true civilisation. Such plates . . .'

I grow mad with disappointment, Johannus! Why did he not speak clearly? Yet I will find out the secret . . .

Memorandum from Peter McFarland, Physics Department, Haverford University, to Professor Charles, Latin, the same Faculty:

Dear Professor Charles:

My reaction is, Damnation! Where is the rest of this stuff?

McFarland.

GIANT KILLER

by A. Bertram Chandler (1912-)

ASTOUNDING SCIENCE FICTION,
October

A. Bertram Chandler is a retired Australian merchant naval officer, whose most famous creations in science fiction are the "Rim Worlds" stories and novels featuring John Grimes. These are entertaining and superior space opera tables that have won Chandler a wide and devoted following. Unfortunately, these books have obscured his shorter fiction on other subjects, which are frequently of a high standard. Particularly noteworthy are "The Cage" (1957), one of the best stories ever on the question of what it means to be human, and the present selection.

"Giant Killer" is a "closed universe" story wherein the characters (or at least some of them) do not realize that their environment constitutes only a small, confined space. It is arguably his finest work of science fiction, although the author is still active and writing in the field.

(I suppose that an editor is allowed to have a favorite story in any anthology he puts together. Generally, if one of my own stories is contained in an anthology I edit, that *is my favorite and since it is generally accepted that I lack modesty, I am allowed to say so.*

Yet even though I have a story in this anthology, I am forced to admit that Chandler's story is my favorite. If you have never encountered it before, read it through to the ending and then with the illumination that comes of that, read it a second time. It then sounds quite different.

The technical problems involved in writing a story of this kind are enormous and Chandler manages them with what seems enviable ease though I know enough about such matters to suppose that behind the scenes he had to do a lot of thinking through a number of sleepless nights. I.A.)

Shrick should have died before his baby eyes had opened on his world. Shrick would have died, but Weena, his mother, was determined that he, alone of all her children, should live. Three previous times since her mating with Skreer had she borne, and on each occasion the old, gray Sterret, Judge of the Newborn, had condemned her young as Different Ones.

Weena had no objection to the Law when it did not affect her or hers. She, as much as any other member of the Tribe, keenly enjoyed the feasts of fresh, tasty meat following the ritual slaughter of the Different Ones. But when those sacrificed were the fruit of her own womb it wasn't the same.

It was quiet in the cave where Weena awaited the coming of her lord. Quiet, that is, save for the sound of her breathing and an occasional plaintive, mewling cry from the newborn child. And even these sounds were deadened by the soft spongy walls and ceiling.

She sensed the coming of Skreer long before his actual arrival. She anticipated his first question and, as he entered the cave, said quietly, "One. A male."

"A male?" Skreer radiated approval. Then she felt his mood change to one of questioning, of doubt. "Is it . . . he—?"

"Yes."

Skreer caught the tiny, warm being in his arms. There was no light, but he, like all his race, was accustomed to the dark. His fingers told him all that he needed to know. The child was hairless. The legs were too straight. And—this was worst of all—the head was a great, bulging dome.

"Skreer!" Weena's voice was anxious. "Do you—?"

"There is no doubt. Sterret will condemn it as a Different One."

"But—"

"There is no hope." Weena sensed that her mate shuddered, heard the faint, silken rustle of his fur as he did so. "His head! He is like the Giants!"

The mother sighed. It was hard, but she knew the Law. And yet—This was her fourth childbearing, and she was never to know, perhaps, what it was to watch and wait with mingled pride and terror while her sons set out with the other young males to raid the Giants' territory, to bring back spoils from the great Cave-of-Food, the Place-of-Green-Growing-Things or, even, precious scraps of shiny metal from the Place-of-Life-That-Is-Not-Life.

She clutched at a faint hope.

"His head is like a Giant's? Can it be, do you think, that the Giants are Different Ones? I have heard it said."

"What if they are?"

"Only this. Perhaps he will grow to be a Gaint. Perhaps he will fight the other Giants for us, his own people. Perhaps—"

"Perhaps Sterret will let him live, you mean." Skreer made the short, unpleasant sound that passed among his people for a laugh. "No, Weena. He must die. And it is long since we feasted—"

"But—"

"Enough. Or do *you* wish to provide meat for the Tribe also? I may wish to find a mate who will bear me sturdy sons, not monsters!"

The Place-of-Meeting was almost deserted when Skreer and Weena, she with Shrick clutched tightly in her arms, entered. Two more couples were there, each with newborn. One of the mothers was holding two babies, each of whom appeared to be normal. The other had three, her mate holding one of them.

Weena recognized her as Teeza, and flashed her a little half smile of sympathy when she saw that the child carried by Teeza's mate would certainly be condemned by Sterret when he choose to appear. For it was, perhaps, even more revolting than her own Different One, having two hands growing from the end of each arm.

Skreer approached one of the other males, he unburdened with a child.

"How long have you been waiting?" he asked.

"Many heartbeats. We—"

The guard stationed at the doorway through which light entered from Inside hissed a warning:

"Quiet! A Giant is coming!"

The mothers clutched their children to them yet more tightly, their fur standing on end with superstitious dread. They knew that if they remained silent there was no danger, that even if they should betray themselves by some slight noise there was no immediate peril. It was not size along that made the Giants dreaded, it was the supernatural powers that they were known to possess. The food-that-kills had slain many an unwary member of the Tribe, also their fiendishly cunning devices that crushed and managled any of the People unwise enough to reach greedily for the savory morsels left exposed on a kind of little platform. Although there were those who averred that, in the latter case, the risk was well worth it, for the yellow grains from the many bags in the Cave-of-Food were as monotonous as they were nourishing.

"The Giant has passed!"

Before those in the Place-of-Meeting could resume their talk, Sterret drifted out from the entrance of his cave. He held in his right hand his wand of office, a straight staff of the hard, yet soft, stuff dividing the territory of the People from that of the Giants. It was tipped with a sharp point of metal.

He was old, was Sterret.

Those who were themselves grandparents had heard their grandparents speak of him. For generations he had survived attacks by young males jealous of his prerogatives as chief, and the more rare assaults by parents displeased by his rulings as Judge of the Newborn. In this latter case, however, he had had nothing to fear, for on those isolated occasions the Tribe had risen as one and torn the offenders to pieces.

Behind Sterret came his personal guards and then, floating out from the many cave entrances, the bulk of the Tribe. There had been no need so summon them; they *knew*.

The chief, deliberate and unhurried, took his position in the center of the Place-of-Meeting. Without orders, the crowd made way for the parents and their newborn. Weena winced as she saw their gloating eyes fixed on Shrick's revolting baldness, his misshapen skull. She knew what the verdict would be.

She hoped that the newborn of the others would be judged before her own, although that would merely delay the death of her own child by the space of a very few heartbeats. She hoped—

"Weena! Bring the child to me that I may see and pass judgment!"

The chief extended his skinny arms, took the child from the mother's reluctant hands. His little, deep-set eyes gleamed at the thought of the draught of rich, red blood that he was soon to enjoy. And yet he was reluctant to lose the savor of a single heartbeat of the mother's agony. Perhaps she could be provoked into an attack—

"You insult us," he said slowly, "by bringing forth *this!*" He held Shrick, who squalled feebly, at arm's length. "Look, oh People, at this *thing* the miserable Weena has brought for my judgment!"

"He has a Giant's head." Weena's timid voice was barely audible. "Perhaps—"

"—his father was a Giant!"

A tittering laugh rang through the Place-of-Meeting.

"No. But I have heard it said that perhaps the Giants, or their fathers and mothers, were Different Ones. And—"

"Who said that?"

"Strela."

"Yes, Strela the Wise. Who, in his wisdom, ate largely of the food-that-kills!"

Again the hateful laughter rippled through the assembly.

Sterret raised the hand that held the spear, shortening his grip on the haft. His face puckered as he tasted in anticipation the bright bubble of blood that would soon well from the throat of the Different One. Weena screamed. With one hand she snatched her child from the hateful grasp of the chief, with the other she seized his spear.

Sterret was old, and generations of authority had made him careless. Yet, old as he was, he evaded the vicious thrust aimed at him by the mother. He had no need to cry orders, from all sides the People converged upon the rebel.

Already horrified by her action, Weena knew that she could expect no mercy. And yet life, even as lived by the Tribe, was sweet. Gaining a purchase from the gray, spongy floor of the Place-of-Meeting she jumped. The impetus of her leap carried her up to the doorway through which streamed the light from Inside. The guard there was unarmed, for of what avail would a puny spear be against the Giants? He fell back before the menace of Weena's bright blade and bared teeth. And then Weena was Inside.

She could, she knew, hold the doorway indefinitely against pursuit. But this was Giant country. In an agony of indecision she clung to the rim of the door with one hand, the other still holding the spear. A face appeared in the opening, and then vanished, streaming with blood. It was only later that she realized that it had been Skreer's.

She became acutely conscious of the fierce light beating around and about her, of the vast spaces on all sides of a body that was accustomed to the close quarters of the caves and tunnels. She felt naked and, in spite of her spear, utterly defenseless.

Then that which she dreaded came to pass.

Behind her, she sensed the approach of two of the Giants. Then she could hear their breathing, and the low, infinitely menacing rumble of their voices as they talked one with the other. They hadn't seen her—of that she was certain, but it was only a matter of heartbeats before they did so. The open doorway, with the certainty of death that lay beyond, seemed infinitely preferable to the terror of the unknown. Had it been only her life at stake she would have returned to face the righteous wrath of her chief, her mate and her Tribe.

Fighting down her blind panic, she forced herself to a clarity of thought normally foreign to her nature. If she yielded to instinct, if she fled madly before the approaching Giants, she would be seen. Her only hope was to remain utterly still. Skreer, and others of the males who had been on forays Inside, had told her that the Giants, careless in their size and power, more often than not did not notice the People unless they made some betraying movement.

The Giants were very close.

Slowly, cautiously, she turned her head.

She could see them now, two enormous figures floating through the air with easy arrogance. They had not seen her, and she knew that they would not see her unless she made some sudden movement to attract their attention. Yet it was hard not to yield to the impulse to dive back into the doorway to the Place-of-Meeting, there to meet certain death at the hands of the outraged Tribe. It was harder still to fight the urge to relinquish her hold on the rim of the doorway and flee—anywhere—in screaming panic.

But she held on.

The Giants passed.

The dull rumble of their voices died in the distance, their acrid, unpleasant odor, of which she had heard but never before experienced, diminished. Weena dared to raise her head once more.

In the confused, terrified welter of her thoughts one idea stood out with dreadful clarity. Her only hope of survival, pitifully slim though it was, lay in following the Giants. There was no time to lose, already she could hear the rising clamor of voices as those in the caves sensed that the Giants had passed. She relinquished her hold on the edge of the door and floated slowly up.

When Weena's head came into sudden contact with something hard she screamed. For long seconds she waited, eyes close shut in terror, for the doom that would surely descend upon her. But nothing happened. The pressure upon the top of her skull neither increased nor diminished.

Timidly, she opened her eyes.

As far as she could see, in two directions, stretched a long, straight shaft or rod. Its thickness was that of her own body, and it was made, or covered with, a material not altogether strange to the mother. It was like the ropes woven by the females with fibers from the Place-of-Green-Growing-Things—but incomparably finer. Stuff such as this was brought back sometimes by the males from their expeditions. It had been believed, once. that it was the fur of the Giants, but now it was assumed that it was made by them for their own purposes.

On three sides of the shaft was the glaring emptiness so terrifying to the people of the caves. On the fourth side was a flat, shiny surface. Weena found that she could insinuate herself into the space between the two without discomfort. She discovered, also, that with comforting solidity at her back and belly she could make reasonably fast progress along the shaft. It was only when she looked to either side that she felt a return of her vertigo. She soon learned not to look.

It is hard to estimate the time taken by her journey in a world where time was meaningless. Twice she had to stop and feed Shrick—fearful lest his hungry wailings betray their presence either to Giants or any of the People who might—although this was highly improbable—have followed her. Once she felt the shaft vibrating, and froze to its matte surface in utter and abject terror. A Giant passed, pulling himself rapidly along with his two hands. Had either of those hands fallen upon Weena it would have been the finish. For many heartbeats after his passing she clung there limp and helpless, scarcely daring to breathe.

It seemed that she passed through places of which she had heard the males talk. This may have been so—but she had no means of knowing. For the world of the People, with its caves and tunnels, was familiar territory, while that of the Giants was known only in relation to the doorways through which a daring explorer could enter.

Weena was sick and faint with hunger and thirst when, at last, the long shaft led her into a place where she could smell the tantalizing aroma of food. She stopped, looked in all directions. But here, as everywhere in this alien country, the light was too dazzling for her untrained eyes. She could see, dimly, vast shapes beyond her limited understanding. She could see no Giants, nor anything that moved.

Cautiously, keeping a tight hold on the rough surface of the shaft, she edged out to the side away from the polished, flat surface along which she had been traveling. Back and forth her head swung, her sensitive nostrils dilated. The bright light confused her, so she shut her eyes. Once again her nose sought the source of the savory smell, swinging ever more slowly as the position was determined with reasonable accuracy.

She was loathe to abandon the security of her shaft, but hunger overruled all other considerations. Orienting her body, she jumped. With a thud she brought up against another flat surface. Her free hand found a projection, to which she clung. This she almost relinquished as it turned. Then a crack appeared, with disconcerting suddenness, before her eyes, widening rapidly. Behind this opening was black, welcome darkness. Weena slipped inside, grateful for relief from the glaring light of the Inside. It wasn't until later that she realized that this was a door such as was made by her own people in the Barrier, but a door of truly gigantic proportions. But all that mattered at first was the cool, refreshing shade.

Then she took stock of her surroundings.

Enough light came in through the barely open doorway for her to see that she was in a cave. It was the wrong shape for a cave, it is true, having flat, perfectly regular walls and floor and ceiling. At the far end, each in its own little compartment, were enormous, dully shining globes. From them came a smell that almost drove the famishing mother frantic.

Yet she held back. She knew that smell. It was that of fragments of food that had been brought into the caves, won by stealth and guile from the killing platforms of the Giants. Was this a killing platform? She wracked her brains to recall the poor description of these devices given by the males, decided that this, after all, must be a Cave-of-Food. Relinquishing her hold of Shrick and Sterret's spear she made for the nearest globe.

At first she tried to pull it from its compartment, but it appeared to be held. But it didn't matter. Bringing her face against the surface of the sphere she buried her teeth in its thin skin. There was flesh beneath the skin, and blood—a thin, sweet faintly acid juice, Skreer had, at times, promised her a share of this food when next he won some from a killing platform, but that promise had never been kept. And now Weena had a whole cave of this same food all to herself.

Gorged to repletion, she started back to pick up the now loudly complaining Shrick. He had been playing with the spear and had cut himself on the sharp point. But it was the spear that Weena snatched, swinging swiftly to defend herself and her child. For a voice said, understandable, but with an oddly slurred intonation, "Who are you? What are you doing in our country?"

It was one of the People, a male. He was unarmed, otherwise it is certain that he would never have asked questions. Even so, Weena knew that the slightest relaxation of vigilance on her part would bring a savage, tooth-and-nail attack.

She tightened her grasp on the spear, swung it so that its point was directed at the stranger.

"I am Weena," she said, "of the Tribe of Sterret."

"Of the Tribe of Sterret? But the Tribe of Sessa holds the ways between our countries."

"I came Inside. But who are you?"

"Tekka. I am one of Skarro's people. You are a spy."

"So I brought my child with me."

Tekka was looking at Shrick.

"I see," he said at last. "A Different One, But how did you get through Sessa's country?"

"I didn't. I came Inside."

It was obvious that Tekka refused to believe her story.

"You must come with me," he said, "to Skarro. He will judge."

"And if I come?"

"For the Different One, death. For you, I do not know. But we have too many females in our Tribe already."

"This says that I will not come." Weena brandished her spear.

She would not have defied a male of her own tribe thus—but this Teeka was not of her people. And she had always been brought up to believe that even a female of the Tribe of Sterrett was superior to a male—even a chief—of any alien community.

"The Giants will find you here." Tekka's voice showed an elaborate unconcern. Then— "That is a fine spear."

"Yes. It belonged to Sterret. With it I wounded my mate. Perhaps he is dead."

The male looked at her with a new respect. If her story were true—this was a female to be handled with caution. Besides—

"Would you give it to me?"

"Yes." Weena laughed nastily. There was no mistaking her meaning.

"Not that way. Listen. Not long ago in our Tribe, many mothers, two whole hands of mothers with Different Ones, defied the Judge of the Newborn. They fled along the tunnels, and live outside the Place-of-Little-Lights. Skarro has not yet led a war party against them. Why, I do not know, but there is always a Giant in that place. It may be that Skarro fears that a fight behind the Barrier would warn the Giants of our presence—"

"And you will lead me there?"

"Yes. In return for the spear."

Weena was silent for the space of several heartbeats. As long as Tekka preceded her she would be safe. It never occurred to her that she could let the other fulfill his part of the bargain, and then refuse him his payment. Her people were a very primitive race.

"I will come with you," she said.

"It is well."

Tekka's eyes dwelt long and lovingly upon the fine spear. Skarro would not be chief much longer.

"First," he said, "we must pull what you have left of the good-to-eat-ball into our tunnel. Then I must shut the door lest a Giant should come—"

Together they hacked and tore the sphere to pieces. There was a doorway at the rear of one of the little compartments, now empty. Through this they pushed and pulled their fragrant burden. First Weena went into the tunnel, carrying Shrick and the spear, then Tekka. He pushed the round door into place, where it fitted with no sign that the Barrier had been broken. He pushed home two crude locking bars.

"Follow me," he ordered the mother.

The long journey through the caves and tunnels was heaven after the Inside. Here there was no light—or, at worst, only a feeble glimmer from small holes and cracks in the Barrier. It seemed that Tekka was leading her along the least frequented ways and tunnels of Skarro's country, for they met none of his people. Nevertheless, Weena's perceptions told her that she was in densely populated territory. From all around her beat the warm, comforting waves of the routine, humdrum life of the People. She knew that in snug caves males, females and children were living in cozy intimacy. Briefly, she regretted having thrown away all this for the ugly, hairless bundle in her arms. But she could never return to her own Tribe, and should she wish to throw in her lot with this alien community the alternatives would be death or slavery.

"Careful!" hissed Tekka. "We are approaching Their country."

"You will—?"

"Not me. They will kill me. Just keep straight along this tunnel and you will find Them. Now, give me the spear."

"But—"

"*You* are safe. There is your pass." He lightly patted the uneasy, squirming Shrick. "Give me the spear, and I will go."

Reluctantly, Weena handed over the weapon. Without a word Tekka took it. Then he was gone. Briefly the mother saw him in the dim light that, in this part of the tunnel, filtered through the Barrier—a dim, gray figure rapidly losing itself in the dim grayness. She felt very lost and lonely and frightened. But the die was cast. Slowly, cautiously, she began to creep along the tunnel.

When They found her she screamed. For many heartbeats she had sensed their hateful presence, had felt that beings even more alien than the Giants were closing in on her. Once or twice she called, crying that she came in peace, that she was the mother of a Different One. But not even echo answered her, for the soft, spongy tunnel walls deadened the shrill sound of her voice. And the silence that was not silence was, if that were possible, more menacing than before.

Without warning the stealthy terror struck. Weena fought with the courage of desperation, but she was overcome by sheer weight of numbers. Shrick, protesting feebly, was torn from her frantic grasp. Hands—and surely there were far too many hands for the number of her assailants—pinned her arms to her sides, held her ankles in a viselike grip. No longer able to struggle, she looked at her captors. Then she screamed again. Mercifully, the dim light spared her the full horror of their appearance, but what she saw would have been enough to haunt her dreams to her dying day had she escaped.

Softly, almost caressingly, the hateful hands ran over her body with disgusting intimacy.

Then—"She is a Different One."

She allowed herself to hope.

"And the child?"

"Two-Tails has newborn. She can nurse him."

And as the sharp blade found her throat Weena had time to regret most bitterly ever having left her snug, familiar world. It was not so much the forfeit of her own life—that she had sacrificed when she defied Sterret—it was the knowledge that Shrick, instead of meeting a clean death at the hands of his own people, would live out his life among these unclean monstrosities.

Then there was a sharp pain and a feeling of utter helplessness as the tide of her life swiftly ebbed—and the darkness that Weena had loved so well closed about her for evermore.

No-Fur—who, at his birth, had been named Shrick—fidgetted impatiently at his post midway along what was known to his people as Skarro's Tunnel. It was time that Long-Nose came to relieve him. Many heartbeats had passed since he had heard the sounds on the other side of the Barrier proclaiming that the Giant in the Place-of-Little-Lights had been replaced by another of his kind. It was a mystery what the Giants did there—but the New People had come to recognize a strange regularity in the actions of the monstrous beings, and to regulate their time accordingly.

No-Fur tightened his grip on his spear—of Barrier material it was, roughly sharpened at one end—as he sensed the approach of somebody along the tunnel, coming from the direction of Tekka's country. It could be a Different One bearing a child who would become one of the New People, it could be attack. But, somehow, the confused impressions that his mind received did not bear out either of these assumptions.

No-Fur shrank against the wall of the tunnel, his body sinking deep into the spongy material. Now he could dimly see the intruder—a solitary form flitting furtively through the shadows. His sense of smell told him that it was a female. Yet he was certain that she had no child with her. He tensed himself to attack as soon as the stranger should pass his hiding place.

Surprisingly, she stopped.

"I come in peace," she said. "I am one of you. I am," here she paused a little, "one of the New People."

Shrick made no reply, no betraying movement. It was barely possible, he knew, that this female might be possessed of abnormally keen eyesight. It was even more likely that she had smelled him out. But then—how was it that she had known the name by which the New People called themselves? To the outside world they were Different Ones—and had the stranger called herself such she would at once have proclaimed herself an alien whose life was forfeit.

"You do not know," the voice came again, "how it is that I called myself by the proper name. In my own Tribe I am called a Different One—"

"Then how is it," No-Fur's voice was triumphant, "that you were allowed to live?"

"Come to me! No, leave your spear. Now come!"

No-Fur stuck his weapon into the soft cavern wall. Slowly, almost fearfully, he advanced to where the female was waiting. He could see her better now—and she seemed no different from those fugitive mothers of Different Ones—at whose slaughter he had so often assisted. The body was well proportioned and covered with fine, silky fur. The head was well shaped. Physically she was so normal as to seem repugnant to the New People.

And yet—No-Fur found himself comparing her with the females of his own Tribe, to the disadvantage of the latter. Emotion rather than reason told him that the hatred inspired by the sight of an ordinary body was the result of a deep-rooted feeling of inferiority rather than anything else. And he wanted this stranger.

"No," she said slowly, "it is not my body that is different. It is in my head. I didn't know myself until a little while—about two hands of feeding—ago. But I can tell, now, what is going on inside your head, or the head of any of the People—"

"But," asked the male, "how did they—"

"I was ripe for mating. I was mated to Trillo, the son of Tekka, the chief. And in our cave I told Trillo things of which he only knew. I thought that I should please him, I thought that he would like to have a mate with magical powers that he could put to good use. With my aid he could have made himself chief. But he was angry—and very frightened. He ran to Tekka, who judged me as a Different One. I was to have been killed, but I was able to escape. They dare not follow me too far into this country—"

Then— "You want me."

It was a statement rather than a question.

"Yes. But—"

"No-Tail? She can die. If I fight her and win, I become your mate."

Briefly, half regretfully, No-Fur thought of his female. She had been patient, she had been loyal. But he saw that, with this stranger for a mate, there were no limits to his advancement. It was not that he was more enlightened than Trillo had been, it was that as one of the New People he regarded abnormality as the norm.

"Then you will take me." Once again there was no hint of questioning. Then— "My name is Wesel."

The arrival of No-Fur, with Wesel in tow, at the Place-of-Meeting could not have been better timed. There was a trial in progress, a young male named Big-Ears having been caught red-handed in the act of stealing a coveted piece of metal from the cave of one Four-Arms. Long-Nose, who should have relieved No-Fur, had found the spectacle of a trial with the prospect of a feast to follow far more engrossing than the relief of the lonely sentry.

It was he who first noticed the newcomers.

"Oh, Big-Tusk," he called, "No-Fur has deserted his post!"

The chief was disposed to be lenient.

"He has a prisoner," he said. "A Different One. We shall feast well."

"*He is afraid of you,*" hissed Wesel. "*Defy him!*"

"It is no prisoner." No-Fur's voice was arrogant. "It is my new mate. And you, Long-Nose, go at once to the tunnel."

"Go, Long-Nose. My country must not remain unguarded. No-Fur, hand the strange female over to the guards that she may be slaughtered."

No-Fur felt his resolution wavering under the stern glare of the chief. As two of Big-Tusk's bullies approached he slackened his grip on Wesel's arm. She turned to him, pleading and desperation in her eyes.

"No, no. He is afraid of you, I say. Don't give in to him. Together we can—"

Ironically, it was No-Tail's intervention that turned the scales. She confronted her mate, scorn written large on her unbeautiful face, the shrewish tongue dreaded by all the New People, even the chief himself, fast getting under way.

"So," she said, "you prefer this drab, common female to me. Hand her over, so that she may, at least, fill our bellies. As for you, my bucko, you will pay for this insult!"

No-Fur looked at the grotesque, distorted form of No-Tail, and then at the slim, sleek Wesel. Almost without volition he spoke.

"Wesel is my mate," he said. "She is one of the New People!"

Big-Tusk lacked the vocabulary to pour adequate scorn upon the insolent rebel. He struggled for words, but could find none to cover the situation. His little eyes gleamed redly, and his hideous tusks were bared in a vicious snarl.

"*Now!*" prompted the stranger. "His head is confused. He will be rash. His desire to tear and maul will cloud his judgment. Attack!"

No-Fur went into the fight coldly, knowing that if he kept his head he must win. He raised his spear to stem the first rush of the infuriated chief. Just in time Big-Tusk saw the rough point and, using his tail as a rudder, swerved. He wasn't fast enough, although his action barely saved him from immediate death. The spear caught him in the shoulder and broke off short, leaving the end in the wound. Mad with rage and pain, the chief was now a most dangerous enemy—and yet, at the same time, easy meat for an adversary who kept his head.

No-Fur was, at first, such a one. But his self-control was cracking fast. Try as he would he could not fight down the rising tides of hysterical fear, of sheer, animal blood lust. As the enemies circled, thrust and parried, he with his almost useless weapon, Big-Tusk with a fine, metal tipped spear, it took all his will power to keep himself from taking refuge in flight or closing to grapple with his more powerful antagonist. His reason told him that both courses of action would be disastrous—the first would end in his being hunted down and slaughtered by the Tribe, the second would bring him within range of the huge, murderous teeth that had given Big-Tusk his name.

So he thrust and parried, thrust and parried, until the keen edge of the chief's blade nicked his arm. The stinging pain made him all animal, and with a shrill scream of fury he launched himself at the other.

But if Nature had provided Big-Tusk with a fine armory she had not been niggardly with the rebel's defensive equipment. True, he had nothing outstanding in the way of teeth or claws, had not the extra limbs possessed by so many of his fellow New People. His brain may have been a little more nimble—but at this stage of the fight that counted for nothing. What saved his life was his hairless skin.

Time after time the chief sought to pull him within striking distance, time after time he pulled away. His slippery hide was crisscrossed with a score of scratches, many of them deep but none immediately serious. And all the time he himself was scratching and pummeling with both hands and feet, biting and gouging.

It seemed that Big-Tusk was tiring, but No-Fur was tiring too. And the other had learned that it was useless to try to grab a handful of fur, that he must try to take his enemy in an unbreakable embrace. Once he succeeded. No-Fur was pulled closer and closer to the slavering fangs, felt the foul breath of the other in his face, knew that it was a matter of heartbeats before his throat was torn out. He screamed, threw up his legs and lunged viciously at Big-Tusk's belly. He felt his feet sink into the soft flesh, but the chief grunted and did not relax his pressure. Worse—the failure of his desperate counterattack had brought No-Fur even closer to death.

With one arm, his right, he pushed desperately against the other's chest. He tried to bring his knees up in a crippling blow, but they were held in a viselike grip by Big-Tusk's heavily muscled legs. With his free left arm he flailed viciously and desperately, but he might have been beating against the Barrier itself.

The People, now that the issue of the battle was decided, were yelling encouragement to the victor. No-Fur heard among the cheers the voice of his mate, No-Tail. The little, cold corner of his brain in which reason was still enthroned told him that he couldn't blame her. If she were vociferous in *his* support, she could expect only death at the hands of the triumphant chief. But he forgot that he had offered her insult and humiliation, remembered only that she was his mate. And the bitterness of it kept him fighting when others would have relinquished their hold on a life already forfeit.

The edge of his hand came down hard just where Big-Tusk's thick neck joined his shoulder. He was barely conscious that the other winced, that a little whimper of pain followed the blow. Then, high and shrill, he heard Wesel.

"Again! Again! That is his weak spot!"

Blindly groping, he searched for the same place. And Big-Tusk was afraid, of that there was no doubt. His head twisted, trying to cover his vulnerability. Again he whimpered, and No-Fur knew that the battle was his. His thin, strong fingers with their sharp nails dug and gouged. There was no fur here, and the flesh was soft. He felt the warm blood welling beneath his hand as the chief screamed dreadfully. Then the iron grip was abruptly relaxed. Before Big-Tusk could use hands or feet to cast his enemy from him No-Fur had twisted and, each hand clutching skin and fur, had buried his teeth in the other's neck. They found the jugular. Almost at once the chief's last, desperate struggles ceased.

No-Fur drank long and satisfyingly.

Then, the blood still clinging to his muzzle, he wearily surveyed the People.

"I am chief," he said.

"You are the chief!" came back the answering chorus.

"And Wesel is my mate."

This time there was hesitation on the part of the People.

The new chief heard mutters of *"The feast . . . Big-Tusk is old and tough. . . . are we to be cheated—?"*

"Wesel is my mate," he repeated. Then— "There is your feast—"

At the height of his power he was to remember No-Tail's stricken eyes, the dreadful feeling that by his words he had put himself outside all custom, all law.

"*Above* the Law," whispered Wesel.

He steeled his heart.

"There is your feast," he said again.

It was Big-Ears who, snatching a spear from one of the guards, with one swift blow dispatched the cringing No-Tail.

"I am your mate," said Wesel.

No-Fur took her in his arms. They rubbed noses. It wasn't the old chief's blood that made her shudder ever so slightly. It was the feel of the disgusting, hairless body against her own.

Already the People were carving and dividing the two corpses and wrangling over an even division of the succulent spoils.

There was one among the New People who, had her differences from the racial stock been only psychological, would have been slaughtered long since. Her three eyes notwithstanding, the imprudent exercise of her gift would have brought certain doom. But, like her sisters in more highly civilized communities, she was careful to tell those who came to her only that which they desired to hear. Even then, she exercised restraint. Experience had taught her that foreknowledge of coming events on the part of the participants often resulted in entirely unforeseen results. This annoyed her. Better misfortune on the main stream of time than well-being on one of its branches.

To this Three-Eyes came No-Fur and Wesel.

Before the chief could ask his questions the seeress raised one emaciated hand.

"You are Shrick," she said. "So your mother called you. Shrick, the Giant Killer."

"But—"

"Wait. You came to ask me about your war against Tekka's people. Continue with your plans. You will win. You will then fight the Tribe of Sterret the Old. Again you will win. You will be Lord of the Outside. And then—"

"And then?"

"The Giants will know of the People. Many, but not all, of the People will die. You will fight the Giants. And the last of the Giants you will kill, but he will plunge the world into—Oh, if I could make you see! But we have no words."

"What—?"

"No, you cannot know. You will never know till the end is upon you. But this I can tell you. The People are doomed. Nothing you or they can do will save them. But you will kill those who will kill us, and that is good."

Again No-Fur pleaded for enlightenment. Abruptly, his pleas became threats. He was fast lashing himself into one of his dreaded fits of blind fury. But Three-Eyes was oblivious of his presence. Her two outer eyes were tight shut and that strange, dreaded inner one was staring at *something*, something outside the limits of the cave, outside the framework of things as they are.

Deep in his throat the chief growled.

He raised the fine spear that was the symbol of his office and buried it deep in the old female's body. The inner eye shut and the two outer ones flickered open for the last time.

"I am spared the End—" she said.

Outside the little cavern the faithful Big-Ears was waiting.

"Three-Eyes is dead," said his master. "Take what you want, and give the rest to the People—"

For a little there was silence.

Then—"I am glad you killed her," said Wesel. "She frightened me. I got inside her head—and I was lost!" Her voice had a hysterical edge. "I was lost! It was mad, mad. *What Was* was a *place*, a *PLACE*, and *NOW*, and *What Will Be*. And I saw the End."

"What did you see?"

"A great light, far brighter than the Giants' lights Inside. And heat, stronger than the heat of the floors of the Far Outside caves and tunnels. And the People gasping and dying and the great light bursting into our world and eating them up—"

"But the Giants?"

"I did not see. I was lost. All I saw was the End."

No-Fur was silent. His active, nimble mind was scurrying down the vistas opened up by the dead prophetess. Giant Killer, *Giant Killer*. Even in his most grandiose dreams he had never seen himself thus. And what was that name?

Shrick? He repeated it to himself—Shrick the Giant Killer. It had a fine swing to it. As for the rest, the End, if he could kill the Giants then, surely, he could stave off the doom that they would mete out to the People. Shrick, the Giant Killer—

"It is a name that I like better than No-Fur," said Wesel.

"Shrick, Lord of the Outside. Shrick, Lord of the World. Shrick, the Giant Killer—"

"Yes," he said, slowly. "But the End—"

"You will go through that door when you come to it."

The campaign against Tekka's People had opened.

Along the caves and tunnels poured the nightmare hordes of Shrick. The dim light but half revealed their misshapen bodies, limbs where no limbs should be, heads like something from a half-forgotten bad dream.

All were armed. Every male and female carried a spear, and that in itself was a startling innovation in the wars of the People. For sharp metal, with which the weapons were tipped, was hard to come by, True, a staff of Barrier material could be sharpened, but it was a liability rather than an asset in a pitched battle. With the first thrust the point would break off, leaving the fighter with a weapon far inferior to his natural armory of teeth and claws.

Fire was new to the People—and it was Shrick who had brought them fire. For long periods he had spied upon the Giants in the Place-of-Little-Lights, had seen them bring from the pouches in their fur little glittering devices from which when a projection was pressed, issued a tiny, naked light. And he had seen them bring this light to the end of strange, white sticks that they seemed to be sucking. And the end of the stick would glow, and there would be a cloud like the cloud that issued from the mouths of the People in some of the Far Outside caverns where it was very cold. But this cloud was fragrant, and seemed to be strangely soothing.

And one of the Giants had lost his little hot light. He had put it to one to the white sticks, had made to return it to his pouch, and his hand had missed the opening. The Giant did not notice. He was doing something which took all his attention—and strain his eyes and his imagination as he might Shrick could not see what it was. There were strange glittering machines through which he peered intently at the glittering Little Lights beyond their transparent Barrier. Or were they on the inside of the Barrier? Nobody had ever been able to decide. There was something alive that wasn't alive that clicked. There were sheets of fine, white skin on which the Giant was making black marks with a pointed stick.

But Shrick soon lost interest in these strange rites that he could never hope to comprehend. All his attention was focused on the glittering prize that was drifting ever so slowly toward him on the wings of some vagrant eddy.

When it seemed that it would surely fall right into the doorway where Shrick crouched waiting, it swerved. And, much as he dreaded the pseudolife that hummed and clicked, Shrick came out. The Giant, busy with his sorcery, did not notice him. One swift leap carried him to the drifting trophy. And then he had it, tight clasped to his breast. It was bigger than he had thought, it having appeared so tiny only in relationship to its previous owner. But it wasn't too big to go through the door in the Barrier. In triumph Shrick bore it to his cave.

Many were the experiments that he, eager but fumbling, performed. For a while both he and Wesel nursed painful burns. Many were the experiments that he intended to perform in the future. But he had stumbled on one use for the hot light that was to be of paramount importance in his wars.

Aping the Giants, he had stuck a long splinter of Barrier material in his mouth. The end he had brought to the little light. There was, as he had half expected, a cloud. But it was neither fragrant nor soothing. Blinded and coughing, Wesel snatched at the glowing stick, beat out its strange life with her hands.

Then—"It is hard," she said. "It is almost as hard as metal—"

And so Shrick became the first mass producer of armaments that his world had known. The first few sharpened staves he treated himself. The rest he left to Wesel and the faithful Big-Ears. He dare not trust his wonderful new power to any who were not among his intimates.

Shrick's other innovation was a direct violation of all the rules of war. He had pressed the females into the fighting line. Those who were old and infirm, together with the old and infirm males, brought up the rear with bundles of the mass-produced spears. The New People had been wondering for some little time why their chief had refused to let them slaughter those of their number who had outlived their usefulness. Now they knew.

The caves of the New People were deserted save for those few females with newborn.

And through the tunnels poured the hordes of Shrick.

There was little finesse in the campaign against Tekka's people. The outposts were slaughtered out of hand, but not before they had had time to warn the Tribe of the attack.

Tekka threw a body of picked spearmen into his van, confident that he, with better access to those parts of Inside where metal could be obtained, would be able to swamp the motley horde of the enemy with superior arms and numbers.

When Tekka saw, in the dim light, only a few betraying gleams of metal scattered among Shrick's massed spears, he laughed.

"This No-Fur is mad," he said. "And I shall kill him with this." He brandished his own weapon. "His mother gave it to me many, many feedings ago."

"Is Wesel—?"

"Perhaps, my son. You shall eat her heart, I promise you."

And then Shrick struck.

His screaming mob rushed along the wide tunnel. Confident the Tekkan spearmen waited, knowing that the enemy's weapons were good for only one thrust, and that almost certainly not lethal.

Tekka scowled as he estimated the numbers of the attackers. There couldn't be that many males among the New People. There couldn't—And then the wave struck.

In the twinkling of an eye the tunnel was tightly packed with struggling bodies. Here was no dignified, orderly series of single combats such as had always, in the past, graced the wars of the People. And with growing terror Tekka realized that the enemy spears were standing up to the strain of battle at least as well as his own few metal-tipped weapons.

Slowly, but with ever mounting momentum, the attackers pressed on, gaining impetus from the many bodies that now lay behind them. Gasping for air in the effluvium of sweat and newly shed blood Tekka and the last of his guards were pressed back and ever back.

When one of the New People was disarmed he fell to the rear of his own front line. As though by magic a fresh fighter would appear to replace him.

Then—"He's using females!" cried Trillo. "He's—"

But Tekka did not answer. He was fighting for his life with

a four-armed monster. Every hand held a spear—and every spear was bright with blood. For long heartbeats he parried the other's thrusts, then his nerve broke. Screaming, he turned his back on the enemy. It was the last thing he did.

And so the remnant of the fighting strength of the Tribe of Tekka was at last penned up against one wall of their Place-of-Meeting. Surrounding them was a solid hemisphere of the New People. Snarl was answered by snarl. Trillo and his scant half dozen guards knew that there was no surrender. All they could do was to sell their lives as dearly as possible.

And so they waited for the inevitable, gathering the last reserves of their strength in this lull of the battle, gasping the last sweet mouthfuls of air that they would ever taste. From beyond the wall of their assailants they could hear the cries and screams as the females and children, who had hidden in their caves, were hunted out and slaughtered. They were not to know that the magnanimous Shrick was sparing most of the females. They, he hoped, would produce for him more New People.

And then Shrick came, elbowing his way to the forefront of his forces. His smooth, naked body was unmarked, save by the old scars of his battle with Big Tusk. And with him was Wesel, not a hair of her sleek fur out of place. And Big-Ears—but he, obviously, had been in the fight. With them came more fighters, fresh and eager.

"Finish them!" ordered Shrick.

"Wait!" Wesel's voice was imperative. "I want Trillo."

Him she pointed out to the picked fighters, who raised their spears—weapons curiously slender and light, too fragile for hand-to-hand combat. A faint hope stirred in the breasts of the last defenders.

"Now!"

Trillo and his guards braced themselves to meet the last rush. It never came. Instead, thrown with unerring aim, came those sharp, flimsy spears, pinning them horribly against the gray, spongy wall of the Place-of-Meeting.

Spared in this final slaughter, Trillo looked about him with wide, fear-crazed eyes. He started to scream, then launched himself at the laughing Wesel. But she slipped back through the packed masses of the New People. Blind to all else but that hateful figure, Trillo tried to follow. And the New People crowded about him, binding his arms and legs with their strong cords, snatching his spear from him before its blade drank blood.

Then again the captive saw her who had been his mate.

Shamelessly, she was caressing Shrick.

"My Hairless One," she said. "I was once mated to *this*. You shall have his fur to cover your smooth body." And then—"Big-Ears! You know what to do!"

Grinning, Big-Ears found the sharp blade of a spear that had become detached from its haft. Grinning, he went to work. Trillo started to whimper, then to scream. Shrick felt a little sick. "Stop!" he said. "He is not dead. You must—"

"What does it matter?" Wesel's eyes were avid, and her little, pink tongue came out to lick her thin lips. Big-Ears had hesitated in his work but, at her sign, continued.

"What does it matter?" she said again.

As had fared the Tribe of Tekka so fared the Tribe of Sterret, and a hand or more of smaller communities owing a loose allegiance to these two.

But it was in his war with Sterret that Shrick almost met disaster. To the cunning oldster had come survivors from the massacre of Tekka's army. Most of these had been slaughtered out of hand by the frontier guards, but one or two had succeeded in convincing their captors that they bore tidings of great importance.

Sterret heard them out.

He ordered that they be fed and treated as his own people, for he knew that he would need every ounce of fighting strength that he could muster.

Long and deeply he pondered upon their words, and then sent foray after foray of his young males to the Place-of Life-That-is-Not-Life. Careless he was of detection by the Giants. They might or might not act against him—but he had been convinced that, for all their size, they were comparatively stupid and harmless. Certainly, at this juncture, they were not such a menace as Shrick, already self-styled Lord of the Outside.

And so his store of sharp fragments of metal grew, while his armorers worked without cessation binding these to hafts of Barrier stuff. And he, too, could innovate. Some of the fragments were useless as spearheads, being blunt, rough, and irregular. But, bound like a spearhead to a shaft, they could deliver a crushing blow. Of this Sterret was sure after a few experiments on old and unwanted members of his Tribe.

Most important, perhaps, his mind, rich in experience but not without a certain youthful zest, busied itself with problems of strategy. In the main tunnel from what had been Tekka's country his females hacked and tore at the spongy wall, the material being packed tightly and solidly into another small tunnel that was but rarely used.

At last his scouts brought the word that Shrick's forces were on the move. Careless in the crushing weight of his military power, Shrick disdained anything but a direct frontal attack. Perhaps he should have been warned by the fact that all orifices admitting light from the Inside had been closed, that the main tunnel along which he was advancing was in total darkness.

This, however, hampered him but little. The body of picked spearmen opposing him fought in the conventional way, and these, leaving their dead and wounded, were forced slowly but surely back. Each side relied upon smell, and hearing, and a certain perception possessed by most, if not all, of the People. At such close quarters these were ample.

Shrick himself was not in the van—that honor was reserved for Big-Ears, his fighting general. Had the decision rested with him alone he would have been in the forefront of the battle—but Wesel averred that the leader was of far greater importance than a mere spear bearer, and should be shielded from needless risk. Not altogether unwillingly, Shrick acquiesced.

Surrounded by his guard, with Wesel at his side, the leader followed the noise of the fighting. He was rather surprised at the reports back to him concerning the apparent numbers of the enemy, but assumed that this was a mere delaying action and that Sterret would make his last stand in the Place-of-Meeting. It never occurred to him in his arrogance that others could innovate.

Abruptly, Wesel clutched his arm.

"Shrick! Danger—from the side!"

"From the side? But—"

There was a shrill cry, and a huge section of the tunnel wall fell inward. The spongy stuff was in thin sheets, and drifted among the guard, hampering their every movement. Then, led by Sterret in person, the defenders came out. Like mountaineers they were roped together, for in this battle in the darkness their best hope lay in keeping in one, compact body. Separated, they would fall easy prey to the superior numbers of the hordes of Shrick.

With spear and mace they lay about them lustily. The first heartbeat of the engagement would have seen the end of Shrick, and it was only the uncured hide of Trilla, stiff and stinking, that saved his life. Even so, the blade of Sterret penetrated the crude armor, and, sorely wounded, Shrick reeled out of the battle.

Ahead, Big-Ears was no longer having things all his own way. Reinforcements had poured along the tunnel and he dare not return to the succor of his chief. And Sterret's maces were having their effect. Stabbing and slashing the People could understand—but a crushing blow was, to them, something infinitely horrible.

It was Wesel who saved the day. With her she had brought the little, hot light. It had been her intention to try its effect on such few prisoners as might be taken in this campaign—she was too shrewd to experiment on any of the New People, even those who had incurred the displeasure of herself or her mate.

Scarce knowing what she did she pressed the stud.

With dazzling suddenness the scene of carnage swam into dull view. From all sides came cries of fear.

"Back!" cried Wesel. "Back! Clear a space!"

In two directions the New People retreated.

Blinking but dogged, Sterret's phalanx tried to follow, tried to turn what was a more or less orderly withdrawal into a rout. But the cords that had, at first, served them so well now proved their undoing. Some tried to pursue those making for the Place-of-Meeting, others those of the New People retiring to their own territory. Snarling viciously, blood streaming from a dozen minor wounds, Sterret at last cuffed and bullied his forces into a semblance of order. He attempted to lead a charge to where Wesel, the little, hot light still in her hand, was retreating among her personal, amazon guards.

But again the cunning—too cunning—ropes defeated his purposes. Not a few corpses were there to hamper fast movement, and almost none of his fighters had the intelligence to cut them free.

And the spear throwers of Shrick came to the fore, and, one by one, the people of Sterret were pinned by the slim deadly shafts to the tunnel walls. Not all were killed outright, a few unfortunates squirmed and whimpered, plucking at the spears with ineffectual hands.

Among these was Sterret.

Shrick came forward, spear in hand, to administer the *coup de grâce.* The old chief stared wildly, then—"Weena's hairless one!" he cried.

Ironically it was his own spear—the weapon that, in turn, had belonged to Weena and to Tekka—that slit his throat.

Now that he was Lord of the Outside Shrick had time in which to think and to dream. More and more his mind harked back to Three-Eyes and her prophesy. It never occurred to him to doubt that he was to be the Giant Killer—although the vision of the End he dismissed from his mind as the vaporings of a half-crazed old female.

And so he sent his spies to the Inside to watch the Giants in their mysterious comings and goings, tried hard to find some pattern for their incomprehensible behavior. He himself often accompanied these spies—and it was with avid greed that he saw the vast wealth of beautiful, shining things to which the Giants were heir. More than anything he desired another little hot light, for his own had ceased to function, and all the clumsy, ignorant tinkerings of himself and Wesel could not produce more than a feeble, almost heatless spark from its baffling intricacies.

It seemed, too, that the Giants were now aware of the swarming, fecund life surrounding them. Certain it was that their snares increased in number and ingenuity. And the food-that-kills appeared in new and terrifying guise. Not only did those who had eaten of it die, but their mates and—indeed all who had come into contact with them.

It smacked of sorcery, but Shrick had learned to associate cause and effect. He made the afflicted ones carry those already dead into a small tunnel. One or two of them rebelled—but the spear throwers surrounded them, their slim, deadly weapons at the ready. And those who attempted to break through the cordon of guards were run through repeatedly before ever they laid their defiling hands on any of the unafflicted People.

Big-Ears was among the sufferers. He made no attempt to quarrel with his fate. Before he entered the yawning tunnel that was to be his tomb he turned and looked at his chief.

Shrick made to call him to his side—even though he knew that his friend's life could not be saved. and that by associating with him he would almost certainly lose his own.

But Wesel was at his side.

She motioned to the spear throwers, and a full two hands of darts transfixed the ailing Big-Ears.

"It was kinder this way," she lied.

But, somehow, the last look that his most loyal supporter had given him reminded him of No-Tail. With a heavy heart he ordered his people to seal the tunnel. Great strips of the spongy stuff were brought and stuffed into the entrance. The cries of those inside grew fainter and ever fainter. Then there was silence. Shrick ordered guards posted at all points where, conceivably, the doomed prisoners might break out. He returned to his own cave. Wesel, when one without her gift would have intruded, let him go in his loneliness. Soon he would want her again.

It had long been Wesel's belief that, given the opportunity, she could get inside the minds of the Giants just as she could those of the People. And if she could—who knew what prizes might be hers? Shrick, still inaccessible and grieving for his friend, she missed more than she cared to admit. The last of the prisoners from the last campaign had been killed, ingeniously, many feedings ago. Though she had no way of measuring time, it hung heavily on her hands.

And so, accompanied by two of her personal attendants, she roamed those corridors and tunnels running just inside the Barrier. Through spyhole after spyhole she peered, gazing in wonderment that long use could not stale at the rich and varied life of the Inside.

At last she found that for which she was searching—a Giant, alone and sleeping. Experience among the People had taught her that from a sleeping mind she could read the most secret thoughts.

For a heartbeat she hesitated. Then—"Four-Arms, Little-Head, wait here for me. Wait and watch."

Little-Head grunted an affirmative, but Four-Arms was dubious. "Lady Wesel," she said, "what if the Giant should wake? What—?"

"What if you should return to the Lord of the Outside without me? Then he would, without doubt, have your hides.

The one he is wearing now is old, and the fur is coming out. But do as I say."

There was a door in the Barrier here, a door but rarely used. This was opened, and Wesel slipped through. With the ease that all the People were acquiring with their more frequent ventures to the Inside she floated up to the sleeping Giant. Bonds held him in a sort of framework, and Wesel wondered if, for some offense, he had been made prisoner by his own kind. She would soon know.

And then a glittering object caught her eye. It was one of the little hot lights, its polished metal case seeming to Wesel's covetous eyes the most beautiful thing in the world. Swiftly she made her decision. She could take the shining prize now, deliver it to her two attendants, and then return to carry out her original intentions.

In her eagerness she did not see that it was suspended in the middle of an interlacing of slender metal bars—or she did not care. And as her hands grabbed the bait something not far away began a shrill, not unmusical metallic beating. The Giant stirred and awoke. What Wesel had taken for bonds fell away from his body. In blind panic she turned to flee back to her own world. But, somehow, more of the metal bars had fallen into place and she was a prisoner.

She started to scream.

Surprisingly, Four-Arms and Little-Head came to her aid. It would be nice to be able to place on record that they were actuated by devotion to their mistress—but Four-Arms knew that her life was forfeit. And she had seen those who displeased either Shrick or Wesel flayed alive. Little-Head blindly followed the other's leadership. Hers not to reason why—

Slashing with their spears they assaulted the Giant. He laughed—or so Wesel interpreted the deep, rumbling sound that came from his throat. Four-Arms he seized first. With one hand he grasped her body, with the other her head. He twisted. And that was the end of Four-Arms.

Anybody else but Little-Head would have turned and fled. But her dim mind refused to register that which she had seen. Perhaps a full feeding or so after the event the horror of it all would have stunned her with its impact—perhaps not. Be that as it may, she continued her attack. Blindly, instinctively, she went for the Giant's throat. Wesel sensed that he was badly frightened. But after a short struggle one of his hands caught the frenzied, squealing Little-Head. Violently, he flung her from him. She heard the thud as her attendant's body struck something hard and unyielding. And the impressions that her mind had been receiving from that of the other abruptly ceased.

Even in her panic fear she noticed that the Giant had not come out of the unequal combat entirely unscathed. One of his hands had been scratched, and was bleeding freely. And there were deep scratches on the hideous, repulsively naked face. The Giants, then, were vulnerable. There might have been some grain of truth after all in Three-Eye's insane babbling.

And then Wesel forgot her unavailing struggle against the bars of her cage. With sick horror she watched what the Giant was doing. He had taken the limp body of Four-Arms, had secured it to a flat surface. From somewhere he had produced an array of glittering instruments. One of these he took, and drew it down the body from throat to crotch. On either side of the keen blade the skin fell away, leaving the flesh exposed.

And the worst part of it was that it was not being done in hate or anger, neither was the unfortunate Four-Arms being divided up that she might be eaten. There was an impersonal quality about the whole business that sickened Wesel—for, by this time, she had gained a certain limited access to the mind of the other.

The Giant paused in his work. Another of his kind had come, and for many heartbeats the two talked together. They examined the mutilated carcass of Four-Arms, the crushed body of Little-Head. Together, they peered into the cage where Wesel snarled impotently.

But, in spite of her hysterial fear, part of her mind was deadly cold, was receiving and storing impressions that threw the uninhibited, animal part of her into still greater panic. While the Giants talked the impressions were clear—and while their great, ungainly heads hung over her cage, scant handbreadths away, they were almost overpowering in their strength. She knew who she and the People were, what their world was. She had not the ability to put it into words—but she *knew*. And she saw the doom that the Giants were preparing for the People.

With a few parting words to his fellow, the second Giant left. The first one resumed his work of dismembering Four

Arms. At last he was finished. What was left of the body was put into transparent containers.

The Giant picked up Little-Head. For many heartbeats he examined her, turning her over and over in his great hands. Wesel thought that he would bind the body to the flat surface, do with it as he had done with that of Four-Arms. But at last he put the body to one side. Over his hands he pulled something that looked like a thick, additional skin. Suddenly, the metal bars at one end of the cage fell away, and one of those enormous hands came groping for Wesel.

After the death of Big-Ears, Shrick slept a little. It was the only way in which he could be rid of the sense of loss, of the feeling that he had betrayed his most loyal follower. His dreams were troubled, haunted by ghosts from his past. Big-Ears was in them, and Big-Tusk, and a stranger female with whom he felt a sense of oneness, whom he knew to be Weena, his mother.

And then all these phantasms were gone, leaving only the image of Wesel. It wasn't the Wesel he had always known, cool, self-assured, ambitious. This was a terrified Wesel—Wesel descending into a black abyss of pain and torture even worse than that which she had, so often, meted out to others. And she wanted him.

Shrick awoke, frightened by his dreams. But he knew that ghosts had never hurt anybody, could not hurt him, Lord of the Outside. He shook himself, whimpering a little, and then tried to compose himself for further sleep.

But the image of Wesel persisted. At last Shrick abandoned his attempts to seek oblivion and, rubbing his eyes, emerged from his cave.

In the dim, half-light of the Place-of-Meeting little knots of the People hung about, talking in low voices. Shrick called to the guards. There was a sullen silence. He called again. At last one answered.

"Where is Wesel?"

"I do not know . . . lord." The last word came out grudgingly.

Then one of the others volunteered the information that she had been seen, in company with Four-Arms and Little-Head, proceeding along the tunnels that led to that part of the Outside in the way of the Place-of-Green-Growing-Things.

Shrick hesitated.

He rarely ventured abroad without his personal guards, but then, Big-Ears was always one of them. And Big-Ears was gone.

He looked around him, decided that he could trust none of those at present in the Place-of-Meeting. The People had been shocked and horrified by his necessary actions in the case of those who had eaten of the food-that-kills and regarded him, he knew, as a monster even worse than the Giants. Their memories were short—but until they forgot he would have to walk with caution.

"Wesel is my mate. I will go alone," he said.

At his words he sensed a change of mood, was tempted to demand an escort. But the instinct that—as much as any mental superiority—maintained him in authority warned him against throwing away his advantage.

"I go alone," he said.

One Short-Tail, bolder than his fellows, spoke up.

"And if you do not return, Lord of the Outside? Who is to be—?"

"I shall return," said Shrick firmly, his voice displaying a confidence he did not feel.

In the more populous regions the distinctive scent of Wesel was overlaid by that of many others. In tunnels but rarely frequented it was strong and compelling—but now he had no need to use his olfactory powers. For the terrified little voice in his brain—from outside his brain was saying *hurry, HURRY*—and some power beyond his ken was guiding him unerringly to where his mate was in such desperate need of him.

From the door in the Barrier through which Wesel had entered the Inside—it had been left open—streamed a shaft of light. And now Shrick's natural caution reasserted itself. The voice inside his brain was no less urgent, but the instinct of self-preservation was strong. Almost timorously, he peered through the doorway.

He smelled death. At first he feared that he was too late, then identified the personal odors of Four-Arms and Little-Head. That of Wesel was there too—intermingled with the acrid scent of terror and agony. But she was still alive.

Caution forgotten, he launched himself from the doorway with all the power of his leg muscles. And he found Wesel, stretched supine on a flat surface that was slippery with blood. Most of it was Four-Arms', but some of it was hers.

"Shrick!" she screamed. "The Giant!"

He looked away from his mate and saw hanging over him, pale and enormous, the face of the Giant. He screamed, but there was more of fury than terror in the sound. He saw, not far from where he clung to Wesel, a huge blade of shining metal. He could see that its edge was keen. The handle had been fashioned for a hand far larger than his, nevertheless he was just able to grasp it. It seemed to be secured. Feet braced against Wesel's body for purchase, he tugged desperately.

Just as the Giant's hand, fingers outstretched to seize him, came down the blade pulled free. As Shrick's legs suddenly and involuntarily straightened he was propelled away from Wesel. The Giant grabbed at the flying form, and howled in agony as Shrick swept the blade around and lopped off a finger.

He heard Wesel's voice: "You are the Giant Killer!"

Now he was level with the Giant's head. He swerved, and with his feet caught a fold of the artificial skin covering the huge body. And he hung there, swinging his weapon with both hands, cutting and slashing. Great hands swung wildly and he was bruised and buffeted. But not once did they succeed in finding a grip. Then there was a great and horrid spurting of blood and a wild thrashing of mighty limbs. This ceased, but it was only the voice of Wesel that called him from the fury of his slaughter lust.

So he found her again, still stretched out for sacrifice to the Giants' dark gods, still bound to that surface that was wet with her blood and that of her attendant. But she smiled up at him, and in her eyes was respect that bordered on awe.

"Are you hurt?" he demanded, a keen edge of anxiety to his voice.

"Only a little. But Four-Arms was cut in pieces . . . I should have been had you not come. And," her voice was a hymn of praise, "you killed the Giant!"

"It was foretold. Besides," for once he was honest, "it could not have been done without the Giant's weapon."

With its edge he was cutting Wesel's bonds. Slowly she floated away from the place of sacrifice. Then: "I can't move my legs!" Her voice was terror-stricken. "I can't move!"

Shrick guessed what was wrong. He knew a little of anatomy—his knowledge was that of the warrior who may be obliged to immobilize his enemy prior to his slaughter—and he could see that the Giant's keen blade had wrought this damage. Fury boiled up in him against these cruel, monstrous beings. And there was more than fury. There was the feeling, rare among his people, of overwhelming pity for his crippled mate.

"The blade . . . it is very sharp . . . I shall feel nothing."

But Shrick could not bring himself to do it.

Now they were floating up against the huge bulk of the dead Giant. With one hand he grasped Wesel's shoulder—the other still clutched his fine, new weapon—and kicked off against the gigantic carcass. Then he was pushing Wesel through the doorway in the Barrier, and sensed her relief as she found herself once more in familar territory. He followed her, then carefully shut and barred the door.

For a few heartbeats Wesel busied herself smoothing her bedraggled fur. He couldn't help noticing that she dare not let her hands stray to the lower part of her body where were the wounds, small but deadly, that had robbed her of the power of her limbs. Dimly, he felt that something might be done for one so injured, but knew that it was beyond his powers. And fury—not helpless now—against the Giants returned again, threatening to choke him with its intensity.

"Shrick!" Wesel's voice was grave. "We must return at once to the People. We must warn the People. The Giants are making a sorcery to bring the End."

"The great, hot light?"

"No. But wait! First I must tell you of what I learned. Otherwise, you would not believe. I have learned what we are, what the world is. And it is strange and wonderful beyond all our beliefs.

"What is Outside?" She did not wait for his answer, read it in his mind before his lips could frame the words. "The world is but a bubble of emptiness in the midst of a vast piece of metal, greater than the mind can imagine. But it is not so! Outside the metal that lies outside the Outside there is nothing. *Nothing!* There is no air."

"But there must be air, at least."

"No, I tell you. There is *nothing.*

"And the world—how can I find words? Their name for the world is—*ship*, and it seems to mean something big going from one place to another place. And all of us—Giants and People—are inside the ship. The Giants made the ship."

"Then it is not alive?"

"I cannot say. *They* seem to think that it is a female. It must have some kind of life that is not life. And it is going from one world to another world."

"And these other worlds?"

"I caught glimpses of them. They are dreadful, dreadful. *We* find the open spaces of the Inside frightening—but these other worlds are *all* open space except for one side."

"But what are we?" In spite of himself, Shrick at least half believed Wesel's fantastic story. Perhaps she possessed, to some slight degree, the power of projecting her own thoughts into the mind of another with whom she was intimate. "What are we?"

She was silent for the space of many heartbeats. Then: "*Their* name for us is *mutants*. The picture was . . . not clear at all. It means that we—the People—have changed. And yet their picture of the People before the change was like the Different Ones before we slew them all.

"Long and long ago—many hands of feedings—the first People, our parents' parents' parents, came into the world. They came from that greater world—the world of dreadful, open spaces. They came with the food in the great Cave-of-Food—and that is being carried to another world.

"Now, in the horrid, empty space outside the Outside there is—light that is not light. And this light—changes persons. No, not the grown person or the child, but the child before the birth. Like the dead and gone chiefs of the People, the Giants fear change in themselves. So they have kept the light that is not light from the Inside.

"And this is how. Between the Barrier and the Far Outside they filled the space with the stuff in which we have made our caves and tunnels. The first People left the great Cave-of-Food, they tunneled through the Barrier and into the stuff Outside. It was their nature. And some of them mated in the Far Outside caves. Their children were—*Different*."

"That is true," said Shrick slowly. "It has always been thought that children born in the Far Outside were never like their parents, and that those born close to the Barrier were—"

"Yes.

"Now, the Giants always knew that the People were here, but they did not fear them. They did not know our numbers, and they regarded us as beings much lower than themselves. They were content to keep us down with their traps and the food-that-kills. Somehow, they found that we had changed. Like the dead chiefs they feared us then—and like the dead chiefs they will try to kill us all before we conquer them."

"And the End?"

"Yes, the End." She was silent again, her big eyes looking past Shrick at something infinitely terrible. "Yes," she said again, "the End. *They* will make it, and *They* will escape it. *They* will put on artificial skins that will cover *Their* whole bodies, even *Their* heads, and *They* will open huge doors in the . . . skin of the ship, and all the air will rush out into the terrible empty space outside the Outside. And all the People will die."

"I must go," said Shrick. "I must kill the Giants before this comes to pass."

"No! There was one hand of Giants—now that you have killed Fat-Belly there are four of them left. And they know, now, that they can be killed. They will be watching for you.

"Do you remember when we buried the People with the sickness? That is what we must do to all the People. And then when the Giants fill the world with air again from their store we can come out."

Shrick was silent awhile. He had to admit that she was right. One unsuspecting Giant had fallen to his blade—but four of them, aroused, angry and watchful, he could not handle. In any case there was no way of knowing when the Giants would let the air from the world. The People must be warned—and fast.

Together, in the Place-of-Meeting, Shrick and Wesel faced the People. They had told their stories, only to be met with blank incredulity. True, there were some who, seeing the fine, shining blade that Shrick had brought from the Inside, were inclined to believe. But they were shouted down by the majority. It was when he tried to get them to immure themselves against the End that he met with serious opposition. The fact that he had so treated those suffering from the sickness still bulked big in the mob memory.

It was Short-Tail who precipitated the crisis.

"He wants the world to himself!" he shouted. "He has killed Big-Tusk and No-Tail, he has killed all the Different Ones, and Big-Ears he slew because he would have been chief. He and his ugly, barren mate want the world to themselves!"

Shrick tried to argue, but Big-Ears' following shouted him down. He squealed with rage and, raising his blade with both hands, rushed upon the rebel. Short-Tail scurried back out of reach. Shrick found himself alone in a suddenly cleared space. From somewhere a long way off he heard Wesel screaming his name. Dazedly, he shook his head, and then the red mist cleared from in front of his eyes.

All around him were the spear throwers, their slender weapons poised. He had trained them himself, had brought their specialized art of war into being. And now—

"Shrick!" Wesel was saying, "don't fight! They will kill you, and I shall be alone. I shall have the world to myself. Let them do as they will with us, and *we* shall live through the End."

At her words a tittering laugh rippled through the mob.

"*They* will live through the End! They will die as Big-Ears and his friends died!"

"I want your blade," said Short-Tail.

"Give it to him," cried Wesel. "You will get it back after the End!"

Shrick hesitated. The other made a sign. One of the throwing spears buried itself in the fleshy part of his arm. Had it not been for Wesel's voice, pleading, insistent, he would have charged his tormenters and met his end in less than a single heartbeat. Reluctantly, he released his hold upon the weapon. Slowly—as though loath to leave its true owner—it floated away from him. And then the People were all around him, almost suffocating him with the pressure of their bodies.

The cave into which Shrick and Wesel were forced was their own dwelling place. They were in pitiable state when the mob retreated to the entrance—Wesel's wounds had reopened and Shrick's arm was bleeding freely. Somebody had wrenched out the spear—but the head had broken off.

Outside, Short-Tail was laying about him with the keen blade he had taken from his chief. Under its strokes great masses of the spongy stuff of the Outside were coming free, and many willing hands were stuffing this tight into the cave entrance.

"We will let you out after the End!" called somebody.

There was a hoot of derision. Then: "I wonder which will eat the other first?"

"Never mind," said Wesel softly. "We shall laugh last."

"Perhaps. But . . . the People. *My* People. And you are barren. The Giants have won—"

Wesel was silent. Then he heard her voice again. She was whimpering to herself in the darkness. Shrick could guess her thoughts. All their grandiose dreams of world dominion had come to this—a tiny cramped space in which there was barely room for either of them to stir a finger.

And now they could no longer hear the voices of the People outside their prison. Shrick wondered if the Giants had already struck, then reassured himself with the memory of how the voices of those suffering from the sickness had grown fainter and fainter and then, at the finish, ceased altogether. And he wondered how he and Wesel would know when the End had come, and how they would know when it was safe to dig themselves out. It would be a long, slow task with only their teeth and claws with which to work.

But he had a tool.

The fingers of the hand of his uninjured arm went to the spearhead still buried in the other. He knew that by far the best way of extracting it would be one quick pull—but he couldn't bring himself to do it. Slowly, painfully, he worked away at the sharp fragment of metal.

"Let me do it for you."

"No." His voice was rough. "Besides, there is no haste."

Slowly, patiently, he worried at the wound. He was groaning a little, although he was not conscious of doing so. And then, suddenly, Wesel screamed. The sound was so unexpected, so dreadful in that confined space, that Shrick started violently. His hand jerked away from his upper arm, bringing with it the spearhead.

His first thought was that Wesel, telepath as she was, had chosen this way to help him. But he felt no gratitude, only a dull resentment.

"What did you do that for?" he demanded angrily.

She didn't answer his question. She was oblivious of his presence.

"The People . . ." she whispered. "The People . . . I can feel their thoughts . . . I can feel what they are feeling. And they are gasping for air . . . they are gasping and dying . . . and the cave of Long-Fur the spearmaker . . . but they are dying, and the blood is coming out of their mouths and noses and ears . . . I can't bear it . . . I can't—"

And then a terrifying thing happened. The sides of the cave pressed in upon them. Throughout the world, throughout the ship, the air cells in the spongy insulation were expanding as the air pressure dropped to Zero. It was this alone that saved Shrick and Wesel, although they never knew it. The rough plug sealing their cave, that, otherwise, would have blown out swelled to meet the expanding walls of the entrance, making a near perfect air-tight joint.

But the prisoners were in no state to appreciate this, even had they been in possession of the necessary knowledge. Panic seized them both. Claustrophobia was unknown among the People—but walls that closed upon them were outside their experience.

Perhaps Wesel was the more level-headed of the pair. It was she who tried to restrain her mate as he clawed and bit savagely, madly, at the distended, bulging walls. He no longer knew what lay outside the cave, had he known it would have made no difference. His one desire was to get out.

At first he made little headway, then he bethought himself of the little blade still grasped in his hand. With it he attacked the pulpy mass. The walls of the cells were stretched thin, almost to bursting, and under his onslaught they put up no more resistance than so many soap bubbles. A space was cleared, and Shrick was able to work with even greater vigor.

"Stop! Stop, I tell you! There is only the choking death outside the cave. And you will kill us both!"

But Shrick paid no heed, went on stabbing and hacking. It was only slowly, now, that he was able to enlarge upon the original impression he had made. As the swollen surfaces burst and withered beneath his blade, so they bulged and bellied in fresh places.

"Stop!" cried Wesel again.

With her arms, her useless legs trailing behind her, she pulled herself toward her mate. And she grappled with him, desperation lending her strength. So for many heartbeats they fought—silent, savage, forgetful of all that each owed to the other. And yet, perhaps, Wesel never quite forgot. For all her blind, frantic will to survive her telepathic powers were at no time entirely in abeyance. In spite of herself she, as always, shared the other's mind. And this psychological factor gave her an advantage that offset the paralysis of the lower half of her body—and at the same time inhibited her from pressing that advantage home to its logical conclusion.

But it did not save her when her fingers, inadvertently, dug into the wound in Shrick's arm. His ear-splitting scream was compounded of pain and fury, and he drew upon reserves of strength that the other never even guessed that he possessed. And the hand gripping the blade came round with irresistible force.

For Wesel there was a heartbeat of pain, of sorrow for herself and Shrick, of blind anger against the Giants who, indirectly, had brought this thing to pass.

And then the beating of her heart was stilled forever.

With the death of Wesel Shrick's frenzy left him.

There, in the darkness, he ran his sensitive fingers over the lifeless form, hopelessly hoping for the faintest sign of life. He called her name, he shook her roughly. But at last the knowledge that she was dead crept into his brain—and stayed there. In his short life he had known many times this sense of loss, but never with such poignancy.

And worst of all was the knowledge that *he* had killed her.

He tried to shift the burden of blame. He told himself that she would have died, in any case, of the wounds received at the hands of the Gaints. He tried to convince himself that, wounds or no wounds, the Giants were directly responsible for her death. And he knew that he was Wesel's murderer, just as he knew that all that remained for him in life was to bring the slayers of his people to a reckoning.

This made him cautious.

For many heartbeats he lay there in the thick darkness, not daring to renew his assault on the walls of his prison. He told himself that, somehow, he would know when the Giants let the air back into the world. How he would know he could not say, but the conviction persisted.

And when at last, with returning pressure, the insulation resumed its normal consistency, Shrick took this as a sign that it was safe for him to get out. He started to hack at the spongy material, then stopped. He went back to the body of Wesel. Just once he whispered her name, and ran his hands over the stiff, silent form in a last caress.

He did not return.

And when, at last, the dim light of the Place-of-Meeting

broke through she was buried deep in the debris that he had thrown behind him as he worked.

The air tasted good after the many times breathed atmosphere of the cave. For a few heartbeats Shrick was dizzy with the abrupt increase of pressure, for much of the air in his prison had escaped before the plug expanded to seal the entrance. It is probable that had it not been for the air liberated from the burst cells of the insulation he would long since have asphyxiated.

But this he was not to know—and if he had known it would not have worried him overmuch. He was alive, and Wesel and all the People were dead. When the mist cleared from in front of his eyes he could see them, their bodies twisted in the tortuous attitudes of their last agony, mute evidence of the awful powers of the Giants.

And now that he saw them he did not feel the overwhelming sorrow that he knew he should have done. He felt instead a kind of anger. By their refusal to heed his warning they had robbed him of his kingdom. None now could dispute his mastery of the Outside—but with no subjects, willing or unwilling, the vast territory under his sway was worthless.

With Wesel alive it would have been different.

What was it that she had said—? *. . . and the cave of Long-Fur the spear maker . . .*

He could hear her voice as she said it *. . . and the cave of Long-Fur the spear maker.*

Perhaps—But there was only one way to make sure.

He found the cave, saw that its entrance had been walled up. He felt a wild upsurge of hope. Frantically, with tooth and claw, he tore at the insulation. The fine blade that he had won from the Inside gleamed dully not a dozen handbreadths from where he was working, but such was his blind, unreasoning haste that he ignored the tool that would have made his task immeasurably shorter. At last the entrance was cleared. A feeble cry greeted the influx of air and light. For a while Shrick could not see who was within, and then could have screamed in his disappointment.

For here were no tough fighting males, no sturdy, fertile females, but two hands or so of weakly squirming infants. Their mothers must have realized, barely in time, that he and Wesel had been right, that there was only one way to ward off the choking death. Themselves they had not been able to save.

But they will grow up, Shrick told himself. *It won't be long before they are able to carry a spear for the Lord of the Outside, before the females are able to bear his children.*

Conquering his repugnance, he dragged them out. There was a hand of female infants, all living, and a hand of males. Three of these were dead. But here, he knew, was the nucleus of the army with which he would reestablish his rule over the world, Inside as well as Outside.

But first, they had to be fed.

He saw, now, his fine blade, and seizing it he began to cut up the three lifeless male children. The scent of their blood made him realize that he was hungry. But it was not until the children, now quieted, were all munching happily that he cut a portion for himself.

When he had finished it he felt much better.

It was some time before Shrick resumed his visits to the Inside. He had the pitiful remnant of his people to nurse to maturity and, besides, there was no need to make raids upon the Giants' stocks of food. They themselves had provided him with sustenance beyond his powers of reckoning. He knew, too, that it would be unwise to let his enemies know that there had been any survivors from the cataclysm that they had launched. The fact that he had survived the choking death did not mean that it was the only weapon that the Giants had at their disposal.

But as time went on he felt an intense longing to watch once more the strange life beyond the Barrier. Now that he had killed a Giant he felt a strange sense of kinship with the monstrous beings. He thought of the Thin-One, Loud-Voice, Bare-Head and the Little Giant almost as old friends. At times he even caught himself regretting that he must kill them all. But he knew that in this lay the only hope for the survival of himself and his people.

And then, at last, he was satisfied that he could leave the children to fend for themselves. Even should he fail to return from the Inside they would manage. No-Toes, the eldest of the female children, had already proved to be a capable nurse.

And so he roamed once more the maze of caves and tunnels just outside the Barrier. Through his doorways and peepholes he spied upon the bright, fascinating life of the Inner World. From the Cave-of-Thunders—though how it had come by its name none of the People has ever known—to the Place-of-Little-Lights he ranged. Many feedings passed, but he was not obliged to return to his own food store. For the corpses of the People were everywhere. True, they were beginning to stink a little, but like all his race Shrick was never a fastidious eater.

And he watched the Giants going about the strange, ordered routine of their lives. Often he was tempted to show himself, to shout defiance. But this action had to remain in the realm of wish-fulfillment dreams—he knew full well that it would bring sure and speedy calamity.

And then, at last, came the opportunity for which he had been waiting. He had been in the Place-of-Little-Lights, watching the Little Giant going about his mysterious, absorbing business. He had wished that he could understand its purport, that he could ask the Little Giant in his own tongue what it was that he was doing. For, since the death of Wesel, there had been none with whom a communion of mind was possible. He sighed, so loudly that the Giant must have heard.

He started uneasily and looked up from his work. Hastily Shrick withdrew into his tunnel. For many heartbeats he remained there, occasionally peeping out. But the other was still alert, must have known in some way that he was not alone. And so, eventually, Shrick had retired rather than risk incurring the potent wrath of the Giants once more.

His random retreat brought him to a doorway but rarely used. On the other side of it was a huge cavern in which there was nothing of real interest or value. In it, as a rule, at least one of the Giants would be sleeping, and others would be engaged in one of their incomprehensible pastimes.

This time there was no deep rumble of conversation, no movement whatsoever. Shrick's keen ears could distinguish the breathing of three different sleepers. The Thin-One was there, his respiration, like himself, had a meager quality. Loud-Voice was loud even in sleep. And Bare-Head, the chief of the Giants, breathed with a quiet authority.

And the Little Giant who, alone of all his people, was alert and awake was in the Place-of-Little-Lights.

Shrick knew that it was now or never. Any attempt to deal with the Giants singly must surely bring the great, hot light foretold by Three-Eyes. Now, with any luck at all, he could deal with the three sleepers and then lie in wait for the Little

Giant. Unsuspecting, unprepared, he could be dealt with as easily as had Fat-Belly.

And yet—he did not want to do it.

It wasn't fear; it was that indefinable sense of kinship, the knowledge that, in spite of gross physical disparities, the Giants and the People were as one. For the history of Man, although Shrick was not to know this, is but the history of the fire-making, tool-using animal.

Then he forced himself to remember Wesel, and Big-Ears, and the mass slaughter of almost all his race. He remembered Three-Eyes' words—*but this I can tell you, the People are doomed. Nothing you or they can do will save them. But you will kill those who will kill us, and that is good.*

But you will kill those who will kill us—

But if I kill all the Giants before they kill us, he thought, then the world, all the world, will belong to the People . . .

And he still hung back.

It was not until the Thin-One, who must have been in the throes of a bad dream, murmured and stirred in his sleep that Shrick came out of his doorway. The keen blade with which he had slain Fat-Belly was grasped in both his hands. He launched himself toward the uneasy sleeper. His weapon sliced down once only—how often had he rehearsed this in his imagination!—and for the Thin-One the dream was over.

The smell of fresh blood, as always, excited him. It took him all of his will power to restrain himself from hacking and slashing at the dead Giant. But he promised himself that this would come later. And he jumped from the body of the Thin-One to where Loud-Voice was snoring noisily.

The abrupt cessation of that all too familiar sound must have awakened Bare-Head. Shrick saw him shift and stir, saw his hands go out to loosen the bonds that held him to his sleeping place. And when the Giant Killer, his feet scrabbling for a hold, landed on his chest he was ready. And he was shouting in a great Voice, so that Shrick knew that it was only a matter of heartbeats before the Little Giant came to his assistance.

Fat-Belly had been taken off guard, the Thin-One and Loud-Voice had been killed in their sleep. But here was no easy victory for the Giant Killer.

For a time it looked as though the chief of the Giants would win. After a little he ceased his shouting and fought with grim, silent desperation. Once one of his great hands caught Shrick in a bone-crushing grip, and it seemed as though the battle was over. Shrick could feel the blood pounding in his head, his eyeballs almost popping out of their sockets. It took every ounce of resolution he possessed to keep from dropping his blade and scratching frenziedly at the other's wrist with ineffectual hands.

Something gave—it was his ribs—and in the fleeting instant of relaxed pressure he was able to twist, to turn and slash at the monstrous, hairy wrist. The warm blood spurted and the Giant cried aloud. Again and again Shrick plied his blade, until it became plain that the Giant would not be able to use that hand again.

He was single-handed now against an opponent as yet—insofar as his limbs were concerned—uncrippled. True, every movement of the upper part of his body brought spears of pain lancing through Shrick's chest. But he could move, and smite—and slay.

For Bare-Head weakened as the blood flowed from his wounds. No longer was he able to ward off the attacks on his face and neck. Yet he fought, as his race had always fought, to his dying breath. His enemy would have given no quarter—this much was obvious—but he could have sought refuge with the Little Giant in the Place-of-Little-Lights.

Toward the end he started shouting again.

And as he died, the Little Giant came into the cave.

It was sheer, blind luck that saved the Giant Killer from speedy death at the intruder's hands. Had the Little Giant known of the pitifully small forces arrayed against him it would have gone hard with Shrick. But No-Toes, left with her charges, had grown bored with the Place-of-Meeting. She had heard Shrick talk of the wonders of the Inside; and now, she thought, was her chance to see them for herself.

Followed by her charges she wandered aimlessly along the tunnels just outside the Barrier. She did not know the location of the doors to the Inside, and the view through the occasional peepholes was very circumscribed.

The she came upon the doorway which Shrick had left open when he made his attack on the sleeping Giants. Bright light streamed through the aperture—light brighter than any No-Toes had seen before in her short life. Like a beacon it lured her on.

She did not hesitate when she came to the opening. Unlike

her parents, she had not been brought up to regard the Giants with superstitious awe. Shrick was the only adult she could remember having known—and he, although he had talked of the Giants, had boasted of having slain one in single combat. He had said, also, that he would, at some time or other, kill all the Giants.

In spite of her lack of age and experience, No-Toes was no fool. Womanlike, already she had evaluated Shrick. Much of his talk she discounted as idle bragging, but she had never seen any reason to disbelieve his stories of the deaths of Big Tusk, Sterret, Tekka, Fat-Belly—and all the myriads of the People who had perished with them.

So it was that—foolhardy in her ignorance—she sailed through the doorway. Behind her came the other children, squealing in their excitement. Even if the Little Giant had not at first seen them he could not have failed to hear the shrill tumult of their eruption.

There was only one interpretation that he could put upon the evidence of his eyes. The plan to suffocate the People had failed. They had sallied out from their caves and tunnels to the massacre of his fellow Giants—and now fresh reinforcements were arriving to deal with him.

He turned and fled.

Shrick rallied his strength, made a flying leap from the monstrous carcass of Bare-Head. But in mid flight a hard, polished surface interposed itself between him and the fleeing Giant. Stunned, he hung against it for many heartbeats before he realized that it was a huge door which had shut in his face.

He knew that the Little Giant was not merely seeking refuge in flight—for where in the world could he hope to escape the wrath of the People? He had gone, perhaps, for arms of some kind. Or—and at the thought Shrick's blood congealed—he had gone to loose the final doom foretold by Three-Eyes. Now that his plans had begun to miscarry he remembered the prophecy in its entirety, was no longer able to ignore those parts that, in his arrogance, he had found displeasing.

And then No-Toes, her flight clumsy and inexpert in these—to her—strange, vast spaces was at his side.

"Are you hurt?" she gasped. "They are so big—and you fought them."

As she spoke, the world was filled with a deep humming

sound. Shrick ignored the excited female. That noise could mean only one thing. The Little Giant was back in the Place-of-Little-Lights, was setting in motion vast, incomprehensible forces that would bring to pass the utter and irrevocable destruction of the People.

With his feet against the huge door he kicked off, sped rapidly down to the open doorway in the Barrier. He put out his hand to break the shock of his landing, screamed aloud as his impact sent a sickening wave of pain through his chest. He started to cough—and when he saw the bright blood that was welling from his mouth he was very frightened.

No-Toes was with him again. "You are hurt, you are bleeding. Can I—?"

"No!" He turned a snarling mask to her. "No! Leave me alone!"

"But where are you going?"

Shrick paused. Then: "I am going to save the world," he said slowly. He savored the effect of his words. They made him feel better, they made him bulk big in his own mind, bigger, perhaps, than the Giants. "I am going to save you all."

"But how—?"

This was too much for the Giant Killer. He screamed again, but this time with anger. With the back of his hand he struck the young female across the face.

"Stay here!" he ordered.

And then he was gone along the tunnel.

The gyroscopes were still singing their quiet song of power when Shrick reached the Control Room. Strapped in his chair, the navigator was busy over his plotting machine. Outside the ports the stars wheeled by in orderly succession.

And Shrick was frightened.

He had never quite believed Wesel's garbled version of the nature of the world until now. But he could see, at last, that the ship was moving. The fantastic wonder of it all held him spellbound until a thin edge of intolerable radiance crept into view from behind the rim of one of the ports. The navigator touched something and, suddenly, screens of dark blue glass mitigated the glare. But it was still bright, too bright, and the edge became a rapidly widening oval and then, at last, a disk.

The humming of the gyroscope stopped.

Before the silence had time to register, a fresh sound assailed Shrick's ears. It was the roar of the main drive.

A terrifying force seized him and slammed him down upon

the deck. He felt his bones crack under the acceleration. True child of free fall as he was, all this held for him the terror of the supernatural. For a while he lay there, weakly squirming, whimpering a little. The navigator looked down at him and laughed. It was this sound more than anything else that stung Shrick to his last, supreme effort. He didn't want to move. He just wanted to lie there on the deck slowly coughing his life away. But the Little Giant's derision tapped unsuspected reserves of strength, both moral and physical.

The navigator went back to his calculations, handling his instruments for the last time with a kind of desperate elation. He knew that the ship would never arrive at her destination, neither would her cargo of seed grain. But she would not—and this outweighed all other considerations—drift forever among the stars carrying within her hull the seeds of the destruction of Man and all his works.

He knew that—had he not taken this way out—he must have slept at last, and then death at the hands of the mutants would inevitably have been his portion. And with mutants in full charge anything might happen.

The road he had taken was the best.

Unnoticed, inch by inch Shrick edged his way along the deck. Now, he could stretch his free hand and touch the Giant's foot. In the other he still held his blade, to which he had clung as the one thing sure and certain in this suddenly crazy world.

Then he had a grip on the artifical skin covering the Giant's leg. He started to climb, although every movement was unadulterated agony. He did not see the other raise his hand to his mouth, swallow the little pellet that he held therein.

So it was that when, at long last, he reached the soft, smooth throat of the Giant, the Giant was dead.

It was a very fast poison.

For a while he clung there. He should have felt elation at the death of the last of his enemies but—instead—he felt cheated. There was so much that he wanted to know, so much that only the Giants could have told him. Besides—it was his blade that should have won the final victory. He knew that, somewhere, the Little Giant was still laughing at him.

Through the blue-screened ports blazed the sun. Even at this distance, even with the intervening filters, its power and heat were all too evident. And aft the motors still roared, and would roar until the last ounce of fuel had been fed into hungry main drive.

Shrick clung to the dead man's neck, looked long and longingly at the glittering instruments, the shining switches and levers, whose purpose he would never understand, whose inertia would have defeated any attempt of his fast ebbing strength to move them. He looked at the flaming doom ahead, and knew that this was what had been foretold.

Had the metaphor existed in his language, he would have told himself that he and the few surviving People were caught like rats in a trap.

But even the Giants would not have used that phrase in its metaphorical sense.

For that is all that the People were—rats in a trap.

WHAT YOU NEED

by Henry Kuttner

ASTOUNDING SCIENCE FICTION,
October

The third story by Kuttner and company in this book is a powerful discussion of the responsibilities and obligations that go with the holding of power. And like much great science fiction, it has a wonderful puzzle quality about it that has tantalized readers since its appearance more than thirty-five years ago. We (at least some of us) know what we want—but do we really know what we need?

(During the first part of the World War II years Unknown *was the most exciting magazine in the world. The paper shortage killed it, but it didn't kill the need to write the type of stories that it printed. Writers who had worked for* Unknown, *who had gotten into the habit of writing "adult fantasy," found that there was no better way of handling certain difficult themes.*

With Unknown *gone, the temptation was to add a touch of science to such a story and write it anyway. I am convinced that Hank wrote this story with* Unknown *in mind. It would take almost nothing in the way of change to make it perfect for that magazine and yet as it stands it is undoubtedly science fiction. I.A.)*

That's what the sign said. Tim Carmichael, who worked for a trade paper that specialized in economics, and eked out a meager salary by selling sensational and untrue articles to the tabloids, failed to sense a story in the reversed sign. He thought it was a cheap publicity gag, something one seldom encounters on Park Avenue, where the shop fronts are noted for their classic dignity. And he was irritated.

He growled silently, walked on, then suddenly turned and came back. He wasn't quite strong enough to resist the temptation to unscramble the sentence, though his annoyance grew. He stood before the window, staring up, and said to himself, " 'We have what you need.' Yeah?"

The sign was in prim, small letters on a black painted ribbon that stretched across a narrow glass pane. Below it was one of those curved, invisible-glass windows. Through the window Carmichael could see an expanse of white velvet, with a few objects carefully arranged there. A rusty nail, a snowshoe and a diamond tiara. It looked like a Dali decor for Cartier or Tiffany.

"Jewelers?" Carmichael asked silently. "But why *what you need*?" He pictured millionaires miserably despondent for lack of a matched pearl necklace, heiresses weeping inconsolably because they needed a few star sapphires. The principle of luxury merchandising was to deal with the whipped cream of supply and demand; few people needed diamonds. They merely wanted them and could afford them.

"Or the place might sell jinni flasks," Carmichael decided. "Or magic wands. Same principle as a Coney carny, though. A sucker trap. Bill the Whatzit outside and people will pay their dimes and flock in. For two cents—"

He was dyspeptic this morning, and generally disliked the world. Prospect of a scapegoat was attractive, and his press card gave him a certain advantage. He opened the door and walked into the shop.

It was Park Avenue, all right. There were no showcases or counters. It might be an art gallery, for a few good oils were displayed on the walls. An air of overpowering luxury, with the bleakness of an unlived-in place, struck Carmichael.

Through a curtain at the back came a very tall man with carefully combed white hair, a ruddy, healthy face and sharp blue eyes. He might have been sixty. He wore expensive but careless tweeds, which somehow jarred with the décor.

"Good morning," the man said, with a quick glance at

Carmichael's clothes. He seemed slightly surprised. "May I help you?"

"Maybe." Carmichael introduced himself and showed his press card.

"Oh? My name is Talley. Peter Talley."

"I saw your sign."

"Oh?"

"Our paper is always on the lookout for possible writeups. I've never noticed your shop before—"

"I've been here for years," Talley said.

"This is an art gallery?"

"Well—no."

The door opened. A florid man came in and greeted Talley cordially. Carmichael, recognizing the client, felt his opinion of the shop swing rapidly upward. The florid man was a Name—a big one.

"It's a big early, Mr. Talley," he said, "but I didn't want to delay. Have you had time to get—what I needed?"

"Oh, yes. I have it. One moment." Talley hurried through the draperies and returned with a small, neatly wrapped parcel, which he gave to the florid man. The latter forked over a check—Carmichael caught a glimpse of the amount and gulped—and departed. His town car was at the curb outside.

Carmichael moved toward the door, where he could watch. The florid man seemed anxious. His chauffeur waited stolidly as the parcel was unwrapped with hurried fingers.

"I'm not sure I'd want publicity, Mr. Carmichael," Talley said. "I've a select clientele—carefully chosen."

"Perhaps our weekly economic bulletins might interest you."

Talley tried not to laugh. "Oh, I don't think so. It really isn't in my line."

The florid man had finally unwrapped the parcel and taken out an egg. As far as Carmichael could see from his post near the door, it was merely an ordinary egg. But its possessor regarded it almost with awe. Had Earth's last hen died ten years before, the man could have been no more pleased. Something like deep relief showed on the Florida-tanned face.

He said something to the chauffeur, and the car rolled smoothly forward and was gone.

"Are you in the dairy business?" Carmichael asked abruptly.

"No."

"Do you mind telling me what your business is?"

"I'm afraid I do, rather," Talley said.

Carmichael was beginning to scent a story. "Of course, I could find out through the Better Business Bureau—"

"You couldn't."

"No? They might be interested in knowing why an egg is worth five thousand dollars to one of your customers."

Talley said, "My clientele is so small I must charge high fees. You—ah—know that a Chinese mandarin has been known to pay thousands of taels for eggs of proved antiquity."

"That guy wasn't a Chinese mandarin," Carmichael said.

"Oh, well. As I say, I don't welcome publicity—"

"I think you do. I was in the advertising game for a while. Spelling your sign backwards is an obvious baited hook."

"Then you're no psychologist," Talley said. "It's just that I can afford to indulge my whims. For five years I looked at that window every day and read the sign backwards—from inside my shop. It annoyed me. You know how a word will begin to look funny if you keep staring at it? Any word. It turns into something in no human tongue. Well, I discovered I was getting a neurosis about that sign. It makes no sense backwards, but I kept finding myself trying to read sense into it. When I started to say 'Deen uoy tahw evah ew' to myself and looking for philological derivations, I called in a sign painter. People who are interested enough still drop in."

"Not many," Carmichael said shrewdly. "This is Park Avenue. And you've got the place fixed up too expensively. Nobody in the low-income brackets—or the middle brackets—would come in here. So you run an upper-bracket business."

"Well," Talley said, "yes, I do."

"And you won't tell me what it is?"

"I'd rather not."

"I can find out, you know. It might be dope, pornography, high-class fencing—"

"Very likely," Mr. Talley said smoothly. "I buy stolen jewels, conceal them in eggs and sell them to my customers. Or perhaps that egg was loaded with miscroscopic French postcards. Good morning, Mr. Carmichael."

"Good morning," Carmichael said, and went out. He was overdue at the office, but annoyance was the stronger motivation. He played sleuth for a while, keeping an eye on Talley's shop, and the results were thoroughly satisfactory—to a certain extent. He learned everything but why.

Late in the afternoon, he sought out Mr. Talley again.

"Wait a minute," he said, at sight of the proprietor's discouraging face. "For all you know, I may be a customer."

Talley laughed.

"Well, why not?" Carmichael compressed his lips. "How do you know the size of my bank account? Or maybe you've got a restricted clientele?"

"No. But—"

Carmichael said quickly, "I've been doing some investigating. I've been noticing your customers. In fact, following them. And finding out what they buy from you."

Talley's face changed. "Indeed?"

"In*deed*. They're all in a hurry to unwrap their little bundles. So that gave me my chance to find out. I missed a few, but—I saw enough to apply a couple of rules of logic, Mr. Talley. *Item*: your customers don't know what they're buying from you. It's a sort of grab bag. A couple of times they were plenty surprised. The man who opened his parcel and found an old newspaper clipping. What about the sunglasses? And the revolver? Probably illegal, by the way—no license. And the diamond—it must have been paste, it was so big."

"M-mmm," Mr. Talley said.

"I'm no smart apple, but I can smell a screwy setup. Most of your clients are big shots, in one way or another. And why didn't any of 'em pay you, like the first man—the guy who came in when I was here this morning?"

"It's chiefly a credit business," Talley said. "I've my ethics. I have to, for my own conscience. It's responsibility. You see, I sell—my goods—with a guarantee. Payment is made only if the product proves satisfactory."

"So. An Egg. Sunglasses. A pair of asbestos gloves—I think they were. A newspaper clipping. A gun. And a diamond. How do you take inventory?"

Talley said nothing.

Carmichael grinned. "You've an errand boy. You send him out and he comes back with bundles. Maybe he goes to a grocery on Madison and buys an egg. Or a pawnshop on Sixth for a revolver. Or—well, anyhow, I told you I'd find out what your business is."

"And have you?" Talley asked.

" 'We have what you need,' " Carmichael said. "But how do you *know?*"

"You're jumping to conclusions."

"I've got a headache—I didn't have sunglasses!—and I don't believe in magic. Listen, Mr. Talley, I'm fed up to the eyebrows and way beyond on queer little shops that sell peculiar things. I know too much about 'em—I've written about 'em. A guy walks along the street and sees a funny sort of store and the proprietor won't serve him—he sells only to pixies—or else he *does* sell him a magic charm with a double edge. Well—*pfui!*"

"Mph," Talley said.

" 'Mph' as much as you like. But you can't get away from logic. Either you've got a sound, sensible racket here, or else it's one of those funny, magic-shop setups—and I don't believe that. For it isn't logical."

"Why not?"

"Because of economics," Carmichael said flatly. "Grant the idea that you've got certain mysterious powers—let's say you can make telepathic gadgets. All right. Why the devil would you start a business so you could sell the gadgets so you could make money so you could live? You'd simply put on one of your gadgets, read a stockbroker's mind and buy the right stocks. That's the intrisic fallacy in these crazy-shop things—if you've got enough stuff on the ball to be able to stock and run such a shop, you wouldn't need a business in the first place. Why go round Robin Hood's barn?"

Talley said nothing.

Carmichael smiled crookedly. " 'I often wonder what the vintners buy one half so precious as the stuff they sell,' " he quoted. "Well—what do *you* buy? I know what you sell—eggs and sunglasses."

"You're an inquisitive man, Mr. Carmichael," Talley murmured. "Has it ever occurred to you that this is none of your business?"

"I may be a customer," Carmichael repeated. "How about that?"

Talley's cool blue eyes were intent. A new light dawned in them; Talley pursed his lips and scowled. "I hadn't thought of that," he admitted. "You might be. Under the circumstances. Will you excuse me for a moment?"

"Sure," Carmichael said. Talley went through the curtains.

Outside, traffic drifted idly along Park. As the sun slid down beyond the Hudson, the street lay in a blue shadow that crept imperceptibly up the barricades of the buildings. Carmichael stared at the sign—WE HAVE WHAT YOU NEED and smiled.

In a back room, Talley put his eye to a binocular plate and moved a calibrated dial. He did this several times. Then, biting his lip—for he was a gentle man—he called his errand boy and gave him directions. After that he returned to Carmichael.

"You're a customer," he said. "Under certain conditions."

"The condition of my bank account, you mean?"

"No," Talley said. "I'll give you reduced rates. Understand one thing. I really do have what you need. You don't *know* what you need, but I know. And as it happens—well, I'll sell you what you need for, let's say, five dollars."

Carmichael reached for his wallet. Talley held up a hand.

"Pay me after you're satisfied. And the money's the nominal part of the fee. There's another part. If you're satisfied, I want you to promise that you'll never come near this shop again and never mention it to anyone."

"I see," Carmichael said slowly. His theories had changed slightly.

"It won't be long before—ah, here he is now." A buzzing from the back indicated the return of the errand boy. Talley said, "Excuse me," and vanished. Soon he returned with a neatly wrapped parcel, which he thrust into Carmichael's hands.

"Keep this on your person," Talley said. "Good afternoon."

Carmichael nodded, pocketed the parcel and went out. Feeling affluent, he hailed a taxi and went to a cocktail bar he knew. There, in the dim light of a booth, he unwrapped the bundle.

Protection money, he decided. Talley was paying him off to keep his mouth shut about the racket, whatever it was. O.K., live and let live. How much would be—

Ten thousand? Fifty thousand? How big was the racket?

He opened an oblong cardboard box. Within, nestling upon tissue paper, was a pair of shears, the blades protected by a sheath of folded, glued cardboard.

Carmichael said something softly. He drank his highball and ordered another, but left it untasted. Glancing at his wrist watch, he decided that the Park Avenue shop would be closed by now and Mr. Peter Talley gone.

"'. . . one half so precious as the stuff they sell.'" Carmichael said. "Maybe it's the scissors of Atropos. Blah." He unsheathed the blades and snipped experimentally at the air. Nothing happened. Slightly crimson around the cheekbones, Carmichael reholstered the shears and dropped them into the side pocket of his topcoat. Quite a gag!

He decided to call on Peter Talley tomorrow.

Meanwhile, what? He remembered he had a dinner date with one of the girls at the office, and hastily paid his bill and left. The streets were darkening, and a cold wind blew southward from the Park. Carmichael wound his scarf tighter around his throat and made gestures toward passing taxis.

He was considerably annoyed.

Half an hour later a thin man with sad eyes—Jerry Worth, one of the copy writers from his office—greeted him at the bar where Carmichael was killing time. "Waiting for Besty?" Worth said, nodding toward the restaurant annex. "She sent me to tell you she couldn't make it. A rush deadline. Apologies and stuff. Where were you today? Things got gummed up a bit. Have a drink with me."

They worked on a rye. Carmichael was already slightly stiff. The dull crimson around his cheekbones had deepened, and his frown had become set. "What you need," he remarked. "Double crossing little—"

"Huh?" Worth said.

"Nothing. Drink up. I've just decided to get a guy in trouble. If I can."

"You almost got in trouble yourself today. That trend analysis of ores—"

"Eggs. Sunglasses!"

"I got you out of a jam—"

"Shut up," Carmichael said, and ordered another round. Every time he felt the weight of the shears in his pocket he found his lips moving.

Five shots later Worth said plaintively, "I don't mind doing good deeds, but I do like to mention them. And you won't let me. All I want is a little gratitude."

"All right, mention them," Carmichael said. "Brag your head off. Who cares?"

Worth showed satisfaction. "That ore analysis—it was that. You weren't at the office today, but I caught it. I checked with our records and you had Trans-Steel all wrong. If I hadn't altered the figures, it would have gone down to the printer—"

"What?"

"The Trans-Steel. They—"

"Oh, you fool," Carmichael groaned. "I know it didn't check with the office figures. I meant to put in a notice to have them changed. I got my dope from the source. Why don't you mind your own business?"

Worth blinked. "I was trying to help."

"It would have been good for a five-buck raise," Carmichael said. "After all the research I did to uncover the real dope— Listen, has the stuff gone to bed yet?"

"I dunno. Maybe not. Croft was still checking the copy—"

"O.K.!" Carmichael said. "Next time—" He jerked at his scarf, jumped off the stool and headed for the door, trailed by the protesting Worth. Ten minutes later he was at the office, listening to Croft's bland explanation that the copy had already been dispatched to the printer.

"Does it matter? Was there—Incidentally, where were you today?"

"Dancing on the rainbow," Carmichael snapped, and departed. He had switched over from rye to whisky sours, and the cold night air naturally did not sober him. Swaying slightly, watching the sidewalk move a little as he blinked at it, he stood on the curb and pondered.

"I'm sorry, Tim," Worth said. "It's too late now, though. There won't be any trouble. You've got a right to go by our office records."

"Stop me now," Carmichael said. "Lousy little—" He was angry and drunk. On impulse he got another taxi and sped to the printer's, still trailing a somewhat confused Jerry Worth.

There was rhythmic thunder in the building. The swift movement of the taxi had given Carmichael a slight nausea; his head ached, and alcohol was in solution in his blood. The hot, inky air was unpleasant. The great Linotypes thumped and growled. Men were moving about. It was all slightly nightmarish, and Carmichael doggedly hunched his shoulders and lurched on until something jerked him back and began to strangle him.

Worth started yelling. His face showed drunken terror. He made ineffectual gestures.

But this was all part of the nightmare. Carmichael saw

what had happened. The ends of his scarf had caught in the moving gears somewhere and he was being drawn inexorably into meshing metal cogs. Men were running. The clanking, thumping, rolling sounds were deafening. He pulled at the scarf.

Worth screamed, ". . . knife! Cut it!"

The warping of relative values that intoxication gives saved Carmichael. Sober, he would have been helpless with panic. As it was, each thought was hard to capture, but clear and lucid when he finally got it. He remembered the shears, and he put his hand in his pocket. The blades slipped out of their cardboard sheath, and he snipped through the scarf with fumbling, hasty movements.

The white silk disappeared. Carmichael fingered the ragged edge at his throat and smiled stiffly.

Mr. Peter Talley had been hoping that Carmichael would not come back. The probability lines had shown two possible variants; in one, all was well; in the other . . .

Carmichael walked into the shop the next morning and held out a five-dollar bill. Talley took it.

"Thank you. But you could have mailed me a check."

"I could have. Only that wouldn't have told me what I wanted to know."

"No," Talley said, and sighed. "You've decided, haven't you?"

"Do you blame me?" Carmichael asked. "Last night—do you know what happened?"

"Yes."

"How?"

"I might as well tell you," Talley said. "You'd find out anyway. That's certain, anyhow."

Carmichael sat down, lit a cigarette and nodded. "Logic. You couldn't have arranged that little accident, by any manner of means. Betsy Hoag decided to break our date early yesterday morning. Before I saw you. That was the beginning of the chain of incidents that led up to the accident. *Ergo*, you must have known what was going to happen."

"I did know."

"Prescience?"

"Mechanical. I saw that you would be crushed in the machine—"

"Which implies an alterable future."

"Certainly," Talley said, his shoulders slumping. "There are innumerable possible variants to the future. Different lines of probability. All depending on the outcome of various crises as they arise. I happen to be skilled in certain branches of electronics. Some years ago, almost by accident, I stumbled on the principle of seeing the future."

"How?"

"Chiefly it involves a personal focus on the individual. The moment you enter this place"—he gestured—"you're in the beam of my scanner. In my back room I have the machine itself. By turning a calibrated dial, I check the possible futures. Sometimes there are many. Sometimes only a few. As though at times certain stations weren't broadcasting. I look into my scanner and see what you need—and supply it."

Carmichael let smoke drift from his nostrils. He watched the blue coils through narrowed eyes.

"You follow a man's whole life—in triplicate or quadruplicate or whatever?"

"No," Talley said. "I've got my device focused so it's sensitive to crisis curves. When those occur, I follow them farther and see what probability paths involve the man's safe and happy survival."

"The sunglasses, the egg and the gloves—"

Talley said, "Mr.—uh—Smith is one of my regular clients. Whenever he passes a crisis successfully, with my aid, he comes back for another checkup. I locate his next crisis and supply him with what he needs to meet it. I gave him the asbestos gloves. In about a month, a situation will arise where he must—under the circumstances—move a red-hot bar of metal. He's an artist. His hands—"

"I see. So it isn't always saving a man's life."

"Of course not," Talley said. "Life isn't the only vital factor. An apparently minor crisis may lead to—well, a divorce, a neurosis, a wrong decision and the loss of hundreds of lives indirectly. I insure life, health and happiness."

"You're an altruist. Only why doesn't the world storm your doors? Why limit your trade to a few?"

"I haven't got the time or the equipment."

"More machines could be built."

"Well," Talley said, "most of my customers are wealthy. I must live."

"You could read tomorrow's stock-market reports if you wanted dough," Carmichael said. "We get back to that old question. If a guy has miraculous powers, why is he satisfied to run a hole-in-the-wall store?"

"Economic reasons. I—ah—I'm averse to gambling."

"It wouldn't be gambling," Carmichael pointed out. " 'I often wonder what the vintners buy . . .' Just what *do* you get out of this?"

"Satisfaction," Talley said. "Call it that."

But Carmichael wasn't satisfied. His mind veered from the question and turned to the possibilities. Insurance, eh? Life, health and happiness.

"What about me? Won't there be another crisis in my life sometime?"

"Probably. Not necessarily one involving personal danger."

"Then I'm a permanent customer."

"I—don't—"

"Listen," Carmichael said, "I'm not trying to shake you down. I'll pay. I'll pay plenty. I'm not rich, but I know exactly what a service like this would be worth to me. No worries—"

"It couldn't be—"

"Oh, come off it. I'm not a blackmailer or anything. I'm not threatening you with publicity, if that's what you're afraid of. I'm an ordinary guy, not a melodramatic villain. Do I look dangerous? What are you afraid of?"

"You're an ordinary guy, yes," Talley admitted. "Only—"

"Why not?" Carmichael argued. "I won't bother you. I passed one crisis successfully, with your help. There'll be another one due sometime. Give me what I need for that. Charge me anything you like. I'll get the dough somehow. Borrow it, if necessary I won't disturb you at all. All I ask is that you let me come in whenever I've passed a crisis, and get ammunition for the next one. What's wrong with that?"

"Nothing," Talley said soberly.

"Well, then. I'm an ordinary guy. There's a girl—it's Betsy Hoag. I want to marry her. Settle down somewhere in the country, raise kids and have security. There's nothing wrong with that either, is there?"

Talley said, "It was too late the moment you entered this shop today."

Carmichael looked up. "Why?" he asked sharply.

A buzzer rang in the back. Talley went through the curtains and came back almost immediately with a wrapped parcel. He gave it to Carmichael.

Carmichael smiled. "Thanks," he said. "Thanks a lot. Do you have any idea when my next crisis will come?"

"In a week."

"Mind if I—" Carmichael was unwrapping the package. He took out a pair of plastic-soled shoes and looked at Talley, bewildered.

"Like that, eh? I'll need—shoes?"

"Yes."

"I suppose—" Carmichael hesitated. "I guess you wouldn't tell me why?"

"No, I won't do that. But be sure to wear them whenever you go out."

"Don't worry about that. And—I'll mail you a check. It may take me a few days to scrape up the dough, but I'll do it. How much?"

"Five hundred dollars."

"I'll mail a check today."

"I prefer not to accept a fee until the client has been satisfied," Talley said. He had grown more reserved, his blue eyes cool and withdrawn.

"Suit yourself," Carmichael said. "I'm going out and celebrate. You—don't drink?"

"I can't leave the shop."

"Well, good-bye. And thanks again. I won't be any trouble to you, you know. I promise that!" He turned away.

Looking after him, Talley smiled a wry, unhappy smile. He did not answer Carmichael's good-bye. Not then.

When the door had closed behind him. Talley turned to the back of his shop and went through the door where the scanner was.

The lapse of ten years can cover a multitude of changes. A man with the possibility of tremendous power almost within his grasp can alter, in that time, from a man who will not reach for it to a man who will—and moral values be damned.

The change did not come quickly to Carmichael. It speaks well for his integrity that it took ten years to work such an alteration in all he had been taught. On the day he first went into Talley's shop there was little evil in him. But the temptation grew stronger week by week, visit by visit. Talley, for reasons of his own, was content to sit idly by, waiting for customers, smothering the inconceivable potentialities of his machine under a blanket of trivial functions. But Carmichael was not content.

It took him ten years to reach the day, but the day came at last.

Talley sat in the inner room, his back to the door. He was slumped low in an ancient rocker, facing the machine. It had changed little in the space of a decade. It still covered most of two walls, and the eyepiece of its scanner glittered under amber fluorescents.

Carmichael looked convetously at the eyepiece. It was window and doorway to a power beyond any man's dreams. Wealth beyond imagining lay just within that tiny opening. The rights over the life and death of every man alive. And nothing between that fabulous future and himself except the man who sat looking at the machine.

Talley did not seem to hear the careful footsteps or the creak of the door behind him. He did not stir as Carmichael lifted the gun slowly. One might think that he never guessed what was coming, or why, or from whom, as Carmichael shot him through the head.

Talley sighed and shivered a little, and twisted the scanner dial. It was not the first time that the eyepiece had shown him his own lifeless body, glimpsed down some vista of probability, but he never saw the slumping of that familiar figure without feeling a breath of indescribable coolness blow backwards upon him out of the future.

He straightened from the eyepiece and sat back in his chair, looking thoughtfully at a pair of rough-soled shoes lying beside him on a table. He sat quietly for a while, his eyes upon the shoes, his mind following Carmichael down the street and into the evening, and the morrow, and on toward that coming crisis which would depend on his secure footing on a subway platform as a train thundered by the place where Carmichael would be standing one day next week.

Talley had sent his messenger boy out this time for two pairs of shoes. He had hesitated long, an hour ago, between the rough-soled pair and the smooth. For Talley was a humane man, and there were many times when his job was distasteful to him. But in the end, this time, it had been the smooth-soled pair he had wrapped for Carmichael.

Now he sighed and bent to the scanner again, twisting the dial to bring into view a scene he had watched before.

Carmichael, standing on a crowded subway platform, glittering with oily wetness from some overflow. Carmichael, in the slick-soled shoes Talley had chosen for him. A commotion in the crowd, a surge toward the platform edge. Carmichael's feet slipping frantically as the train roared by.

"Good-bye, Mr. Carmichael," Talley murmured. It was the farewell he had not spoken when Carmichael left the shop. He spoke it regretfully, and the regret was for the Carmichael of today, who did not yet deserve that end. He was not now a melodramatic villain whose death one could watch unmoved. But the Tim Carmichael of today had atonement to make for the Carmichael of ten years ahead, and the payment must be exacted.

It is not a good thing to have the power of life and death over one's fellow humans. Peter Talley knew it was not a good thing—but the power had been put into his hands. He had not sought it. It seemed to him that the machine had grown almost by accident to its tremendous completion under his trained fingers and trained mind.

At first it had puzzled him. How ought such a device to be used? What dangers, what terrible potentialities, lay in that Eye that could see through the veil of tomorrow? His was the responsibility, and it had weighed heavily upon him until the answer came. And after he knew the answer—well, the weight was heavier still. For Talley was a mild man.

He could not have told anyone the real reason why he was a shopkeeper. Satisfaction, he had said to Carmichael. And sometimes, indeed, there was deep satisfaction. But at other times—at times like this—there was only dismay and humility. Especially humility.

We have what you need. Only Talley knew that message was not for the individuals who came to his shop. The pronoun was plural, not singular. It was a message for the world—the world whose future was being carefully, lovingly reshaped under Peter Talley's guidance.

The main line of the future was not easy to alter. The future is pyramid shaping slowly, brick by brick, and brick by brick Talley had to change it. There were some men who were necessary—men who would create and build—men who should be saved.

Talley gave them what they needed.

But inevitably there were others whose ends were evil. Talley gave them, too, what the world needed—death.

Peter Talley had not asked for this terrible power. But the key had been put in his hands, and he dared not delegate such authority as this to any other man alive. Sometimes he made mistakes.

He had felt a little surer since the metaphor of the key had occurred to him. The key to the future. A key that had been laid in his hands.

Remembering that, he leaned back in his chair and reached for an old and well-worn book. It fell open easily at a familiar passage. Peter Talley's lips moved as he read the passage once again, in his room behind the shop on Park Avenue.

"And I say also unto thee, that thou art Peter. . . . And I will give unto thee the keys of the Kingdom of Heaven. . . ."

DE PROFUNDIS

by Murray Leinster

THRILLING WONDER STORIES,
Winter

Murray Leinster's third contribution to the best of 1945 is a powerful first-"person" story of an individual with a problem. The quotes around person are there because this is one of those rare stories which is told from the point-of-view of the alien. *1940s science fiction usually stressed ideas over character development, but not in the case of "De Profundis."*

(It is possible to have the essentials of an "alien intelligence" story without ever leaving Earth. "Giant Killer" was one example and this is another.

There is a certain opportunity for satire in having a thoughtful, inquiring intelligence utterly ignorant of matters which the reader takes for granted. We cannot help but smile or titter at the mistakes the alien makes, the false conclusions he comes to.

And yet such a story does not [or should not] serve to be merely a vehicle of amusement to us. Rather it should give rise to the question: What is it that we don't understand that would amuse someone who knows more than we do? What false conclusions do we come to out of ignorance? In short, in what way do we play the fool?

This we can be sure of. We would never play the fool as intensely as we do, if we could only get it through our heads that the possibility of playing the fool exists. I.A.)

I, Sard, make report to the Shadi during Peace Tides. I have made a journey of experiment suggested by the scientist Morpt after discussing with me an Object fallen into Honda from the Surface. I fear that my report will not be accepted as true. I therefore await the consensus on my sanity, offering this report to be judged science or delirium as the Shadi may elect. . . .

I was present when the Object fell. At the moment I was in communication with the scientist Morpt as he meditated upon the facts of the universe. He was rather drowsy, and his mind was more conscientious than inspiring as he reflected—for the benefit of us, his students—upon the evidence of the Caluphian theory of the universe, that it is a shell of solid matter filled with water, which being naturally repelled from the center, acquires pressure, and that we, the Shadi, live in the region of greatest pressure. He almost dozed off as he reflected for our instruction that this theory accounts for all known physical phenomena, except the existence of the substance gas, which is neither solid nor liquid and is found only in our swim-bladders. For this reason, it is commonly assumed to be our immortal part, rising to the center of the universe when our bodies are consumed, and there exists forever.

As he meditated, I recalled the Morpt exercises by which a part of this gas may be ejected from a Shadi body and kept in an inverted receptacle while the body forms a new supply in the swim-bladder. I waited anxiously for Morpt's trenchant reasoning which denies that a substance—however rare and singular—which can be kept in a receptacle or replaced by the body can constitute its vital essence.

These experiments of Morpt's have caused great disturbances among scientific circles.

At the moment, however, he was merely a drowsy instructor, sleepily thinking a lecture he had thought a hundred times before. He was a little annoyed by a sharp rock sticking into his seventh tentacle, which was not quite uncomfortable enough to make him stir.

I lay in my cave, attending anxiously. Then, abruptly, I was aware that something was descending from above. The instinct of our race to block out thought-transference and seize food before anyone else can know if it operated instantly. I flowed out of my cave and swept to the space below the Object. I raised my tentacles to snatch it. The whole process was automatic—mind-block on, spatial sensation extended to the fullest, full focused reception of mental images turned upon the sinking Object to foresee its efforts to escape so that I could anticipate them—but every Shadi knows what one does by pure instinct when a moving thing comes within one's ken.

There were two causes for my behavior after that automatic reaction, however. One was that I had fed, and lately. The other was that I received mental images from within the Object which were startlingly tuned to the subject of Morpt's lecture and my own thoughts of the moment. As my first tentacle swooped upon the descending thing, instead of thoughts of fright or battle, I intercepted the message of an entity, cogitating desparingly, to another.

'My dear, we will never see the Surface again,' it was thinking.

And I received a dazzling impression of what the Surface was like. Since I shall describe the Surface later, I omit a description of the mental picture I then received. But it gave me to pause. I believe fortunately. For one thing, had I swept the Object into my maw as instinct impelled, I believe I would have had trouble digesting it. The Object, as I soon discovered, was made of that rare solid substance which only appears in the form of artifacts. One such specimen has been repeatedly described by Glor. It is about half the length of a Shadi's body, hollow, pointed at one end, with one of its sides curiously flat with strangely shaped excrescences, openings, and two shafts and one hollow tube sticking out of it.

As I said, the Object was made of this rare solid material. My spatial sense immediately told me that it was hollow. Further, that it was filled with gas! And then I received conflicting mental images which told me that there were two living creatures within it! Let me repeat—there were two living entities within the Object, and they lived in gas instead of water!

I was stunned. For a long time I was not really aware of anything at all save the thoughts of the creatures within the Object. I held the Object firmly between two of my tentacles, dazed by the impossible facts I faced. I was most incautious. I could have been killed and consumed in the interval of my bewilderment. But I came to myself and returned swiftly to my cave, carrying the Object with me. As I did so, I was aware of startled thoughts.

'We've hit bottom—no! Something has seized us. It must be monstrous in size. It will soon be over, now. . . .'

Not in answer, but separately, the other entity thought only emotional things I cannot describe. I do not understand them at all. They represent a psychology so alien to ours that there is no way to express them. I can only say that the second entity was in complete despair, and therefore desired intensely to be clasped firmly in the other entity's two tentacles. This would constitute complete helplessness, but it was what the second creature craved. I report the matter with no attempt to explain it.

While flowing into my cave, I knocked the Object against the top of the opening. It was a sharp blow. I had again an impression of despair.

'This is it!' the first creature thought, and looked with dread for an inpouring of water into the gas-filled Object.

Since the psychology of these creatures is so completely inexplicable, I merely summarize the few mental images I received during the next short period, which served to explain the history of the Object.

To begin with, it had been a scientific experiment. The Object was created to contain the gas in which the creatures lived, and to allow the gas to be lowered into the regions of pressure. The creatures themselves were of the same species, but different in a fashion for which we have no thought. One thought of itself as 'man', the other as 'woman'. They did not fear each other. They had accompanied the Object for the purpose of recording their observations in regions of pressure. To make their observations, the Object was suspended by a long tentacle from an artifact like the one of Glor's description.

When they had observed, they were to have been returned to the artifact. Then the gas was to be released, and they would rejoin their fellows. The fact that two creatures could remain together with safety for both is strange enough. But their thoughts told me that forty or fifty others of the same species awaited then on the artifact, all equally devoid of the instinct to feed upon each other.

This appears impossible, of course, and I merely report the thought-images I received. However, while at the full length of the tentacle which held it, the tentacle broke. The Object therefore sank down into the regions of pressure in which we Shadi live. As it neared solidity, I reached up and grasped it and miraculously did not swallow it. I could have done so with ease.

When, in my cave, I had attended for some time to the thoughts coming from within the Object, I tried to communicate. First, of course, I attempted to paralyze the creatures with fear. They did not seem to be aware of the presence of mind. I then attempted, more gently, to converse with them. But they seemed to be devoid of the receptive faculty. They are rational creatures, but even with no mind-block up, they are completely unaware of the thoughts of others. In fact, their thoughts were plainly secret from each other.

I tried to understand all this, and failed. At long last a proper humility came to me, and I sent out a mental call to Morpt. He was still drowsily detailing the consequences of the Caluph theory—that in the center of the universe the gas which has escaped from the swim-bladders of dead Shadi has gathered to form a vast bubble, and that the border between the central bubble and the water is the legendary Surface.

Legends of the Surface are well-known. Morpt reflected, in sleepy irony, that if gas is the immortal part of Shadi, then since two Shadi who see each other instantly fight to the death, the bubble at the center of the universe must be the scene of magnificent combat. But his irony was lost upon me. I interrupted to tell him of the Object and what I had already learned from it.

I immediately felt other minds crowd me. All of Morpt's pupils were instantly alert. I blanked out my mind with more than usual care—to avoid giving any clue to the whereabouts of my cave—and served science to the best of my ability. I told, freely, everything I knew.

Under other conditions, I would have been proud of the furor I created. It seemed that every Shadi in the Honda joined the discussion. Many, of course, said that I lied. But I was fed, and filled with curiosity. I did not reveal my whereabouts to those challengers. I waited. Even Morpt tried to taunt me into an incautious revelation and went into a typical Shadi rage when he failed. But Morpt is experienced and huge. I could not hope to be the one to live did we meet each other outside of the Peace Tides.

Once I had proved I could not be lured out, however, Morpt discussed the matter dispassionately and in the end suggested the journey from which I have just returned. If, despite my caution where other Shadi were concerned—all of Morpt's pupils will recognize the challenging irony with which he thought this—if, despite my caution, I was not afraid to serve science, he advised me to carry the Object back to the Heights. From the creatures within it I should receive directions. From their kind I had my strength and ferocity as protections. From the Heights, themselves, Morpt urged his exercises as the only possible safeguards.

As I knew, said Morpt, the gas in our swim-bladders expands as pressure lessens. Normally, we have muscles which control it so that we can float in pursuit of our prey or sink to solidity at will. But he told me that as I neared the Heights I would find the pressure growing so small that in theory even my muscles would be unable to control the gas. Under such conditions I must use the Morpt exercises and release a portion of it. Then I could descend again.

Otherwise, I might actually be carried up by my own expanding gas, it might repture my swim-bladder and invade other body cavities and expand still further, and finally carry me with it up to the Surface and the central bubble of Caluph's theory.

In such a case, Morpt assured me wittily, I would become one Shadi who knew whether Caluph was right or not, but I would not be likely to return to tell about it. Still, he insisted, if I paused to use his exercises whenever I felt unusually buoyant, I would certainly carry the Object quite near the Surface without danger and so bring back conclusive evidence of the truth of error of the entire Caluphian cosmology, thus rendering a great service to science. The thoughts coming from within the Object should be of great assistance in the enterprise.

I immediately determined to make the journey. For one thing, I was not too sure that I could keep my whereabouts hidden, if continually probed by older and more experienced minds. Only exceedingly powerful minds, like those of Morpt and the other instructors, can risk exposure to constant hungry inspection. Of course, they find the profit in their instructorships in such slips among their students. . . .

It would be distinctly wise for me to leave my cave, now that I had called attention to myself. So I put up my mind-block tightly and with the Object clutched in one tentacle, I flowed swiftly up the slope which surrounds Honda before other Shadi should think of patrolling it for me—and each other.

I went far above my usual level before I paused. I went so high that the gas in my swim-bladder was markedly uncomfortable. I did the Morpt exercises until it was released. It was strange that I did this with complete calm. But my curiosity was involved now, and we Shadi are inveterate seekers. So I found it possible to perform an act—the deliberate freeing of a part of the contents of my swim-bladder—which would have filled past generations of Shadi with horror.

Morpt was right. I was able to continue my ascent without discomfort. More, with increasing Height, I had much for my mind to think of. The two creatures—the man and the woman—in the Object were bewildered by what had happened to their container.

'We have risen two thousand feet from our greatest depth,' the man said to the woman.

'My dear, you don't have to lie to make me brave,' the woman said. 'I don't mind. I couldn't have kept you out of the bathysphere, and I'd rather die with you than live without you.'

Such thoughts do not seem compatible with intelligence. A race with such a psychology would die out. But I do not pretend to understand.

I continued upward until it was necessary to perform the Morpt exercises again. The necessary movements shook the Object violently. The creatures within speculated hopelessly upon the cause. These creatures not only lack the receptive faculty, so that their thoughts are secret from each other, but apparently they have no spatial sense, no sense of pressure and apparently fail of the cycle of instincts which is so necessary to us Shadi.

In all the time of my contact with their minds, I found no thought of anything approximating the Peace Tides, when we Shadi cease altogether to feed and, therefore, instinctively cease to fear each other and intermingle freely to breed. One wonders how their race can continue without Peace Tides, unless their whole lives are passed in a sort of Peace Tide. In that case, since no one feeds during the Peace Tides, why are they not starved to death? They are inexplicable.

They watched their instruments as the ascent went on. Instruments are artifacts which they use to supplement their defective senses.

'Four thousand feet up,' said the man to the woman. 'Only heaven knows what has happened!'

'Do you think there's a chance for us?' the woman said yearningly.

'How could there be?' the man demanded bitterly. 'We sank to eighteen thousand feet. There is still almost three miles of water over our heads, and the oxygen won't last forever. I wish I hadn't let you come. If only you were safe!'

Four thousand feet—whatever that term may mean—above the Honda, the character of living things had changed. All forms of life were smaller, and their spatial sense seemed imperfect. They were not aware of my coming until I was actually upon them. I kept two tentacles busy snatching them as I passed. Their body lights were less brilliant than those of the lesser creatures of the Honda.

I continued my flowing climb toward the Surface. From time to time, I paused to perform the Morpt exercises. The volume of gas I released from my swim-bladder was amazing. I remember thinking, in somewhat the ironic manner of Morpt himself, that if ever Shadi possessed so vast an immortal part, the central bubble must be greater than Honda itself! The creatures inside the Object now watched their instruments incredulously.

'We are up to nine thousand feet,' said the man dazedly. 'We dropped to eighteen thousand, the greatest depth in this part of the world.'

The thought 'world' approximates the Shadi conception of 'universe,' but there are puzzling differences.

'We've risen half of it again,' the man added.

'Do you think that the ballast dropped off and we will float to the Surface?' asked the woman anxiously.

The thought of 'ballast' was of things fastened to the Object to make it descend, and that if they were detached, the Object would rise. This would seem to be nonsense, because all substances descend, except gas. However, I report only what I sensed.

'But we're not floating,' said the man. 'If we were, we'd rise steadily. As it is, we go up a thousand feet or so and then we're practically shaken to death. Then we go up another thousand feet. We're not floating. We're being carried. But only the fates know by what or why.'

This, I point out, is rationality. They knew that their rise was unreasonable. My curiosity increased. I should explain how the creatures knew of their position. They have no spatial sense or any sense of pressure. For the latter they used instruments—artifacts—which told of their ascent. The remarkable thing is that they inspected those instruments by means of a light which they did not make themselves. The light was also made by an artifact. And this artificial light was strong enough to be reflected, not only perceptibly, but distinctly, so that the instruments were seen by reflection only.

I fear that Kanth, whose discovery that light is capable of reflection made his scientific reputation, will deny that any light could be powerful enough to make unlighted objects appear to have light, but I must go even further. As I learned to share not only consciously formed thoughts but sense-impressions of the creatures in the Object, I learned that to them, light has different qualities. Some lights have qualities which to them are different from other lights.

The light we know they speak of as 'bluish.' They know additional words which they term 'red' and 'white' and 'yellow' and other terms. As we perceive difference in the solidity of rocks and ooze, they perceive differences in objects by the light they reflect. Thus, they have a sense which we Shadi have not. I am aware that Shadi are the highest possible type of organism, but this observation—if not insanity—is important matter for meditation.

But I continued to flow steadily upward, pausing only to perform the necessary Morpt exercises to release gas from my swim-bladder when its expansion threatened to become uncontrollable. As I went higher and ever higher, the man and woman were filled with emotions of a quite extraordinary nature. These emotions were unbearably poignant to them, and it is to be doubted that any Shadi has ever sensed such sensations before. Certainly the emotion they call 'love' is inconceivable to Shadi, except by reception from such a creature. It led to peculiar vagaries. For example, the woman put her twin tentacles about the man and clung to him with no effort to rend or tear.

The idea of two creatures of the same species pleasurably anticipating being together without devouring each other—except during the Peace Tides, of course—is almost inconceivable to a Shadi. However, it appeared to be part of their normal psychology.

But this report grows long. I flowed upward and upward. The creatures in the Object experienced emotions which were stronger and ever stronger, and more and more remarkable. Successively the man reported to the woman that they were but four thousand of their 'feet' below the Surface, then two thousand, and then one. I was now completely possessed by curiosity. I had barely performed what turned out to be the last needed Morpt exercise and was moving still higher when my spatial sense suddenly gave me a new and incredible message. Above me, there was a barrier to its operation.

I cannot convey the feeling of finding a barrier to one's spatial sense. I was aware of my surroundings in every direction, but at a certain point above me there was suddenly—nothing! Nothing! At first it was alarming. I flowed up half my length, and the barrier grew nearer. Cautiously—even timorously—I flowed slowly nearer and nearer.

'Five hundred feet,' said the man inside the Object. 'My heavens, only five hundred feet! We should see glimmers of light through the ports. No, it's night now.'

I paused, debating. I was close enough to this barrier to reach up my first tentacle and touch it. I hesitated a long time. Then I did touch it. Nothing happened. I thrust my tentacle boldly through it. It went into Nothingness. Where it was there was no water. With an enormous emotion, I realized that above me was the central bubble and that I alone of living Shadi had reached and dared to touch it. The sensation in my tentacle within the bubble, above the Surface, was that of an enormous weight, as if the gas of departed Shadi would have thrust me back. But they did not attack, they did not even attempt to injure me.

Yes, I was splendidly proud. I felt like one who has overcome and consumed a Shadi of greater size than himself. And as I exulted, I became aware of the emotions of the creatures within the Object.

'Three hundred feet!' said the man frantically. 'It can't stop here! It can't! My dear, fate could not be so cruel!'

I found pleasure in the emotions of the two creatures. They felt a new emotion, now, which was as strange as any of my other experiences with them. It was an emotion which was the anticipation of other emotions. The woman named it.

'It is insane,' she told the man, 'but somehow I feel hope again.'

And in my pleasure and intellectual interest it seemed a very small thing for one who had already dared so greatly to continue the pleasures I felt. I flowed further up the slope. The barrier to my spatial sense—the Surface—came closer and ever closer.

'A hundred feet,' said the man in an emotion which to him was agony, but because of its novelty was a source of intellectual pleasure to me.

I transferred the Object to a forward tentacle and thrust it ahead. It bumped upon the solidity which, here approached and actually penetrated the Surface. The man experienced a passion of the strong emotion called 'hope'.

'Twenty-five feet!' he cried. 'Darling, if we start to go down again, I'll open the hatch, and we'll go out as the bathysphere floods. I don't know whether we're near shore or not, but we'll try.'

The woman was pressed close against him. The agony of hope which filled her was a sensation which mingled with the high elation I felt over my own daring and achievement. I thrust the Object forward yet again. Here the Surface was so near the solidity under it that a part of my tentacle went above the Surface. And the emotions within the Object reached a climax. I thrust on, powerfully, against the weight within the Bubble, until the Object broke the surface, and then on and on until it was no longer in water but in gas, resting upon solidity which was itself touched only by gas.

The man and woman worked frantically within the Object. A part of it detached itself. They climbed out of it. They opened their maws and uttered cries. They wrapped their tentacles about each other and touched their maws together, not to devour but to express their emotions. They looked about them, dazed with relief, and I saw through their eyes. The Surface stretched away for as far as their senses reported, moving and uneven, and yet flat. They stood upon solidity from which things projected upward. Overhead was a vast blackness, penetrated by innumerable small bright sources of light.

'Thank God!' said the man. 'To see trees and the stars again.'

They felt absolutely secure and at peace, as if in a Peace Tides enhanced a thousand fold. And perhaps I was intoxicated by my own daring or perhaps by the emotions I received from them. I thrust my tentacles through the Surface. Their weight was enormous, but my strength is great also.

Daringly I heaved up my body. I thrust my entire forepart through the Surface and into the central bubble. I was in the central bubble while still alive! My weight increased beyond computation, but for a long, proud interval I loomed above the Surface I saw with my own eyes—all eighty of them—the Surface beneath me and the path of solidity on which the man and the woman stood. I, Sard, did this!

As I dipped below the Surface again I received the astounded thoughts of the creatures.

'A sea-serpent,' thought the man, and doubted his own sanity as I fear mine will be doubted. 'That's what did it.'

'Why not, darling?' the woman said calmly. 'It was a miracle, but people who love each other as we do simply couldn't be allowed to die.'

But the man stared at the Surface where I had vanished. I had caught his troubled thought.

'No one would believe it. They'd say we're insane. But confound it, here's the bathysphere, and our cable did break when we were above the Deep. When we're found, we'll simply say we don't know what happened and let them try to figure it out.'

I lay resting, close to the Surface, thinking many things. After a long time there was light. Fierce, unbearable light. It grew stronger and yet stronger. It was unbearable. It flowed down into the nearer depths.

That was many tides ago, because I dared not return to Honda with so vast a proportion of the gas in my swim-bladder released to the central bubble. I remained not too far below the Surface until my swim-bladder felt normal. I descended again and again waited until my 'immortal part' had replenished itself. It is difficult to feed upon such small creatures as inhabit the Heights. It took a long time for me to make the descent which by Morpt's discovery had been made so readily as an ascent. All my waking time was spent in the capture of food, and I had little time for meditation. I was never once full-fed in all the periods I paused to wait for my swim-bladder to be replenished. But when I returned to my cave, it had been occupied in my absence by another Shadi, I fed well.

Then came the Peace Tides. And now, having bred, I lay my report of my journey to the Surface at the service of all the Shadi. If I am decreed insane, I shall say no more. But this is my report. Now determine, O Shadi: Am I mad?

I, Morpt, in Peace Tides, have heard the report of Sard and having consulted with others of the Shadi, do declare that he has plainly confounded the imagined with the real.

His description of the scientific aspects of his journey, which are not connected with the assumed creatures in the Object, are consistent with science. But it is manifestly impossible that any creature could live with its fellows permanently without the instinct to feed. It is manifestly impossible that creatures could live in gas. Distinction between light and light is patent nonsense. The psychology of such creatures as described by Sard is of the stuff of dreams.

Therefore, it is the consensus that Sard's report is not science. He may not be insane, however. The physiological effects of his admitted journey to great Heights have probably caused disorders in his body which have shown themselves in illusions. The scientific lesson to be learned from this report is that journeys to the Heights, though possible because of the exercises invented by myself, are extremely unwise and should never be made by Shadi. Given during the Peace Tides. . . .

PI IN THE SKY

by Fredric Brown

THRILLING WONDER STORIES,
Winter

A popular target of science fiction writers during the 1950s and early 1960s was the advertising industry, which came under heavy attack, especially in the pages of Horace Gold's Galaxy Science Fiction. *The acknowledged leader in the attack was Frederik Pohl, who in books and stories like* The Space Merchants *(1953, with C. M. Kornbluth), "Happy Birthday, Dear Jesus," and "The Tunnel Under the World" (to name only a few) took apart the whole production-consumption process and its underlying assumptions. Many other writers, from Ann Warren Griffith ("Captive Audience") to John Jakes ("The Sellers of the Dream"), also explored this industry and its tactics.*

But long before the trend, there was Fred Brown and "Pi in the Sky."

(How great are the wonders of semantics. Call it "advertising" and, as Marty says, intellectual types like writers can find no words too harsh to condemn it, no story techniques too cutting to satirize it. [I've done it myself.]

On the other hand, call it "promotion" and the writers all flock to take part. How ardently they condemn the cleanser manufacturers for hawking their wares. How even more ardently they condemn the publishers for not hawking their wares enough.

It depends on whose ox is gored, I suppose. Fred

Pohl is indeed the acknowledged leader, but I once saw a schedule of one of Fred's promotion tours for one of his books. I think he stopped in every town with a population of over 4,000, and what do you think he did in each one of them—advertised his book, of course.

Now as for me, I don't travel, so I don't engage in such low shenanigans, but I'm not a model of virtue either. I don't think there's a writer in the world who discusses himself as much as I do—and that's advertising, too. I.A.)

Roger Jerome Phlutter, for whose absurd name I offer no defense other than that it is genuine, was, at the time of the events of this story, a hardworking clerk in the office of the Cole Observatory.

He was a young man of no particular brilliance, although he performed his daily tasks assiduously and efficiently, studied the calculus at home for one hour every evening, and hoped some day to become a chief astronomer of some important observatory.

Nevertheless, our narration of the events of late March in the year 1987 must begin with Roger Phlutter, for the good and sufficient reason that he, of all men on earth, was the first observer of the stellar aberration.

Meet Roger Phlutter.

Tall, rather pale from spending too much time indoors, thickish shell-rimmed glasses, dark hair close-cropped in the style of the nineteen eighties, dressed neither particularly well nor badly, smokes cigarettes rather excessively. . . .

At a quarter to five that afternoon, Roger was engaged in two simultaneous operations. One was examining, in a blink-microscope, a photographic plate taken late the previous night of a section in Gemini. The other was considering whether or not, on the three dollars remaining of his pay from last week, he dared phone Elsie and ask her to go somewhere with him.

Every normal young man has undoubtedly, at some time or other, shared with Roger Phlutter his second occupation, but not everyone has operated or understands the operation of a blink-microscope. So let us raise our eyes from Elsie to Gemini.

A blink-mike provides accommodation for two photographic plates taken of the same section of sky, but at different times. These plates are carefully juxtaposed and the operator may alternately focus his vision, through the eyepiece, first upon one and then upon the other, by means of a shutter. If the plates are identical, the operation of the shutter reveals nothing, but if one of the dots on the second plate differs from the position it occupied on the first, it will call attention to itself by seeming to jump back and forth as the shutter is manipulated.

Roger manipulated the shutter, and one of the dots jumped. So did Roger. He tried it again, forgetting—as we have—all about Elsie for the moment, and the dot jumped again. It jumped almost a tenth of a second.

Roger straightened up and scratched his head. He lighted a cigarette, put it down on the ashtray, and looked into the blink-mike again. The dot jumped again, when he used the shutter.

Harry Wesson, who worked the evening shift, had just come into the office and was hanging up his topcoat.

"Hey, Harry!" Roger said. "There's something wrong with this blinking blinker."

"Yeah?" said Harry.

"Yeah. Pollux moved a tenth of a second."

"Yeah?" said Harry. "Well, that's about right for parallax. Thirty-two light years—parallax of Pollux is point one oh one. Little over a tenth of a second, so if your comparison plate was taken about six months ago when the earth was on the other side of her orbit, that's about right."

"But Harry, the comparison plate was taken night before last. They're twenty-four hours apart."

"You're crazy."

"Look for yourself."

It wasn't quite five o'clock yet, but Harry Wesson magnanimously overlooked that, and sat down in front of the blink-mike. He manipulated the shutter, and Pollux obligingly jumped.

There wasn't any doubt about it being Pollux, for it was far and away the brightest dot on the plate. Pollux is a star of 1.2 magnitude, one of the twenty brightest in the sky and by far the brightest in Gemini. And none of the faint stars around it had moved at all.

"Um," said Harry Wesson. He frowned and looked again. "One of those plates is misdated, that's all. I'll check into it first thing."

"Those plates aren't misdated," Roger said doggedly. "I dated them myself."

"That proves it," Harry told him. "Go on home. It's five o'clock. If Pollux moved a tenth of a second last night, I'll move it back for you."

So Roger left.

He felt uneasy somehow, as though he shouldn't have. He couldn't put his finger on just what worried him, but something did. He decided to walk home instead of taking the bus.

Pollux was a fixed star. It couldn't have moved a tenth of a second in twenty-four hours.

"Let's see—thirty-two light-years," Roger said to himself. "Tenth of a second. Why, that would be movement several times faster than the speed of light. Which is positively silly!"

Wasn't it?

He didn't feel much like studying or reading tonight. Was three dollars enough to take Elsie out?

The three balls of a pawn-shop loomed ahead, and Roger succumbed to temptation. He pawned his watch, and then phoned Elsie. Dinner and a show?

"Why certainly, Roger."

So, until he took her home at one-thirty, he managed to forget astronomy. Nothing odd about that. It would have been strange if he had managed to remember it.

But his feeling of restlessness came back as soon as he had left her. At first, he didn't remember why. He knew merely that he didn't feel quite like going home yet.

The corner tavern was still open, and he dropped in for a drink. He was having his second one when he remembered. He ordered a third.

"Hank," he said to the bartender. "You know Pollux?"

"Pollux who?" asked Hank.

"Skip it," said Roger. He had another drink, and thought it over. Yes, he'd made a mistake somewhere. Pollux couldn't have moved.

He went outside and started to walk home. He was almost there when it occurred to him to look up at Pollux. Not that, with the naked eye, he could detect a displacement of a tenth of a second, but he felt curious.

He looked up, oriented himself by the sickle of Leo, and then found Gemini—Castor and Pollux were the only stars in Gemini visible, for it wasn't a particularly good night for seeing. They were there, all right, but he thought they looked a little farther apart than usual. Absurd, because that would be a matter of degrees, not minutes or seconds.

He stared at them for a while, and then looked across to the dipper. Then he stopped walking and stood there. He closed his eyes and opened them again, carefully.

The dipper just didn't look right. It was distorted. There seemed to be more space between Alioth and Mizar, in the handle, than between Mizar and Alkaid. Pheeda and Merak, in the bottom of the dipper, were closer together, making the angle between the bottom and the lip steeper. Quite a bit steeper.

Unbelievingly, he ran an imaginary line from the pointers, Merak and Dubhe, to the North Star. The line curved. It had to. If he ran it straight, it missed Polaris by maybe five degrees.

Breathing a bit hard, Roger took off his glasses and polished them very carefully with his handkerchief. He put them back on again and the dipper was still crooked.

So was Leo, when he looked back to it. At any rate, Regulus wasn't where it should be by a degree or two.

A degree or two! At the distance of Regulus! Was it sixty-five light years? Something like that.

Then, in time to save his sanity, Roger remembered that he'd been drinking. He went home without daring to look upward again. He went to bed, but couldn't sleep.

He didn't feel drunk. He grew more excited, wide awake.

He wondered if he dared phone the observatory. Would he sound drunk over the phone? The devil with whether he sounded that way or not, he finally decided. He went to the telephone in his pajamas.

"Sorry," said the operator.

"What d'ya mean, sorry?"

"I cannot give you that number," said the operator, in dulcet tones. And then, "I am sorry. We do not have that information."

He got the chief operator, and the information. Cole Observatory had been so deluged with calls from amateur astronomers that they had found it necessary to request the telephone company to discontinue all incoming calls save long distance ones from other observatories.

"Thanks," said Roger. "Will you get me a cab?"

It was an unusual request, but the chief operator obliged and got him a cab.

He found the Cole Observatory in a state resembling a madhouse.

The following morning most newspapers carried the news. Most of them gave it two or three inches on an inside page, but the facts were there.

The facts were that a number of stars, in general the brightest ones, within the past forty-eight hours had developed noticeable proper motions.

"This does not imply," quipped the *New York Spotlight*, "that their motions have been in any way improper in the past. 'Proper motion' to an astronomer means the movement of a star across the face of the sky with relation to other stars. Hitherto, a star named 'Barnard's Star' in the constellation Ophiuchus has exhibited the greatest proper motion of any known star, moving at the rate of ten and a quarter seconds a year. 'Barnard's Star' is not visible to the naked eye."

Probably no astronomer on earth slept that day.

The observatories locked their doors, with their full staffs on the inside, and admitted no one except occasional newspaper reporters who stayed a while and went away with puzzled faces, convinced at last that something strange was happening.

Blink-microscopes blinked, and so did astronomers. Coffee was consumed in prodigious quantities. Police riot squads were called to six United States observatories. Two of these calls were occasioned by attempts to break in on the part of frantic amateurs without. The other four were summoned to quell fistfights developing out of arguments within the observatories themselves. The office of Lick Observatory was a shambles, and James Truwell, Astronomer Royal of England, was sent to London Hospital with a mild concussion, the result of having a heavy photographic plate smashed over his head by an irate subordinate.

But these incidents were exceptions. The observatories, in general, were well-ordered madhouses.

The center of attention in the more enterprising ones was the loudspeaker in which reports from the Eastern Hemisphere could be relayed to the inmates. Practically all observatories kept open wires to the night side of Earth, where the phenomena were still under scrutiny.

Astronomers under the night skies of Singapore, Shanghai and Sydney did their observing, as it were, directly into the business end of a long-distance telephone hookup.

Particularly of interest were reports from Sydney and Melbourne, whence came reports on the southern skies not visible—even at night—from Europe or the United States. The Southern Cross was by these reports, a cross no longer, its Alpha and Beta being shifted northward. Alpha and Beta Centauri, Canopus and Achernar all showed considerable proper motion—all, generally speaking, northward. Triangulum Australe and the Magellanic Clouds were undisturbed. Sigma Octanis, the weak pole star, had not moved.

Disturbance in the southern sky, then, was much less than in the northern one, in point of the number of stars displaced. However, relative proper motion of the stars which were disturbed was greater. While the general direction of movement of the few stars which did move was northward, their paths were not directly north, nor did they converge upon any exact point in space.

United States and European astronomers digested these facts and drank more coffee.

Evening papers, particularly in America, showed greater awareness that something indeed unusual was happening in the skies. Most of them moved the story to the front page—but not the banner headlines—giving it a half-column with a runover that was long or short, depending upon the editor's luck in obtaining statements from astronomers.

The statements, when obtained, were invariably statements of fact and not of opinion. The facts themselves, said these gentlemen, were sufficiently startling, and opinions would be premature. Wait and see. Whatever was happening was happening fast.

"How fast?" asked an editor.

"Faster than possible," was the reply.

Perhaps it is unfair to say that no editor procured expressions of opinion thus early. Charles Wagren, enterprising editor of the *Chicago Blade*, spent a small fortune in long-distance telephone calls. Out of possibly sixty attempts, he finally reached the chief astronomers of five observatories. He asked each of them the same question.

"What, in your opinion, is a possible cause, any possible cause, of the stellar movements of the last night or two?"

He tabulated the results.

"I wish I knew."—Geo. F. Stubbs, Tripp Observatory, Long Island.

"Someboly or something is crazy, and I hope it's me—I mean I."—Henry Collister McAdams, Lloyd Observatory, Boston.

"What's happening is impossible. There can't be any cause."—Letton Tischauer Tinney, Burgoyne Observatory, Albuquerque.

"I'm looking for an expert on Astrology. Know one?"—Patrick R. Whitaker, Lucas Observatory, Vermont.

Sadly studying this tabulation, which had cost him $187.35—including tax—to obtain, Editor Wangren signed a voucher to cover the long distance calls and then dropped his tabulation into the wastebasket. He telephoned his regular space-rates writer on scientific subjects.

"Can you give me a series of articles—two-three thousand words each—on all this astronomical excitement?"

"Sure," said the writer. "But what excitement?" It transpired that he'd just got back from a fishing trip and had neither read a newspaper nor happened to look up at the sky. But he wrote the articles. He even got sex appeal into them through illustrations, by using ancient star-charts showing the constellation in dishabille, by reproducing certain famous paintings such as "The Origin of the Milky Way" and by using a photograph of a girl in a bathing suit sighting a hand telescope, presumably at one of the errant stars. Circulation of the *Chicago Blade* increased by 21.7%.

It was five o'clock again in the office of the Cole Observatory, just twenty-four and a quarter hours after the beginning of all the commotion. Roger Phlutter—yes, we're back to him again—woke up suddenly when a hand was placed on his shoulder.

"Go on home, Roger," said Mervin Armbruster, his boss, in a kindly tone.

Roger sat upright suddenly.

"But Mr. Armbruster," he said, "I'm sorry I fell asleep."

"Bosh," said Armbruster. "You can't stay here forever, none of us can. Go on home."

Roger Phlutter went home. But when he'd taken a bath, he

felt more restless than sleepy. It was only six-fifteen. He phoned Elsie.

"I'm awfully sorry, Roger, but I have another date. What's going on, Roger? The stars, I mean."

"Gosh, Elsie—they're moving. Nobody knows."

"But I thought all the stars moved," Elsie protested. "The sun's a star, isn't it, Once you told me the sun was moving toward a point in Samson."

"Hercules."

"Hercules, then. Since you said all the stars were moving, what is everybody getting excited about?"

"This is different," said Roger. "Take Canopus. It's started moving at the rate of seven light-years a day. It can't do that!"

"Why not?"

"Because," said Roger patiently, "nothing can move faster than light."

"But if it is moving that fast, then it can," said Elsie. "Or else maybe your telescope is wrong or something. Anyway, it's pretty far off, isn't it?"

"A hundred and sixty light-years. So far away that we see it a hundred and sixty years ago."

"Then maybe it isn't moving at all," said Elsie. "I mean, maybe it quit moving a hundred and fifty years ago and you're getting all excited about something that doesn't matter anymore because it's all over with. Still love me?"

"I sure do, honey. Can't you break that date?"

" 'Fraid not, Roger. But I wish I could."

He had to be content with that. He decided to walk uptown to eat.

It was early evening, and too early to see stars overhead, although the clear blue sky was darkening. When the stars did come out tonight, Roger knew, few of the constellations would be recognizable.

As he walked, he thought over Elsie's comments and decided that they were as intelligent as anything he'd heard at Cole. In one way they'd brought out one angle he'd never thought of before, and that made it more incomprehensible.

All these movements had started the same evening—yet they hadn't. Centauri must have started moving four years or so ago, and Rigel five hundred and forty years ago when Christopher Columbus was still in short pants if any, and Vega must have started acting up the year he—Roger, not

Vega—was born, twenty-six years ago. Each star out of the hundreds must have started on a date in exact relation to its distance from Earth. Exact relation, to a light-second, for checkups of all the photographic plates taken night before last indicated that all the new stellar movements had started at 4:10 a.m. Greenwich time. What a mess!

Unless this meant that light, after all, had infinite velocity.

If it didn't have—and it is symptomatic of Roger's perplexity that he could postulate that incredible "if"—then—then what? Things were just as puzzling as before.

Mostly, he felt outraged that such events should happen.

He went into a restaurant and sat down. A radio was blaring out the latest composition in dissarythm, the new quarter-tone dance music in which chorded woodwinds provided background patterns for the mad melodies pounded on tuned tomtoms. Between each number and the next a phrenetic announcer extolled the virtues of a product.

Munching a sandwich, Roger listened appreciatively to the dissarythm and managed not to hear the commercials. Most intelligent people of the eighties had developed a type of radio deafness which enabled them not to hear a human voice coming from a loudspeaker, although they could hear and enjoy the then infrequent intervals of music between announcements. In an age when advertising competition was so keen that there was scarcely a bare wall or an unbillboarded lot within miles of a population center, discriminating people could retain normal outlooks on life only by carefully cultivated partial blindness and partial deafness which enabled them to ignore the bulk of that concerted assault upon their senses.

For that reason a good part of the newscast which followed the dissarythm program went, as it were, into one of Roger's ears and out of the other before it occurred to him that he was not listening to a panegyric on patent breakfast foods.

He thought he recognized the voice, and after a sentence or two he was sure that it was that of Milton Hale, the eminent physicist whose new theory on the principle of indeterminacy had recently occasioned so much scientific controversy. Apparently, Dr. Hale was being interviewed by a radio announcer.

"—a heavenly body, therefore, may have position or velocity, but it may not be said to have both at the same time, with relation to any given space-time frame."

"Dr. Hale, can you put that into common everyday language?" said the syrupy-smooth voice of the interviewer.

"That is common language, sir. Scientifically expressed, in terms of the Heisenberg contraction-principle, then *n* to the seventh power in parentheses, representing the pseudo-position of a Diedrich quantum-integer in relation to the seventh coefficient of curvature of mass—"

"Thank you, Dr. Hale, but I fear you are just a bit over the heads of our listeners."

"And your own head," thought Roger Phlutter.

"I am sure, Dr. Hale, that the question of greatest interest to our audience is whether these unprecedented stellar movements are real or illusory?"

"Both. They are real with reference to the frame of space but not with reference to the frame of space-time."

"Can you clarify that, Doctor?"

"I believe I can. The difficulty is purely epistemological. In strict causality, the impact of the macroscopic—"

" 'The slithy toves did gyre and gimble in the wabe,' " thought Roger Phlutter.

"—upon the parallelism of the entrophy-gradient."

"Bah!" said Roger, aloud.

"Did you say something, sir?" asked the waitress. Roger noticed her for the first time. She was small and blonde and cuddly. Roger smiled at her.

"That depends upon the space-time frame from which one regards it," he said, judicially. "The difficulty is epistemological."

To make up for that, he tipped her more than he should have, and left.

The world's most eminent physicist, he realized, knew less of what was happening than did the general public. The public knew that the fixed stars were moving, or that they weren't. Obviously Dr. Hale didn't even know that. Under a smoke screen of qualifications, Hale had hinted that they were doing both.

Roger looked upward, but only a few stars, faint in the early evening, were visible through the halation of the myriad neon and spiegel-light signs. Too early yet, he decided.

He had one drink at a nearby bar, but it didn't taste quite right to him so he didn't finish it. He hadn't realized what was wrong, but he was punch-drunk from lack of sleep. He merely knew that he wasn't sleepy anymore and intended to keep on walking until he felt like going to bed. Anyone hitting him over the head with a well-padded blackjack would have been doing him a signal service, but no one took the trouble.

He kept on walking and after a while, turned into the brilliantly lighted lobby of a cineplus theater. He bought a ticket and took his seat just in time to see the sticky end of one of the three feature pictures. Several advertisements followed which he managed to look at without seeing.

"We bring you next," said the screen, "a special visicast of the night sky of London, where it is now three o'clock in the morning."

The screen went black, with hundreds of tiny dots that were stars. Roger leaned forward to watch and listen carefully—this would be a broadcast and visicast of facts, not of verbose nothingness.

"The arrow," said the screen, as an arrow appeared upon it, "is now pointing to Polaris, the pole star, which is now ten degrees from the celestial pole in the direction of Ursa Major. Ursa Major itself, the Big Dipper, is no longer recognizable as a dipper, but the arrow will now point to the stars that formerly composed it."

Roger breathlessly followed the arrow and the voice.

"Alkaid and Dubhe," said the voice. "The fixed stars are no longer fixed but—" The picture changed abruptly to a scenc in a modern kitchen. "—the qualities and excellences of Stellar's Stoves do not change. Foods cooked by the superinduced vibratory method taste as good as ever. Stellar Stoves are unexcelled."

Leisurely, Roger Phlutter stood up and made his way out into the aisle. He took his pen-knife from his pocket as he walked toward the screen. One easy jump took him up onto the low stage. His slashes into the fabric were not angry ones. They were careful, methodical cuts intelligently designed to accomplish a maximum of damage with a minimum expenditure of effort.

The damage was done, and thoroughly, by the time three strong ushers gathered him in. He offered no resistance either to them or to the police to whom they gave him. In night court, an hour later, he listened quietly to the charges against him.

"Guilty or not guilty?" asked the presiding magistrate.

"Your Honor, that is purely a question of epistomology," said Roger earnestly. "The fixed stars move, but Corny Toasties, the world's greatest breakfast food, still represents the pseudo-position of a Diedrich quantum-integer in relation to the seventh coefficient of curvature!"

Ten minutes later, he was sleeping soundly. In a cell, it is true, but soundly nonetheless. The police left him there because they had realized he needed to sleep. . . .

Among other minor tragedies of that night can be included the case of the schooner *Ransagansett*, off the coast of California. Well off the coast of California! A sudden squall had blown her miles off course, how many miles the skipper could only guess.

The *Ransagansett* was an American vessel, with a German crew, under Venezuelan registry, engaged in running booze from Ensenada, Baja California, up the coast to Canada, then in the throes of a prohibition experiment. The *Ransagansett* was an ancient craft with four engines and an untrustworthy compass. During the two days of the storm, her outdated radio receiver—vintage 1955—had gone haywire beyond the ability of Gross, the first mate, to repair.

But now only a mist remained of the storm, and the remaining shreds of wind were blowing it away. Hans Gross, holding an ancient astrolabe, stood on the deck waiting. About him was utter darkness, for the ship was running without lights to avoid the coastal patrols.

"She clearing, Mister Gross?" called the voice of the captain from below.

"Aye, sir. Idt iss glearing rabidly."

In the cabin, Captain Randall went back to his game of blackjack with the second mate and the engineer. The crew—an elderly German named Weiss, with a wooden leg—was asleep abaft the scuttlebutt—wherever that may have been.

A half hour went by. An hour, and the captain was losing heavily to Helmstadt, the engineer.

"Mister Gross!" he called out.

There wasn't any answer and he called again and still obtained no response.

"Just a minute, mein fine feathered friends," he said to the second mate and engineer, and went up the companionway to the deck.

Gross was standing there staring upward with his mouth open. The mists were gone.

"Mister Gross," said Captain Randall.

The second mate didn't answer. The captain saw that his second mate was revolving slowly where he stood.

"Hans!" said Captain Randall, "What the devil's wrong with you?" Then he, too, looked up.

Superficially the sky looked perfectly normal. No angels flying around nor sound of airplane motors. The dipper— Captain Randall turned around slowly, but more rapidly than Hans Gross. Where was the Big Dipper?

For that matter, where was anything? There wasn't a constellation anywhere that he could recognize. No sickle of Leo. No belt of Orion. No horns of Taurus.

Worse, there was a group of eight bright stars that ought to have been a constellation, for they were shaped roughly like an octagon. Yet if such a constellation had ever existed, he'd never seen it, for he'd been around the Horn and Good Hope. Maybe at that— But no, there wasn't any Southern Cross!

Dazedly, Captain Randall walked to the companionway.

"Mister Weisskopf," he called. "Mister Helmstadt. Come on deck."

They came and looked. Nobody said anything for quite a while.

"Shut off the engines, Mister Helmstadt," said the captain. Helmstadt saluted—the first time he ever had—and went below.

"Captain, shall I vake opp Veiss?" asked Weisskopf.

"What for?"

"I don't know."

The captain considered. "Wake him up," he said.

"I think ve are on der blanet Mars," said Gross.

But the captain had thought of that and rejected it.

"No," he said firmly. "From any planet in the solar system the constellations would look approximately the same."

"You mean ve are oudt of der cosmos?"

The throb of the engines suddenly ceased and there was only the soft familiar lapping of the waves against the hull and the gentle familiar rocking of the boat.

Weisskopf returned with Weiss, and Helmstadt came on deck and saluted again.

"Vell, Captain?"

Captain Randall waved a hand to the afterdeck, piled high with cases of liquor under a canvas tarpaulin. "Break out the cargo," he ordered.

The blackjack game was not resumed. At dawn, under a sun they had never expected to see again—and, for that matter, certainly were not seeing at the moment—the five unconscious men were moved from the ship to the Port of San Francisco Jail by members of the coast patrol. During the night the *Ransagansett* had drifted through the Golden Gate and bumped gently into the dock of the Berkeley ferry.

In tow at the stern of the schooner was a big canvas tarpaulin. It was transfixed by a harpoon whose rope was firmly tied to the after-mast. Its presence there was never explained officially, although days later Captain Randall had vague recollection of having harpooned a sperm whale during the night. But the elderly able-bodied seaman named Weiss never did find out what happened to his wooden leg, which is perhaps just as well.

Milton Hale, Ph.D., eminent physicist, had finished broadcasting and the program was off the air.

"Thank you very much, Dr. Hale," said the radio announcer. The yellow light went on and stayed. The mike was dead. "Uh—your check will be waiting for you at the window. You—uh—know where."

"I know where," said the physicist. He was a rotund, jolly-looking little man. With his bushy white beard, he resembled a pocket edition of Santa Claus. His eyes twinkled and he smoked a short stubby pipe.

He left the soundproof studio and walked briskly down the hall to the cashier's window. "Hello, sweetheart," he said to the girl on duty there. "I think you have two checks for Dr. Hale."

"You are Dr. Hale?"

"I sometimes wonder," said the little man. "But I carry identification that seems to prove it."

"Two checks?"

"Two checks. Both for the same broadcast, by special arrangement. By the way, there is an excellent revue at the Mabry Theater this evening."

"Is there? Yes, here are your checks, Dr. Hale. One for seventy-five and one for twenty-five. Is that correct?"

"Gratifyingly correct. Now about the revue at the Mabry?"

"If you wish I'll call my husband and ask him about it," said the girl. "He's the doorman over there."

Dr. Hale sighed deeply, but his eyes still twinkled. "I think he'll agree," he said. "Here are the tickets, my dear, and you can take him. I find that I have work to do this evening."

The girl's eyes widened, but she took the tickets.

Dr. Hale went into the phone booth and called his home. His home, and Dr. Hale were both run by his elder sister. "Agatha, I must remain at the office this evening," he said.

"Milton, you know you can work just as well in your study here at home. I heard your broadcast, Milton. It was wonderful."

"It was sheer balderdash, Agatha. Utter rot. What did I say?"

"Why, you said that—uh—that the stars were—I mean, you were not—"

"Exactly, Agatha. My idea was to avert panic on the part of the populace. If I'd told them the truth, they'd have worried. But by being smug and scientific, I let them get the idea that everything was—uh—under control. Do you know, Agatha, what I meant by the parallelism of an entropy-gradient?"

"Why—not exactly."

"Neither did I."

"Milton, have you been drinking?"

"Not y— No, I haven't. I really can't come home to work this evening, Agatha. I'm using my study at the university, because I must have access to the library there, for reference. And the star-charts."

"But, Milton, how about that money for your broadcast? You know it isn't safe for you to have money in your pocket when you're feeling—like this."

"It isn't money, Agatha. It's a check, and I'll mail it to you before I go to the office. I won't cash it myself. How's that?"

"Well—if you must have access to the library, I suppose you must. Good-bye, Milton."

Dr. Hale went across the street to the drug store. There he bought a stamp and envelope and cashed the twenty-five dollar check. The seventy-five dollar one he put into the envelope and mailed.

Standing beside the mailbox he glanced up at the early evening sky—shuddered, and hastily lowered his eyes. He took the straightest possible line for the nearest tavern and ordered a double Scotch.

"Y'ain't been in for a long time, Dr. Hale," said Mike, the bartender.

"That I haven't, Mike. Pour me another."

"Sure. On the house, this time. We had your broadcast tuned in on the radio just now. It was swell."

"Yes."

"It sure was. I was kind of worried what was happening up there, with my son an aviator and all. But as long as you scientific guys know what it's all about, I guess it's all right. That was sure a good speech, Doc. But there's one question I'd like to ask you."

"I was afraid of that," said Dr. Hale.

"These stars. They're moving, going somewhere. But where they going? I mean, like you said, if they are."

"There's no way of telling that exactly, Mike."

"Aren't they moving in a straight line, each one of them?"

For just a moment the celebrated scientist hesitated.

"Well—yes and no, Mike. According to spectroscopic analysis, they're maintaining the same distance from us, each one of them. So they're really moving—if they're moving—in circles around us. But the circles are straight, as it were. I mean, it seems that we're in the center of those circles, so the stars that are moving aren't coming closer to us or receding."

"You could draw lines for those circles?"

"On a star-globe, yes. It's been done. They all seem to be heading for a certain area of the sky, but not for a given point. In other words, they don't intersect."

"What part of the sky they going to?"

"Approximately between Ursa Major and Leo, Mike. The ones farthest from there are moving fastest, the ones nearer are moving slower. But darn you, Mike, I came in here to forget about stars, not to talk about them. Give me another."

"In a minute, Doc. When they get there, are they going to stop or keep on going?"

"How the devil do I know, Mike? They started suddenly, all at the same time, and with full original velocity—I mean, they started out at the same speed they're going now—without warming up, so to speak—so I suppose they could stop just as unexpectedly."

He stopped just as suddenly as the stars might. He stared at his reflection in the mirror back of the bar as though he'd never seen it before.

"What's the matter, Doc?"

"Mike!"

"Yes, Doc?"

"Mike, you're a genius."

"Me? You're kidding."

Dr. Hale groaned. "Mike, I'm going to have to go to the university to work this out. So I can have access to the library and the star-globe there. You're making an honest man out of me, Mike. Whatever kind of Scotch this is, wrap me up a bottle."

"It's Tartan Plaid. A quart?"

"A quart, and make it snappy. I've got to see a man about a dog-star."

"Serious, Doc?"

Dr. Hale sighed audibly. "You brought that on yourself, Mike. Yes, the dog-star is Sirius. I wish I'd never come in here, Mike. My first night out in weeks, and you ruin it."

He took a cab to the university, let himself in, and turned on the lights in his private study and in the library. Then he took a good stiff slug of Tartan Plaid and went to work.

First, by telling the chief operator who he was and arguing a bit, he got a telephone connection with the chief astronomer of Cole Observatory.

"This is Hale, Armbruster," he said. "I've got an idea, but I want to check my facts before I start to work on it. Last information I had, there were four-hundred sixty-eight stars exhibiting new proper motion. Is that still correct?"

"Yes, Milton. The same ones are still at it—no others."

"Good. I have a list of them. Has there been any change in speed of motion of any of them?"

"No. Impossible as it seems, it's constant. What is your idea?"

"I want to check my theory first. If it works out into anything, I'll call you." But he forgot to.

It was a long, painful job. First he made a chart of the heavens in the area between Ursa Major and Leo. Across that chart he drew 468 lines representing the projected path of each of the aberrant stars. At the border of the chart, where each line entered, he made a notation of the apparent velocity of the star—not in light-years per hour—but in degrees per hour, to the fifth decimal.

Then he did some reasoning.

"Postulate that the motion which began simultaneously will

stop simultaneously," he told himself. "Try a guess at the time. Let's try ten o'clock tomorrow evening."

He tried it and looked at the series of positions indicated upon the chart. No.

Try one o'clock in the morning. It looked almost like—sense!

Try midnight.

That did it. At any rate, it was close enough. The calculation could be only a few minutes off one way or the other and there was no point now in working out the exact time. Now that he knew the incredible fact.

He took another drink and stared at the chart grimly.

A trip to the library gave Dr. Hale the further information he needed. The address!

Thus began the saga of Dr. Hale's journey. A useless journey, it is true, but one that should rank with the trip of the messenger to Garcia.

He started it with a drink. Then, knowing the combination, he rifled the safe in the office of the president of the university. The note he left in the safe was a masterpiece of brevity. It read:

Taking money. Explain later.

Then he took another drink and put the bottle in his pocket. He went outside and hailed a taxicab. He got in.

"Where to, sir?" asked the cabby.

Dr. Hale gave an address.

"Fremont Street?" said the cabby. "Sorry, sir, but I don't know where that is."

"In Boston," said Dr. Hale. "I should have told you, in Boston."

"Boston? You mean Boston, Massachusetts? That's a long way from here."

"Therefore we better start right away," said Dr. Hale, reasonably. A brief financial discussion and the passing of money, borrowed from the university safe, set the driver's mind at rest, and they started.

It was a bitter cold night, for March, and the heater in the taxi didn't work any too well. But the Tartan Plaid worked superlatively for both Dr. Hale and the cabby, and by the time they reached New Haven, they were singing old-time songs lustily.

"Off we go, into the wide, wild yonder . . ." their voices roared.

It is regrettably reported, but possible untrue, that in Hartford Dr. Hale leered out of the window at a young woman waiting for a late streetcar and asked her if she wanted to go to Boston. Apparently, however, she didn't, for at five o'clock in the morning when the cab drew up in front of 614 Fremont Street, Boston, only Dr. Hale and the driver were in the cab.

Dr. Hale got out and looked at the house. It was a millionaire's mansion, and it was surrounded by a high iron fence with barbed wire on top of it. The gate in the fence was locked and there was no bell button to push.

But the house was only a stone's throw from the sidewalk, and Dr. Hale was not to be deterred. He threw a stone. Then another. Finally he succeeded in smashing a window.

After a brief interval, a man appeared in the window. A butler, Dr. Hale decided.

"I'm Dr. Milton Hale," he called. "I want to see Rutherford R. Snively, right away. It's important."

"Mr. Snively is not at home, sir," said the butler. "And about that window—"

"The devil with the window," shouted Dr. Hale. "Where is Snively?"

"On a fishing trip."

"Where?"

"I have orders not to give out that information."

Dr. Hale was just a little drunk, perhaps. "You'll give it out just the same," he roared. "By orders of the President of the United States."

The butler laughed. "I don't see him."

"You will," said Hale.

He got back in the cab. The driver had fallen asleep, but Hale shook him awake.

"The White House," said Dr. Hale.

"Huh?"

"The White House, in Washington," said Dr. Hale. "And hurry!" He pulled a hundred dollar bill from his pocket. The cabby looked at it, and groaned. Then he put the bill into his pocket and started the cab.

A light snow was beginning to fall.

As the cab drove off, Rutherford R. Snively, grinning, stepped back from the window. Mr. Snively had no butler.

If Dr. Hale had been more familiar with the peculiarities of the eccentric Mr. Snively, he would have known Snively kept no servants in the place overnight, but lived alone in the big house at 614 Fremont Street. Each morning at ten o'clock, a small army of servants descended upon the house, did their work as rapidly as possible, and were required to depart before the witching hour of noon. Aside from these two hours of every day, Mr. Snively lived in solitary splendor. He had few, if any, social contacts.

Aside from the few hours a day he spent administering his vast interests as one of the country's leading manufacturers, Mr. Snively's time was his own and he spent practically all of it in his workshop, making gadgets.

Snively had an ashtray which would hand him a lighted cigar any time he spoke sharply to it, and a radio receiver so delicately adjusted that it would cut in automatically Snively-sponsored programs and shut off again when they were finished. He had a bathtub that provided a full orchestra accompaniment to his singing therein, and he had a machine which would read aloud to him from any book which he placed in its hopper.

His life may have been a lonely one, but it was not without such material comforts. Eccentric, yes, but Mr. Snively could afford to be eccentric with a net income of four million dollars a year. Not bad for a man who'd started life as the son of a shipping clerk.

Mr. Snively chuckled as he watched the taxicab drive away, and then he went back to bed and to the sleep of the just.

"So somebdy has things figured out nineteen hours ahead of time," he thought. "Well, a lot of good it will do them!"

There wasn't any law to punish him for what he'd done. . . .

Bookstores did a landoffice business that day in books on astronomy. The public, apathetic at first, was deeply interested now. Even ancient and musty volumes of Newton's *Principia* sold at premium prices.

The ether blared with comment upon the new wonder of the skies. Little of the comment was professional, or even intelligent, for most astronomers were asleep that day. They'd managed to stay awake the first forty-eight hours from the start of the phenomena, but the third day found them worn out mentally and physically, and inclined to let the stars take care of themselves while they—the astronomers, not the stars—caught up on sleep.

Staggering offers from the telecast and broadcast studios enticed a few of them to attempt lectures, but their efforts were dreary things, better forgotten. Dr. Carver Blake, broadcasting from KNB, fell soundly asleep between a perigee and an apogee.

Physicists were also greatly in demand. The most eminent of them all, however, was sought in vain. The solitary clue to Dr. Milton Hale's disappearance, the brief note "Taking money. Explain later," wasn't much of a help. His sister Agatha feared the worst.

For the first time in history, astronomical news made banner headlines in the newspapers.

Snow had started early that morning along the northern Atlantic seaboard and now it was growing steadily worse. Just outside Waterbury, Conn., the driver of Dr. Hale's cab began to weaken.

It wasn't human, he thought, for a man to be expected to drive to Boston and then, without stopping, from Boston to Washington. Not even for a hundred dollars.

Not in a storm like this. Why, he could see only a dozen yards ahead through the driving snow, even when he could manage to keep his eyes open. His fare was slumbering soundly in the back seat. Maybe he could get away with stopping here along the road, for an hour, to catch some sleep. Just an hour. His fare wouldn't ever know the difference. The guy must be loony, he thought, or why hadn't he taken a plane or a train?

Dr. Hale would have, of course, if he'd thought of it. But he wasn't used to traveling and besides there'd been the Tartan Plaid. A taxi had seemed the easiest way to get anywhere—no worrying about tickets and connections and stations. Money was no object, and the plaid condition of his mind had caused him to overlook the human factor involved in an extended journey by taxi.

When he awoke, almost frozen, in the parked taxi, that human factor dawned upon him. The driver was so sound asleep that no amount of shaking could arouse him. Dr. Hale's watch had stopped, so he had no idea where he was or what time it was.

Unfortunately, too, he didn't know how to drive a car. He took a quick drink to keep from freezing, and then got out of the cab, and as he did so, a car stopped.

It was a policeman—what is more it was a policeman in a million.

Yelling over the roar of the storm, Hale hailed him.

"I'm Dr. Hale," he shouted. "We're lost. Where am I?"

"Get in here before you freeze," ordered the policeman. "Do you mean Dr. Milton Hale, by any chance?"

"Yes."

"I've read all your books, Dr. Hale," said the policeman. "Physics is my hobby, and I've always wanted to meet you. I want to ask you about the revised value of the quantum."

"This is life or death," said Dr. Hale. "Can you take me to the nearest airport, quick?"

"Of course, Dr. Hale."

"And look—there's a driver in that cab, and he'll freeze to death unless we send aid."

"I'll put him in the back seat of my car, and then run the cab off the road. We'll take care of details later."

"Hurry, please."

The obliging policeman hurried. He got back in and started the car.

"About the revised quantum value, Dr. Hale," he began, then stopped talking.

Dr. Hale was sound asleep. The policeman drove to Waterbury airport, one of the largest in the world since the population shift from New York City northwards in the 1960's and 70's had given it a central position. In front of the ticket office, he gently awakened Dr. Hale.

"This is the airport, sir," he said.

Even as he spoke, Dr. Hale was leaping out of the car and stumbling into the building, yelling, "Thanks," over his shoulder and nearly falling down in doing so.

The warm-up roaring of the motors of a superstratoliner out on the field lent wings to his heels as he dashed for the ticket window.

"What plane's that?" he yelled.

"Washington Special, due out in one minute. But I don't think you can make it."

Dr. Hale slapped a hundred-dollar bill on the ledge. "Ticket," he gasped. "Keep the change."

He grabbed the ticket and ran, getting into the plane just as the doors were being closed. Panting, he fell into a seat, the ticket still in his hand. He was sound asleep before the hostess strapped him in for the blind take-off.

A little while later, the hostess awakened him. The passengers were disembarking.

Dr. Hale rushed out of the plane and ran across the field to the airport building. A big clock told him that it was nine o'clock, and he felt elated as he ran for the door marked "Taxicabs."

He got into the nearest one.

"White House," he told the driver. "How long'll it take?"

"Ten minutes."

Dr. Hale gave a sigh of relief and sank back against the cushions. He didn't go back to sleep this time. He was wide awake now. But he closed his eyes to think out the words he'd use in explaining matters.

"Here you are, sir."

Dr. Hale gave the driver a bill and hurried out of the cab and into the building. It didn't look like he expected it to look. But there was a desk and he ran up to it.

"I've got to see the Preisdent, quick. It's vital."

The clerk frowned. "The president of what?"

Dr. Hale's eyes went wide. "The president of the— Say, what building is this? And what town?"

The clerk's frown deepened. "This is the White House Hotel," he said, "Seattle, Washington."

Dr. Hale fainted. He woke up in a hospital three hours later. It was then midnight, Pacific Time, which meant it was three o'clock in the morning on the Eastern Seaboard. It had, in fact been midnight already in Washington, D. C., and in Boston, when he had been leaving the Washington Special in Seattle.

Dr. Hale rushed to the window and shook his fists, both of them, at the sky. A futile gesture.

Back in the East, however, the storm had stopped by twilight, leaving a light mist in the air. The star-conscious public thereupon deluged the weather bureaus with telephone requests about the persistence of the mist.

"A breeze off the ocean is expected," they were told. "It is blowing now, in fact, and within an hour or two will have cleared off the light fog."

By eleven-fifteen the skies of Boston were clear.

Untold thousands braved the bitter cold and stood staring upward at the unfolding pageant of the no-longer-eternal stars. It almost looked as though an incredible development had occurred.

And then, gradually, the murmur grew. By a quarter to twelve, the thing was certain, and the murmur hushed and then grew louder than ever, waxing toward midnight. Different people reacted differently, of course, as might be expected. There was laughter as well as indignation, cynical amusement as well as shocked horror. There was even admiration.

Soon in certain parts of the city, a concerted movement on the part of those who knew an address on Fremont Street, began to take place. Movement afoot in cars and public vehicles, converging.

At five minutes to twelve, Rutherford R. Sniveley sat waiting within his house. He was denying himself the pleasure of looking until, at the last moment, the thing was complete.

It was going well. The gathering murmur of voices, mostly angry voices, outside his house told him that. He heard his name shouted.

Just the same he waited until the twelfth stroke of the clock before he stepped out upon the balcony. Much as he wanted to look upward, he forced himself to look down at the street first. The milling crowd was there, and it was angry. But he had only contempt for the milling crowd.

Police cars were pulling up, too, and he recognized the Mayor of Boston getting out of one of them, and the Chief of Police was with him. But so what? There wasn't any law covering this. Then having denied himself the supreme pleasure long enough, he turned his eyes up to the silent sky, and there it was. The 468 brightest stars spelling out:

USE
SNIVELY'S
SOAP

For just a second did his satisfaction last. Then his face began to turn apoplectic purple.

"My God!" said Mr. Sniveley. "It's spelled wrong!"

His face grew more purple still and then, as a tree falls, he fell backward through the window.

An ambulance rushed the fallen magnate to the nearest hospital, but he was pronounced dead—of apoplexy—upon entrance.

But misspelled or not, the eternal stars held their position as of that midnight. The aberrant motion had stopped and again the stars were fixed. Fixed to spell—USE SNIVELY'S SOAP!

Of the many explanations offered by all the sundry who professed some physical and astronomical knowledge, none was more lucid—or closer to the actual truth—than that put forward by Wendell Mehan, president emeritus of the New York Astronomical Society.

"Obviously, the phenomenon is a trick of refraction," said Dr. Mehan. "It is manifestly impossible for any force contrived by man to move a star. The stars, therefore, still occupy their old places in the firmament.

"I suggest that Sniveley must have contrived a method of refracting the light of the stars, somewhere in or just above the atmospheric layer of earth, so that they appear to have changed their positions. This is done, probably, by radio waves or similar waves, sent on some fixed frequency from a set—or possibly a series of 468 sets—somewhere upon the surface of the earth. Although we do not understand just how it is done, it is no more unthinkable that light rays should be bent by a field of waves than by a prism or by gravitational force.

"Since Sniveley was not a great scientist, I imagine that his discovery was empiric rather than logical—an accidental find. It is quite possible that even the discovery of his projector will not enable present-day scientists to understand its secret, any more than an aboriginal savage could understand the operation of a simple radio receiver by taking one apart.

"My principal reason for this assertion is the fact that the refraction obviously is a fourth-dimensional phenomenon or its effect would be purely local to one portion of the globe. Only in the fourth dimension could light be so refracted. . . ."

There was more, but it is better to skip to his final paragraph:

"This effect cannot possibly be permanent—more permanent, that is, than the wave-projector which causes it. Sooner or later, Sniveley's machine will be found and shut off, or it will break down or wear out of its own volition. Undoubtedly it includes vacuum tubes, which will some day blow out, as do the tubes in our radios. . . ."

The excellence of Dr. Mehan's analysis was shown, two months and eight days later, when the Boston Electric Co. shut off, for non-payment of bills, service to a house situated at 901 West Rogers Street, ten blocks from the Sniveley mansion. At the instant of the shut-off, excited reports from the night side of Earth brought the news that the stars had flashed back into their former positions instantaneously.

Investigation brought out that the description of one Elmer Smith, who had purchased that house six months before, corresponded with the description of Rutherford R. Sniveley, and undoubtedly Elmer Smith and Rutherford R. Sniveley were one and the same person.

In the attic was found a complicated network of 468 radio-type antennae, each antenna of different length and running in a different direction. The machine to which they were connected was not larger, strangely, than the average ham's radio projector, nor did it draw appreciably more current, according to the electric company's record.

By special order of the President of the United States, the project was destroyed without examination of its internal arrangement. Clamorous protests against this high-handed executive order arose from many sides. But inasmuch as the projector had already been broken up, the protests were of no avail.

Serious repercussions were, on the whole, amazingly few.

Persons in general appreciated the stars more, but trusted them less.

Roger Phlutter got out of jail and married Elsie. Dr. Milton Hale found he liked Seattle, and stayed there. Two thousand miles away from his sister Agatha, he found it possible for the first time to defy her openly. He enjoys life more but, it is feared, will write fewer books.

There is one fact remaining which is painful to consider, since it casts a deep reflection upon the basic intelligence of the human race. It is proof, though, that the President's executive order was justified, despite scientific protests.

That fact is as humiliating as it is enlightening. During the two months and eight days during which the Sniveley machine was in operation, sales of Sniveley Soap increased 915%!